A RIVER THAT IS CONGO:

OF CHIEFS AND GIANTS

Paul J. Stam

ALL THINGS THAT MATTER PRESS

A RIVER THAT IS CONGO: OF CHIEFS AND GIANTS

ISBN: 9780988542792

Library of Congress Control Number: 2013906023

Cover Design by All Things that Matter Press

Published in 2013 by All Things that Matter Press

Memorabilia

These former precious things,
Memorabilia once kept,
Of things, and lands where giants walked,
And where mere mortals wept.
They are no more, for they are lost,
In the shifting folds of time,
Forevermore obliterated,
In the stream of memory's slime.

1879

CHAPTER ONE

Ronzozo, first son of Chief Kimulu and chief-to-be, stood in the center of the front rank of warriors along the crest of the hill. The rising sun cast diagonal shadows to the slopes across the valley. Directly behind them, hidden in the ravine, were five hundred more warriors. An equal number of warriors were also hidden behind the hill at the other end of the ravine.

The first rank of the enemy crested the hill on the other side of the valley and the warriors started beating their shields in unison and shouting, Kufu. Kufu. Kufu. Kufu. Ronzozo watched with anxious uneasiness as rank upon rank came over the crest, each rank joining the others, beating on their shields and shouting their threat. Their numbers swelled until there were more than four times as many warriors on the opposite hill as there were on his side. He breathed a sigh of relief and smiled with secret confidence. Just as his father had predicted, Dumodo's warriors would fight the old way, not holding anything in reserve. They were not being cunning.

For half an hour the opposing forces stood at the tops of their respective hills chanting their threat of; Kill, Kill, Kill, Kill. Ronzozo stood shouting with the rest of them, looking back and forth from the enemy and to his father standing up in his tepoi to his right. He felt safe now, the bodies of the warriors on each side of him touching his body. He could smell the palm oil they had rubbed on themselves and this gave him a feeling of safety in their closeness. If a spear were to come flying toward them it would hit someone else, but everyone was thinking the same thing.

Their common sense told them if a spear was coming right for them, there would be no way to dodge it if they stayed pressed close together. Over and over again his father explained it to him, to the chiefs and to the warriors, and yet he knew the impulse would be to stay bunched together. It was just this impulse on the part of the enemy that would be their defeat.

He saw his father raise his right hand, the Gangilo held above his head. His father pointed with his left hand toward the other side and the right arm came down. Ronzozo raised his spear over his head, gave a shout, and they started running down the hill. Their movement was like a trigger releasing the enemy and the two opposing forces rushed toward each other to the valley below.

Ronzozo and all his forces were halfway down the hill when he saw the reserves running up the other side to get in position to come against Dumodo's warriors on the flank and from behind. The reserves ran with stealth and bent low with no shouting that would let the enemy know they were there. Halfway down the hill Ronzozo and those with him stopped. Those in the ranks behind turned when he stopped and started running back up the hill, while those in the front rank spread out. Dumodo's warriors interpreted their action first as fear, and then as retreat, and some of them started running ahead, wanting to be the first to have a kill.

Ronzozo found himself on the side of the hill feeling vulnerable and exposed. The rest of the warriors were to the side and behind him, spread out just the way they were trained to do. The only protection he had was his own weapons. Around his waist he had the skin of the leopard he had killed in becoming a man. Strapped to his left arm was his shield, buffalo hide stretched over a wooden frame. In his left hand was his battle-axe. The handle was carved out of ebony shaped to fit perfectly into his right hand. It felt awkward held in his left hand.

In his right hand he held his spear, the same one with which he killed his manhood leopard. The blade was the length of a man's arm and as wide as a woman's hand at the base. The shaft was more than six feet long. A casing of beaten iron covered the butt as a counter-balance to the blade.

He gave a yell and started running down the hill headed for the closest of the enemy warriors. When they were thirty paces apart, he saw the enemy make the turn of his body, the change from a straight-on run to a sideways run, the arm going back and then coming forward throwing the spear. It was a good throw. The warrior didn't even break stride in throwing, and Ronzozo watched the spear flying toward him, side stepped, heard the swish of air as it went by, and then the thud as it entered the ground behind him.

The warrior kept coming toward him, his shield protecting his body, his battle-axe in his raised hand. With his spear held close to his body like a lance, Ronzozo had the advantage of reach, but it was hard to control the spear. If he missed, the enemy's axe could slash right through his shield and take off his arm or his head. The warrior kept coming, looking right into his eyes. Ronzozo made a jab with his spear at the warrior's face and the enemy raised his shield to deflect the thrust. Ronzozo drew back, dropped the point, and thrust forward, sliding under the shield into the man's stomach. He felt the blade ease through the flesh, the shaft twist a little in his hand as the blade hit and was deflected by a bone. He saw the warrior's eyes get wide and white in disbelief; the battle-axe fell from his hand. Ronzozo pulled out his spear, slashing downward as he did so, laying open the man's abdomen, cutting the thong that held the leather skirt in place. The skirt fell to the ground before the man did and then the severed bluish-white guts spilled out onto the bloody ground. The smell of offal, blood, fear and death filled Ronzozo's nostrils.

He had just an instant to look around him, to see blood and slaughter everywhere, and then there was another one upon him. He came at Ronzozo with his spear held above his head. He thrust and Ronzozo deflected the spear with his shield. He thrust again; each time staying just out of reach of Ronzozo's spear. He thrust a third time and Ronzozo let the blade penetrate his shield. He turned, twisting, the wooden frame of his shield, wedging against the spear, acting like a fulcrum against the shaft and blade. The warrior was pulled forward holding on to his spear and Ronzozo thrust forward with his. It went through the dry leather shield and he heard the groan as the spear entered the warrior's chest. The warrior let go of his own spear, turned and fell, jerking the spear from Ronzozo's hand. The man rose to a kneeling position trying to draw the spear from his chest. Ronzozo removed the spear that was caught in his own shield and threw it to the ground. He took his battle-axe in his right hand and swung at the kneeling man, the inside curve of the ax fitting the roundness of the man's neck. The man's head fell forward, blood spurted upward landing on Ronzozo's hand. The body fell and in that instant Ronzozo sensed there was someone behind him.

He swung around. The blade was coming toward his face. Too late to deflect it with the shield, he swung at it with his ax and shattered the shaft. He swung again, shattering the top of the enemy's shield. The warrior swung at him with a stubby battle-axe and Ronzozo swung in return. He felt the backside of his blade cut into the flesh of the enemy's arm. The enemy's fingers released their hold and the battle-axe fell to the ground. Ronzozo swung again. The enemy tried to dodge backward, but he was too late, the point of the ax entered at the middle of the neck, passed through and the head fell backwards, still attached by a flap of flesh at the back of the neck. The man fell forward, spurting blood all over Ronzozo as he fell.

Ronzozo stood and looking around him. He saw human bodies were spread everywhere. The sound of groaning was deafening. One warrior of his own tribe was sitting up with a diagonal slash across his abdomen, his hands pressed against his stomach, and his fingers spread across the opening trying to keep his guts from spilling out.

When he looked back to the left there was an enemy leaping over a fallen warrior, rushing toward him from behind, his spear tucked under his arm, his shield waving back and forth with the swinging of his left arm. Ronzozo turned just in time for his shield to intercept the blade aimed at the middle of his back. Even as he twisted around, he raised his right arm to swing the ax, pushing the shield downward and with it the blade of the spear so it missed his chest and abdomen and, instead, entered the upper outside of his left thigh. He felt the cold-hot fire of the blade in his flesh, followed by the ripping of the barbs and then the stretching and pulling of the flesh. The man kept pushing forward. Ronzozo felt himself falling backwards and he swung the ax with all his might. The blade entered at the small of the warrior's waist, passing through the point coming out at the man's navel, and leaving his whole left side split open. The man would not let go of his spear, and the force of his forward motion drove the blade of the spear deep into the ground, pinning Ronzozo to the spot.

Ronzozo lay with the weight of the other man pressing down on him. It was good, even with the pain of the gash in his leg, to lay still and rest for a moment. Straight above him he saw that the carrion birds circled. He sensed, more than felt or heard, when the man on top of him died, a relaxing through the man's whole body. He looked down at the top of the man's head, which rested on his shoulder, saw some white hairs, and thought he had killed a man old enough to be his father.

The man lay so Ronzozo's left arm with the shield attached was immovable. He stretched his neck looking around as far as he could to make sure no one was anywhere close to attack him and then released his grasp on the battle-axe. With his right hand he tugged and pushed, trying little by little to roll the warrior off of him. Each movement increased the excruciating pain of the spear rubbing on his wound. Finally, the man rolled off landing on his back next to him, his left arm and shield still lying across Ronzozo. He swung the arm and shield off.

Ronzozo moved his left arm causing a pain that almost made him faint. He knew that if he fainted he'd bleed to death. He slid his right hand between the shield and his body and undid the lashing holding the shield to his left arm. With his thigh still pinned to the ground, he pushed himself, inch by painful inch, up to a sitting position. He had to fight to keep from fainting.

The spear had gone through the shield, through his thigh, and into the ground. When he moved, even a little bit, the spear jerked and sent shocks of pain thorough him. He forced himself to consciousness, overpowering the pain and the waves of fainting. Sitting up with both hands free he was able to lift his shield, sliding it along the shaft of the spear, doing his best to keep from jiggling it. The slightest movement of the shield jerked the spear so it tore at his flesh. He raised shield till it was high enough he could look under it and see the wound.

Most of the blade was buried deep in the ground with the barbs still in the backside of his thigh with the shaft coming out the front. He couldn't pull the spear out because the barbs would catch his flesh, tearing it to shreds. With the blade buried so deep in the ground, there was no way to pull the spear all the way through. The only thing to do was to try and cut, or break, the shaft off as close to his leg as he could and then try to lift himself off the imbedded blade.

With his battle-axe he enlarged the hole in the shield and was able to lift it up and over the butt of the spear. He examined the grain of the wood of the shaft wondering if it would be better to try and chip at it with his battle-axe or sever it with one powerful blow. But, if he were able to cut through with one blow he might also cut right through and hit himself.

He held the shaft with his left hand just above his leg. He swung his battle-axe, hitting the shaft at an angle following the grain of the wood. The pain from the shaft's movement flooded through him. He closed his eyes and yelled, both to keep from fainting and in defiance.

The blow didn't sever the wood, but it went far enough through that he was able to break it. He flung the shaft away from him and then sat for a moment staring at the stub sticking out of his thigh, trying to work up the energy to lift himself up and off of it. He looked around, realizing sitting up showed the enemy he wasn't dead and vulnerable to attack. But the fighting was moving away from him up the valley.

He heard a yell and looking in his father's direction saw the reserves come over the hill. The enemy saw them coming and started running away, throwing down their spears and shields so they could run faster. All of Kimulu's forces were in pursuit. Spears landed in the backs of fleeing warriors, some from those thrown down from the panicked enemy. His father had won. The pursuit would continue until sundown or until there was no one left to pursue. He looked toward his father again and wondered if he could recognize him if he happened to look his direction. No! He was too far away.

With both hands he raised his left knee, the movement sending shots of pain throughout his body as the flesh rubbed on the shaft. He brought his right knee up even with the other, put his hands on either side of him and raised himself. With the spear shaft removed the blood oozed in a steady flow from the wound. He forced himself to sit up and clasped his left hand over the back opening in his thigh and his right hand over the front opening. After a while the bleeding slowed and he took off the leopard skin from around is waist and wrapped it as tight as he could around his leg, lashing it in place. He lay back. He could relax now and not bleed to death.

***

The last of the pursuing warriors passed in front of Kimulu and he sat down and motioned for his bearers to set him down. He stepped out of his tepoi and started toward the battlefield. "I go to find my son," he said and motioned for them to join the others in pursuit of the enemy.

The warriors of Kimulu won a great victory that day. They followed the warriors of Dumodo and the slaughter continued until there were no more warriors to chase. None were left to die of their injuries. Before the sun set, all Dumodo's warriors had their heads separated from their bodies, thus preventing forever the possibility of their entering into fellowship with their ancestors, destined forever to wander headless in the realm of the unknown.

1883

CHAPTER TWO

Light from the flames of the small fire flickered against the black, mud walls of the hut. The smoke curled upwards feeling its way along the bare pole rafters until it found the hole in the thatch at the peak of the roof where all the rafters came together. Close to the wall, opposite the entrance, a young girl lay on a woven straw mat, her stomach protruding high above her with the new life in her. She was fifteen years old. She was the third and youngest wife of Ronzozo, first son of Chief Kimulu and Chief-to-be. Next to her an old woman, her hair gray, her flesh loose and sagging, squatted, her arms wrapped around her knees, her chin resting on her folded arms, as she stared into the small flames of the fire.

The girl's body tensed, her knees came up, her fists clutched the edge of the straw mat, her face contorted with the pain, and her buttocks rose off the ground in her effort to bring the child forth. The old woman turned her head to look at her. The contraction passed; the girl's body went limp, her legs straightened out, and she again lay flat on the mat taking long, deep breaths. She had not made a sound. To cry out while giving birth would only tell the evil spirits a child was being born.

Excited voices could be heard outside the hut and the old woman got up and went out, stooping almost double to get through the low entrance. Outside the whole village was bathed in moonlight. In front of the entrance was another fire. Next to it, a young man sat on his heels, his arms extended in front of him and his hands clasped around the shaft of a spear, the butt of which rested on the ground. Not far away, halfway to the next hut, a group of women stood talking in hushed, but excited tones. The old woman stood in the shadows listening for a moment and then went back inside. She sat down next to the girl and sighed, resigned to the loss of what she and the girl had hoped for said, "Shushi has brought forth a man child."

The girl turned her head. "How know you this?"

"It is the talk."

"Go! Tell Mukulu to go to my husband and say to him Meli, his third wife, has brought forth her first born; a man-child."

The old woman looked at her and said, "If the child you bare is a girl you will be put away, cast out for telling this lie. No village will have room for you."

"I will bear a son," the girl growled. "Tell Mukulu to go. He is to run. He is to stop and talk to no one. He must run quickly. He must get there before the messenger of Shushi gets there ..." Another contraction started. "Go!" she hissed at the old woman and then clamped her mouth shut pushing with the contraction.

The old woman went out and spoke to the young man sitting next to the fire. He got up and walked around to the back of the hut where the talking women wouldn't see him leave and then broke into a long-legged run, his spear in his right hand swinging as he ran. He was thankful for the full moon. Any other time he wouldn't be out at night and not go so far from the village, but he knew the importance of his mission. His sister had just given birth to a son. He had no time to lose. He had to be first at the meeting of the Chiefs at the Valley of the Yellow Flowers. If he got there first, he'd be uncle to the one who would someday be chief of the Five Tribes.

Ahead of him, Mukulu saw Shushi's runner. His running was controlled and steady, pacing himself for the distance. Does his throat also burn? Were his legs as tired? Mukulu had run fast to catch up with Shushi's runner and he wondered if he had the strength to pass him? Step by weary step the distance between them shortened. Shushi's runner turned to look, and then for some reason Mukulu couldn't understand, stopped and waited for him. A short distance away Shushi's runner called, "Is the child well?"

Mukulu didn't answer until he was up to him and then said, "The child is well," and passed by him. The other started running again. From time to time Mukulu looked over his shoulder and each time the distance between them was greater.

The sun was coming up when he entered the Valley of the Yellow Flowers. The warriors stationed on the perimeters called to him, and he called back, "Ronzozo, Chief-to-be, has a son." By the time he got to the place of meeting, the chiefs were already seated on their mats. They kept him waiting for a few minutes while they became silent, and then Chief Kimulu motioned for him to come into the place of meeting.

"What say you?" Kimulu asked.

"I have been sent to tell Ronzozo he has a son. A man-child born to him by his wife Meli. The child is well and strong."

The chiefs smiled and nodded, expressing their approval and congratulated the father. And even while they were nodding and smiling, Shushi's runner burst through the circle of warriors, and gasping for breath said, "Shushi has born Ronzozo, Chief-to-be, a son. A man-child! Ronzozo's son by Shushi is first born!"

"It is a lie. Meli was first to give birth. Did not I arrive first with the word?"

"You did pass me in the way and out-run me, but the son of Shushi is first born. All in the village know I did leave first to bring you word."

"All in the village did sleep. Even you did sleep while I ran. Only now, at this time, in this place have I seen you," Mukulu argued.

"Quiet!" The firm voice of Chief Kimulu brought a hush over the gathering. "My son, Ronzozo, Chief-to-be, has two sons on the same day, but of different mothers born. What say you to that, my son?"

Ronzozo stood up, standing with his weight on his right leg favoring the left. He crossed his arms over his chest and looked around. All the chiefs were looking at him. He knew it would be difficult to ever find out which wife had given birth first. His father had put him on the spot in front of the other chiefs to test him, proving him. He let his arms drop to his side and said, "My son by my wife Shushi shall be called Kusala. And my son by my wife Meli shall be called Kitomolo."

It was quiet for a while, and then his father said, "And who do you name Chief-to-be after you; Kusala or Kitomolo?"

He folded his arms over his chest again and stood for a moment looking beyond them to the distant hills. He turned back and looked at his father, then around at each of the other chiefs and said, "Kusala and Kitomolo shall be equal sons until the day they become men. He who kills his leopard first and becomes a man first shall be named Chief-to-be. I, Ronzozo, have spoken it."

The rest of the chiefs smiled and grunted their approval. It was a good decision. Ronzozo, first son of Kimulu and chief-to-be, had answered with wisdom.

1900

CHAPTER THREE

Chief Kimulu was dead. The stars were past the midpoint in the night sky, but the first cock had not yet crowed. The sorrowful wailing of the women began to float like sediment in the fluidity of the dark night. Whenever a man entered the place of death, a full-chested roar of agony would splash like a heavy stone of torment into the night. He would raise his voice once or twice in respectful sorrow and then sit down with the other men to listen with respect to the incessant wailing of the women. The wailing couldn't be heard beyond the village, but the drums would carry the message to all the other villages of the tribe, to the clans and to the little four and five family villages. Because it was Chief Kimulu who had died, other distant villages would pick up the message and beat the drums until the first gray of morning when all would know Kimulu, Chief of the Five Tribes, Ruler of the North, Protector of the Lands, had gone to be with his ancestors.

In her hut, Meli, third wife of Ronzozo, knew as soon as she heard the first beats of the drum that her father-in-law had died. He had been attacked with fever three days ago and had started vomiting and been unable to eat. The batu-na-dawa had come and made the cuts in his body to release the evil spirits, but the drums now told her the power of the evil spirits was greater than the knowledge of the batu-na-dawa.

She was in awe of death and had a fear of the realm of the ancestors as she walked toward the place of death, but she also had a sense of satisfaction and expectation. The death of Kimulu was the first step necessary for her son, Kitomolo, to becoming chief. Her husband would have to die next. Right now, she was just one of many wives to Ronzozo, but she was the only mother of Kitomolo. When he became chief she would be the most important woman in the tribe. A man might have many wives, but he had only one mother. She would not contribute to anyone's death because of the vengeance of the ancestral spirits, but in her heart, she wished Ronzozo's death would come soon.

When she entered the hut, Kimulu's body was already wrapped in the burial mats. Ronzozo, and the other men sat cross-legged to one side of the pole bed on which the chief's body lay. Out of respect, they sat on the ground rather than on the low stools they usually carried with them. She picked her way through the women, and sat down close to Ronzozo's other wives. She sat with her legs together and stretched straight out in front of her, which was the proper way for a woman to sit. Her wailing combined with that of the other women, and her body swayed back and forth in rhythm with theirs. From the string around her waist she took a small, hand-forged iron knife and started making small nicks in the flesh just above her breasts to show the genuineness of her grief. Little driblets of blood flowed over and around her breast, along her torso to her hips and thighs, and to the ground.

CHAPTER FOUR

The dancing and celebrating for the new chief had gone on for eight days. Ronzozo now sat in the place of chief. Behind him was his new house, built on the spot where the old house had been, the place of the chief's house. Beside, and behind him on carved stools, sat the elders of the village. In front of him were the chiefs and delegates from other tribes and villages.

Ronzozo looked over the crowd before him. He was chief, but he was also young. He had seen only twenty-eight seasons and, although under ordinary circumstances he would have been allowed to speak in the meetings of the council, his words would not have carried much weight. He was chief, and it was known he was a great warrior. There were many songs and stories praising him and telling of the battle with Dumodo's tribes.

He got up from where he was sitting, went over to Ngawaika and said, "The responsibility thrust upon me is beyond my years. So I ask you now, because you are the eldest of all here and because of your friendship with my father, you will give me counsel when you see I have need of it."

Ngawaika nodded and the other elders grunted their approval. He went to each of the elders reminding them of something important in their lives and asking them for their counsel. Those younger than himself he ignored. Even the older delegates from other tribes were given special recognition.

He sat down and the delegates and chiefs started bringing their gifts: baskets of corn, millet, and fufu. There were skins of all kinds, elephant tusks, and carved stools. The elder from Chief Kesalengo was the last to bring forward his gift. It was wrapped in a mat and all had wondered what it was. The elder unwrapped it slowly and with care. Waving it above his head for all to see and said, "This is a weapon of white people."

There was hushed and skeptical talk at the mention of white people. They had heard stories that there were humans who were completely white, not just wearers of white coverings like those to whom Dumodo's tribes used to sell the people they took captive. Ronzozo took the gift, examining it from barrel tip to butt and thought, Is Kesalengo trying to make a fool of me? He walked around the circle of elders showing them the gift. If none of them knew what it was or how to use it, then there would be no shame in his not knowing. Ngawaika ran an old withered hand over the scarred but smooth stock and nodded a little. Another elder took the gun from Ronzozo; looked at one side, then the other, and then held the end of the barrel up to his face and squinted, trying to look down the hollow of the barrel. Shaking his head, he handed it back to Ronzozo. None of the elders understood the gun.

Ronzozo stood for a short time handling Kesalengo's gift while the elders and chiefs looked on. For many seasons the talk of white people had increased, but never until now had he, or any of them, seen one or anything belonging to one. What he held in his hand was a little frightening because it belonged to the unknown. Running his hand back and forth along the gun he accidentally pushed the right way on the bolt and it flew open. He jumped a little in surprise. Looking into the chamber, he could see the light coming down the barrel. He pushed forward on the bolt and it slid back into place. He slid the bolt back again and tried to look down the barrel. He turned to the delegate who had given it to him. "How does the white man's weapon work?"

"It is said that with a great noise it throws a round rock which cannot be seen until it hits you."

"Have you brought us any of these rocks?"

The man shook his head, embarrassed, and Ronzozo thought, Kesalengo has sent me a bow without any arrows. But for a bow I could make arrows.

"Have you ever seen this weapon throw its little round rocks and make its great noise?"

Again, the man shook his head.

"Thank the great Chief Kesalengo for this gift." There was no sarcasm, but genuine appreciation in his voice. He had heard of the killing-sticks before, but didn't know anyone who had ever seen one. He waited for a moment and then started speaking, talking in a voice just loud enough for the elders to hear him. He was not addressing the crowd. He was not speaking to the women and children.

"For many season we have heard talk of white men. Many say there cannot be such a thing for we have not seen it. But each passing season the talk has become more. Much of the talk is of the evil they do. That is the way of talk, for one fears what they do not know. One speaks only evil of that which he fears. But for good, or for evil, the white man is real."

He paused for a moment and said, "If you have a seed you know there must also have been a plant to produce the seed." He held the gun above his head. "Chief Kesalengo has given a seed that is of the white man."

The elders nodded and grunted their agreement.

"As the Five Tribes we have withstood those who would come against us. We came against Dumodo when he stole our people to sell to those of the white robes. It was said those of the white robes had such a killing stick. I think it would be a good thing then if the chiefs and elders of the Five Tribes came together to share what each knows of the white man. And so, I ask that two days after the third full moon from now the chiefs and elders of the Five Tribes meet at the Valley of the Yellow Flowers to renew, again, our covenants of friendship, and talk in council."

1901

CHAPTER FIVE

Harry VanVeldt walked behind his wife, Alma, along the narrow, snaking pathway. Ahead of them the column of almost five hundred people stretched out in single file for more than a mile. Ten feet in front of them the bare back and shoulders of the last porter glistened with sweat in the mid-morning sun, the shadow from the load he carried on his head crossing his back as he turned one way or another.

The only load Harry carried was a Springfield Krag rifle. He carried it at his waist, balanced in the crook of his arm, the butt extending behind him, the barrel pointed forward and downward. He was a tall, thin man with sharp features, deep-set hazel eyes and a square chin. He was clean-shaven with straight, black hair hidden under the Wolsey helmet that pointed front and kept his face in a cool shadow. His once white shirt was now a yellow-gray and there were dark sweat stains under the arms. His heavy brown trousers were tucked into the knee-high boots. Looking past his wife, he could see the column, the figures becoming increasing smaller with the distance, moving into the valley and up the next hill where the front of the column disappeared over the other hilltop.

Alma walked in front of Harry, her swinging hips causing the long skirt to swish back and forth above the grass alongside the path. She was considered by many to be too attractive to be a missionary. As a toddler she had a round, cherubic face which couldn't help but remind people of the cupids depicted on valentine cards of the era. As she grew older, the roundness changed to oval with large, brown eyebrows, long lashes, and gray eyes with flecks of gold. Her heavy, dark-brown hair had a soft natural wave to it. She had a full-lipped, wide mouth, which was a deep pink and a creamy-white complexion that burned easily in the sun. She always had a hint of a smile and the general softness of her face belied her iron will. She stood almost a full head shorter than her husband, but she carried herself with such self-confidence she gave the impression of being taller than she was.

Behind Harry, in a low voice, Watsumdumu sang a work chant and would interrupt his chant to give a piece of advice. "Not good have wives and toto after Bashindi, Bwana Van. Best send wives and toto home." As far as Harry could tell he would take up the chant where he had interrupted it, and sing for a while, and then, "Not good stay long Bashindi, Bwana Van. Leave Bashindi soon, soon. Little rest make men strong. Too long rest make men lazy, good for nothing. Not stay long Bashindi."

The other missionaries were interspersed among the porters with Harry and Alma at the end of the column and Reverend Scott at the front right behind the guide. Watsumdumu was in charge of the safari. He was a freed slave from Zanzibar who, at the age of sixteen, was a porter with Stanley's trans-Africa expedition twenty-five years before. He had been Reverend Scott's safari marshal each time Scott went in to establish the stations at Jikobe and Mbundu.

Not everybody in the safari was paid. Two-thirds of the people were wives and children. Often the load the wife carried was greater than that of her hired husband. The wife would have the family bedding and pots on her head, an infant strapped to her back, and another child walking along side that she would sometimes have to be pick up and carry.

Watsumdumu kept the safari moving ahead at a steady pace. At the start of the march he would be at the front, just behind the guide. After a while he would step out and stand alongside the path. He always wore a colorful shirt and loose Arab style pantaloons. He would stand with his arms folded across his chest, his scimitar stuck in the waistband, eyeing each person who passed by him. After a while he would step back into the line for a mile or two, and then step out again to let the safari pass by him. Often times he would pick up one of the children and carry them for a while. By the time the two-hour march ended, he would be at the rear of the column. While everyone else sat next to their load during the morning rest period, he would walk to the front of the mile long column, ready to give the signal to march again. Because their destination was less than half a day's march away, there was no rest period today and so he now walked along behind Harry.

They crested a small hill and ahead of them they could see some whitewashed buildings. Just to the side of those buildings was a level stretch of brilliant green. A herd of elephants, following each other in a column, appear as a frieze separating the green flatland from the blue of Lake George. Beyond that, blending into the sky and yet separate from it, was the purple of the distant Congo Mountains. "Bashindi! Bwana, George Nyanza!" Watsumdumu said catching up with them and pointing to the town and lake beyond it.

Harry and Alma stopped, letting the safari go on ahead of them. Watsumdumu waited for a moment, and then went around them leaving them alone. Harry reached over and took Alma's hand and they both looked beyond the green hills and the blue of Lake George, to the purple mountains of Congo, taking deep breaths to control their emotions. Harry wasn't sure just how Alma felt, but he was filled with excitement, but also trepidation. He had never been sure he was called to be a missionary. All the others in the party claimed they were sure of their calling, but he wasn't. He didn't feel prepared for the life of a missionary.

It was while he was a pre-med student at Columbia University he met Alma. As far as he could tell she had always desired to be a missionary and defied her parents by marrying him and sailing for Africa. It would have been hard for him to know which of those two things; marrying him, or going to Africa, made her parents the angriest. But Alma was like that. Once she made up her mind to something, nothing could dissuade her from it. She was one of those who made things happen, while he was one who let them happen. After pre-med, Harry continued training at Bellevue for a year while Alma finished at Columbia. When the Central Africa Mission accepted them, he wasn't certain he was ready to go. He was not an adventurer, but Alma couldn't wait to get started.

Standing there holding Alma's hand, he was apprehensive and uncertain. They were scheduled to go and establish a new station in the northeast corner of the Congo Free State where, in all probability, no white man had ever been before. Just a week ago John Scott, when he learned Alma was pregnant, had suggested Harry and Alma remain at Mbundu. It was the second station opened, located in the Kenya highlands where the temperature was pleasant, and lacked the mosquitoes and disease of the lowlands. There was a hospital, a school, and several missionary families. It was a safe and comfortable place for their first child to be born. When Scott had suggested maybe it would be better if they stayed at Mbundu, Alma had looked at her husband and asked, "Is this what you want, Harry?"

He would liked to have said, "Yes" but instead said, "I think that's for you to decide, dear."

"You're the leader," Alma said, turning to Reverend Scott, "and we'll do whatever you say, John, you know that. But, I'd like to have more reasons as to why you think we should stay here?"

"As I said, I just thought it would be easier for you and safer for the baby."

"I didn't know we came out here because it was safe. Having babies is a function of being a married woman. I assume when you, and the Board, decided it would be best to send out couples, you also understood there would be a good likelihood they would have children."

"Well, yes, but …" he said frowning and spreading his hands and taken back a little by her response. "Your assignment is a little different. Starting a new station is fraught with dangers and hardships. That is why I suggest you stay here until the child is older."

"How much older? A year? Ten Years? When do you think it'll be safe for a baby or a child? Are you going to reassign people every time some wife gets pregnant? What if the other women all got pregnant in the next two or three months? Would you sit back and wait until it was safe for the babies before you opened more stations? Are you going to have the work of the mission stop because some wife becomes pregnant?"

"I just thought—"

"I know. You were thinking of the baby and me and I appreciate that. Believe me, I appreciate it, but babies are born in this country every day."

"That's different. They are natives."

Alma smiled. "A native is one who is born in a place. If my child is born here then it, too, will be a native. I see women walking along with loads on their heads and babies strapped to their backs. If I have to, I'll strap my baby to my back like the native women do and go wherever I have to go, but don't let a baby, mine or anyone else's, stop us from doing what God has called us to do."

Alma had always been strong willed and had no allusions as to what the life would be like. She was told at the beginning they would be living in tents, and after that in wattle and thatch huts. "Wattle and thatch" was Scott's phrase. She guessed he thought it sounded better than "grass and mud" huts. In time they could start building their permanent homes. No one had ever told her it would be easy, and she was looking forward to it as an adventure.

Alma Kelly had always lived in comfort. The Kellys were Irish. "Orange Irish," her mother always reminded Alma. They attended the First Presbyterian Church. It was there at the age of twelve, after listening to a missionary, that Alma Gertrude Kelly decided she was going to be a missionary. Her parents didn't think she was serious. It was just a childhood fantasy. But she never changed her mind. They weren't pleased when she enrolled at Columbia University. While at Columbia, she met Harry VanVeldt. She invited him to a meeting at the New York Missionary Training College.

Alma didn't let Harry come to the house when she announced to her parents they were going to be married. Her parents didn't approve of Harry. Her father had even said something to the effect that Harry was after her money. She knew Harry had an inordinate respect for authority and might obey her father if he forbade Harry to marry

Alma. It was good Harry was not there because her parents said she wasn't to marry him or go to Africa. They accused her of being ungrateful and that she was throwing her life away. They even threatened to disown her until Alma ended the discussion by saying, "Dad, Mother, I love you both. But I'm going to live my life my way and marry whom I please and do what I please. You can either have hard feelings about it, or accept it graciously." Her parents accepted it, but not graciously.

Her parents didn't come to the dock to bid her farewell when the ship sailed. "For me to be at the sailing would give the impression I approve of this whole thing, and I don't," Mrs. Kelly said with a strong nod of her head.

"Mother, I'm going to be gone for years. Can't you at least yield enough to come down to the boat and see us off?"

"No! I want my last sight of you to be standing here in this house where you belong, not setting off on some ship for God knows where!"

Now, looking at the mountains that were part of the country in which she would establish a home for her family, she wondered if her parents' feelings would soften when they received the letter telling them she was pregnant.

They started after the others, both of them feeling a strange affinity for the mountains on the other side of Lake George. For as long as they were at Bashindi, the weather would never again be clear enough for them to see those mountains. When they left they would be moving away from them to the northeast. It would be forty years before they would see them. But for as long as they lived, and for all the other wonders they would see, they would never forget that first sight of the purple mountains of Congo, and the feelings of excitement, hope, fear and awe that first sight evoked.

CHAPTER SIX

Cloudless, blue skies, the faint smell of the smoke from the cooking fires, and the stronger pungent smell of corn beer lingered in the still air. Even this early in the morning the whole village was congregated, filled with excitement. It was a great day in the village, in the tribe, and even in the Five Tribes, for this was the day he who became a man first would become chief-to-be.

Kusala walked along the edge of the crowd acknowledging the greetings of those who called to him. Young children reached out to touch him and the girls eyed him as he passed and whispered to each other giggling behind their hands. If he happened to look at one of them she would turn away and look down at the ground.

He came to where his mother sat in front of her hut. His sisters were all there with her. His mother handed him a gourd of water flavored with lemon grass. He lifted the gourd to his mouth, swished the liquid around his mouth, and spit it out on the ground as a sacrifice and gift to the spirits. He raised the gourd again, drank a few swallows, and handed it back to his mother. "Beware of the hyena," she said taking the gourd. She always referred to his half bother, Kitomolo, as the hyena. "He will try to steal this day from you."

"I have no fear! I am the better one. He is no hunter." Being her only son, he had made her proud. He'd had to do it for she had no other sons from whom she could expect manly things. He was not the great warrior his father, Ronzozo, was, but aside from his father, there was none that could hunt or bring back meat for the village cooking fires the way Kusala did.

"It is not in the hunting he will steal the day," she said. She had always maintained that Meli, Kitomolo's mother, was the most devious woman she had ever known, and Kitomolo was worse than his mother.

Across the compound he saw Kitomolo laughing and joking with his brothers and friends. Kitomolo's brothers were also a hurt to his mother. Except for Kusala, she was able to present Ronzozo with nothing but girls. Meli had given Ronzozo five sons. But after today, none of that would be important. By the end of the day Sushi would be mother of Kusala, Chief-to-be, and Meli and her five sons would only be as important as Kusala permitted them to be.

Kusala turned and walked away when Ronzozo came out of the Chief's hut. Ronzozo was limping a little, favoring his left leg. He walked over to his tepoi, sat down, and his warriors raised him to their shoulders. He raised his hand and the crowd quieted. "Today my sons hunt to become men. Because they are of the same day born, he who kills a leopard and becomes a man first shall be chief after me. I, Ronzozo, have spoken it."

The crowd cheered and they started out of the village, Kusala and Kitomolo in front, their father behind them in the tepoi, and the rest of the young warriors on either side almost equally divided in their loyalties. Kusala's three friends were right behind him. Their spears were weighted and balanced as closely as possible to Kusala's. If he needed more than one spear, he could grab anyone of them and have no concern it would have an unfamiliar weight and feel.

At mid-day, from a small rise, they saw a group of leopards lying peacefully and content on the plain far below them. A male and three females stretched out sleeping on their sides in the sun while the kittens played and tumbled in the circle made by the adults. The two brothers moved forward staying hidden in the grass, their friends following behind while Ronzozo and the rest of the warriors took cover to watch from the top of the hill.

Kusala crawled forward on his hands and knees. He knew his brother was off to his right, crawling along as he was, but he did not look that direction, but only at the leopard. The male rolled up so he was lying on his belly with his legs under him, his head up, looking around. The breeze brought Kusala the smell of the leopards. The male was alert but not wary. Now was the time to throw. If they tried to get any closer the leopards might become aware of them and bolt. Kusala could just make it from there. It was farther than his brother could throw, but he could make it.

He drew back and threw; the spear flew with accurate speed from his hand. He saw his spear making its arc and then to the right of him he saw his brother's spear wobbling through the air. He couldn't understand why Kitomolo had thrown. Kitomolo had to know the distance was too great for him. What a fool! His spear wobbles as if thrown by a woman, Kusala thought.

He saw his own spear enter the male leopard's ribs. The leopard roared and the females and kittens ran away while the male bit and clawed at the spear imbedded in his side. Kusala threw a second spear and saw it enter just forward of the hips. The third entered the stomach. He took the forth spear and ran forward with his three friends behind him.

When he got to the leopard he held the spear out in front of him with both hands, the butt clamped against his body by his arm. The leopard made a feeble attack toward him and he thrust the spear in at the base of the neck to the heart. The blood spurted out, and he knew he had hit home. The animal kept pushing toward him, the blood was gushing out of his throat, but there was not much strength left in him. Still holding onto the spear, Kusala kept stepping back with the advance of the leopard until it crumpled and fell over on its side.

He looked around, but his brother was nowhere to be seen. There should have been shouting from the hill, but there was no shouting. He pulled his own spear from the leopard's side and his three friends, with their spears still stuck in the leopard, lifted it to their shoulders and followed Kusala to where his father and the warriors were waiting. Kitomolo was standing next to his father and the warriors looked at Kusala blank-faced. They dropped the leopard in front of the Chief and Kusala said, "I have killed my leopard. I am first to become a man."

"Kitomolo accuses you of bending the blade of his spear so it does not fly right. How do you answer this?" Chief Ronzozo asked.

Kusala remembered his mothers words and a cold fear came over him as he said, "All know I am the better hunter. I have no need to harm his spear. If his spear does not fly right it is because he cannot throw it."

"Look! It is bent!" Kitomolo said holding up his spear. All have seen its crooked path. You did this to my spear so I could not kill a leopard first. All did see I threw my spear first."

Kusala stood trembling with anger. "You lie! If your spear is bent you did it yourself to put the blame on me knowing you could not win without trickery."

"It is enough," the Chief said. "Talk no more. It will be decided in council."

In the council Kitomolo's friends testified that the night before the hunt they had seen Kusala outside Kitomolo's hut. They saw him in the darkness with Kitomolo's spear across his knees. The elders asked questions over and over again. Kusala was alone all night so there was no one to say he did not leave his hut. His only defense against the lies was that he was a better hunter; all the elders knew that, so why should he resort to such trickery? After many hours the elders agreed the batu-na-dawa would have to be called to cast the bones to decide the truth.

The batu-na-dawa and council were up all night. The bones did not have an easy time discovering the truth. It was dawn when friends brought Kusala word the council was coming out. Kusala stepped out of his man's hut. Across the clearing Kitomolo was standing in front of his own hut. The villagers began to assemble and Ronzozo came out. The crowd quieted and Ronzozo spoke. "It has been decided in council that because Kusala did by trickery try to become chief after me, he shall not be chief though he did first become a man. Kitomolo is Chief-to-be. I, Ronzozo, have spoken it."

Kusala couldn't believe what he heard. How could this be? Could not the bones discover his brother's lies? There was nothing left. Even the bones could not be trusted. Even the batu-na-dawa and his bones could be bought.

A shout went up and some of the warriors started to dance in celebration. Some of those standing on Kusala's side of the clearing edged their way to the other side. The Chief raised his hand again for quiet. "It is the law that he who tries to steal the place of chief shall be put to death unless the chief say he may live. It has been decided that at midday, when the sun is overhead and the shadows under foot, Kusala shall for two days be hunted and if found, killed. He who gives Kusala refuge, acts against me. He who hunts him not, also acts against me. If he has not been found when the sun is overhead of the second day, he may return and live in peace as son of the Chief and brother to the Chief-to-be. He is free to go and find his place of hiding and none may start to hunt until the sun is overhead. I, Ronzozo, have spoken it."

Kusala looked at the crowd around him. His father had been given him half a day to escape. He could run in a straight line, and always be half a day ahead of everybody else, but that would not prove anything. He had to show them he was better than his brother.

He pulled the reed door in place to close his hut and, taking his spear, ran from the village. He ran in a straight line until he was out of sight and then started making a loop, coming in on his own track. He jumped from rocks to rock, ran in the streams, swung from one vine to the next above the streams. Every time he made a turn he noted the exact spot where he did it. There were others in the village as good at following a trail as he, but he would make this one hard to follow and then come back along it, right through those who were hunting for him back to his hut.

It was dark when he emerged from the stream where he had relieved himself to confuse Kumiliki's dog. He was in the highest branches of a tree when Kumiliki and his dog and most of the others passed right below him. The dog ran in circles below, sniffing and scratching the dirt, before they moved on. By then he had been all the way to the Lake of Many Tears and back.

Between midnight and the coming of day he was back where he had made his first turn. In the darkness he had to be extra careful in following his track back to the village. Within a few hundred feet of the village he fell to his hands and knees. There was no reason to worry about the track here. This close to the village all tracks were covered by other people passing.

He was almost back to his hut when a woman came out of hers. He lay flat on the ground, motionless, while she walked past him to relieve herself in the brush on the edge of the village. She returned, and he crawled, stopping every few seconds to listen. He got to the back of his hut and, pressing himself against the wall, crawled around and slid in behind the reed door. He pulled the door closed behind him and then sat back smiling, pleased with himself. He had only to wait now until midday.

Through the cracks in the door he watched it get light. He waited, checking from time to time through the cracks, until the shadow of his hut's roof was straight down without any slant. He waited a little longer until he knew for sure midday had come and gone, and then relaxed the hold on his spear, suddenly aware he was hungry. He stepped out and went over to his mother's hut and told his sisters to bring him some food and water, making sure everyone in the village saw that just after noon of the second day Kusala was back at the village.

It was late afternoon when Kitomolo and the rest of the hunters returned. Kusala sat in the shadows of his hut looking through the door until Kitomolo was there.

He stepped out and said "Sene, Kitomolo."

Kitomolo looked at him, but said nothing.

"I greet Kitomolo, Chief-to-be."

"Sene, Kusala."

"I am alive."

Kitomolo didn't answer.

"At midday of the second day I came from my hut and walked the village. There are many here did see me."

"I have heard it so."

"While you did search the rocks and waters of the Lake of Many Tears I did sleep in my hut." He laughed as he said it, but for some reason no one was laughing with him. "Even with Gulu, and Kumiliki's dog to help you, you could not find me. All know that next to me, Gulu is the best hunter. Yet I did sleep in the village while you did search the night through."

The whole crowd was quiet, listening to him. "You cannot throw a spear, yet you are Chief-to-be. You are not yet a man, yet you are Chief-to-be. You cannot hunt, yet you are Chief-to-be. Your enemy sleeps in your own village and you look for him elsewhere." He turned to look at the gathered crowded and shouted, "Is this he you would have as Chief-to-be?"

He paused for a moment before he went on, sensing the crowd's hostility. In trying to make a fool of Kitomolo, he had made a fool of all who had hunted him, and they resented it. He was trying hard to think of what he could say to bring the people around to him when he heard his father's voice.

"Kusala." He turned and looked at his father standing in the door of the Chief's house. "You do cause trouble and rise up against the word of your Chief. You do stir up the people to go against the word of their chief. Leave this village and do not return again to this place until you can live in peace with your brother. I, Ronzozo, have spoken it."

He reached for his spear and almost gave the challenge but stopped himself just in time. It was one thing to try to influence the chief by the will of the people, but it was death to challenge a chief. He looked around and saw the resentment in the faces of the warriors. They now considered him an enemy, but even worse was the knowledge he had been the favored of his father and was now banished from the village, the tribe and his father. His father had staged the leopard hunt knowing Kusala would win and then given him another chance with a half-day start before Kitomolo could hunt him. But now there were no more chances. Kitomolo would be chief, and there was nothing he could do to change it. His brother would be chief because of his cunning and guile, not his ability and skill. Nothing could be depended upon. Even the bones of the batu-na-dawa could not be trusted.

He went over to his mother's hut. She was sitting on the ground by the entrance, her legs together and straight ahead of her, her back curved, her head down, her forearms running parallel to her thighs until her hands rested, palms down, on her knees. Her breast, flat and elongated from giving suck to so many children, hung down, the nipples touching the tuft of withered banda leaves clustered like a nest in her lap.

He stood looking down at her, controlling the anger within him. He had to control the anger. To give way to it would only cause her more agony. From the earliest days of understanding she had told him he was first born. There were rumors Kitomolo was born a day later than Meli said he was. Only Meli's mother was with her when she had given birth to Kitomolo. Ronzozo himself was at a meeting of the chiefs of the Five Tribes.

"You were right," he said to the silent figure. She didn't answer or even nod her head. "I shall not rise against my father," he said, "but on the day he dies I shall return and take what is mine."

He waited for some response, some encouragement, but she didn't raise her head to even look at him. He turned and left the village. He felt no fear. He would survive. Worse than any fear was the emptiness, a sense of loss, of having been abandoned. Never again would he be able to aspire to anything in any village. Even in the small villages he would always be a stranger, the one not of the clan. Because he had defied his father, there would never be a place for him in the council of the elders. He would wander from village to village, allowed to live, to eat the food of the village if the times were good, but he wouldn't be allowed to build a hut, and if he didn't have a hut, he wouldn't be able to take a bride. No father would give his daughter to a man who didn't have a house for her.

CHAPTER SEVEN

The rain was always there; sometimes more, and sometimes less, but it was always there. There was a long time of singing hymns and choruses after dinner. John Scott was sharing a devotional as he did every evening after dinner. Alma didn't listen much. She was thinking about the rain and wondering what it would be like to be living in tents in this kind of weather. She shifted in the hard wooden chair wishing Reverend Scott would finish his little talk. She was tired, and wanted to get to bed. She hadn't told anyone, but she'd had a couple of little contractions earlier that day.

The meeting broke up a little before nine and there was the general hubbub as those who had to go to other houses pulled on slickers and boots and lighted lanterns. She stood by the door watching the others leave, glad she and Harry didn't have to walk through the rain and mud to get to their rooms.

When the others left she followed Harry into their dark room. She watched him strike a match, which, because of the dampness, only left a little trail of sparks to glow for a second along the side of the box, and then the match died. He took another one. It blazed when he struck it, bringing a flash of light to the dimness of the room. He lifted the chimney off the lamp, touched the match to the wick, which caught, and the light in the room increased. He set the chimney back in place; the light became even brighter. He turned the wick up a little and set the open box of matches close to the light so the warmth of the lamp would drive the dampness out of the matches.

They quickly got undressed and into their nightgowns, spurred on by the damp chill of the room. Harry waited until she was in bed before he blew out the light. The bed bounced as he made his way across it to snuggle up to her, his knees bent to the shape of hers, his stomach against her back, his arm across her waist with his hand open against the fullness of her belly.

Her sleep was disturbed by a feeling of being cold. He had turned over, away from her, and she pushed herself across the bed until her back was pressed against the warmth of his and she felt a contraction, stronger than she had ever felt before. It was a cramp that seemed to start at her backbone with the pain crawling around her hips to end up below her stomach. She waited for a moment and then it was gone.

She waited until she'd had three of the cramps and then she called him, "Arrie." When he didn't respond she poked him in the back and spoke a little louder. "Arrie? Arrie?"

"Huh? What?" He turned over and sat up.

"I think it's time."

"Huh? Oh!" He started to get up, running a long fingered hand through his straight black hair, getting his legs tangled in the bedding in his eagerness. "What's happened?"

"I've had three contractions. Strong ones. I had a couple earlier today, too, but not like these."

He got up, and went over to light the lamp, fumbling with four matches before he got it lit. The light came up in the room and he went over and sat down on the edge of the bed. "Now just relax," he said, and she smiled thinking he was the one who was excited. "All we can do right now is wait."

By seven o'clock all the missionaries that gathered at the Jones' house for breakfast knew Alma had started labor. By eight o'clock all the mission natives knew of it. By nine o'clock those who came to the dispensary for treatment were taking the news back to the their villages. In the cookhouse, kettles of hot water were set on the side of the stove to keep hot and the cradle Samuel Jones had made for their daughter, Melody, was brought in.

At five in the afternoon, thirteen hours after Alma woke Harry, the baby was born. It was a textbook delivery. The head, the shoulders, the body, and just before Harry pulled the tiny legs free Sarah cried, "It's a girl, Alma. A perfectly beautiful girl."

Sarah swabbed the baby's mouth, it cried and started breathing. Harry tied off and cut the cord, wrapped the baby in a warm towel, carried it around to show Alma and then gave the baby to Sarah to clean and weigh. Harry went and stood by the bed holding Alma's hand while the women hurried around cleaning and straightening the bed.

"She's beautiful, isn't she," Alma said smiling.

"Yes she is," he answered pushing the heavy, damp, brown hair away from her forehead. "Now get some rest. We'll bring the baby to you in a little while to be fed."

"What are we going to name her?" she asked.

"What do you want?"

"Rebecca Julianna," she said as she fell asleep.

It was a combination they had never discussed. For some reason he got all choked up. He didn't know if it was because the baby now had a name, or the name itself; Rebecca, the bride sought for Isaac, and Julianna, after his mother.

An hour later Sarah Jones lifted little Rebecca out of the cradle and brought her over to Alma for her first feeding. Harry was sitting on the edge of the bed. He helped prop the pillow up behind Alma and then sat facing her. She pushed the nightgown to one side exposing the pregnant breast and then reached for her baby, holding it for the first time, cradling it in the crook of her arm. She smiled down at her baby, directing its mouth toward her nipple. The tiny hand pressed against the fullness of her breast, the pink lips closing around the nipple, and the sucking mouth began drawing its life from her. The instant Rebecca started to suck it was as though a strange warm feeling came from those tiny lips to her nipple, passing through her breast along her stomach to her innermost being.

She looked down at her child; sucking, swallowing, sucking, swallowing, sucking, swallowing, and then Rebecca coughed, spitting up the thick, yellow milk through her mouth and nose. The baby started to cry.

"Arrie! What's wrong?"

"Nothing, Darling," he said covering his own concern. "She just tried to swallow too fast and got a little milk down her windpipe." He took Rebecca, holding her cradled in his arm while he wiped her mouth and face and Alma cleaned the spit-up milk from her body and nightgown. She took the baby back, putting her to nurse on the other side. As soon as Rebecca's lips touched her nipple she felt that same special affinity for her daughter. She was beautiful. She was perfect. She sucked strongly, eagerly at the nipple. Alma was sure she could feel the milk flowing out of her into her child and then Rebecca spit up again. She looked at her husband and saw the concern on his face. In a wail of fear she said "Arrieee ... There's something wrong!"

Sarah Jones came in and stood by them, watching.

He took the baby again, cleaning it, and then sat down on the bed alongside his wife. He handed Rebecca back to Alma, and put one arm around her, supporting her and holding her for strength against his fears. "Now don't let her have too much," he said. "Just let her have one or two swallows and then pull her away."

It seemed so cruel. The little mouth would just start to suck and then Harry would move Rebecca's mouth away and she would start to cry. "No, not yet. Give her time to swallow it," he said, his hand over Alma's preventing her from moving the little head back to her breast. Sometimes he waited more than a minute and then would say, "All right. Let her have just a little now," and then right away he would pull Rebecca's head away again.

"What do you think is wrong, Arrie?"

"I don't know."

"But you have an idea," she said trying to hide her concern.

He shook his head, his black hair swinging across his brow. He didn't know what to say and permitted her to put the baby to her breast again for an instant. She felt Rebecca suck and then Rebecca's head jerked as she spit up.

"Here, give her to me," Sarah Jones said. She took the wailing Rebecca, cradling her in her arm, carrying her over to the cradle and put her in it. Harry leaned forward holding Alma to him, her head resting on his shoulder, her hands clutching at him. They didn't say anything for fear it might bring about what they feared. From the living room they could hear the singing as the evening devotions started, singing without Harry's trumpet to lead them.

"Just let her rest awhile, and we'll try again a little later," Sarah said. "You get some rest, too, Alma." She went around the room straightening things, fluffed the pillows, and said, "Now try to get some sleep. I'll come in and wake you when it's time for her next feeding." She turned the lamp down and left the room.

"What's wrong with her, Arrie?" Alma asked.

"Nothing. She's just having a little trouble swallowing. It's not unusual in newborns," he said lying and smiling. "She'll be fine. Now get some rest." He lay down on his back bringing her to him, her head on his shoulder, her arm across his chest.

"Why is she still crying?"

"She's just angry because we woke her up. She'll fall asleep any minute now," he said and Rebecca, tired from trying to nurse and from crying, stopped crying and fell asleep. "See, didn't I tell you?"

He felt her breathe a sigh of relief and a little while later she, too, was asleep. He lifted her arm from across his chest and, being careful not to wake her, slid his shoulder out from under her head. She mumbled but didn't wake up. He put on his shoes and went out through the side door to the porch. He didn't want to see them. Didn't want to answer their questions or see their looks of pity. He stood there trying to keep his mind from dwelling on what he suspected, saying over and over again, "Oh, God, straighten it out. Don't let anything be wrong. Make everything right. Please, God! Please, God! Please, God!" All around him was the sound of the water pouring off the roof into the rushing stream in the ditch. From time to time, a gust of wind would blow a fine spray of water against him, chilling him, giving his physical body the same chilling sensation as was inside him.

He went back in through the door of the pantry to the dining room. From there he could see them all on their knees praying; praying for a miracle, praying for wisdom and understanding, praying for strength, comfort, and peace. But most of all they were praying for a miracle and he knew Sarah had told them. He didn't know what she had told them, but they wouldn't be praying for a miracle if she had said everything was all right. She didn't need any medical training to know the food was not getting to the stomach.

From where she was kneeling with the others she lifted her head and saw him. She came and sat down at the table next to him. "Do you know what's wrong?" she asked in a matter-of-fact way.

He looked at her sitting next to him, her hands folded on the table in front of her, her head turned to look at him. She wasn't a large woman, but an aura of strength emanated from her. Her blond hair was pulled back from her face and tied in a bun at the back of her head. The gaze of the large, blue eyes intent, and showed neither pity nor resignation. She was the kind who believed you did what you could and left the rest to God. She and her husband had come to Africa eight years before with the first party in 1893. She was a practical woman; one of those determined to survive, and so she did. She had no medical training, but she ran the mission infirmary because there was no one else to do it. She had sent off for medical books and had studied after they got to the field. "Do you know what's wrong?" she asked again, and her attitude helped Harry to view Rebecca as a patient and not as his daughter.

"It's a constriction, or a blockage of the esophagus."

"Is there anything that can be done? Medically I mean."

"Not that I know of."

She sat there staring at her hands for a moment. "Maybe if we feed her just one swallow at a time. If we feed her a spoonful at a time it may seep through. What do you think?"

He smiled, not a real smile, but a twisting of the mouth in resignation and nodded. He got up when she did and went back to the bedroom. His clothes were too damp to lie down on the bed so he sat in the chair next to the table with the lamp on it. He sat staring at his wife. How am I going to tell her? What am I going to tell her? He got up and went and stood with the lamp in his hand looking into the cradle. Rebecca was sleeping with her fist clenched next to her face. She looked so perfect, so complete, so healthy. He stood looking at her for a long time, and then went, and sat down again.

It was ten-thirty when Sarah came back in carrying a fresh kettle of hot water. She poured some of the water into the basin and set the kettle down. She dampened a washcloth, and went to the edge of the bed. "Alma." Sarah shook her gently. "It's time to feed Rebecca again. Here's a washcloth. Wipe your face. You'll feel better."

Alma sat up and ran the washcloth all over her face and neck. "I'm sorry to wake you, Alma. It'll only be for a minute and then you can go back to sleep," she said, getting Rebecca from the cradle. Alma put Rebecca to her breast and, more asleep than awake, watched the baby suck and take a swallow and then Sarah took the baby away and it started to cry. Alma looked up wondering what was happening. "She can only have a little bit at time. You go back to sleep. I'll bring Rebecca back to you for more in an hour."

"Can't I hold her?"

"No. You need your rest. You can hold her next time. I'll take Rebecca out until she stops crying," she said, and Alma lay back on the bed, disappointed, and fell asleep.

Sarah brought the baby in again at eleven-thirty and twelve-thirty for a swallow of milk. At the twelve-thirty swallow Rebecca again spit up. They could not hide the truth. If there was any food getting to the stomach it was so little it would only prolong the inevitable.

Sarah took the crying baby out of the room and Harry sat down on the edge of the bed. He reached out and took Alma's hands in his and she saw the tears well up and then overflow. She didn't look into his eyes, but down at his hands as though she expected those hands to do something. He saw her body shake with her grief and the clenched lips which refused to add her wailing to that of the baby's, so all he could hear was a whimper. He felt inadequate and frustrated. There was nothing he could do to help his child. Clinically, he knew that within three to seven days his child would starve to death and there was nothing he, or any other human being, could do. And although he hadn't said anything to Alma, she also knew and there was no way he could comfort her. He could hold her, he could sympathize, he could empathize, he could, and did, share her fear, but that was not comfort. The only thing that could comfort them was if someone could correct what was wrong. That would be comforting.

Nor could they blame Africa for it. It wouldn't have made any difference if Rebecca had been born in London, or New York, or Zurich; in the best hospital in the world, there was nothing anyone could have done. He sat there for a while holding back the tears, and then he could control himself no longer. He slid off the bed and knelt at the edge of it. His head rested on his arms and his body racked with the sobs that came from deep within him. He wanted to pray, but all he could do was sob, "Oh, God. Oh, God. Oh please, God. Oh, God." He thought he should be strong for her sake, but he couldn't help himself. He felt her stroking his head and he reached out and took his hand in hers.

From the living room, Alma could hear the faint cries of the child she longed to hold. Seeing her husband on the floor next to her, she knew there was no hope. He had not said anything to her, had not made any explanation, but the fact he was there told her there was no hope. If there were any medical procedure that had even the remotest possibility of saving their child, he would have been making preparations to perform it, rather than kneeling by the bed weeping.

Dave Robins stuck his head in and then walked around the foot of the bed. He started for the cradle, stopped, looked at them, and then came over and knelt down beside Harry. He didn't say anything, didn't pray, just knelt next to Harry with one arm around him. After several minutes he lifted his head and kissed Harry on the back of the head. He reached over and took one of her hands, held it for a minute, and then got up and carried the cradle out of the room. He was crying when he left the room. He was the last person she would have expected to act that way. Rough, tough, Dave Robins, with his silly cowboy boots, unruly red hair, freckled, pie-shaped face, and eyes that always seemed to be squinting into his precious Colorado sun had cried for them. The tears had ran across his freckled cheeks to drop on Harry's head and on her hand. He had walked out carrying the cradle, not bothering to try and wipe the tears from his face, and she knew those tears were not for himself, but for them.

Rebecca Julianna VanVeldt lived for five days before she starved to death. After the first twenty-four hours, Sarah Jones stopped taking Rebecca into Alma to be fed because of the emotional strain. Instead, she tried to feed the baby cow's milk with an eyedropper. During the first three days Rebecca cried to be fed until she grew too tired, and then she would fall asleep. Her crying became weaker until she had no strength. She just lay there with eyes sunken into her head, the flesh melting away so they could see the blood moving through the tiny vessels and the outlines of the bones through the thin infant skin.

They used a packing case for a coffin which rested in the living room for two days while they waited for the rains to let up, but they couldn't wait any longer. In the morning the grave was dug at the top of a rise not far from the infirmary. When they got there in the early afternoon there were several inches of water standing in the bottom of the grave. None of the women went to the graveside. Dave Robins carried the coffin. It was too small for more than one person to carry. They walked in single file, each wearing a slicker, and carrying a black umbrella. They gathered around the hole that was twice as big as the coffin and four feet deep. Dave slipped and almost fell in the mud when he set the coffin down. Reverend Scott preached the graveside service, but those on the other side of grave couldn't hear him because of the noise of the rain falling on their umbrellas. When they put the coffin in the grave, it floated on the water in the bottom for a while, and then settled to the bottom. Harry was glad Alma was not there. They walked away, a single file of black umbrellas, the mud squishing around their feet leaving the natives to throw the mud back into the hole.

***

The rain had stopped two days before and things were beginning to dry out. That morning Harry had taken Alma to see where Rebecca Julianna was buried. Walking there the path had been slippery in spots and the little mound of black-brown earth was damp and cold. Alma had reached down and placed her hands on it and, when she stood up, the dirt was still on her hands. She didn't want to rub it off. The two of them stood there, letting the tears flow, and then went back to the house, not wanting to talk to anyone else.

That same afternoon they sat around the dining room table with Scott at the head. Outside, beyond the porch, all the trees, shrubs, grass and even the other buildings glowed with the warmth of the afternoon sun.

Harry didn't know why Scott had called the meeting, but since the Fenkins and the Jacksons were not there, Harry was afraid it was more bad news. He was sure of it when Scott opened the meeting with a prayer asking The Almighty for guidance, wisdom and strength. Scott kept his head bowed and his eyes closed for some time after he said the "Amen."

They all sat looking at him, waiting, and when he did look up he stared at each of them for a moment, his brow furrowed as though trying to grasp something he didn't understand. His voice quavered with hurt emotion when he said, "I can't think of a kind way to say this so I'll just speak it out, but the Jacksons and the Fenkins came to me this morning and informed me they were not going on. They are even now making arrangements for porters and a guide to take them back—"

Exclamations of shocked unbelief interrupted him and he raised a hand to quiet them while his other hand touched a handkerchief to his eyes to wipe the tears. "I tried to dissuade them of course, but they were adamant. Please don't take offense at this Alma, Harry," he said looking at each of them with tears running down his cheeks, "but I think the death of little Rebecca awakened them to the fact that where we are headed is even more remote and perilous than here and that maybe frightened them."

The four of them stared at him, stunned, and yet admitting and understanding their own uncertainty.

"I have, of course, cabled the home office of these developments. But the question before you is whether you want to go on. I want you to think hard about this and pray about it before you decide—"

"I don't have to pray about it," Alma said interrupting him. "I am not going to let someone else's action influence what I believe God has called us to do. Isn't that right, Harry?"

He nodded, but he wished he was as certain as she seemed to be.

"My guess is they will reply that the decision is up to us. There are some options to consider. We can all quit and go back home and that will be the end of it for a while, anyway. Or you four can stay here and help with the work of this station while I go back and find some more people who will help us go and establish the new station. Lastly, the five of us would decide to go forward. If that were the case I would stay on with you. Watsumdumu would not be happy with the responsibility of bringing the porters back out, but I'm confident he could do it."

"You mean the five of us would be out there in the middle of nowhere without anyone knowing where we are?" Laura asked with an anxious frown.

"Laura," Scott said reaching over to squeeze her hand, "even now others are being trained to help with the work. As you all know we would be making maps as we go in, just as the Joneses and I did when we first came in to establish this station. The only difference is that instead of eight people staying to establish a station, there would be only the five of us, and instead of my leading the safari out, Watsumdumu would do it."

"Yeah, well that's something we really have to pray about, isn't it," Dave Robins said as he squinted looking out the window.

1902

CHAPTER EIGHT

Harry VanVeldt and Dave Robins stood on the shore of the river. They had made their way north along Lake Albert until the lake became the Nile River. On the other side the sun was going down behind the trees. On either side of them the long, round-bottomed, dugout canoes were pulled up on the shore in preparation for the next day's crossing. Behind them were their own tents, the encampment of the safari, and the buildings of the Murchison Falls garrison.

"Tomorrow we will be in the Congo," Dave said, his eyes squinting against the setting sun, his hair having an even redder glow to it. They waited for the sun to disappear below the horizon and then went back to camp.

Alma, wearing a dress that came well below the tops of her knee-high boots as protection against the mosquitoes, sat in one of the camp chairs trying to read by the dim light of the kerosene lantern hanging from the tent post. The gold flecks in her gray eyes seemed brighter than the glow from the dim lamp. Harry pulled a chair up to the camp table, ran his hands through his black hair pushing it away from his eyes, took out a pad of paper and started to write. With his left hand he not only held the pad of paper, but also steadied the table against the motion of his writing.

Fort Murchison Falls
Buganda Province (via Mombasa)
British East Africa, Africa
January 27, 1902

Dear Pop, Mom, and all the dear ones at home:
We haven't heard from you since the last pile of letters which we received over a month ago while we were still at Bashindi. Nor can I imagine when we will hear from you next. We were all hoping something would catch up with us before we leave tomorrow morning. Now there is no telling how many months or even years it will be

before we hear from you again. As always I am enclosing the pages of the daily journal for the past week.

It is hard to believe how little is known about the area into which we will be going. Maybe that is why King Leopold was so willing to give the mission a grant. Everything on the British side of the Nile is well marked, but thirty miles west of the river the map is a blank.

The British Colonial office has asked us to make maps of the area through which we pass. As I mentioned in last week's letter, Dave and I have been taking instruction on how to use the sextant and mercury basin from Reverend Scott. Now it seems we will not only need that skill to find our destination, but also for making maps. Seeing us practicing with the sextant and basin, the authorities here ask Reverend Scott if we would be willing and interested in making maps for them. We spent several hours with the resident cartographer getting some helpful hints and getting supplies. Upon agreeing to make maps we were offered an escort of native soldiers. Apparently, they want to make certain our maps of the area return safely. They also made it clear the soldiers were under our command, and not a British incursion into Leopold's Congo. For that reason the soldiers will not be in uniform. When those soldiers return with our maps, the British will have a better knowledge of Leopold's territory than the King of the Belgians himself has.

Having decided to accept the military escort, we also thought it would be reasonably safe for the families of the porter to accompany their men if they so desired. With that news the morale of the porters immediately improved.

Thank you again for all your letters. Share this with all the family. The journals will bring you up-to-date on our daily happenings. How we rejoice with you all, and especially with John and Sarah, at the birth of Elizabeth Ruth.

The loss of Rebecca Julianna is still hard to bear, but Alma is doing remarkably well.

This letter will be sent out with the next post from the fort. I don't know when you will hear from us next.

We pray for all of you daily. Pray for us that our Lord will find us faithful, for I know that within myself I am totally inadequate.

Your loving son, Arrie.

***

Flowing from Lake Albert to the Mediterranean, the Nile River, through the centuries, has been the site of more disaster, death, slavery, conquest, defeat, anguish and cruelty than any other one river in the world. On its banks have raged innumerable wars. At one end the battles of the Pharaohs, Caesars, Alexander, Turks, Arabs, crusaders and at the other end, tribal chieftains and Arab warlords. Kingdoms: black, white, and brown have come to power, and passed away. Persecuted slaves have died by the millions. People have been slaughtered on its banks, drowned in its cataracts, and disappeared in its swamps. It abounds with disease; sleeping sickness, malaria, bilharzia, and is infested with mosquitoes, leeches, parasites, savage flesh-eating fish and vicious crocodiles. Yet, in the morning sunlight, it lay there; calm as silk, placid as butter, with no evidence of the violence of which it was capable or that it even flowed.

The tranquility of the river was disturbed by the first of the canoes breaking the glassy surface. The dugout canoes, some as short as thirty feet and some as long as seventy, were all as round as the tree trunks from which they were carved. There was nothing in the canoes to keep them stable except the instinctive sense of balance of the paddlers who shifted their body weight to compensate for any imbalance.

John Scott, Harry and Alma went across in the first wave of some forty canoes with John in one canoe and Harry and Alma in another. Watsumdumu and the Robins were last on the British side of the river to come over with the last wave of canoes. Each canoe was filled half with paddlers and half with cargo and passengers. The passengers sat on their bundles with their hands resting on the gunwales. If they slid their hands over the side just a little they could touch the water just six inches below. They sat tense and stiff, fearful any movement they made would overturn the canoe.

In their canoe, Alma sat with her hands folded around her helmet in her lap, her wavy, brown hair caressed by the early morning breeze. Her eyes showed the excitement she felt with the prospect of the crossing and with the idea that when she touched land again, she would be in Leopold's Congo Free State.

In front of her, six paddlers bent in unison, dipping the paddle into the water and then leaning into the paddle propelling the canoe forward. Behind her, the other passengers and the cargo, were six other paddlers. They sang a chant in harmony with all the other paddlers in the other canoes, the ones in back singing a line, and the paddlers in front answering with the next line of the chant.

The canoe touched the bank and the paddlers in front jumped out and pulled it up on the bank. Alma walked forward, picking her way through the water in the bottom of the canoe and holding up her skirt, stepped over the side to the soft earth of the riverbank. With all of the passengers out they were able to pull the canoe up to dry land and the cases and bundles were unloaded, the porters carrying them well away from the water's edge. She sat down on one of the boxes and squeezed the water out of the bottom of her skirt, resolving that tomorrow she would wear the men's trousers she had bought so many months before. Where they were going there wouldn't be anyone who might consider it improper for a woman to wear trousers.

In front of her, John Scott walked back and forth talking to the porters, to Harry and to her while the canoes went back for the next load. He couldn't hide his excitement. He was a small, wiry man in his mid forties with gray beginning to show in his brown hair. He seemed to be like a bird that wanted to look everywhere at the same time with his dark, piercing eyes. His head jerked a little as he looked from one object to the next trying to see if anything needed his immediate attention.

It was almost noon when the last of the supplies and men came across. In one of the canoes, a porter, in his eagerness to get to shore, jumped over the side just as the canoe touched the muddy bank, tipping the canoe over. The passengers scrambled frantically, some pushing through the water to the shore, others trying to save some of the cargo. John Scott rushed in to get a box that was floating away. Flailing his arms, he kept following the box as it floated on the current until he was up to his neck in the river. He stood there, knee deep in mud, neck deep in water, as the box, with mocking defiance, floated away from him while at the same time sinking below the surface. He stood there angry and frustrated. On shore everyone kept shouting for him to come back, warning him there were crocodiles in the river. He came out wet, muddy and despondent and dropped to the ground.

They unpacked the items that had fallen into the river and spread them out to dry and Harry instructed Watsumdumu to get the tents set up. Scott objected and Harry said, "You have to get dry clothes on you and the supplies have to dry out. No sense rushing just to have some things mildew and rot on us. Tomorrow will be soon enough."

CHAPTER NINE

Kusala squatted low in the grass sitting on his heels. To the right of him the sun was just coming over the edge of the earth creating long shadows of trees, boulders, and of the animals that made their way toward the watering hole. Behind him was a visible path where his passing had wiped dew from the blades of grass. Everything—the earth, the trees, the boulders and even the animal he was going to kill—was content and at peace.

A herd of gazelle started to move with precise steps away from the watering hole. Two lingered a little longer, their heads down drinking the water. The last one to stop raised his head and, when he saw the others were leaving, turned with a jump, slipping in the trampled mud at the water's edge, almost falling and then loped after the others.

They moved along in a single file, walking with a slow, delicate, prancing gait. A few lowered their heads to take a bite of grass, but most of them kept their heads held high, sniffing the wind, heading for better pasture. Kusala moved bent low through the grass toward that point where they would pass by him.

The last one in the herd was a yearling buck. There were larger gazelle in the herd, but if he tried to get one of those, one in the back might see the spear flying through the air, get scared and spook the rest.

The last gazelle passed him. He slid his left foot forward, shifting his position as his right arm went back, jostling the spear until it settled balanced in his hand. At the same time his left arm rose, forming a straight line from the right hand that held the spear through his shoulder line to the tip of the fingers of his left hand. He threw, rising out of the grass as he did so. The spear flew through the air as his body settled back into the protective covering grass. He waited, watching the spear arc through the sky, and then start to descend. The spear entered at an angle just forward of the hip.

The gazelle gave a bleat, bounded once in the air, and then the whole herd leapt away in fear. He stood up and watched them leave. There was no hurry. With each bounding leap of the animal, the end of the spear rose and fell, slashing back and forth inside the gazelle. The animal would run until it was too weak to go any further, and then it would die.

He walked along, whistling as he followed the gazelle. When he could no longer see the animal, the trail of blood was easy to follow. He found it lying on its side with its legs straight out. It raised its head and thrashed its legs a little trying to get up. It was too weak and its head fell back to the ground. He took a hand-forged, hook-shaped knife from the cord around his waist and, kneeling with one knee on the animal's nose, his left hand on the tip of a horn, kept the head pinned to the ground. With his right hand he made a small cut in the gazelle's neck. The blood came from the wound in slow spurts. He let the knife drop and cupping his hand to catch the blood, bent over and drank of it as it flowed from the wound. The blood was warm and tasted good. The blood had the life and the spirits of the gazelle and in drinking it they would become a part of him. The gazelle was young, strong, swift, and agile and he drank those traits into himself along with the life and nourishment of the blood. He drank, receiving the sharpness of eye and the swiftness of hoof to mingle with those abilities that were already his.

The blood stopped flowing and he picked up the knife and moved to the back of the animal to yank the spear from its side. He squatted and made a cut starting just back of the rib cage and sawed at the skin and flesh with the crude, hooked knife, cutting open the belly. There was the smell of blood and raw flesh, and the smell of excrement where the slashing blade of the spear had cut open the intestines.

The flies swarmed and buzzed around. They gathered at the dead animals eyes, nose and mouth, at the cut in the throat, around the tail area, but landed in swarms on the guts being pulled out of the carcass. With each movement of his hand they would rise in protest at being disturbed, the sound of their wings a droning in the stillness.

He pulled the guts from the carcass and then wiped the inside of the cavity the best he could with tufts of grass. He stood and walked around to the other side and, reaching over, took hold of the front and back legs and rolled the carcass over, the flies swarming and buzzing. Kneeling down he picked up the lifeless, 120-pound carcass and maneuvered it onto his shoulders. With the legs hanging down in front of him, he shifted it until it was balanced around his neck and then took some lengths of grass and tied the legs together in front of him. With his left hand holding the hooves of the gazelle and his right hand carrying the spear like a staff, he started for the village.

***

It was a good day. The spirits were favorable to him. The sun was not yet halfway to its midday height and he was returning with meat for the village. It was a pleasant village with only eight families, all the same clan. At first they had accepted him because he was the son of Ronzozo. There was an abandoned, rundown hut, which the chief of the village, the head of the clan, had said he could use. They hadn't expected him to stay more than a night or two. The second day he went hunting and brought his kill back to the village. Little by little they let him know there was no need for him to move on and they had begun to accept him for himself, even though he wasn't of their clan.

He came to a stream and lowered the carcass into it. Little crayfish ran away to hide under rocks. The great multitude of flies that were concentrated inside the carcass buzzed in protest when they were engulfed in the water, while the rest floated away. He let the water wash away all the blood. When the carcass was clean, he started bathing himself, his head and neck, arms and legs. Lifting the dripping carcass to his shoulders, he started for home.

It was a little after midday when he entered the village. There was something different. The children didn't run out to meet him. The men greeted him, but this time no one walked along side to talk about the hunt.

The village chief rose up from the shade of the granary where he was sitting. Kusala lowered the animal to the ground in front of the chief who would divide it among the villagers. He saw Akudru emerge from the shadows of the granary and he knew Akudru had not come as a friend, but as a bringer of bad news.

They stood facing each other while the villagers gathered to hear what was said. He knew it must be bad for Akudru was having trouble saying it. "What is it you have come to say?" Kusala asked.

"Your mother is dead."

Those words fell like a heavy boulder inside him. All people die, but somehow he thought his mother would go beyond everyone else. "When did she die?"

"Three days ago. A little before midday."

Akudru had not wasted any time. It was a good two days journey to Ronzozo's village. "How came this thing to be?"

"Your sister said it to me to say to you. She was by your mother's side, both of them grinding corn. Your mother cried 'Eeeeyowww' and put her hand to her head. When she tried to get up she could not, but fell on her side. The batu-na-dawa came and cut her in many places to let the evil spirits out, but they would not leave. He could not drive them out. She died that same day."

Kusala walked away from the small crowd of villagers and went to his hut. He went inside, sat down on the ground, his knees up, his arms wrapped around his knees. Outside the door Akudru squatted on his heels, close to his friend, but not interfering with his feelings. Kusala sat looking out the door.

It had to be witchcraft. It was well known everything had spirits in it. There were good spirits and there were bad spirits. The earth was the mother of all the good spirits. That was why when people died they were buried in the earth so their body could return to the good spirits. There were witches who could influence and sometimes even control bad spirits. Witch experts could be hired to counteract the influence of witches. Anybody could be a witch. A man, or a woman, or a boy, or a girl, but it was well known the witch substance in boys and girls was not strong. Only a member of the chief's family could not be a witch. Since the chief decided if a person was a witch, he could not be a witch himself. A person was a witch by heredity. A father passed his witch substance on to his sons and a mother passed her witch substance on to her daughters. A father could not pass it to a daughter and a mother could not pass it to a son, for the witch substance of men was different from that of women.

He sat in his hut knowing all this, things he had known from his earliest childhood. Yet knowing all this, he was convinced his brother Kitomolo had performed witchcraft to kill his mother. But this could not be, for Kitomolo was of the chief's family, and chiefs cannot be witches. Yet he could think of no one else who would have wanted to perform witchcraft on his mother. This had not been a weak kind of witchcraft that only made her sick. This was witchcraft to kill her. The only way Kitomolo could be a witch is if he were not truly Ronzozo's son, if Meli, Ronzozo's third wife, had lain with some other man, a man who was a witch. It was well known the witch substance passed on in this way was the most powerful kind.

The sun was low in the sky when Kusala came out of his hut. Akudru came and stood next to him. "Who sent you to me, Akudru?" Kusala asked.

"I have said, your sister."

"And my father? What did he at the death of my mother?"

"The death dance was well done. The burying also."

"Who led the death dance, her daughters? Was nothing said that her only son should be there?"

"If it was said, it was not heard by me. The death was quick. There was not time for you to get there."

He knew Akudru was trying to keep peace, to make excuses. "And Kitomolo, what did he?"

"He danced as did your father in honor of your mother."

A girl approached from one of the huts and he knew she was coming to tell them they would be welcome to eat at their cooking fire. "Go and eat, Akudru. I have no stomach for food. Then stay the night with me and leave in the morning. Go to my father and say to him that in four days when the sun is high in the sky, I, Kusala, will come to him. If he will see me, so be it. If he will kill me, so be it, but I do come."

***

It was obvious from the surprised looks on the faces of the villagers they were not told he was coming. He walked down the center of the ilolo toward his father's house. He stopped ten feet in front of his father's hut. He stood, holding his spear in his right hand, the butt of the spear resting close to his foot, his arm outstretched so the spear angled away from him. He stood there waiting, not moving. He knew those inside could see him and were watching him. Because he was in the bright sun, all he could see was the darkness of the doorway.

The sun was overhead when he arrived, but was halfway toward the earth when his father stepped out of the hut. Ronzozo stood just outside the door still in the shade of the small porch that encircled the hut. "Kusala?" Ronzozo spoke the name as a question even though he knew it was his son.

"It is I, Kusala, first born son of Chief Ronzozo."

His father stared at him. He knew his father was angered by his answer, but he had to answer that way in case Kitomolo should hear him. Now that Ronzozo had come out, the men of the village began to gather, forming a large circle around Kusala. If Ronzozo gave the word he would not be able to escape.

"I, Ronzozo, Chief of the Five Tribes, said to Kusala not to come again to this place if you do not come in peace. Do you come in peace, Kusala?"

"I come to see the place of my mother's burying, to mourn along with my father at her dying, and to accuse him who worked the witchcraft that killed my mother."

Ronzozo stood for a moment and then walked with dignity, despite his limp, down the incline until he stood before his son. Looking into his eyes he spoke in low tones so the warriors standing in the circle could not hear what he said. "And who is it you accuse of this witchcraft?"

"Kitomolo."

Kusala could see the anger in his father's eyes, but there was no other indication that might have been seen by the warriors.

"He is my son. He cannot be a witch," Ronzozo said through clenched teeth.

Kusala knew Ronzozo comprehended all of the implications of the accusation he made, but still he went on. "If he is not truly your son, if he was fathered by another who is a witch, he could have done it."

Ronzozo raised his arms and put his hands on Kusala's shoulders. To those standing by it might have looked like act of affection, but he squeezed so hard Kusala had to work to keep from wincing. "I, Ronzozo, Chief of the five tribes tell you this. It is only because you are my son that you are still alive. I told you once you could return when you came in peace. You did not come in peace. So I tell you now, you are never to return unless I, Ronzozo, Chief of the Five Tribes, send for you. On the day you do come without being called you shall surely die. I, Ronzozo, have spoken it."

Kusala looked into his father's eyes and knew he had gambled and lost. He had known when he came his father would not accept his accusation. "I have heard what my father has said. Now let Ronzozo, Chief of the Five Tribes, hear what Kusala, firstborn son of Ronzozo, would say. After today Ronzozo shall never again see the face of his first born son, Kusala. I will respect and defend my father the Chief. May you live long and have a good life. On the day I hear of your death, I will do the death dance and mourn for you and my mourning will be true and deep. But know you this, on the day you are buried I shall start calling warriors and will make war on Kitomolo and I shall sit in the place of chief, which is rightfully mine. Know you this, too. I do not come again to this village except to kill my brother. Look you well and see what you may see, for today is the last day you shall look on the face of your firstborn son. I, Kusala, have spoken it."

Ronzozo dropped his arms and Kusala turned and walked away. The warriors parted to let him pass through. He walked the length of the village the way he had come. He did not turn to look back, but he knew his father was still standing in the same place watching him leave.

CHAPTER TEN

The country was rolling hills. For the most part, they followed native paths that were headed in the northwest direction they wanted to go. They crossed small streams, some of them beginning to dry up with the coming of the dry season. At each stream Dave would find a small, smooth stone, and drop it in his pocket.

"You going to pick up a stone at every stream we come to?" Laura asked. She was a large woman who was raised on a ranch in Colorado. Her face and arms had an everlasting tan. Her blond hair was cut short and hidden most of the time under her cowboy style hat. She had soft, doe-like brown eyes that gave the impression of being surprised by something.

"Only if they're pretty," he replied. "Look at this one. I've never seen a stone that color red."

"And just how long you going to keep them?"

"Till they get too heavy to carry."

"Well, don't expect me to carry any of them for you."

"Don't worry, my dear, I won't"

Every morning, just as it was beginning to get light but still dim enough to see the stars, they would take out the mercury basin and sextant and take star sights to get their position. On the sheets of paper provided by the cartographer at Murchison Falls, they would plot their position and make notations of the streams they crossed and any other significant landmarks.

They passed little villages; some close by, some far away. They were careful not to walk through yam fields or plantain groves or anything else that looked like a garden. Sometimes people from the villages came out and stood at a distance to watch them pass. Other times, small groups of the curious would follow them for short distances. Most of the villages were small and far apart, so it came as a frightening surprise when they got up on the tenth day after crossing the Nile to discover they were surrounded by warriors. Dave estimated there were a thousand or more just standing there, silently watching. They were not brandishing their weapons or shouting, just standing fifty yards away encircling the safari's encampment. They waited for the warriors to leave while the precious cool of the morning was being wasted, but the warriors stayed fixed.

"I think we should just break camp and try to go," Dave Robins said. "If they don't let us pass then we can try and figure out what they want."

They broke camp and started out with Harry at the front of the line playing his trumpet. Over and over again he played Onward Christian Soldiers, swinging the trumpet from left to right with each step as he used to do when he marched the streets of Newark and Paterson with the Salvation Army Band. He started up the hill toward the warriors who stood waiting. When he was fifty feet away, the warriors slowly parted to let them through.

All day the warriors followed alongside, keeping their distance but always there. With that many warriors, the game was frightened away long before they got to it and so they didn't kill any food that day. When they stopped for the noon rest period, the warriors closed the ring around them and then opened it again when they got started after the break. The ring closed again in the evening and no one slept well that night.

Next morning when they started to make preparations to get underway the warriors started shouting and pounding on their shields. When Harry started to take out his trumpet, Watsumdumu put a hand on his shoulder and said, "Dey no make way today, Bwana Van. Dey want make talk-talk. Dey say how much we give dem to cross land."

"How much do you think they want?" Dave Robins asked.

"Dey want all. We give only little. Dey 'fraid of guns, but not real 'fraid. Dey not know for real 'bout gun. First we show dem 'bout gun, den we make talk."

They had to wait the whole day to show them "bout gun." They had camped in a little grassy meadow not far from a stream. The evening before they had dipped what water they needed as they were crossing, but now the warriors prevented them getting to the stream. As soon as the warriors started shouting all the great birds had taken off, so there was not a bird or animal around to be used to demonstrate what the guns could do.

They spent the day there. Once Watsumdumu tried to lead a group of people to get water, but the warriors shouted and shook their spears at them as they approached and wouldn't let them through. Another time Watsumdumu and a few of the soldiers went to the warriors and tried to talk with them, but the warriors just stood silent and unresponsive. There was nothing they could do but wait.

As evening approached the birds returned to the trees. Herons and cranes stood in the upper most branches, dark silhouettes on long spindle-like legs, large plump bodies, and long necks supporting small heads with long beaks. They turned on their stick-like legs or set the long bill to scratching the chest or back, their movements accentuated against the endless orange of the evening sky.

Watsumdumu left the camp with the sergeant and three soldiers. They walked toward the stream and, from time to time, Watsumdumu would raise his arm and point to the trees. By the time they got halfway to the stream the warriors were looking toward the trees.

The soldiers formed a straight line and raised their rifles to their shoulders. The sergeant gave the order and five rifles fired with one sound and everyone saw three birds fall from their places in the tops of the trees. An instant later there was the muffled, whirring, thunder of thousands of powerful wings beating the air. The rest of the birds rose like a dark cloud into the brilliant orange of the evening sky. They went back to camp knowing some of the warriors would go to find the birds.

The slow beating of the drum announced the coming of the chief. They heard the drums from a great distance at first, and then growing louder until the steady beat became distinct. When the drumming stopped, Watsumdumu said, "Chief here now," though no one in camp had seen him or the drummers.

The chief arrived late in the morning, but it was not until mid afternoon that the drumming started again. The warriors started down until they were half way to the camp and then they stopped; the front part of the mass opening and pulling back a little until the chief, sitting in a tepoi carried on the shoulders of some men, could be seen in front of them. The drumming stopped. The tepoi was lowered to the ground, and Watsumdumu said, "We go make talk, talk now."

They started up the hill with Watsumdumu in front, his pantaloons type pants catching on the knee-high grass, followed by the three missionary men and three porters carrying gifts. The sergeant, with a few soldiers, followed behind them. Watsumdumu stopped fifteen feet from where the chief sat in his chair. On his head the chief had a headdress made of long white feathers, and around his waist he had a dhoti of blue and white cloth reaching down to his ankles. His chest was bare except for a necklace made of lions' teeth. In his left hand he had an elephant tail fly chaser that he swung back and forth to chase the flies away as he stared at them. On either side, and behind him, were several men who were also clothed in a wrap-around dhoti of cloth, evidence of trade with the Arabs. Most of them stood holding spears. Watsumdumu stepped forward, raised his hand and said, "Jambo." There was no response. The chief and warriors just stared at him. From his early travels with Stanley, Watsumdumu had learned greetings in several languages. He tried all the other greetings he knew and, when there was still no response, stepped aside.

John Scott took the bundle from the porter behind him and handed it to Watsumdumu who set it on the ground in front of the chief. One of the warriors picked it up and Watsumdumu stepped forward again and untied the four corners of the small, bright red piece of cloth, letting the material fall open exposing the small burlap sack. He untied the string around the top of the sack and reached in and took out a small kernel of rock salt. Behind the chief there was a low murmur of approval as they all recognized what it was. The chief nodded, and the warrior set it down on the ground close to the chief.

The next gift was a dhoti of bright red cloth in which the chief didn't show any interest. The third gift was a machete. With exaggerated motion Watsumdumu drew the blade out of its case. It was a heavy machete, eighteen inches long and a quarter of an inch thick along the back of the blade and razor sharp. He took a swing at some nearby tall grass and the grass fell away as the blade passed. He put it back in its case and handed it to the warrior, who handed it to the chief.

The chief inspected the machete, examining both sides of the blade and the handle and checking its sharpness with his thumb. He finally spoke in a loud, animated way. As he spoke his warriors nodded and grunted their approval.

"Did anyone understand him at all?" Scott asked when the chief finished. Everyone shook their heads. It took more than an hour to find one of the porters named Nginga, who seemed to know enough of the language to get by. Through Nginga and Watsumdumu the palavering could start in earnest, but with long pauses since everything said had to go through two interpreters, from Scott to Watsumdumu to Nginga to the chief and back again.

The chief was angry and wanted to know why they had killed his birds, and how they did it. Three warriors came out with the birds. They held them by the heads holding their hands almost shoulder high, the long necks of the birds stretched out by the weight of the body, the tail feathers dragging on the ground. The birds were blood stained and dirty, but it was obvious the feathers of the chief's headdress came from the same kind of birds.

Watsumdumu apologized for the death of the birds. His explanation of how they were killed was not one of which Reverend Scott would have approved. "The mondeli," Watsumdumu said, "are in control of some quick and powerful spirits. They used the sticks like the ones the soldiers are holding to send those spirits where they wanted them to go. The spirits escape with a great noise and kill whatever the sticks are pointed at. The white man can lend you the stick, but the stick is not any good without the spirits. Only they have the cases that hold the spirits. If the mondeli trust you, they will let you use the stick and spirits to kill things." It took a long time for this explanation, phrase by phrase to be conveyed to the chief. "Yes, the spirits could kill a man, or a leopard, or even an elephant from far away."

After three days of small talk and lots of bargaining done through Nginga and Watsumdumu, the chief decided they could cross his land in exchange for an additional machete in payment for the birds that were killed. For payment to cross his lands they would have to give him fifty dhotis of cloth, ten more pounds of salt, a bag of assorted beads, and one roll of copper wire. In return, to assure their safe passage across his lands, he gave them a long, carved staff with some copper wire wound around the top.

All the palavering held them up almost a week and they were eager to get started again. They got underway at first light with John Scott walking in front carrying the rod the chief gave them. They hadn't walked a hundred yards when the warriors stopped them, and then the chief stepped out in front of them. He was dressed the same as the day before, except he held a spear in his left hand and the new machete hung from a rope around his waist. He said something, and Nginga was called for. The chief wanted to see how the gun worked. It was obvious they were not going to be allowed to leave until the chief saw for himself what the gun could do.

They found a large clay pot and one of the porters ran ahead to where there was a low, scraggly shrub. He set the wide mouthed pot upside down over the some of the branches. From that distance the soot-covered pot was just a little black spot in the gray-brown field of dried grass.

Dave motioned the chief over to watch him put the shell in the chamber and slide the bolt closed. "Are you sure you can hit it?" Scott asked.

"When you needed meat for the pot have I ever missed?"

"An antelope is a lot bigger than a jug."

"Scottie, I've told you more than once that when I was a kid I had to shoot squirrels, and rabbits for the supper pot, and I had to account to my daddy for every shell. One rabbit for every shell. Believe me, I can do it. What? You want one of the soldiers to do it instead?"

"No. No. It's just that this is very important."

"So was getting a rabbit for the supper pot."

He raised the rifle to his shoulder and the chief leaned forward almost touching the end of the barrel. Dave lowered the rifle, the chief looking at him, frowning, and Dave said, "Watsumdumu, tell him not to get so close."

"He wants to see it jump out of the gun, Bwana."

"Didn't you tell him it moved too fast for him to see it?"

"Yes, Bwana, but he say chief see everything."

"Then tell him," Dave said, "to stand behind me, looking over my shoulder. That way he can see the bullet leave the gun and go to the pot."

"Ndio, Bwana," Watsumdumu said smiling, and gave the message to Nginga who spoke it to the chief.

The chief stepped in behind Dave, his chin almost on Dave's shoulder. Dave fired, and the chief jumped back, startled. He had not been there when the birds were shot, so he had no idea of how loud the gun could be. Around him the warriors were laughing and from the stream there was the screaming and squawking of startled birds and the sound of beating wings as they took to the air. The chief kept staring at the spot where the pot had been. He then ordered three men to go and bring him the pot. When they returned all they had were a few pieces and not enough to make up the whole pot. They gave the chief the pieces they had found and Watsumdumu and Nginga tried to explain how the bullet's impact had shattered and scattered the pieces.

The chief scowled at the few pieces brought to him, threw them on the ground and then shouted something. Two frightened boys, between eight or nine years of age, came out from among the warriors. They walked forward looking around at everyone, each followed by a warrior with the point of a spear at the middle of the boy's back. One warrior said something, and the boys stopped ten feet in front of the chief and got on their knees. They knelt with their legs tucked under them, their buttocks resting on their ankles, their backs straight, their bodies leaning forward a little, their arms straight with their hands resting on their knees, their heads down.

The chief walked around behind the two boys. He handed his spear to one of the warriors and untied the machete from around his waist. He pulled the machete from its leather case. He handed the case to another warrior, and then with both hands swung the machete. The blade curved through the air hitting the boy's neck at the base of the skull. The head seemed to jump up a little before it fell forward, bounced on the boy's knee, and rolled a short distance. Blood spurted from an artery. The headless body stayed erect for an instant and then the straight arms seemed to buckle and the body fell forward. The blood was no longer spurting, but just a little flowed onto the pressed down grass.

The second boy stared at his brother and then screamed and started to get up to run, but the warrior behind set the blade of his spear down hard on the boy's shoulder, and the boy sat back down in the grass, his body shaking with terror. The chief took the case back from the warrior and slid the still bloody machete back into it.

It had happened so fast and unexpectedly it was over before the missionaries realized it. Laura Robins turned away and vomited and Alma gasped and slumped fainting to the ground. The men, feeling a little sick, watched as the chief walked toward them. He stopped in front of Reverend Scott, and said something and waited for the translation.

"Chief say with spear, arrow, or big knife he can kill man. Now he want Bwana Dave kill other boy with gun," Watsumdumu said.

Scott started bellowing and shaking his fists. Watsumdumu reached over and placed a hand on Scott's and said, "It more bettah, Bwana, you no shout." The argument between Scott and the chief had to go through Watsumdumu and Nginga, which considering Scott's tone of voice, was fortunate.

"He saw what happened to the pot. There is no reason to shoot the boy."

"He say even goat can kick and break pot. To kill animal is more hard and to kill man is most hard of all."

"Ask him how we killed the birds. Can he kill birds with a spear, or arrow, or machete from as far away as we did?"

The chief talked for a long time becoming more irritated. Watsumdumu translated. "He say spear kill more far than knife, and arrow more far than spear. How far gun can kill he not know. He not know if gun kill birds. He not see. He say Bwana Dave not kill boy, we not go."

"Tell him," Scott said, "yesterday we entered into a treaty with him, and he gave us his word we could go. Will he go back on his word in front of all his warriors?"

"I not think good to say that, Bwana Scottie."

"Say it," Scott yelled. It was obvious the chief was displeased.

"He say he keep his word. He let us go when we kill boy."

Dave Robins turned and walked away and the discussion stopped as everyone, including the chief, watched him walk away. He went the short distance to where their packs were and handed the porter his rifle and took the shotgun. He broke it, slipping a shell into each of the barrels and walked back to where the others were standing. He raised the gun to his shoulder and then quickly aimed it skyward and everybody looked up at three large, black hawks gliding in circles above them. He fired one barrel and then the other and two of the three hawks came tumbling from the sky. He lowered the gun and held it pointed toward the chief. He stood that way for a moment and then handed the gun to Watsumdumu and headed toward the chief.

"Watsumdumu, tell the chief I will not hurt him," Dave said walking toward the chief, his right hand open, held out toward the chief, while his other hand was in the left pouch pocket of his bush jacket where his fingers caressed the smoothness of half a dozen smooth pebbles.

When he was in front of the chief, he removed his left hand from his pocket and held his hands, palms open, fingers spread in front of the chief. He turned them back and forth so the chief could see both the palm and the back. He reached toward the chief, putting his left hand on the chief's chin as though to steady his head. He didn't say anything, but just kept smiling and nodding his head. The warriors crowded around, their spears pointed at him, ready to jump on him, if he did anything wrong. Dave reached behind the chief's ear and pulled his hand away holding a small, smooth, white pebble between his thumb, and first finger. There were "ohs" and "ahs" and excited chatter from the warriors standing close by. Dave held the pebble toward the chief indicating he should take it. The chief opened his hand and Dave placed the pebble in his palm.

Dave opened his own mouth wide indicating he wanted the chief to do the same, and when the chief opened his mouth Dave put two fingers into the chief's mouth. He ran his finger around between the upper teeth and the inside of the cheek. When he brought his fingers out of the chief's mouth there was a smooth, round, reddish-brown pebble in his hand. He showed it to those standing by and then dropped it next to the other one in the chief's hand. While the chief was staring at the two pebbles, Dave reached behind the other ear, and produced a third pebble. He dropped the pebble in the chief's hand and then, so Reverend Scott would not hear him said, "Watsumdumu, tell the chief if those stones had remained in his head he would have soon died. I have saved his life."

The chief turned, shaking the hand holding the stones, to talk to the elders and the close by warriors. They were all talking at once and too fast for Nginga to understand much of what they were saying. When they quieted down the chief raised his arms above his head, the machete in one hand and the pebbles in the closed fist of the other and spoke. When he was through, Watsumdumu translated. "He say he give boy to Bwana Dave. Bwana Dave save chief's life, chief give Bwana Dave boy's life. Now we go quick now. We take boy," Watsumdumu said motioning for the porters to pick up their loads.

"We can't just take the boy with us," Scott said.

"He not belong here, Bwana," Watsumdumu said, "If we not take him they say Bwana Dave not want him because he have bad spirits and they kill him. We go quick now."

The boy, naked even of a string around his waist, walked in front of the Robins. Every few minutes he would turn his head and look with curiosity and fear at his new master. Dave had told Watsumdumu to tell the boy he was free to go, but instead, with Nginga translating, Watsumdumu had told the boy Bwana Dave was his new master. That if he was obedient, and diligent he would be well treated, seldom beaten and never again would he be threatened with being killed. He told the Robins the boy did not want to go free. Out of gratitude for saving his life he wanted to forever be their slave.

There was no maliciousness in Watsumdumu's manipulation. From Nginga he had learned the boy didn't know how to get back to his village. Without a village the boy would, without question, be taken prisoner again or killed. He and the other boy were given to the chief in payment for some wrong, maybe an accidental death. Watsumdumu himself had been a life payment. When he was six years old, his uncle had accidentally killed a man from another village while hunting. His village had decided since it was Watsumdumu's uncle who had killed the man, and since Watsumdumu's mother had died soon after he was born and all the women in the village were raising him because his father had not yet taken another wife, it was appropriate that Watsumdumu be the life payment.

The next time they stopped Laura found a piece of cloth for the boy to wrap around his waist, and said, "I think we'll call him Moses. Doesn't he look like those pictures they have in Bible story books of young Moses with his head shaved and a red cloth around his waist?"

CHAPTER ELEVEN

The hills became steeper, the ravines deeper. Many of the ravines showed signs of having had streams in them during the wet season, but now the streams beds were dry. All the grass was hard and brittle from the dry-season sun. Above them a colorless sky, almost the color of a white sun, with not a single cloud to suggest there might someday be some relief, burned down on them. It was as though the sky itself was the source of the heat. Black bodies glistened in the sweat that drained out of them. The clothing of the missionaries was darkened with sweat stains mixed with the dust rising from a thousand passing feet. The dust rose and hung like a cloud over the column with no breath of air to disperse it.

Watsumdumu spent most of his time at the front of the column now, his leather-slipper covered feet taking the first step into the dry and brittle grass. Behind him were the missionaries, their leather boots breaking the grass down even more so those following would not cut their bare feet on the razor sharp grass. By the time the first twenty or thirty people had passed, there was a clear path of dry, black earth.

The column moved along like a never-ending worm undulating up and down the terrain. In the middle of safari, four men carried John Scott on a makeshift stretcher. He had not been feeling well and had been suffering from diarrhea even when they were dealing with the chief. For several days he'd had to be carried on the stretcher. Blood had appeared in his stools, and when Harry examined a specimen under the microscope, there was no doubt Reverend Scott had contracted bilharzia. He had probably swallowed some river water when he went into the Nile to save a box. Now he also had symptoms of malaria and was running a fever of between a 102 and 103 degrees.

The words flew from persons to person along the column, "Trees!" "Lots of trees!" "Water!" "Big stream!" With each word of description from the front of the safari, those at the back took heart. It was more than half an hour before those at the end of the column crested the hill and saw for themselves the green valley of water and trees.

After the dryness, and scarcity of water for the past week, it was an oasis so perfect many of them couldn't believe there was water deep enough to sit in and so many trees no one had to spend the day in the sun. A mile upstream they found where the game came to drink, and two miles downstream, they found a grove of plantain trees. There was plenty of food and water and the perfect place to stay until John Scott was well enough to travel again. Upstream three of the soldiers shot enough game so there was plenty for everyone to eat all they wanted. The camp settled down that night, happy that the next day was Sunday. Even if Reverend Scott became well enough to travel, they wouldn't be carrying their loads on a Sunday.

In Scott's tent Watsumdumu and Harry took turns with Dave and Moses sitting up with John Scott. Every few hours he was given medicine and forced to drink cup after cup of water. On one side of the cot, one of them kneeled dipping a cloth into a bucket of water and sponging down Scott's body, while on the other side of the cot the other one stood fanning with a large woven mat trying to get Scott's temperature down. From time to time, they would change places to relieve the tired arms of the one who was fanning. Scott suffered from cramps and vomiting, both of which racked his body.

The sun came up white and hot as it did every morning, and they clustered under the shade of the trees. This morning there should have been the pleasant leisureliness of Sunday, but instead, there was concern. Laura and Alma sat in the camp chairs watching Watsumdumu supervising the breakfast preparations while Dave and Moses were again fanning and sponging Reverend Scott who lay naked on his cot except for a towel across his hips. The flaps of his tent were open, inviting any benevolent breeze to pass through and help with the cooling process. From time to time, a porter would come by, look in, express his concern, and then walk away to discuss the seriousness of the situation. Laura and Alma couldn't help with Scott, because as with many of the porters, it was forbidden for a married woman in any way to touch or handle a man not her husband or blood relative. It would have been considered as bad as adultery, and so they sat there, concerned and wishing they could be of more use.

In the middle of the afternoon, Harry took out his trumpet and started to play. He played softly, melodiously. It was a form of prayer, soothing and edifying. The porters started gathering around to listen, as they always did when the trumpet was played. He had taken the trumpet out and started playing for his own benefit, to release the tension and to express something to God who alone could understand. Even as he played, standing with his feet apart, the trumpet pointed upward, his eyes closed, his yearning and doubts welled up from his soul and out the bell of the horn. It was not what he played so much, as the way he played it. The floating notes seemed to hang in the air as though you could reach out and gather them, with a gentle touch, holding them in your cupped hands, because if you closed you hands even a little, they would be crushed and shatter like delicate crystal.

It was while Harry was playing that Dave noticed Scott's urine was darker than normal. It was one of the things Harry had told them to be looking for, but now that he noticed it, he couldn't bring himself to mention it while the music floated like a benediction over the camp. That evening, just before dinner, when Scott again relieved himself, lying on his side at the edge of the cot because he was too weak to get up, the fluid that flowed into the pot was a dark, blackish-red color, and the missionaries knew he had black-water fever. Considering his past illnesses and his general condition, it would take a miracle for him to live.

As far as Moses was concerned, Bwana Scott had died. That did not mean it was time to bury him, but it was the point at which there was no hope of recovery. When someone didn't eat any more, vomited, but nothing came up, could not get up from their bed and their bodies shook with chills while at the same time burning with fever, then they had finished to die. For Moses, the shaking of the chills was evidence of the evil spirits fighting inside Bwana Scott's body, and when the urine came out that frightening dark color, without question, the evil spirits had done their worst. It was time to move the body outside of the camp so when he was fully dead, the evil spirits would not enter someone nearby and kill them, too.

After someone was dead, the evil spirits would look for someone else to move into. When all life left the body it could be brought back to the village because the spirits that had killed him were gone. The man's own spirits would stay there to see that the body was treated with respect and the burying was done correctly. When the body was properly buried, his spirit would join the spirits of the ancestors. At certain times the spirit would return to be near its old body. Faithful sons would bring bowls of yams, or manioc, and bowls of beer or palm wine to the grave as a present to the spirit. That's the way it had always been in his village.

But Moses wasn't in his village. He was with the mondeli who had strange customs and frightening ways. But he understood that by some magic they had saved his life. The fact that he was living on bought time was no consolation when he was forced to be this close to a person, a mondeli, who had finished to die. He realized they did not require him to spend any more time with Bwana Scott than they did, so he surmised they had a magic that would keep the evil spirits from entering those close by. But did that magic work as well for black men as for white men? When Watsumdumu told him they wouldn't be moving the next day, he knew the mondeli also understood Bwana Scott had finished to die, and he dreaded the thought that he might be the one next to Bwana Scott when all life left him.

***

Harry VanVeldt sat on a campstool at the foot of the fresh dug grave. Fifty-six hours before he woke up in the middle of the night with violent nausea. The contractions of his vomiting seemed to empty not only the contents of his stomach, but also the air from his lungs. He just finished vomiting when he had an attack of diarrhea. The vomiting and diarrhea continued through the night until there was nothing left in him, and even then the body tried to expel what wasn't there. He grew weak from the spasms. He was acutely thirsty, but every time he drank it would only stay down for a minute or so, and he would throw up again. As he gradually began to feel better, they assumed he must have been poisoned by something he ate. He was recovering, but still very weak.

He sat with his feet flat on the ground, elbows on his knees, hands clasped in front of him, his thin body leaning forward, tired and weak. Everyone had tried to discourage him, but he had insisted he had to be there. He came supported on one side by a porter, and on the other by Watsumdumu. Moses had walked behind carrying the campstool for him to sit on. Dave had walked in front carrying the wasted body of John Scott. The body lay wrapped in a dhoti of mericani on top the mound of earth next to the open grave. As weak as he was, Harry had to be there. Six hours ago the person who had brought him to this place; physically, mentally, and spiritually, had died. During the last couple of days he had wondered what they would do; most of the time thinking about how they would get back. He was there now to covenant with himself that they should go on.

Harry sat looking into the hole, too weak even to raise his head and look at Dave Robins. He didn't really hear the Scriptures read or what Dave said. Harry looked up when Dave set the book and his helmet down on the ground. He watched Dave and Watsumdumu reach over and pick up the body by taking hold of the extra material at each end. The bundle sagged like a body in a hammock. They walked sideways, Watsumdumu moving between Harry and the grave, and then they knelt down. They reached down into the grave as far as they could before letting go of the bundle. It dropped the remaining short distance landing with a quiet thud. They stood up, looked for one last time into the grave, and then Watsumdumu turned to help Harry up while Dave picked up his bible and helmet. Four porters started shoveling the dirt back into the hole and Harry walked with fear of the uncertainty of what was ahead.

CHAPTER TWELVE

The dry season fires had passed through burning everything in their path. The sun, a white heat in the center of the palest of skies, glared down with a fierce fury on a land so flat it seemed to blend unbroken into the endless sky. The flatness was interrupted from time to time by erratically scattered outcroppings of rocks, or abrupt craggy hills that burst out of place and looked more like the tantrum strewn toys of some mythological god-child than natural formations. In every direction, as far as they could see, was the fire swept paleness of the land. Sometimes there was the twisted blackness of a charred acacia tree whose twigs rose up from the fat trunks like grotesque, twisted, multi-fingered hands reaching out from the flat earth to take something, anything from the totally empty sky.

They plodded along discouraged and tired. With each step a little cloud of gray ash would rise around their feet. The next person would stir the ash even more, the cloud rising higher in the still air until by the seventh or eighth person the cloud of dust was head high. It required more than twenty dhotis of mericani cut up into foot squares to give everyone a cloth to cover their nose and mouth. But that didn't protect the eyes, nor was the noon break much relief. It was a time when they could sit for a while in the shade of their mats, when the water rations were handed out, when they didn't have to put one foot ahead of the other, but it was also a time when any little movement stirred up the dust which settled on their food and put a film on the top of their precious water ration. They sat with nothing to do except watch the sweat make little trails through the dust on their arms and bodies. They wondered if it wouldn't be better to just keep going and get to the camp site that much sooner.

For weeks they marched on, just one or two days a week, then waiting while the scouts went ahead to find the next place with a stream where they could camp. They didn't cover more than fifteen miles a week. Across the burned out wasteland they crawled, one thousand feet stirring up the powdery ash as they went. Only the first ten in line were visible, each one in line less distinct than the one before until almost all the five hundred people were just shadowy impressions in the drawn out cloud of dust. But after they had passed and the dust had settled, there was an ash-cleared path of red earth to show their passing. None saw the path except God and an occasional circling vulture.

It was while they were stopped for their noon break Moses said, "Soon come rain today."

Rain. It was their preoccupation. They thought of little else; while eating, while walking, and they dreamed of it at night. When they woke up in the morning their first thought, their first hope was it would rain that day. No one paid any attention to Moses' comment but took it as his inability to yet communicate.

They left the stopping place fearful of leaving and fearful of staying. They didn't want to stay there; it was just less horrendous than the alternative of walking through the self-made dust cloud. But they had to go on to the promise of water and trees, and so they walked, squint-eyed, lids and corners of their eyes caked with grime, eyes burning, nose and throat scorched, despite the square of mericani tied over their faces.

A sudden chill passed through the column. Each felt it and thought it was exclusive to themselves and wondered if they were coming down with an attack of malaria. Only Moses, knowing what it portended, smiled and wondered why the others showed no reaction.

Watsumdumu was the first to see it. Now in the burnt out land with no dry grass that needed to be broken down, he was again in the habit of going to the head of the safari. His blouse and baggy trousers gray from the dust, his eyes squinting, standing with his legs apart, watching the dim, cloud-shrouded figures pass by him. When the last person was past he would overtake the column to the front, his slipper covered feet kicking up a little dust trail of his own. He stopped, and turned to watch the safari pass and yelled, "Bwana, look!" pointing back the way they had come.

It wasn't much, just a darker line of gray delineating the gray whiteness of the earth from the whiteness of the sky. From then on those in front would turn to look back past the line of dust to the horizon. The strip of gray grew wider, started to have irregularity of line which changed and grew into mounds, and peaks and spirals, all the time growing darker, armored clouds marching against the sun, battle lines advancing, wave after wave of formations rolling forward with indomitable force. Across the burned out vastness, they could see the shadow advancing, moving forward, coming toward them, unwavering and unhindered by the heat, or sun, or dust.

They stopped, the long line of march coming together, loads dropped, raising their own clouds of dust. The silent, boiling, rolling churning clouds advanced against the afternoon sun, pushing back its heat, the shadow getting closer, then it was over them, blotting out the white heat, sheltering them in the shade of gray-black clouds. They wanted to shout, but instead stood awed to silence, wonder, and gratitude.

The first drops fell slowly, one at a time, large as cherry pits, making a plopping sound, raising little coronets of dust like perfectly piled dirt rings around an ant hole, the big drop of water, dust covered, lying in the center of the piled up rim of ash. The drops started coming faster, heavier; the first downpour of the rainy season had come. The dry season was over. They started to laugh, holding out their arms to expose as much of themselves as possible to the rain.

After the initial downpour, it slacked off a little to a steady, heavy rain, cleansing the air of heat and dust, nourishing the earth, washing their bodies and refreshing the spirit. The rain came pure, fresh, clean, and indiscriminating. They stayed there, not going any farther. There was no need to press on to the water supply. The water had come to them. They put out jugs, pots, canvas washbasins, and canvas bathtubs. They laughed as they slid around in the newly formed mud as they set up camp.

The rain stopped just after sundown, the stars glowed brilliant and clear, and when the sun came up in the morning, it sent rays of light through horizon clouds. The higher the sun climbed, the bluer became the sky. They walked that day without the pieces of mericani over their faces, breathing in the clean moist smelling air. They didn't stop for the midday rest, but kept going, passing up the stream that was the previous day's destination. They kept going until they saw the clouds forming, and then they stopped to have the camp set up before the rain started.

Each morning before the light obliterated the stars they would set up the mercury basin and plot their way toward the land granted to the Central African Mission by King Leopold of the Belgians. They recorded the change in the terrain that rose and fell with no real hills or valleys. It was dotted with clumps of bushes or isolated, thick-trunked trees. All the trees, grass and shrubs were green with new rains. In the sea of low waving grass there was, from time to time, a patch of yellow, or blue, or violet flowers, all the patches alive, and buzzing with pollen-laden bees. Sometimes there would be a pile of rocks or just one rock as big as a house sitting by itself.

Out of that vibrant new greenness there appeared a rising, indistinct and hazy blue on the horizon. For three weeks they kept moving toward it, and at the end of each day it was clearer, more defined, waiting for them. The hill seemed to lie on the plain rather than rise out of it. It looked like some great two-humped camel had settled down for a while to rest. In one direction the long neck was stretched out along the ground with the head disappearing in the earth and the neck sloping up to the first hump. The second hump dropped off abruptly at the rump.

As they got closer the smooth silhouette of the reclining camel was replaced by the jagged irregularity of craggy, rock formations. The tops of the two humps were mostly bare rock with the base and saddle between being covered with trees, shrubs and grass. At the base and in the center, just below the saddle of this mile long extrusion, a stream broke out of the ground. They set up camp by the stream. While the porters worked, Watsumdumu and the missionaries started for the top. The climb up the side was steeper than it looked and they had to grab hold of boulders, rocks and shrubs to pull themselves along. From the saddle the climb was less steep, but they had to crawl between, around and over boulders and rocks. They pushed and pulled each other up to the highest boulder and then stood panting and tired, turning in a slow circle to look in every direction.

Not too far from where the camp was being set up there was a faint symmetry of formation in the growing grass that only could have been seen from above. It meant a village had once been there. Maybe a fire, or a plague, or sickness had driven them away, but the fact that a village had once been there indicated the hill was not sacred or forbidden.

From where they stood they seemed to be able to see forever. They could see outlines of distant villages and streams meandering across the flatness of the country. To the north were distant blue hills and to the east were dome shaped hills strange in symmetry and similarity. They turned around several times, looking every direction, and knew they had arrived.

1903

CHAPTER THIRTEEN

Laura Robins was confronted with an openness that was frightening in its endlessness. She grew up seeing mountains on every side of her, mountains with character and personality, mountains that were referred to by name. Here there was nothing, just endlessness. A great distance away there were some irregularities in the straight line of the horizon that might have been considered mountains, but they were so far away as to be more imaginary than real.

In all the months of traveling, there was a destination, a direction, with the continual need to think about what they were doing that did not leave time for emotionalism or introspection. Now that they had arrived, she had time to think and she had never felt more isolated, frustrated, and alone. People always surrounded her, but they were not her people. In one direction there was the continual activity of the porters going up and down the zigzag path carrying the poles for their houses. In the other side of the hill, the path was filled with the curious coming to look at the white people, always watching, watching and giggling at the white people as they washed their face, brushed their teeth and combed their hair. A few of them were induced to help with the offer of beads, a piece of cloth or a length of wire, but most of the time they were content to sit and watch. At any time of day, they might stick their heads inside the tent flap to see what was going on inside. It was all Watsumdumu and Moses could do to keep them out of the tents.

She sat in her tent with a desperate longing to go back to those familiar mountains of home, to feel a chill wind in the winter and see the snow, first on the mountains and then on her doorstep. Would she ever see those things again, or would they just be familiar childhood memories growing less and less familiar? Did she belong here? At one time she had thought all of her life was a preparation for coming to this place, but now she wasn't at all certain. She felt out of place and unsure. If any of the others felt the same way, they hadn't given any indication of it, and so she felt worse that she should be the only one who couldn't take it.

She sat on her cot with her booted feet flat on the ground, her head buried in her hands, her short blond hair sticking out through her fingers, her body shaking with sobs. She hoped no one would hear her or come in. She didn't know where the others were; probably doing something useful, but all she could do was sit there feeling sorry for herself, and feeling useless.

Some sound caught her attention and she raised her head and through her tears saw a black head stuck through the flaps staring at her. The head withdrew almost the moment she looked up and she dropped her head to her hands and started crying that much harder. God, I don't belong here. I'm sorry, but I've made a mistake. I'm sorry, I'm sorry, I'm sorry.

She had started out for Africa with all the vision, myths, and legends. With her vision she could overlook what she had heard about the heat, dirt, disease, poverty, and ignorance. She was young enough to have dreamed that in the years ahead she would be able to look back, with her husband, and know what they had done was noble, and Godly. They would be able to look back and know they had driven back disease and ignorance and would be remembered as the ones who had brought the light and the message of salvation. She was able to maintain that vision until just after John Scott died and she had faced the truth.

The truth was she hated Africa, the real Africa, the Africa behind the vision, and the dreams, and the calling. She hated the heat, the dust, and the clockwork rains. She hated the endless skies, the dry season fires and the mosquitoes, the snakes, the spiders and all the other creepy-crawly things. She hated the loneliness, no neighbors to meet in town on a Saturday afternoon or in church on Sunday morning. No neighbors who would come galloping over the fields or down the roads in wagons and buggies if she rang the big bell by the front door long and hard because of some emergency. She would talk to Dave and together they would go back with the porters. The porters were hesitant to leave without a white man to lead them. Once they got to Murchison Falls she would convince Dave they had to go home.

The face appeared at the flap again. She waved her hand motioning for the head to leave, but instead the flap was pushed back and a woman stepped in. She was middle aged, her breast sagging flat on her chest. She was naked except for a string around her waist that held the tuft of leaves in front between her legs. In one hand she carried some kind of fruit Laura had never seen before and in the other a small cluster of flowers. Laura straightened up feeling angry and superior. She waved for her to go, but the woman continued toward her, smiling. She knelt down next to the cot, setting the flowers on the ground, and started pealing the fruit. She smiled, making clucking sounds, her filed teeth gleaming against her black lips. With one hand she raised the partially pealed fruit to Laura's lips, like a mother trying to comfort a child with a morsel of food. Laura turned her head away and the woman followed with the fruit touching it to Laura's lips. Laura gave up and took a bite of the fruit and a smile spread over the woman's whole face. The fruit had a tart sweetness to it and Laura wondered if there was some significance to that. She took the rest of the fruit from the woman, holding it by the section that still had the skin on it and pealed and ate the rest of it. When she was through, the woman put out her hand to take the skin like a mother taking the leftover refuse from a child. The woman picked up the flowers, got up, and walked out of the tent.

Laura laid back on the cot, swinging her booted feet up, put her hands behind her head, and fell asleep. She woke up a short time later, conscious of the heat in the tent and thought she'd had a dream until she stepped out and saw the little cluster of flowers stuck in the rope hole of the flap. She pulled the flowers out, holding them with both her hands to her face, inhaling the strange, indefinable fragrance, a fragrance of Africa.

She looked around at the group of curiosity filled natives who were looking at her, smiling at her, but she couldn't distinguish the face of the woman who had come into her tent. She would like to have been able to thank her in some way, a touch, a gesture, but she wasn't there, so Laura smiled at all of them.

Two weeks later, Watsumdumu and the others left as the sun was coming up just as they would have on any day's trek. The only loads they had were the little bundles of extra instruments that belonged to the garrison at Fort Murchison Falls. In addition to the sextants, mercury basin, and pedometers, there was a bundle of the charts they had made and letters. The missionaries lined up to shake hands with each of the porters and soldiers as they filed by and to pat the heads of the children. It was like family leaving, people they had come to know, to depend on and love. Watsumdumu stood with his arms folded across his chest, his white blouse and floppy trousers now turned gray. When all of the almost five hundred people had passed by, it was Watsumdumu's turn to shake hands. They held on to his hand with both of theirs, reluctant for the separation to be complete, and then he, too, turned and followed the others.

They climbed the hill standing in front of their tents and then, as the long grass hid the heads and shoulders, climbed to the highest rocks. The shoulders and heads shrunk to dots, and then disappeared into the never-ending vastness. They were alone. Now there was no chance of saying or writing any more, and they wondered if they had written enough. Were the charts good enough so the next group would have no trouble finding them? There was a letter to King Leopold stating the exact location of where they had established the station. There were letters to their families, and with those letters, was the hope they would not be left forever alone, that those various pieces of paper were a connection to others who would not let them remain alone.

1904

CHAPTER FOURTEEN

Ronzozo sat in his low chair looking out over the village. His left leg was stretched out in front, and to one side of him. It was not a dignified position, but if he sat for too long with his knee bent he started to get pain and cramps in his thigh from the old wound he had received in the battle with Dumodo. It was good, sometimes, to sit this way in council for it reminded the others he had proven himself a great warrior in battle. Many of these little village chiefs had not even been there, but they had all heard the stories. It was not a serious pain, just the evil spirits that had been attached to the spear and had entered him. They were trapped in his leg and were trying to get out.

He put both hands under his knee, pulling his leg up until it matched the bend of the other, and then, leaning forward, pushed himself up from the low chair. The village chiefs looked at him and understood he was just relieving his leg and kept on talking. He walked around the circle of the council hut, limping a little as he went, the spirits in the old wound sending sharp, jabbing pains every time he put his weight it.

The discussion continued behind him, the voices raised, the arms waving. The talk had gone on long enough. It was time to come to agreement. Those who were opposing him did it to side with Kitomolo. They wanted to be known as loyal to the chief-to-be so when Kitomolo came to power they would be remembered and favored. He remembered those kinds. He'd had them when he was young.

Most of the village chiefs felt as he did. In his heart he wished the mondeli had not come. He had thought at first they were just passing through as they had through the lands of Unjubu and Musemude. But he knew they were not just passing through when they moved their cloth houses to the top of the hill. When those who had carried their things left, he knew the mondeli had come to stay with staying.

It would be nothing to wipe them out. It would be easy to stir the people up, to convince them there was a danger in letting the mondeli stay. That's what Kitomolo wanted to do, kill the mondeli, burn their cloth houses and let that be the end of it. But that would not be the end of it. If these mondeli were able to get here, others would be able to do it. The gun given him by the representative of Chief Kesalengo still hung in his hut. Kesalengo, the last of those who had united with his father's father had died a month after he had sent the gun. Many seasons after he had received the gun the mondeli had come, and some from his own village had told him of hearing the great noise and seeing large animals fall dead a great distance away.

There was no question he wished they hadn't come, for their coming meant change, and change always brought with it uncertainties and trouble. But that change would come because of them was not enough reason in Ronzozo's eyes to destroy them. If the change did not come now, it would come later with those who followed them. There was also a certain respect on his part for their indomitableness. He had heard stories of how, after the fires had passed, they had kept moving, always in the same direction. After the fires one might take the path to a close by village, but one did not go great distances until the rains came again. But they had kept going, always the same direction, nothing stopping them.

There was also with that respect a certain mysticism. Reports from the villages showed the mondeli had been heading straight for the Hill of Two Streams. How could they have known how to get there if they had never seen it before? Yet they had gone right to it, their trail always headed for it. He didn't think it was just an accident their march was always toward it. There were also the legends and stories about the Hill of Two Streams.

It was said that in the days when his father's father, Chief Limu, ruled, there was a village alongside the stream that came from the middle of the hill. One night there was a rumbling and a shaking of the earth. Things leaning against the walls fell over, and those who tried to get up found it hard to stand. The shaking stopped, and then there was a great crashing and rumbling sound. When they looked out of their huts, a great stone, larger than four huts put together, came rolling through the village. It went through the ilolo of the village, not hitting a single hut. When the sun came up they could see the path of broken trees and crushed grass down the side of the mountain and then on the other side of the village to the place where the great stone came to rest. The only damage in the village was a few broken pots. The batu-na-dawa walked around the great stone many times working his dawa and said it was a warning they were not to stay there. That no one was hurt or even huts destroyed meant it was a warning from the good spirits. The village moved away, and the hill was left to itself. It was not a cursed place, nor was it sacred. It was safe to drink the water from the springs, and hunters chased their prey up its sides. Now the mondeli had come there. It was said they had put their cloth houses in the same place where the great boulder had been. Had the spirits been saving the hill for them? It was said they had strong dawa that could heal sickness and sores and take away pain. There was too much about them he didn't understand. If they were favored of the spirits, it would be foolish to come against them.

He turned back and sat down in his chair. He raised his hand, and the others fell silent. "We have worried this thing for two days. It is time now to decide what we will do. It is not good for us to come against them for no reason. We are not like the Buganda who take pleasure in killing people. But neither do we need to help them. We will tell our people they may go to them, they may get the dawa, they may trade, but they should not help them to build houses for they have not yet come to us to get permission to build their village."

CHAPTER FIFTEEN

There is stability in regularity. Their lives have settled into a regular pattern. There is the regular arrival of those who want treatment at the "dispensary." That's what they call the open tent where they have set up two boxes to act as a table. The natives arrive with fevers and weaknesses, with grotesque sores and pustules, with fingers and toes or even a whole hand or foot missing. Their faces and bodies are mutilated with leprosy. Others have legs swollen to four times the normal size with elephantiasis and the filarial worm. Keloids grow out of parts of their body like knots on a tree.

They treat what they can, anyway they can, cleaning sores and wrapping them with bandages made from strips of mericani. Each time a medicine is dispensed, there is the subconscious question of how and when it is going to be replaced. They try to save the bandages. When a patient returns with a bandage still on, it's taken off. The area with the worst stains is cut away and then it's dropped into the pot of boiling water to be sterilized and used again. They have learned not to give a second bandage if the patient doesn't return with the first one, and so, sometimes, they come back carrying the bandage while flies cover the sore. They have yet to learn they must keep the dressing on and the wound clean without knowing the language. The natives are willing to stand and watch the mondeli for hours on end and to be treated for their illnesses, but they refuse to try to communicate.

The descent from the hill is another regular ritual. They all go down together after dispensary is over. The women walk behind with smudged and stained helmets on their heads that will never be white again and hoes on their shoulders. Every day the women enter a battle with the land. Their arms swing the hoes, the blades hitting and pulling, hitting and pulling, turning up fresh dirt and mangling young plants that have thrived on that land for centuries and are now considered weeds. The jodhpurs and boots they wore traveling have been replaced with cooler loose blouses and skirts without petticoats. Perspiration dampens their blouses. With each stroke of the hoe hitting the ground there is a jarring to their arms and chests. From time to time, one of them stops and leans the handle of the hoe against her waist. With one hand she removes the helmet from her head and with the other takes a piece of mericani from her waistband and wipes her face and neck. They wonder sometimes if guaranteed seeds, bought in London, tested in India, will produce in Central Africa. They cut the weeds to make room for the tender shoots from the guaranteed seeds. Not one soul has been saved and not a single word of the language has been learned. Still, in the cool of the morning, they battle against the weeds.

The men wear khaki helmets and carry a five-gallon pail in each hand. Only Moses does not wear a covering of any kind on his head. While the women go to the garden to continue where they left off the day before, the men go to the full flowing stream and, standing on a protruding rock, fill their buckets. The path dips and turns, and the water splashes over the edge onto their legs and boots and on Moses' bare feet. Four times they make the trip up the hill with their burden of water, but there is no thought of moving their tents down the hill closer to their garden and water. The water ritual happens every day of the week. They don't hoe their garden, or open the dispensary, or cut poles for their homes on Sunday, but they do fetch water.

Moses doesn't comprehend the need for so much water. They are always splashing it over their arms and faces and throwing out what is left in the basin. Saturday is the worst because extra water is needed for his owners' baths. They bathe in turns with their own two pails of water, one hot and one cold. He doesn't understand why he pours the water into the canvas tub clear and dumps it out gray. He thinks it must have something to do with keeping them white. It cannot only have to do with cleanliness, for then they would do as he does and go stand in the stream to bathe.

Each day he learns more of his owners' ways and language. He can't think of them in any way except owning him. They tell him he is free, but he doesn't comprehend the word. He saw his brother's head cut off, but by some miracle having to do with them, he's still alive. He has never been treated better in his whole life, and for just that reason he does not trust his situation. He has no thought of running away. Although he is beginning to understand and speak their language, he doesn't understand them. He expects any day he may be given away to correct an insult, or, as part of a gift for their right to build their village where their cloth huts now stand.

Moses carries water, cuts poles for their houses, learns their language, cooks for them, and sometimes even sits at the table to eat with them, but he does not understand them. They tell him of heaven and hell, and he nods his head agreeing with what they say, not wanting to displease them. At night he goes to the storage tent, which is his place to sleep. He lies down on comfortably arranged dhotis of cloth and wonders if tomorrow is the day he will be sold or given away.

CHAPTER SIXTEEN

They sat to one side in the eating tent in case a sudden gust of wind blew the rain in on them. In the plain below were the herds, heads down under some of the larger trees in an attempt to keep dry.

The sound of steady raindrops hitting the canvas should have been soothing, but it wasn't. It only reminded them of how little they've gotten done that day. They are no further along than they were the day before. The natives come for treatment, but they can't get them to do anything, nor have they learned any of the language. They've gone to the various villages they can see from the top of the hill to try and get some kind of agreement, some kind of permission to build their station, but the chief and his elders sit around nodding and smiling. There was no way to know what they were saying, and so the palaver was meaningless. Because they don't have permission to build, the poles have not been set in the ground, but lay in piles behind the tents starting to be eaten by termites.

They're all discouraged, and Harry would like to tell them what had happened that morning, but there is nothing to tell. He's gotten into the habit of getting up before sunrise and climbing to the highest rock of the highest hump of the camel like extrusion on which they've decided to build and live. Their thinking was that a light, or a station, set upon a hill cannot be hidden.

From what he has come to think of as his *prayer rock*, Harry can see the light of day as it spreads over the earth. This morning the sun came up new and fresh, sending rays of celestial light through the holes and separations in the clouds before it broke over the horizon, changing the clouds to gold-rimmed, pink and orange shaded domes and turrets. In the sheer beauty of the beginning of the day, the sense of futility often vanishes. He thinks from time to time of encouraging the others to join him, but he fears if they were all there, the splendor and beauty of it would somehow be diminished.

Every morning is special, revitalizing, but this morning was extraordinary. The sun burst over the horizon and instead of reaching for his Bible first as he usually does, he reached for the case next to him and took out the trumpet. He placed the mute in the bell, licked his lips while pushing a lank of black hair out of his eyes, and raised the trumpet to his lips. The tones came out soft, and pure, and worshipful, and he heard the words in his mind with each note:

I come to the garden alone,
While the dew is still on the roses,
And the voice I hear, falling on my ear,
The Son of God discloses.
And He walks with me, and He talks with me,
And He tells me I am His own;
And the joy we share as we tarry there,
None other has ever known.

He plays the hymn over and over again, for some reason unable to play any other.

He speaks, and the sound of His voice,
Is so sweet the birds hush their singing,
And the melody that He gave to me
Within my heart is ringing.
And He walks with me, and He talks with me,
And He tells me I am His own;
And the joy we share as we tarry there,
None other has ever known.

I'd stay in the garden with Him
Though the night around me be falling,
But He bids me go; though the voice of woe
His voice to me is calling.
And He walks with me, and He talks with me,
And He tells me I am His own;
And the joy we share as we tarry there,
None other has ever known.

When he lowered the instrument, he felt at peace and content. He removed the mute and was turning to place it in its place in the case when he saw the man. He was a tall man, or maybe it was the way he stood, straight with his feet together.

Instead of the usual leaves or bark cloth, he had a skin of a leopard wrapped around his waist. In his right hand, with its butt resting on the rock, was a long spear. Harry had no idea how long the man was there. He was standing thirty feet away. They stared at each other for a long time, and when Harry smiled and nodded in greeting, the native just stared at him without changing expression. He stood so still he gave the impression of being more a statue than a living man. He was beautiful, with broad shoulders, strong arms, and legs. His face was not expressionless so much as not affected by anything he saw or heard.

Harry put the trumpet away, closed the lid snapping the latches, and all the time from the corner of his eye he could see the man standing there, unmoving, watching him. He picked up the Bible and started reading it. Every time he turned a page, he couldn't help but glance in that direction, and the man was still there just as before. Half an hour later Harry closed the Bible, picked up his trumpet and started down the steep hill with the man still standing there. He didn't look back to see if the man turned his head to watch him leave.

When he got back down he wanted to tell Alma about the man, but there wasn't anything to tell except that he had seen a man at his *prayer rock.* Before he could say anything about the morning, she had told him she thought she was pregnant again. They had all expressed their joy, and happiness, and now, sitting in the dampness of the tent with the rain falling outside, his impression of that morning didn't seem significant or even real. What was real was the fact they were still living in tents and his wife was going to have a baby.

Harry went to his *prayer rock* the next morning hoping to see the man again. From time to time he would lift his head from his reading and look around expecting to see the man behind him. He played the trumpet again, waiting for the native to arrive as though something, he didn't know exactly what, depended on the man being there.

He came down from his *prayer rock* with a feeling of disappointment. Then, as he entered the camp, he became apprehensive because the natives who always gathered, laughing and giggling to watch them eat breakfast, were silent. Harry came around one of the tents and saw the man. He stood unmoving, his arms folded across his chest, his spear stuck in the ground next to him. Harry smiled, feeling much better. He walked over to the man, his hand up, palm open, to show there was no hidden weapon, in the accepted method of first meeting, but the native just stared at him.

"We tried that," Dave said coming up behind him.

Harry lowered his hand, and the two men just stared into each other's eyes for a long time, and then Harry turned and went over and sat down at the table.

"What do you think?" Dave asked.

"That man," Harry said smiling with a secret understanding, "is going to teach us the language."

For the next three days he was there when Harry came down from the hill. He stayed, standing in one place, not moving, seeming to not even be breathing, until after they went to bed at night. The big difference was there was less talking and laughing among the other natives. Those who lined up for medical treatment glanced at the man from time to time as though expecting him to interfere.

Harry and Dave tried to talk with him, offered him a cup of their precious tea, indicated he should come and sit at the table with them as Moses did, but he just stood watching them. They enticed Moses to try and talk to him. Moses used what languages he knew, but Moses was uncomfortable in front of the man. He didn't tell them it was just such a man, not in size or looks, but in demeanor, who made the decision to give his brother and him as a life payment for the man his uncle accidentally killed.

Few natives hung around to watch on Sundays because all the white people did was sit in the shade of their cloth houses. But the man was still there; standing in the same place he always stood. "Well, let's try again," Harry said after they had concluded their Sunday morning devotions. They all walked out to the man as they had done so often before and, one at a time, stepping in front of him, introduced themselves.

Harry pointed to himself and said, "Harry. Harry." Alma pointed to herself, "Alma. Alma." Moses pointed to himself. "Mbekede. Mbekede," he said using his pre-missionary name as he was instructed to do. Dave and Laura stepped up, and when they had given their names, Harry pointed to each of them saying the name, and then pointed to the man waiting for him to give his name.

They had gone through the same ritual so many times before that they were surprised when the man nodded and unfolded his arms. He clenched his right fist and struck it against his chest and spoke for the first time. In a deep resonant voice, as though addressing an audience he said, "Kusala! Ngy azi Kusala. Mototo miboko na Ronzozo. Ngy azi Kusala."

They went through the names again and started pointing at objects. They got him to come and sit on the stool in the tent and Harry ran to the storage tent and got a notebook. He came back and set it on the table in front of him, ran his finger along the binding to press back the pages and then, at the top of the first page printed, VOCABULARY OF THE NORTHEAST CONGO AREA.

That evening Kusala ate by the fire with Moses, and slept that night in the supply tent. Next morning when it was time for the dispensary to open, Kusala stood at the head of the table telling the next person in line when they could come for treatment. When it was time to go for water, he said something and four men picked up the buckets to go get the water. Some were put to work clearing grass and others started cutting poles. At the end of the day when Dave brought out the bag of beads and bolts of cloth to pay people for their work,

Kusala stepped in and handed each worker what he thought they should have. The next day there were three times as many people as there were the day before. When the dispensary was opened, Kusala stood at the front of the line extracting a payment of food: a hand of bananas, Papaya, a half dozen eggs, or something else from each waiting patient.

During the week grass was cleared and the ground leveled where their houses were to stand. Poles piled up. Vines, an inch in diameter and up to thirty feet long, lay like piles of rope next to the poles. Women sat talking and laughing while they stripped the bark from the vines, the thin strands of bark to be used as cords. A pile of clay from a pit by the stream on the other side of the hill grew higher each day as women climbed the hill with a basket of clay on their heads, the gray water oozing from between the weave of the baskets, leaving their heads and bodies streaked with gray. They chanted as they climbed the hill and gave a shout when they emptied their basket on the growing pile of clay. Others brought bundles of long grass that would be used for thatch.

By the end of the second week poles were set in the ground eighteen inches apart. The vines were woven through the poles. Clay filled in the cracks between the vines and the walls were smoothed inside and out. By the end of the fourth week they could move in. There were two huts close together with the doors facing each other. Between the two huts there were poles supporting a thatch roof that extended over the entrances. In each hut there was a window eighteen inches wide and three feet high. The builders did not approve of the windows or the high doors that Dave showed he wanted by undoing the woven vines they had already done. To them, they were openings that could let in a goat, a hyena, or even a leopard. The entrances were so wide and high a buffalo could walk in. The natives also insisted the buildings be round instead of square. The missionaries thought it was because the vines would not bend at a ninety-degree angle without breaking. The real reason was the natives believed a room should not have sharp corners because it was impossible to drive a demon out of a corner. But if the walls were curved you could drive them along the curve of the wall to the door and out.

They moved in, the VanVeldts in one hut and the Robins in the other. The table and chairs from the eating tent were put in the covered area between the two huts. The first night the mosquitoes swarmed through the open doors and windows while they were getting undressed and had them covered with bites before they were able to get under the mosquito nets. The next day the tents were cut up to use the netting in the windows and the canvas as a door flap.

In the days that followed, structures continued to go up. Kusala built his house down by the stream. They built a hut as a storehouse where Moses slept. The dispensary was a roof with no walls, just post holding up the roof. During the day, while all this work was going on, Harry followed the natives with a notebook in his hand, writing the phonetic sounds he heard. In the evening, when the other natives had left, they would sit at the table with Kusala, refining and defining the sounds Harry had written down. Two months after Kusala arrived Harry delivered the first Sunday message standing under a tree. He stumbled over some of the words and his audience sometimes laughed when he least expected them to. The next day Laura and Alma started teaching some children the alphabet.

CHAPTER SEVENTEEN

"A safari, Uncle Harry, a safari." Moses burst into the dispensary shed waving his arms while trying to run one direction and pointing behind him at the same time. Harry looked up from where he was taking a dressing off a festering knee and Moses repeated what he had said.

It had been almost three years since they crossed the Nile and in all that time they had not seen a white person except themselves. He finished dressing the sore and left the dispensary stopping by their hut to pick up the binoculars on his way to joining the rest of the spectators at the rim of the station.

Even before he raised the binoculars to his eyes he knew they were headed toward the east. Where have you come from? Could you have come up the Congo River and then across country? Impossible. Stanley proved how impractical, almost impossible, it was to try and hack your way through the great Ituri Forest.

Through the binoculars he picked up the white man in front. The man carried his gun over his right shoulder, the barrel forward, the wrist resting on the barrel and the hand hanging down, the butt of the rifle protruding behind him. On his head he had a round, flat-topped hat with a peak in front and piece of cloth hanging down in back to shade his neck from the sun. Behind him was a gun bearer with two more guns.

Harry moved the glass past the gun bearer, past the porters carrying boxes and tents, to the porters carrying tusks. An elephant hunter! He handed the binoculars to Alma and went into their rooms to get the mirror. He started flashing with the mirror and after a while, Dave, who was watching through the binoculars, announced the hunter had seen the flashing and was coming toward them. They sent Moses and Kusala, with twenty curious natives tagging along, with a note, which in French simply said, "We would be delighted if you would join us for lunch."

The hunter got to the top of the hill rushing around Kusala to meet them. "Je suis Leo Papadopolis," he said every time he put his hand out to shake hands. Laura said something to Alma in English, and he beamed even more and said, "Oh, you are English. I speak English, too. Speak English better than anything else." There was a staccato to his speech, and he seemed to almost bounce as he spoke each short sentence. He shook hands with Alma. "Alma VanVeldt," he said repeating the name. "Leo Papadopolis. Grew up speaking English. My mother was English." He tipped his cap with his left hand as he shook hands with the women.

Leo Papadopolis was an average size man with black eyes and wavy black hair that reached almost to his shoulders. There was a compression line in his hair where his cap sat on his head. He was dark complexioned and gestured a lot when he talked. His eyes sparkled when he smiled and he exuded an excitement that was contagious.

He shook hands all around a second time saying, "I'm Leo Papadopolis," and repeating their names as though to assure himself they were really there, and then started hugging everyone, hesitating at Alma as though wondering if he should hug a pregnant woman. Alma set his mind at ease by throwing her arms around him.

"Papadopolis, that's a Greek name, isn't it?" Harry said.

"Yes. Yes. My father was Greek. My mother was English."

"Well, Greek or English, we're delighted to see you," Harry said motioning for everyone to follow as he headed for the shade of the shed area between their huts.

"May I get you a cup of water?" Alma said as soon as they were all seated.

"Do you have any tea?"

"All out, I'm afraid. Out of tea, coffee, sugar, salt, out of everything except what we raise ourselves or trade for with the natives."

"Oh, I can give you some sugar and salt," he said jumping up and went to the edge of the shed and called to his porters. A couple of them came over carrying a large chop box and he started rummaging through it. "Sugar. Here's couple pounds of sugar you can have—"

"Oh, no we couldn't take that," Alma said interrupting him.

"Without coffee or tea to put it in, who needs it? My cook just steals it anyway. And here's a little salt. Can't spare too much of that."

"I don't suppose you have any matches," Harry said.

"No. Never have enough of them. Take what you want out of there, Mrs. VanVeldt, Mrs. Robins. I have another chop box that should last me until I get to the Khor Gomor where I can replenish," he said stepping away from the box and sitting down.

The two women just stood there looking from him to the box and he said, "Please, take what you want."

They started looking through it. There wasn't a whole lot; some spices, cans of squash and pumpkin and other things they were raising in their garden, but Laura squealed with delight when she found a can of salmon.

"How long have you folks been here?"

"Almost two years now," Laura said, "and you are the first other person we've seen in all that time. Another white person, I mean. How long have been in these parts?"

"Came through these parts on my way west six months ago to hunt elephants."

"I haven't seen any elephants around here," Dave said.

"Not in this area. No elephants here. West of here. An area called Zandeland. Heard about it from a customs official in Khartoum. I was on my way back when I saw the flashing of your mirror."

It was after lunch when they were telling Leo about when they first arrived that Leo said, "I ask you, Mrs. VanVeldt, what right do you have to be here?" He pointed to the ground, "To build houses on this land?"

"We have a grant to this land signed by King Leopold himself," she said turning her head as though surprised by his questions.

"Ah, Mrs. VanVeldt, with all due respect, as far as the Belgians, or the English, or the Germans, or the Portuguese, or the Americans are concerned, your grant is valid. But they are not here, and the natives know nothing about grants and deeds. They don't deal with deeds."

He paused while he uncrossed and crossed his legs the other direction. "To them the land is a god. The earth is one of their good gods. From it comes all the food they eat. It gives life to the seeds they plant. It gives grass for the animals they kill and eat. It provides the vines and the mud for the walls of their huts and grass for the roof. It provides the clay for pots in which they cook their food and carry their water.

"Because of this, the land belongs to everyone. No one can own any part of it. It belongs to everyone. And one of the functions of a chief is to protect the land for everybody. Even the chief does not own land, so you see there is no such thing as deeds and titles. There are territorial boundaries, but those are limits of a chief's influence rather than land area.

"Now if you plant a tree it is yours, but not the land it grows on. Plant a crop, it is yours, but not the land. Build a house, it is yours, but not the land it sits on. The reason the tree, the crop, and house are yours is because you put something of yourself into it. But you can't put anything of yourself into the earth. It is, and was, always there. The land belongs to everybody equally and the chief is custodian of the land on behalf of his people. Surely when you were in East Africa they told you about palavering with the chiefs before doing anything."

"We've tried," Dave said. "At first we didn't know the language, but now that we've learned the language we've gone to three villages to try and palaver, but they don't seem to understand."

"Maybe they don't have the authority. Maybe a bigger chief has told them not to deal with you."

"What do we do?"

"What you have to do is go see a Chief Ronzozo. You should have done it as soon as you got here, got permission to build your houses."

"How could we have done that? We didn't even know the language," Laura said.

"Oh, Mrs. Robins, you can always communicate with someone if you really want to. I got permission to cross his lands and I don't know the languages of this area."

"How did you do it?"

"Mostly sign language, but that's beside the point. You know the language now. You'd better try to negotiate with him. He is a powerful chief. I don't know how far his influence goes, but it goes a long way."

"Can you take us to this Ronzozo?"

Leo pursed his lips, hesitated for an instant and said, "I could, but I don't think I should. He's only two days away from here. Any native can guide you to his village."

"Why don't you want to go back there?" Laura asked turning her head and looking sideways at him.

"I have no proper gift to give him. I gave him a music box last time and I have nothing that would be better than that which I don't need myself. He desperately wants a gun. He showed me an old relic of one he has hanging in his hut. But don't ever give him a gun. Not that he'll attack you with it, but because once the shells are gone he'll be back for more. If you can't give him more shells he will begin to be upset by the gift rather than pleased."

Leo left two days later with packets of mail, letters to families, the mission board, and to friends in England. It was a large bundle because there were journals and letters that were saved up for the past two years. They stood watching him leave feeling much the same way they had when Watsumdumu left, except this time they were sure they would see him again. He knew the way in and had promised to contact the Mission's representative in London and, if there were any missionaries waiting to come out, to bring them with him when he returned.

CHAPTER EIGHTEEN

"Darling, I think it's time."

Harry sat up fumbling to untuck the mosquito netting. "When did it start?"

"I don't know. Not too long after we went to bed."

In the darkness, with his legs still under the blankets and the mosquito netting between Alma and himself, he leaned over and found his boots. He turned each of them over and shook them vigorously to remove any scorpions or centipedes before pulling them on. He carried the lamp out to where the cooking fire was and, with a twig, got a flame from the coals to light the lamp. Leo was able to supply them with some more lamp oil, but he, too, had run out of matches. He went back into the room and said, "How frequent are they?"

"I don't know exactly. I couldn't see the clock in the dark, but they're pretty regular now. Not real close, but regular."

He set the lamp down next to the clock on the packing crate and was relieved to see it was almost 4:30. Be light soon, he thought. Mosquitos bad. They'll be gone when the sun comes up. Don't be born till after sunup.

He went back out and gathered wood to build up the fire and the noise he made brought Dave, wrapped in a blanket to protect against the mosquitoes, out from his hut.

"She's started labor," Harry said.

"Here, I'll take care of the fire and heating the water, you go back to her."

Harry ducked back through the flap of canvas door and, getting under the mosquito net, sat down on the bed next to her and held her hand. Laura came in bringing their lantern and stood at the foot of the bed. "It's going to be all right," she said, and although Harry appreciated her desire to be an encouragement, he resented her voicing what they all feared. How can you know that it will be all right, he wanted to say.

"I've been praying," she said as though reading his thoughts.

We've all been praying, he thought. Oh, God, don't let it happen again. Don't let anything be wrong with this child.

From the other side of the canvas door Dave said, "The water's getting hot. Is there anything else I should do?"

"No. I guess everything is ready," Harry said, but he wished Sarah Jones was there. He was trained in delivering children in his time at

Bellevue, and he had assisted when Sarah had delivered Rebecca Julianna, but now it was all up to him. "You can come in if you want to, Dave," Harry said wanting him to be there.

Through the netting over the window they could see the gray of the beginning of the day. Dave went over and looked out the window. A hint of yellow appeared on the upper frame, and Dave said, "Come here, Harry."

Harry slipped out from under the mosquito net and went and stood by Dave. The first curved edge of the sun was breaking above the horizon. There were no clouds, just the golden sun emerging into their life. He rolled up the netting covering the window and leaned out. Directly above were some high clouds, all of them reflecting the glow of the sun. He turned back, feeling relieved and happy, knowing he would never forget the sunrise of the day his perfectly healthy son was born and wondering why he had thought it would be a boy.

According to the black-faced, white-numbered clock on the packing case next to the bed, the birth of Peter John VanVeldt took place at eight forty-two in the morning. All other activities on the station stopped while they waited for the baby to be born. The news the white woman was going to have a baby spread to the villages and natives started to arrive, climbing the hill to stand behind those who were there before them. They assumed, as was customary with them, that the baby would be brought out to be shown to them, and they want to see for themselves if white people were born white or became lighter as they grew older.

Except for being in a mud hut, it was in every way an easy birth. As soon as the baby was cleaned, Harry handed him to Alma to nurse. Alma took the baby in her arms and put him to her breast. Harry sat next to her with his arm on the pillow behind her head. The baby started to suck, its tiny fist clutching and kneading the full breast. They all waited, watching, and with each successive sucking of the tiny lips they relaxed more and more. Alma shifted him to the other side and the smiles came to their faces, hesitant at first and then broad, relieved smiles. He stopped nursing, his eyes closed, his nostrils moving with his breathing, and Alma said, "He's all right, isn't he." It was an affirmation rather than a question.

"Yes, praise God, he's perfectly healthy," Harry said and tears came to Alma's eyes and dropped one-by-one from her cheeks to the arm of her tiny son. Harry took Peter out for all the natives to see and they started dancing and chanting. He took the little baby back into the house and Laura took the baby and put him in the cradle Dave and Harry had made out of a packing crate.

Two weeks after the birth of Peter John a messenger arrived informing them Ronzozo, Chief of the Five Tribes, was now willing to talk to them. They were to be at Ronzozo's village in ten days. Watching the messenger head back down the path, Harry said laughing, "Well, it seems the birth of our son has even softened the heart of the great Chief Ronzozo."

The birth of Peter made it easier for Chief Ronzozo to convey his decision regarding the whites to the other chiefs and elders. Up until Peter's birth he had explained the presence of the whites as visitors, or even trespassers, which he could ignore, and refuse to see, thereby avoiding the decision to either refuse or permit them to stay. But now that one of them had been born in his territory, he considered the child as one of his subjects and had to deal with the child's parents accordingly.

***

They sat in the dimness of the council house, sitting on mats with their knees spread and their feet tucked under their thighs in the way of men. Men sat that way so they could rest their arms on their knees during long hours of talking. But Dave and Harry were the only ones wearing shoes and the soles of the shoes cut into the flesh of their thighs. They wished Kusala were there so they could ask him if it were all right to sit some other way. But for some reason they couldn't understand why Kusala had refused to accompany them. He told them what gifts to take, how the meeting would go, and how they should act, but refused to go with them.

For three days they sat in council. The first two days were filled with long speeches. There were questions concerning Peter John and then long speeches by the various chiefs congratulating Harry. At other times they just sat, staring into the fire, while the logs on the fire settled tiredly, releasing sparks that floated toward the roof.

At noon of the third day the chiefs gave their decisions. "Yes, they would be allowed to build their houses and plant their gardens. They could teach their signs to any who wanted to learn. They could hand out their dawa to any sick who wanted it. The limits for their village for houses, gardens, corrals, granaries and all other activity except the grazing of herds, which had no limit, was to be one half of a quarter day's walk in all directions from the top of the hill."

Everyone stood up and the batu-na-dawa was called. He entered pushing his staff in ahead of him. It was decorated at the top with the hairs of an elephant's tail. Below was a cluster of clay bells and charms. He was naked except for a cord around his waist from which hung a piece of bark cloth in front and three pouches. He shook his staff over the fire a couple of times and then handed it to the boy who had come in with him. From the cord around his waist he took a small, crude, hand-forged blade and, reaching for Ronzozo's left hand, made a cut in the flesh of the index finger between the first and the second knuckle. There were scars there from previous incisions. Ronzozo held his hand over the fire while the batu-na-dawa reached for Harry's left hand and made a similar cut. He slid the knife back between the flesh of his hip and the cord. From one of the pouches he took a stick a little over a man's hand long and as big around as two fingers. He held it over the fire and the two men took hold of it with their left hands, the incisions touching each other, the blood mixing as it flowed over the rod to drop into the fire.

They raised their right hands, and Ronzozo said, "I Ronzozo, Chief of the Five Tribes, Protector of the lands and the peoples from the Valley of the Yellow Flowers to the Great River and from the place of the Yellow Earth to place of the Great Trees, before the Council of Chiefs and Elders, do give permission to this mondeli Van to use the lands at the Hill of Two Streams. He may build houses and villages for his family and followers so long as they are loyal to me and the council of the Five Tribes. It shall be to them and to their children to use from this time forward until they, of their own free will, shall walk away to go to another place leaving behind them the land of all the peoples. To this I cut this agreement and to this our bloods mix. I, Ronzozo, have spoken it."

The others standing around grunted in agreement and then it was Harry's turn. He raised his right hand a little higher and said the things Kusala had told him to say, "I, Harry VanVeldt of the mondeli, as head of my family, and leader of those who will join me, do promise to support Chief Ronzozo, and the council of the Five Tribes. We shall care for the land entrusted to us and shall help the peoples of the Five Tribes in all ways we can. As they welcome us, we honor them. This agreement shall be to me and to my children and to those who join me and to their children from this time forward. To this I cut this agreement with Chief Ronzozo and the Council of the Five Tribes, and to this our bloods mix."

The batu-na-dawa took the short rod and put it into its pouch. He reached into another pouch and took out some filaments of a spider's nest and pressed the white filaments against the cuts to stop the bleeding. With that, the ceremony was over. They had permission to remain and establish the station.

1905

CHAPTER NINTEEN

Harry and Dave sat in the thatch-covered area between their two huts. It had been almost a year since they received permission from Ronzozo to established the station and not much was done since then. There were some more buildings, except they weren't buildings at all. The church was nothing more than some poles holding up a thatched roof. It was the second such church and twice as big as the first one which had been destroyed by termites. During the week it was used as a school where Laura and Alma taught the Children. There were some other such sheds, but the dispensary was now used for storage since there was no more medicine to dispense.

The significant changes were that a large area was cleared not far from the buildings and natives now hoed and watered the garden while Alma and Laura taught school. A few families had attached themselves to the station and there was a small village on either side of the hill close to the streams that ran in opposite directions from the hill.

The wet season had just ended leaving all the land still green, but the heat of the dry season was beginning to set in. It was the after-lunch time of day when most people and animals looked for shade to get away from the heat. Alma, who was expecting again, little Peter, and Laura were all inside the huts taking a nap. Dave sat on a low native stool leaning back against the mud wall of their hut. His head was back against the wall, his eyes closed, his arms resting on his knees, his hands hanging down.

Harry sat in the tattered camp chair, his elbows on his knees, and his chin in his hands. Long strands of black hair hung down on either side of his face which he didn't bother to push away from his eyes. He sat looking across the grass filled plain, not discouraged, but wondering about a great many things, for all of which he did not have an answer. There was no reason to be discouraged, but at the same time there was no reason for any great expectations. They were surviving, but not accomplishing much.

On the table next to him were Flemish, French, English and Latin Bibles and the pads of paper on which he was working on the translation of the New Testament. He thought he should get back to work, while at the same time wondering if his work would ever see the ink of a printing press, or if the New Testament would ever be in the hands of the people.

For some time he had been watching a man headed toward them along one of the many paths that wove through the waist high grass. They had been on some of those paths when Kusala took them hunting and had walked for almost two days along a path when they had gone to Ronzozo's village to get permission for the station. To see a native walking one of the paths was not unusual except that this native would run for a while, then walk a little while, and then run again. Harry didn't know how long he had been watching the man, but that was not normal action, even for a native, in the noontime heat of the day.

He got up, went inside through the canvass flap, careful not to make any noise that would wake up Alma or Peter, and got the binoculars. He's carrying something. What is that? A basket? A piece of wood? A pouch? It doesn't look native, whatever it is, he said to himself.

"Dave, what do you make of this?" he said lowering the field glasses.

"Huh," Dave said opening his eyes and leaning away from the wall.

"Come look at this."

Dave pushed himself up off the stool and walked over to where Harry was standing, squinting as he looked the direction Harry was pointing. He took the glasses, looked through them for a moment and said, "Looks to me like someone coming this way."

"What's he carrying?"

"Don't know."

Harry took the glasses and looked through them again. "It's some kind of a pouch; canvas, or maybe leather. But it isn't native. We've got to call the girls."

The man ran up the hill, holding out the pouch when he saw them, staggering the last few steps. Harry and Dave ran out to meet him.

"Leopopo say give to you," the man said and then flopped down in the shade of the hut. Harry and Dave recognized Mbiyama, Leo's gun bearer.

Dave went over and dipped a gourd into one of the clay water pots and brought it to the man while Harry tried to untie the string around the pouch, but his hands were shaking so much with excitement he couldn't control them and had trouble undoing Leo's knots. He held the pouch while Alma untied the string.

They all sat down around the table and Harry reached in and took out the bundle of papers. It had been so long since they'd had any word from anyone. They were all shaking with anticipation. Harry started to read the top paper, but his eyes were so full of tears he couldn't read it and handed it to Alma. "Here, you read it," he said.

She started to read. "We should be there within two days of when Mbiyama delivers this to you. I have lots of supplies and some people for you. I have separated out some of the letters I thought would be of most interest. I have sack full of mail. Signed Leo," she added.

They sat there, all of them crying with joy and disbelief. They moved the Bibles and pads of translation out of the way and spread the letters out on the table, turning them over so they could see who they were from, trying to make out the return addresses through the distortion of tears, each of them trying to decide which letter they wanted to read first.

***

It was mid-morning when they saw the front of Leo's safari headed toward them. They stood for a while at the top of the second hump, looking at the safari through the binoculars, passing them from one person to the next. After half an hour they couldn't wait and went down the hill, Mbiyama leading them along the path. When they were fifty yards from Leo and his group they started shouting to each other, but with all of them shouting at once they couldn't make out what the people in the other group were saying except for an occasional word. When they were within ten yards of each other, Harry, and those with him, stopped as though they were afraid if they touched those people they would and disappear. The newcomers also stood, and stared at the four of them.

The newcomers had all seen the pictures in the mission files, but these people, dressed in worn-out khaki and wearing dirt-stained helmets were not the same as the men and women in suits and fashionable dresses they had seen in the professional portraits of them. They had read the letters and journals sent to the home office. They knew about Rebecca Julianna's death, John Scott's death, how Moses had come to join them and the relief and excitement expressed in those letters when they finally got to their destination. To an extent, they had come to revere these people. Now they were face to face with them and the respect and reverence they had for them was not diminished by what they saw. They all thought, if these four could do it, I can do it.

For both the Robins and the VanVeldts, the six newcomers were not just strangers, but more like distant relatives they had always know were out there somewhere but had never met. They examined the newcomers, not with any question as to whether or not they were capable, but with a deep sense of gratitude. Regardless of their abilities they had volunteered to come to help, to work together, live together and overcome together.

Leo bounded forward. "What is it, Reverend VanVeldt? Do you not like what I've brought you?" he said in his staccato way of speaking while reaching out to shake hands. "Ah, Mrs. VanVeldt, you look just the way you did last time I saw you," he said looking at her waist and referring to the fact that she was pregnant the last time he was there. He bent over to kiss her hand.

He still seemed to almost bounce with excitement as he spoke, the flap on the back of his Foreign Legion style cap swinging as his head went back and forth between the two groups of people. He shook hands with Dave and Laura, while at the same time motioning with the other hand for people to come forward.

"Thank you, Lord. Thank you, Lord," Harry kept exclaiming, and then they were all rushing through the grass toward each other, throwing their arms around the complete strangers, hugging each other, going from one person to the next without yet knowing their names.

They quieted down a little and Harry said, "Welcome, everyone. Welcome. You have no idea how glad we are to see you."

"I think we have some idea," an average sized man said. He spoke in a slow meditative way. "I am Dr. Ralph Schwartz," He took off his helmet as he spoke revealing a mop of fine, brown hair, "and this is my wife, Rosemary."

"Harry, Doctor, Rosemary" Alma interrupted, "can we please get to the house where we can sit in the shade to make introductions and talk instead of standing here in this hot sun?"

They all started toward the station, Harry walking with Leo, leaving Alma, Dave and Laura to answer the newcomers' questions. It was not that he didn't want to talk to them, but rather that he was so overjoyed to see them he was afraid he would not be able to control his emotions. He would have time later to get to know them. "Thank you, Leo. You said you'd bring help and you have," Harry said with the tears overflowing the eyelids that were supposed to keep them back.

For three years they had managed to survive. The four of them had stood at the top of the hill to which the newcomers were now walking and had watched Watsumdumu and those on whom they had come to depend walk away to disappear into the high grass. They stood, afraid and uncertain, that those on whom they were still depending to tell others where they were would not make it.

They had watched Leo leave with their bundles of journals and letters and had, again, wondered if he really would see they got to the right people. If this stranger, who had come out of nowhere, had to choose between delivering his ivory or the bag of letters from some people the rest of the world had forgotten about, wouldn't he choose his ivory?

During those three years, with all the unspoken fears, was the constant realization that a savage to whom they had come to preach, who had not yet admitted to accepting their doctrine, was keeping them alive. If it hadn't been for Kusala, they wouldn't have survived.

Walking toward the hill, Harry wondered what the outcome would have been if little Peter had been born in a tent rotting with holes and blight instead of in a hut. They always referred to those structures as "the house", but it was nothing more than two mud huts with a shed connecting them. They had watched with dread as their bolts of Mericani, bags of beads, coils of copper wire and everything else they brought as trade goods steadily disappeared. Those were the things they needed to have the garden hoed, the water carried, make needed repairs and buy food so Laura and Alma could teach the women and children.

When everything was gone, Kusala kept people hoeing the garden, bringing the water and doing what had to be done. When the ammunition they depended on for meat was expended, he would disappear for a day or two and then arrive back with an antelope over his shoulders. He shared his kill with everyone, but he was the one who had kept them alive. No, there was no way Dr. Schwartz and the others could know how he, Alma, Dave and Laura felt. Dr. Schwartz and those with him were their rescuers, but Kusala was their savior.

In the next three days two more safaris arrived with equipment and supplies. Better, in some ways than all the equipment, medical supplies and building tools, was that half of the porters who brought in the equipment were going to stay right there as workers. Leo didn't need all of them to bring out the ivory. He would take them with him when he came back through on his way out.

For Harry and the others it was as though for three years they had been sitting on eggs waiting for them to hatch and, all at once, there were new chicks running about everywhere. It was all the four of them could do to keep the chicks together and safe. With each new box and bundle the newcomers couldn't wait to unpack. Leo left early in the morning three days after he had arrived and headed for Zandeland

and elephant hunting, leaving behind a hundred and three men to help build the station.

***

They all sat under the shed in various kinds of camp chairs around Bill Pontier's table which had replaced Harry's termite eaten one. Hanging well below the grass of the roof, four lanterns glowed brightly with the new abundance of lamp oil. "Now this is just a preliminary sketch, mind you, but it will give you an idea of what can be done," Bill said spreading a sheet of paper onto his camp table and they all stood up and pressed in to view it. It was a map of sorts, with a road running down the center of the top of the hill. There were overlapping circle makings for the large trees and squares indicating buildings. Off to each side of the sheet were the streams with little circles indicating the huts in the villages.

Bill Pontier was a giant of a man, six feet nine inches tall with broad shoulders and strong arms and large hands. He was from San Diego where his father was in the construction business. From the time he was fourteen he worked in construction after school and during the summers. His hair was yellow-blond on top of a long face with a straight prominent nose and deep-set, blue eyes.

"Doc and Rosemary came by while I was drawing this and when I explained what it was they said they wanted the hospital right here at the end of the station, right here just before it slopes down to the field. Is that okay with everyone?"

He looked around and, when there were no objections, looked at harry and said, "Harry, where do you want the director's house?"

The day they had arrived Bill said while they were shaking hands, "Well, well, Mr. VanVeldt, somehow you do not resemble what I thought the director of the Congo field would look like. How do you want us to address you, as Director VanVeldt, Reverend VanVeldt, or Mr. VanVeldt?"

"Call me Harry, but what's this about Director."

"We were told more than once that you are director of the Congo Field."

"Huh," Harry grunted. "The Congo Field, huh? Well, there's not a whole lot here to direct, now, is there? But please, just call me Harry."

Harry laughed. "To be honest with you, I haven't given much thought to being director or where the director should live."

"Then I think it should go right here," Bill said pointing to the other end of the hill from the hospital. "For the past two mornings I've seen you climb that hill early in the morning. This way you won't have so far to climb," he said smiling.

"What are we going to build these houses with; mud and sticks?" Laura asked looking sideways at him.

"Oh, with bricks," Sylvia said. Bill and I took a walk down to each of the streams. There's lots of good clay there."

Sylvia Pontier was a slim, tall woman, not as tall as her husband, but well over six feet. She had long black hair pulled straight back that hung down to her waist. She had dark, almost black eyes, straight nose, prominent cheekbones and a wide, sensuous mouth.

"Sylvia is a potter," Bill said. "We'll look over the crates and we'll have to cut some of them up to make forms for the bricks. Look over the wooden cases you have and decide which ones you don't have to keep until your house is built—"

"We've already unpacked some we won't need again," Doc said interrupting him.

"Good. We'll start with those tomorrow. I'll need some of you to help me because the natives won't know how to use the tools, but they can certainly start collecting the mud. It's the beginning of the dry season and so we don't have to worry about keeping the new bricks out of the rain. After they're sun dried we'll bake them in kilns and hopefully we'll start building in six to seven months."

Looking down on the station from his *prayer rock* early the next morning, Harry saw the entire top of the hill filled with tents. For centuries invading forces had moved into an area and lived in tents; kept their supplies, equipment, cannons and gunpowder dry in tents until they built their city. The building of a city was about to begin and God had sent Bill Pontier to do it.

CHAPTER TWENTY

It had been three months since Doc and Rosemary and the others first arrived. It was three months of getting settled and two hours every afternoon of learning the language. When Doc and Rosemary first opened the dispensary, Moses and Laura helped them as interpreters and in the process became efficient as medical assistants and even assisting in surgery. Now, after three months, Laura and Moses would have charge of changing dressings and hand out medications while Doc and Rosemary went on their first medical safari.

***

They left as the sun was just edging over the horizon. Kusala was in front, behind him Harry, followed by Doc and Rosemary and the porters carrying all the supplies: tents, food, medicine, instruments, bandages and dressings, lanterns and kerosene for the lanterns, everything needed for living and caring for the sick. They went down the hill and through the Kakwa village to follow a footpath that led away from the Hill of Two Streams.

They passed through several of the small, three and four family villages where the packs of Basenji dogs rushed out to meet them without barking, but showing their teeth. The children trailed after for a mile or so after they had passed through. By the middle of the afternoon a small group of sick and hobbling were following behind.

They arrived at their destination at sundown, a large village about twenty miles from the mission and set up camp. The villagers stood around watching, knowing why they had come and wondering if they dared bring the sick, or if it was true what the batu-na-dawa had said about the munganga putting demons into their bodies and they would die, burning with inside fire. Because of what the batu-na-dawa and the chief said, none from this village had ever been to the mission for treatment, but they had heard about the munganga and his dawa, that he had strong dawa that could remove the sickness.

They were up before dawn the next morning. The porters set up the large open tent where surgery would be performed, built fires under the large galvanized tubs for sterilizing the sheets and gowns and arranged the boxes of instruments and supplies where Harry and Doc told them to. Some of the boxes were placed around the edge of the tent to keep the natives from crowding into the surgery area. They finished all the preparations and then stopped to have breakfast.

The line was not long when they went to the row of boxes forming a counter where the villagers were lined up. There were those from other villages who had followed them, but not many from the village itself. The witch doctor had convinced his village of the evil intentions of the munganga.

The last person in line was a woman. She stood staring at him, refusing to speak, while the doctor tried to find out what was wrong. She had no sores to be seen and she looked healthy. He took her temperature, felt her pulse, took her blood pressure, listened to her heart and lungs and finally she shrugged her shoulders and said, "It is my husband. He has finished to die and we have moved him from the village."

"When did you see him last?" Doctor asked pulling on the lobe of his right ear.

"Last evening," she said and the doctor thought the man might have died in the night.

"Where is he?"

"He is this way," she said and started walking away. They walked with her, Dr. Schwartz asking questions, most of which she answered with a shrug. She didn't know. Couldn't remember when it had started. The demon had entered him and he had started to die. "Yes. He was very hot when the demon first entered him. He burned with the demon's fires at night and shook with the cold in the mornings."

"Did he cough out his food?"

She nodded her head.

"When did it start?"

"When the demon entered him."

"How many days ago did the demon enter him?"

"Who can know when a demon enters," she said and Doc gave up asking questions.

A hundred yards from the village they found her husband, a wasted, bone-skinny man, lying on his right side on a crude, pole platform six feet off the ground. The doctor set up the wobbly pole ladder lying nearby and climbed up to examines the man. He knelt beside the man, the platform shaking every time he moved. He listened with the stethoscope and then asked the man to take a deep breath. The man shook his head, refusing to do as he was asked.

"Does it hurt to breathe?" Doctor asked and the man nodded. The doctor felt along the man's chest and abdomen and the man jerked a little once and cried out in pain.

"Well?" Rosemary asked when Doctor finally straightened up from examining the man.

"Amoebic abscess of the liver," he said matter-of-factly as he started down the ladder.

"Any hope?" Harry asked.

"All the hope in the world if we take care of it right away. The symptoms are common to a lot of other things. Because of the fever cycle, it is often confused with acute malaria, but I'm sure this is an abscess of the liver. I'll know for sure as soon I make a diagnostic aspiration," he said.

When he told them to bring the man back to the village there was an immediate clamor from his wife and the village natives. They didn't want him in the village. If he died there the demon might enter someone else and they would get the same illness.

"I will kill the demon and take it out," Doc said.

They still refused, arguing and shaking their fingers at him.

"I won't let the demon enter any of you. I will be the closest to it. If it could enter anyone it would be me." No matter what he said they refused to have the man brought back to the village. "Well, we'll have to do it here," he said.

It took a couple of hours to make all the preparations, carry the two boxes and the slab that made up the operating table, set up the aspirating syringe and other instruments, lifting the patient down from the platform and washing and preparing him for the procedure. They crowded around the table, Dr. Schwartz and Rosemary wearing their white helmets, Harry with a stained brown helmet on his head. Rosemary and Harry were on either side of Dr. Schwartz while on the other side of the table a porter held the patient in a sitting position while another one held his right arm up and out of the way.

The morning sun was burning down on them and trickles of sweat were running down their necks and backs. Dark splotches of perspiration spread wider on the bent backs. Half an hour later they were able to relax. Dr. Schwartz put his hands on his hips and leaned back. "Must have gotten four pints out of there," he said to no one in particular and shaking his head a little.

A couple of porters wrapped the man in a white sheet to keep the flies off him and lifted him back to the platform. They tied some slim poles to the larger corner post and stretched a sheet between them to give him some shade. They collected the equipment and went back to the village, leaving the patient's wife sitting on the ground under the platform. She returned to the village in the evening telling everyone the demon had been driven out and her husband was asking for food.

During the night the word spread and the next morning the lines of patients that filed by the boxes seemed endless. One of the patients was the man from the platform, helped along by a brother on each side holding him. The doctor gave him an emetine injection and told them to bring him back that afternoon when he aspirated a pint of the thick, sticky, cocoa-brown pus.

The whole village was at the service that evening. They stayed in that village three more days, clinic in the morning, surgery in the afternoon, and services every night. When they ran out of supplies they broke camp and headed back to the station.

1908

CHAPTER TWENTY-ONE

Harry and Alma, with three-year-old Peter John between them, stood at the ship's rail. Harry was holding on to Peter John's collar to keep him from leaning out to far. There was a light breeze blowing on the Hudson, which added to the cold of that September day.

There were almost two hundred people on the dock to welcome Harry and Alma home after more than eight years separation. The whole family, all thirty-six of them, seemed to be trying to outdo each other with their waving. On the ship Harry and Alma waved, threw kisses, and tried to sort out the crowd on the dock. "Harry, can that be Henry's John? I can't believe it. He's almost as tall as his father."

In addition to the family, there were all the VanVeldt employees who had been given the day off and their way paid to New York. To one side was the ten-piece band and all the workers from the Place of Hope Mission that Pop VanVeldt had started. In front and center of the crowd was Pieter VanVeldt with his wife Julianna on one side and the mayor of the city of Paterson on the other.

The ship eased toward the dock, the fenders groaning and squeaking in doing their job of protecting the brittle iron hull from the hardness of the concrete dock. Harry picked up Peter John and headed with Alma to where the gangplank was being lowered. The customs and immigration officials in their dark uniforms and peaked caps came aboard, followed by Pieter VanVeldt. He stepped on deck and swept the hat off his head before throwing his long arms around Harry, Alma and little Peter all at once. He hung on to them, pressing his cheek against each of theirs and then stepped back and took little Peter. Peter John put one hand on his grandfather's cheek and said, "Grandpa?"

"Yah. Is Grandpa."

Pieter VanVeldt was a tall, raw-boned man, an inch taller than his tallest son. Despite his great height, he had a head too large for his slim frame. His head was topped with a pronounced widow's peak that was thinning and beginning to gray. His gray eyes were expressive and had in them something that disturbed those who didn't know him. They were never known to harden, or to become too intent or piercing, but shone with an assurance that came from knowing what he wanted and a determination to see it fulfilled.

"Come. Come," he said leading the way over to the chief immigration officer who scanned their papers and then let them go ashore.

There was the usual struggle of everyone pushing forward to greet them, and then Pop, still holding little Peter, said, "Arrie, Alma, come" and started through the crowd. The crowed opened as he approached and closed again after they had passed. They made their way to the only car on the edge of the crowd. The driver looked down from his perch behind the wheel of the Model G Cadillac as Pop VanVeldt, still holding little Peter, reached over and opened the carriage door and then held out his hand to help Alma's mother step down.

Alma rushed forward and threw her arms around her mother who was embarrassed by the display. "Oh, Mama, Mama, it's so good to see you," she said stepping back while the tears started to flow.

"Please, Dear, you know I prefer you call me 'mother'. It's good to see you, too. You're looking well." From inside her purse she took an embroidered handkerchief and, holding it out said, "Here, Dear, dry those tears." and then turning to Pop VanVeldt said, "And this is Peter?"

"Say hello to your grandmother, son," Harry said.

"Hello," Peter John said turning away.

She took a hand and touched his cheek. "You are such a lovely child." She said it as though she was surprised he was completely normal, as though being born in Africa should have tainted him somehow. "Would you like to come and visit me some time?"

Little Peter just stared at her.

"We'll have such a good time together. Do you have a kiss for me?" she said leaning toward him. His grandfather pushed Peter John toward her a little and he leaned forward in his grandfather's arms and kissed her cheek.

"Well, dear, you must call sometime," Mrs. Kelly said reaching out and lightly touching Alma's hand.

"I will, Mother. I will."

"Thank you for inviting me here today," Mrs. Kelly said formally to Pop VanVeldt. "I'm sorry my husband and I will not be able to attend your banquet this evening." She turned then and climbed back into the car.

They watched the car pull away and Harry put an arm around Alma who had started crying again. Pop put an arm around her from the other side. "Is a beginning, Yah? Is a beginning. She vill vant to hold her grandson."

Alma nodded, smiling through the tears. "Thank you, Pop."

***

In the weeks following their arrival Harry preached, spoke or lectured, four to five times a week. It started when he was asked to give a "little talk" at the arrival banquet. The account of their arrival and excerpts of the remarks he made at the employees banquet appeared in the Saturday paper with the closing line, "Mr. Harry VanVeldt is an accomplished lecturer and this reporter was held captivated as he related incident after incident of his experiences in the most interior places of Africa. He will be the speaker Sunday morning at the Hawthorne Christian Church." The church was packed that Sunday.

Everybody was interested in Africa. The President was planning a trip to Africa and his trip had created a great deal of interest everywhere. People wanted to hear from someone who had been in the Congo. The first week in October Harry spoke in Park Street Church in Boston Sunday morning, then in Marblehead in the evening, New Haven on Tuesday, Hartford on Wednesday, Atlantic City YMCA on Thursday, and then the after-dinner speaker at the Explorers Club in Washington on Friday. The next morning he was in Philadelphia to give his report to a specially called meeting of the Board of Directors at the Mission headquarters.

On Sunday, October 18, 1908, while Harry was reviewing his notes on what he was going to say that morning at a Sunday morning service, the Belgian Parliament, half way around the world, was voting in favor of annexing the Congo as a Belgian colony, thus ending twenty-three years of King Leopold's reign as sole owner and sovereign of almost 1 million square miles in the middle of Africa, the largest privately owned domain in the world. Harry preached that morning unaware that Leopold's *Congo Free State* had become the *Belgian Congo.*

With Harry gone so much of the time, Alma handled the invitations to speak and made the bookings. On the first Monday in November, the day before Election Day, she sat with the appointment book, the box of notepaper and the mail from the past Friday, Saturday and that morning in front of her. She started arranging the envelopes in the order of the date they were mailed. She felt there was a certain impartial fairness to that. She picked up an envelope and hesitated when she saw the District of Colombia postmark. She looked at the return address on the back. There was no name, just 1600 Pennsylvania Avenue and below that, Washington, D.C. There was something vaguely familiar about the address, but she didn't know anyone in Washington. Just because it was from the nation's capitol, she violated her sense of fair play and opened it before sorting through the rest of the mail. She unfolded the sheet of paper and stared in unbelief at the top of the page with the simple words: THE WHITE HOUSE. Underneath was scrawled the date and she thought for a moment she had opened someone else's mail and then saw in the same slanted scrawl the salutation, Dear Mr. VanVeldt.

She got up from the desk and ran into the dining room where Harry was answering letters that needed to be answered by him. She held the letter out in front of her. "Harry, Harry. You got a letter from the President."

"President of what? The mission?"

"No. President Roosevelt."

"Oh, is that so," he said not believing her, "what does it say?"

"I haven't read it yet," she said handing him the letter. He held it so they both could see it and he started reading it aloud.

Dear Mr. VanVeldt,

The Friday before last a friend of mine attended a meeting of the Explorers Club here in Washington, which you addressed on the subject of your experiences in Central Africa. From what he said I understand most of your time was spent in the Congo, but that you are also familiar with the British East Africa.

As you may have heard, I will soon be leading an expedition for the collection of specimens for the National Museum under the auspices of the Smithsonian Institute. I have many experienced and capable advisors, but I would like to talk with someone who has returned from there as recently as you have.

With the elections just a few days away I will be very busy between now and then and immediately following. The best time for me would be Monday or Tuesday just before Thanksgiving. Possibly you and your wife could join me here for lunch on one of those days. My aide, Captain Fitzhugh Lee, will be expecting your call. If both those days are not good for you, Captain Lee will know my schedule and hopefully another time can be scheduled.

I look forward to meeting with you.

Sincerely,

Theodore Roosevelt

"I can't believe it," she said. "Lunch with President Roosevelt at the White House."

Harry smirked, "But I thought we agreed we wouldn't go anywhere Thanksgiving week. Just stay home."

"We agreed you wouldn't go off by yourself that week, that we'd spend the whole week together."

***

They sat in an anteroom waiting to be shown into lunch with the President. Alma looked toward a wall mirror and, as she had done several times before, put her hand to her hat, an arrangement of feathers and velvet that matched the velvet of her dress. She was wearing a long-sleeved, high-necked dress with a four strand pearl choker around the material at the neck. It was a dress her mother had helped her select for the occasion, designed to, as much as possible, hide the fact she was pregnant. Her mother had also loaned her the pearl choker for the occasion. It was wonderful what a difference an invitation to lunch with the President could make in her parent's attitude toward Harry.

As long time Republicans who voted for Roosevelt when he first ran for governor of New York, and every time he ran since then, they not only envied Harry and Alma this singular honor, but also concluded there might be something to Harry VanVeldt they had not recognized.

A man held the door for them showing them into the office. The President was just coming around the edge of the desk as they entered and Alma had the impression, from the way he tugged at the bottom of his coat and shrugged his shoulders, that he had just slipped into his jacket. He came across the room, his hand extended. There was energy in the way he walked and talked, but he was shorter than Alma expected. He was not a short man, of average height, but she just expected he would be taller than everyone else.

He turned and introduced them to his son. "And this is my son, Kermit. He's in his first year at Harvard." There was a smile on his face and a father's pride when he said, "He's hardly gotten started at Harvard and can't wait to get out early."

The President led the way into an adjoining room where a table was set for the four of them. Until the soup was served, the conversation was mostly Alma talking with Kermit about Harvard and then the President started asking questions. They were the kind of questions asked by someone who had found out all they could about the subject and Harry wondered if there was much Alma and he could add to what the President already knew about Kenya. They had gotten to the dessert when the President asked, "And how long do you think it will take to make Africa a white man's land?"

"Well, I don't know that we should make it a white man's land."

"Of course we should. Where would this nation be today if we had left it to the Indians? We have to bring Africa into the twentieth century."

"We've hardly entered it ourselves," Alma said.

The President looked at her for an instant and then laughed. "How true. How true," he said.

"Well, as a missionary, I believe the most important thing is their salvation, but next to that is education. I'm not just talking about reading and writing. That is needed, but there also has to be a practical curriculum. We have a school at our headquarters station of Jikobe, in Kenya, called CAM Institute. The C.A.M. does not stand for Central Africa Mission, but for Commercial, Agricultural and Mechanical Institute. Governor Jackson has been there several times and often brings visitors to see it as a model of an educational institution meeting the needs of the people. If you can at all make it, you should try to visit it. It is in the highlands so the weather is moderate and there is an abundance of game in the area. Governor Jackson would probably be glad to take you there and we would be honored to have you.

"Education is the key. As I pointed out to the members of our board, if the education the mission provides is considered indispensable, then the missionaries will always be allowed to stay. I will say this, Mr. President, but the Leopold regime has had no interest in educating the natives and I doubt that is going to change even though the country has now become a colony. All education is left to the missionaries. Education is the key, Mr. President. The educational system can always be a place for American influence in a country," Harry said, knowing that America having influence everywhere was something Teddy Roosevelt believed in.

When Harry explained that in the Congo all education was provided by missions and told him of the problem they were having getting permission to open new stations, the President said, "Well, I'll write King Leopold and see what I can do. When you get back home call my aide, Captain Fitzhugh Lee, and give him particulars of the original grant, you know, dates, boundaries, that sort of thing, so I can include them in my letter. Jog old Leopold's memory a bit, eh? I know control of the Congo is now with the parliament, but Leopold still has a lot of influence. Captain Lee will be expecting your call. We'll get you those stations. A few more spots of American influence, aye?"

They left after an hour and a half with the President. They felt exhilarated as anyone might after having had lunch with him, but with the excitement there was also a confidence. The President was an opinionated man and bold when stating and arguing his opinions. He believed absolutely that everything America did was right and better than any other country could do. If possible, the whole world should conform to the United States. His confidence was infectious and left you, even if you did not agree with him, confident of yourself. They left believing he would get them the permission to open the new stations.

1909

CHAPTER TWENTY-TWO

A ten-fifteen on Thursday, February 25, 1909, the postman rang the doorbell. He always rang the bell to announce the mail had arrived, but this morning he waited. All the neighborhood knew the VanVeldts had lunch with the President. When Alma answered the door he held out the small bundle of letters and said, "Good morning Mrs. VanVeldt. I thought the top one might be important. It's from the White House." She left the postman standing in the open doorway as she ran back into the house shouting, "Harry. Harry. It's a letter from the President."

She stood next to him, impatient for him to hurry, but he would not be hurried. It had been three months since the lunch with the President. They had called Captain Lee with the information as soon as they got home. When they didn't hear anything, they began to think the President had forgotten his promise. Harry put his arm around her and, holding the letter so she could see it, started reading out loud.

Dear Mr. and Mrs. VanVeldt:

I want to thank you for coming to Washington to meet with me and for all the valuable information that time together provided me.

I am happy to inform you I received, just yesterday, a letter from His Majesty, King Leopold of the Belgians, informing me the Belgian government would soon be sending to your home office in Philadelphia authorization for your mission to open new stations in the Northern Congo. I am very happy about this. It was one of those things I wanted to be sure was wrapped up before I left office.

In a month I shall be leaving for my Africa trip and I'm sure you can understand how eager I am. I want to thank you again for all the help and suggestions you contributed when last we met.

I shall be leaving from New York on Monday, March 29, aboard the HAMBURG. We shall be sailing at noon, so if you and your wife would like to come by the ship in the morning, it would be pleasant to see you again.

Sincerely, T.R.

They didn't make it to T.R.'s sailing. They sent a messenger with a note thanking him for the invitation and explaining why they couldn't make it. On Sunday, March 28th at eight-thirty in the morning, as they were getting ready to go to church, Alma started labor. By nine o'clock Pop and Mama VanVeldt were there with the midwife, Pop making Harry stay in the living room with him. It made no difference to Pop that Harry had delivered Rebecca Julianna and Peter John.

"Is not in Africa now you are. Out of da vay of da vomen you will stay." Pop made Harry stay where he could see him while he called the rest of the family. To each of them he said, "And vhat is it you can here do? Go first to church, then come over. Yah, yah, all is fine."

At 2:07 p.m. Daniel Philip VanVeldt was born. Mama VanVeldt, with strands of graying hair hanging loose around her face from the bun at the back of her neck, came half way down the stairs and leaned over the balustrade to announce his birth. Both the mother and baby were doing fine. No, there was no need for the doctor to come up. He had been called more as a friend of the family than to deliver a baby and 'just in case.' No, Harry could not come up yet, and he sat back down a little piqued that as her husband, he should be prevented from going to see his son until the women said he could.

CHAPTER TWENTY-THREE

Moses lay flat on his back in his bed in the Robins' house feeling alone and confused. The missionaries told him repeatedly God had saved his life for a special purpose. He had never forgotten the day when he knelt down in the grass and saw his brother's head cut off. He was eight years old when that happened; at least that was what he was told. They had settled on the date the chief gave him to the Robins as the day on which they celebrated his birthday and established 1895 as the year of his birth.

He was told he was saved by a miracle, but he also knew it was a miracle aided by a gun and sleight of hand. That didn't mean he was any less alive, but he was not sure he wanted to be alive. That was one of the things that confused him. He also felt guilty because he had been told it was a sin to wish he were dead. He didn't wish to be dead exactly, he just wished he had never been born.

He also felt ungrateful for his feelings. Ever since he had escaped being killed he had been treated well, better than any other native he knew. In the beginning he had stayed with Watsumdumu and the conditions there were better than the soldiers or the porters had. After Watsumdumu and the others left, he stayed in the storage tent and then in a room in the back of the dispensary. It was then he started sitting at the table with them instead of having a plate of food by himself. Soon after Peter John was born, he moved in with the Robins house. He had never been told, but he somehow knew the Robins could not have children, and after Peter was born, they had decided to make him their child and raise him as their own. He was like the missionaries in every way except in color. New missionaries who arrived treated him nicely, but he knew he made them uncomfortable. They didn't know how to handle a savage who lived, talked, ate and behaved like a white.

It was after Uncle Harry and Aunt Alma had left to go to the United States that Moses started to have some physical changes which were also confusing. Hair started growing between his legs and under his arms. He was afraid to ask Uncle Dave about it and so he had shown it to Kusala who assured him it was perfectly normal. It was a sign of him becoming a man. Since it was obvious to Kusala Bwana Dave was not telling Moses things he should know, Kusala took it upon himself to instruct Moses. He told him that soon he would have evidence of his man's fluid and of the way it was with women and men. Soon after Kusala talked to him, Moses had a strange dream. He dreamt a group of girls were reaching for him. He was embarrassed because he didn't have any clothes on which, even in the dream, he knew to be wrong. Then suddenly he was unable to keep from urinating right in front of all the girls. When he awoke he remembered the dream. It was pleasant remembering and he realized it was not urine that wet the bed but his man's fluid.

He looked at the girls differently than before. Sometimes they stood, three or four at a time, staring boldly at him and giggling with each other. He always wore clothes just like Uncle Dave and Uncle Harry did. Most of the girls wore nothing at all except for the little bunch of leaves in front between their legs, and he wondered if it was his clothes that made them stand and stare at him giggling. When they giggled, or ran, or slapped each other playfully, their firm young breast bounced and their swaying buttocks beckoned him.

At night he lay in his white man's bed and thought of the girls. He thought of them in ways he was sure Uncle Dave and Uncle Harry would say were sinful. But he couldn't help thinking of them. In his dreams they touched him and played with him until his hand replaced the one he was dreaming about, and he would have the wonderful release of his man's fluid. He was certain he was sinning when he did that. He didn't want to sin, but he couldn't stop thinking of the girls.

Doctor and nurse Schwartz had always treated him the same way Uncle Harry and Aunt Alma and the Robins did. The Pontiers and the Langtrees, who had arrived with the Schwartz's, treated him nicely, but he knew he made them uncomfortable. Of the latest group of missionaries who came in with Leo, only Mrs. Wilson seemed totally at ease with him. He felt comfortable with Mrs. Wilson. She never treated him as though he were different from anyone else.

1912

CHAPTER TWENTY-FOUR

It had been seven years since Leo brought in the first group of missionaries. Since then Leo had brought in three more groups including the last trip two years ago when Harry and Alma returned from their furlough. Harry had not seen Leo since they returned with him and they sat now in Harry's office at the back of the building that was the church on Sundays and the school all the other days of the week. It was the first brick building erected after Bill Pontier arrived. "Yes, Harry, I'm quitting elephant hunting," Leo said.

"Do you mean right now or after this one last trip to Zandeland?"

"Right now."

"What are you going to do?"

"After I take my porters back and pay them off, I'm going to Khartoum and get my wife."

"Wife," Harry exclaimed, "You never told us you were married."

"Well, I am and I've palavered with Kitomolo and I can pretty much build a house anywhere I want to," Leo said, his body bobbing in his excitement as he talked.

"Why that's wonderful," Harry exclaimed with a smile brightening his whole face. Then it faded and he looked sidewise at Leo and said, "Do you mean to tell me you made this last trip just to bring in that last batch of people? You're not going on from here to do some hunting?"

"Nope, Harry. My hunting days are over. I promised you I'd bring this group in and I did."

Harry looked at him and thought it was Leo who had built the station; not Alma and he, not Dave and Laura, not even Bill and Sylvia Pontier who had arrived seven years before with Doc and Rosemary and the others. In those seven years Bill Pontier had designed and built all the buildings on the station. There was the church and school in which they were now sitting, a hospital, a print shop and homes for each of the missionaries. Bill may have directed the natives, and even trained them to make and lay brick, but it was Leo who had left a hundred of his porters to work with Bill that first year. Since then, Harry had often tried to reimburse Leo for their wages and Leo had always put him off.

"Leo, Leo, Leo, you never cease to surprise me. Well, we'll have to walk around the station and you can decide where you want your house and we'll get Bill right on it."

"Oh, I'm not going to live here, Harry. Did you know your station here is less than four miles from the Anglo Egyptian Sudan border?"

"Well, I knew it was kind of close, but I thought maybe forty or fifty miles. Are you sure it's only four miles from here to the boarder?"

"Less than four miles, Harry," Leo said jumping up and knocking over the chair he was sitting in. He stopped long enough to right the chair and went on, "and there's going to be a government boarder post not far from here. Last time I was in London I learned the British and Belgian government had entered into some kind of an agreement to build a road connecting Stanleyville on the Congo River with Juba on the Nile and the Belgian part of the road is going to go right by here. Did you know that, Harry?"

"Well, I heard something about a road," he said. "About a year ago I was asked by Kitomolo to go and meet an army coming this way. There had been some kind a fight and some natives had killed a white engineer who was building a road. Boma thought there was going to be an uprising and Kitomolo was ready to go to war if he had to, but didn't want to. The officer they sent was Pierre d'Entremont. Do you know him at all?"

"No. Name sounds familiar, but I don't think I know him."

"He only had a hundred or so tukutuku with him. Certainly not enough soldiers if he really thought there was going to be an uprising. He negotiated with Kitomolo for laborers to build a road.

"Sad thing happened while he was here. Got a letter telling him his wife had died. Sad, very sad," Harry said shaking his head. "I really liked the man."

"That's the road I'm talking about, Harry. That's why I have to get back to London, or maybe even to Brussels, and find out where exactly the government border post is going to be. That's where I'm going to build my house."

"And then what are you going to do?"

"Open a store," Leo said waving his arms excitedly.

"Leo, you're a hunter, not a merchant."

"But I can do it, Harry. Believe me, I can do it," Leo said with a smug smile. "I ran a shop once."

Leo Papadopolis was born in Dar es Salaam. His father was a Greek merchant, and his mother was the daughter of a British soldier and an Indian mother from Zanzibar. They moved to Mombasa when Leo was just two. Both his parents died in a cholera epidemic when he was eighteen. He had grown up thinking he would always be in their store. But when his parents died, the store had to be sold to pay debts, and that was when he started hunting professionally.

Leo started hunting in Zandeland a year after the missionaries arrived at their hill. He was on his way back out when he saw the flashing of the mirror.

1913

CHAPTER TWENTY-FIVE

It was teatime. Moses was not interested in the things the missionaries talked about around the teacart. From where he was playing with Peter John and Daniel Philip he heard his name mentioned and moved to where he could better hear them. The missionaries were discussing plans for the Robins' to go on furlough again. Moses was not pleased with the idea of the Robins' being gone. The Robins' often introduced Moses to new arrivals as their son, and they treated him as their son, but they couldn't take him with them when they went to the United States. The first time Dave explained that without a birth certificate they couldn't get a passport or visa for him, and without a passport and visa he couldn't travel. Standing there with Uncle Harry and Aunt Alma as the Robins' left with Leo, he knew he didn't belong with them. He didn't belong anywhere.

Like the last time, he would probably have to live with the VanVeldts while the Robins were away. He was not looking forward to that. The VanVeldt home was crowded and noisy with four children. Peter and Daniel were loud, rough and tumble boys. He would probably have to share the room with the boys. Three-year-old Ruth was always clamoring for attention and it seemed to Moses that one-year-old Sara never stopped her crying.

"When would you like Moses to move over here?" Alma asked while she handed baby Sarah to Harry to hold while she poured the tea.

"Probably the day before we leave," Laura said.

"Oh, let Moses stay with us," Lillian said, putting her plump little hand on Alma's arm. "We have plenty of room, and it will be easier for you, with the new baby and all, if Moses stays with us."

Moses' heart started beating faster when Mrs. Wilson said that. She was attractively full and had the habit of placing her soft, little hand on his arm when she was talking with him, which she did with everyone. Her sparkling blue eyes gleamed through the thickest of girlish long lashes. She looked and acted so much like a girl it was hard sometimes for Moses to think of her as a married woman. He often fantasized about what she would look like if she wore no more clothes than the native girls did.

"Are you sure?" Alma asked.

"Oh, yes. We'd love to have him, wouldn't we, Ernest."

Lillian was four years younger than Ernest. She was in her final year at the Greenbrier School for Girls when Ernest started courting her. He was the son of the minister of the church she and her parents attended. She had never thought of him romantically. She had always thought of him as a rather effeminate milksop.

She agreed to marry Ernest for no other reason than she saw him as a means of getting to places that were exciting. When she was a child she often spent time in the patients' waiting room of her father's office looking at the National Geographic Magazine. She dreamed and fantasized about going to the places the magazine pictured: Africa, Borneo and islands of the South Pacific and other places where the pictures showed people without any clothes. She was fourteen when she started watching Buck in his room above the garage. He was black and six years older than she was and did the outdoor chores around the house.

Lillian and Earnest sailed two weeks after they were married. Lillian didn't expect Ernest to be an ardent lover, but she did expect their marriage would be consummated before they were half way across the Atlantic. Ernest considered it a sin to get pleasure from the sex act. Consequently, he didn't try to give his wife any pleasure, nor did they have sex often.

"If you like," Earnest said. Moses could tell Mr. Wilson was not at all pleased with Lillian's suggestion.

"It's all settled then," Lillian said.

"We'll have to see what Moses has to say, but if he has no objections, I don't see why it wouldn't be all right," Harry said.

***

From the moment Moses moved in with the Wilsons his one obsession was seeing Mrs. Wilsons without any clothes on. He knew when he could do it, but for a month he struggled knowing his desires were a sin. During the day he would plan how he was going to see her and then when the time came, he stayed in the darkness of his room, fearing what would happen to him if he were caught.

Baths in the Wilson house were on Wednesdays and Saturdays. When Moses moved in with them, he continued to take his bath between tea time and dinner. Ernest Wilson took his bath right after dinner. On Wednesday evening he had to go to a staff meeting at the VanVeldt house. Only the men went to staff meetings. Lillian usually took her bath after Ernest left just before going to bed. The last thing the houseboys did on Wednesdays and Saturdays was to empty Ernest's bath water and set up the bath for Mrs. Wilson with cold water in the tub and three kettles of hot water next to it, then they left.

A month after moving in with the Wilson's, Moses' desire overcame his fear. He sat in his room after dinner waiting anxiously for Ernest to leave. From the windows of his room Moses watched Ernest walk the path to the VanVeldt house half a mile away. He waited a little longer after the light from the lantern disappeared behind the shrubs along the road and then got up and went out onto the back porch. He was cautious and alert as he crept along the back porch, stopping at every imagined noise, his body shaking with both fear and excited anticipation.

He turned the corner of the porch and saw the glow of the light from the bathroom shining through the screen door. A mat hung down along the outside edge of the porch opposite the door to provide privacy for the bathroom while still permitting the door to be open for coolness. He crept forward, looking over his shoulder from time to time. He squatted down at the edge of the screen door, his heart pounding, his knees shaking.

The mosquitoes buzzed heavily around the door and started biting him. He didn't dare slap at them for fear the sound would betray him. He squatted, leaning forward, his head turned to see into the bathroom. The tub was there with the bath-mat next to it and three kettles with tiny wisps of steam still coming from the spouts.

It seemed forever before she came through the door opposite him. She was wearing a robe, and when he saw her he pulled back fearful she would see him. He eased forward to look again. She was standing by the washstand pouring cold water into the basin. She bent over picking up one of the kettles and poured a little hot water into the basin. She pushed the collar of her robe away from her neck and washed her face. She patted her face dry and then emptied the basin into the slop pail turning his direction to do it and he jerked back.

He leaned forward cautiously and saw her at the end of the tub pouring in the hot water. She finished and walked around to the side of the tub with her back to him. She kicked off her slippers stepping onto the bathmat while at the same time letting the robe slide down her shoulders and off her arms. She put it on the stool next to the bathtub. She stood with her back to him, the creamy skin glowing in the soft lamplight. She raised a leg over the edge of the tub, and tested the water with her foot, swinging the foot back and forth to mix the water. She placed the foot in the tub, followed by the other foot turning to the side as she did it so he saw her from the side.

He squatted there breathing through his mouth, almost panting, his heart pounding even harder than it had before as she bent over to place a hand on each side of the galvanized tub, her full breast hanging down, and then lowered herself into the water. Sitting in the tub she was hidden except for her shoulders and head.

She finished bathing finally and stood up and turned to get the towel. She stood facing him. The lamplight glowed on her wet body. For the first time he saw the wet, yellow blond hair between her legs. He was afraid she would look toward the door and see him, but he couldn't stop looking at her. He watched transfixed as she dried herself. When she was through drying she put on her robe and then, picking up the towel, sat down on the stool to dry her feet before she put them into the slippers. He pulled back, stood up and walked around the porch to his room, burning with desire.

The oil lamp was still burning on his desk and the lessons for the next day were still out. He had left them just that way so he could run back and look like he had been studying. He was just going to put them away when he heard her outside his open door saying, "Moses, may I come in."

He swung around suddenly, startled, forgetting she could not know what he had been thinking and then sat down quickly at his desk. "Yes, of course. Yes. Yes. Please come in."

She was wearing the robe that just a few minutes before he had watched her put on. She sat down in the other chair, the robe pulled tightly around her. She sat with her hands folded in her lap looking at him for almost a minute and then said in a voice soft as velvet quietly, "Moses, were you watching me bathe?"

"No! Of course not," he blurted. "What makes you think a thing like that?" His heart was pounding and he felt his face getting hot. The words didn't come out sounding exactly the way he thought they would.

"I saw you outside the door, Moses." She said it calmly, and fear fell on him like a smothering blanket.

"I'm sorry. I'm sorry. I'll never do it again..."

She interrupted him. "You'd better blow the light out," she said, and he looked at her trying to understand.

"We have some important things to talk about and it might not look good if someone were to walk by and see me in your room."

He leaned up from his chair and blew out the flame.

"How long have you been watching me, Moses?"

In the darkness he could dimly see her sitting across from him. "Just tonight," he said.

"Why did you watch me, Moses?"

He didn't answer.

"There are so many native girls you could look at without having to hide by the door. If you wanted to, you could go down to the stream and watch them bathe. Why do you like to watch me?" Her voice was soft and caressing, and as she talked he became less afraid. Her talking about it brought back visions of what he had seen. "You liked watching me, didn't you?"

"Oh, yes," he said and then was afraid he had answered too eagerly.

"You also like looking at the native girls, don't you?" He didn't answer, and she went on, "When you stand by the doorway and look into my classroom is it to look at Ruta and Maria and the others?" She paused again, and then asked, "Have you ever been with any of them?"

"Oh, no! Never! I've never been with anyone."

"I just don't understand why with all the girls who never wear any clothes who you could look at, you want to look at me?" He thought she sounded more pleased than angry. "Did you watch me the whole time I was taking my bath?"

He didn't answer.

"You must be honest with me, Moses, you must answer me. Did you watch me the whole time I was taking my Bath?"

"Yes," he said, his voice quavering.

She kept asking her questions; listing everything he had seen while watching her. In her listing of them he remembered it all and became more excited as though he were watching it all over again. "What were you thinking when you were watching me, Moses?"

He didn't answer, but sat there looking across the darkness at her. In the stillness of the night he could hear her breathing as she waited for an answer. He couldn't tell her what he had been thinking, but he thought she must surely know.

"What were you thinking when you were watching me, Moses?" she asked again. "What were you thinking?"

"I don't know."

"Watching me, did you think you might like to touch me?"

"I guess so."

"Where did you want to touch me, Moses?" She asked. She kept asking him, listing all the places she had touched herself when she bathed.

"Oh, Please, Mrs. Wilson, don't ask any more questions. I know it was wrong and I'll never do it again."

"I have to ask these questions, Moses, to know what kind of a man you are. I'm not asking these questions because I'm angry with you,

Moses. I'm not going to tell anyone else what you tell me. But I have to know. Did you want to kiss me?"

"Yes."

He waited to hear what she would say next and when she did speak her voice was soft and soothing, but he heard her clearly say. "I liked having you watch me. I wanted you to watch me."

He gasped, his heart pounding, feeling the shaking of desire start in his body again. He knew he had heard her correctly, but he still couldn't believe it.

"Would you like to touch me now," she said standing. In the darkness he saw the robe fall to the floor. She started toward him, and he got up awkwardly, knocking over the chair he had been sitting in. She took hold of his hands and directed them behind her while putting her arms around him.

From then on Wednesday nights became their time together. In a few weeks Lillian was demanding more than just Wednesday night. She found occasions to make love almost daily, some daringly defiant in the chance of being discovered. Within six months he began to wish Dave and Laura would return sooner than was expected so he could move out of the Wilson house.

1917

CHAPTER TWENTY-SIX

Preparations for the arrival Samuel and Sarah Jones started three weeks before they arrived. Everyone who had come in by way of Kenya, rather than with Leo, had stayed with the Joneses on their way in. Harry and Alma, particularly, were looking forward to seeing them. The guesthouse was whitewashed inside and out. They didn't know how long the Joneses would be staying, but three days or three months the attitude was one of not being able to do enough for them.

Alma would have liked to have had a specific date for their arrival so she could do the slaughtering the day before they arrived and have fresh meat for their first day there. As it was, she decided to have chicken the first day, and six pullets had already been selected to have their heads cut off. In the meantime, the chosen chickens were put in a separate pen and fed grain in the hopes they would fatten up a little and be tender when served.

Samuel and Sarah Jones arrived Wednesday afternoon. All the missionaries on the station were invited to that first dinner at Harry and Alma's. During the first week they were invited to dinner at a different home every evening. After the first week, people tried to avoid Samuel who was making suggestions and criticizing everyone and everything on the station. To an extent, Alma thought she understood the reason for the change in Samuel, but she felt sorry for the rest of the missionaries.

The Joneses had always been special to her and Harry. It was the Joneses who had been there to support and comfort them when Rebecca Julianna died. What bothered Alma the most was Samuel mostly found fault with the way Harry did things, and, he was not afraid to criticize Harry in front of the others. Samuel was also particularly hard on Melody. Harry and Alma had always remembered her to be radiantly happy, but now she was quiet and sullen most of the time. Peace only came when Samuel Jones left from time to time to visit other stations. Harry guessed that at those stations also Samuel was criticizing Harry, but the peace when he was away was worth it.

"He's afraid," Alma said one night as they lay under the mosquito listening to little Sarah snoring in her crib.

"Afraid," Harry exploded. "What in the world of?"

"Getting old."

"Old? He's only ten years older than I am for crying out loud."

"Yes, but like you, he came out and started something, and watched it grow. He's gotten used to being the top man. Remember how we worshiped him when we first met him. Now he's loosing all of that. He's going back to where he will be one man of a dozen or so. He'll express his opinion along with the rest of them, but the decision will not be his."

"There was no reason for them to leave. They could have stayed out another twenty years, until they died if they wanted to, but they decided to return to the States," Harry said with decided scorn. "No one made them do it."

"I think the reason for it is they couldn't stand the idea of being separated from Melody. She has to go back to the States for schooling. She should've been sent home long ago, but they could never bring themselves to send her away. They idolized the girl. Samuel, more than Sarah. Without understanding, or knowing it, he resents Melody for making him give up what he loves and really wants. That's why he is so hard on her and she doesn't know how to take it. Up to now he has given her anything she wanted, and now, suddenly, she can't do anything that pleases him. He also resents you because you still have what he's given up. He can't quite bring himself to leave. That's why there's always one more station he wants to visit. So be patient with him, dear."

"I don't know if I can."

"Of course you can. And just remember, if they ever offer you a place on the Board, turn it down."

"Don't worry. I most assuredly will."

"Sometimes I wake up at night dreading when we're going to have to leave the children. Up to now it has always been in the future, but it's getting closer now. Next time we go to the States P.J. will be thirteen. We'll have to leave him there to go to school. Danny will be eleven. I suppose we could bring him back and then send him to the States with someone else going on furlough when he's thirteen, but I think it would be good for P.J. and Danny to be together, to have each other. Ruth and Sarah will come back with us, of course, but sometimes I wake up at night and cry at the idea of deserting our two boys in some foreign land. Oh, I know, they'll be with your folks or mine. I know we've never talked about it before. I try not to think of it too much, but I think I can understand why Samuel and Sarah decided to give up everything here. We'll still have the girls with us when we leave the boys, but all they have is Melody."

Harry lay in the darkness looking up at the mosquito netting above him listening to his wife talking, and he, too, had tried not to think of when they would have to be separated from their children. But it was something that came to every missionary or colonialist eventually, unless like the Joneses, they gave up everything to be with their children.

***

During the dry season, Saturday afternoon was a time when all the station gathered at the VanVeldt home for tea and tennis. The native-made wicker chairs and the teacart were moved from the porch to the shade of the mango trees that grew to one side of the tennis court. The mototos, naked except for a loincloth, gathered along the hedges at the ends of the court ready to shag balls.

Mabel Guetz arrived with Doc and Rosemary. Mabel was puffing and perspiring from the mile walk. She breathed a loud sigh of relief as she settled into the wicker chair, which creaked protesting her more than two hundred pounds.

The others arrived and Bill Pontier said, "On our way over here we were talking about Leo marrying one of Ronzozo's daughters."

"I don't see that it's any of our business," Mabel said in her gravelly voice as she started to fan herself with a woven, heart-shaped fan.

"It may not be any of our business," Lillian Wilson said turning her head quickly causing her blond ringlets to bounce defiantly, "but it interests us enough that we're talking about it, aren't we."

"Well, yes, it does interest us," Laura Robins said. "But you certainly can't be concerned that some white trader is marrying a native. The reason we're interested is because Leo is a friend of ours, and we're always interested when a friend of ours gets married."

"Oh, no! It's not that. It's that he already has a wife. There must be some law against having two wives. It's his having two wives that has us talking." There was a certain excitement in Lillian's voice.

"I'm sure there must be such a law in Lisbon, or Paris, or maybe even in New York," Alma said quietly as she measured the tealeaves into the pot. Lillian looked at Alma curiously, wondering if there was something in the way Alma said it she didn't understand.

"But aren't we under Belgian Law out here?" Lillian asked.

"The Belgians would be wanting us to think so," Dave Robbins said sarcastically reaching for one of the tennis racquets.

"Well, actually," Doc said slowly and deliberately, "there are two sets of laws: the colonial and the native law. Leo has chosen to operate under the native law."

"But he's not a native." Lillian said.

"Of course he is," Ernest said trying to display his wife's ignorance. "A native is one who is born in a place. He was born in Africa, so he is a native. Since we were not born here, we're not."

"I know that. You know what I mean," she said.

"What you mean," Alma said, "is that he's not black."

"As I see it," Samuel Jones said, "it is not a matter of black or white, or colonial law or native law." Samuel was a large man with curly, blond hair that was beginning to turn gray. He had a wonderfully sonorous voice. He spoke pompously and had a habit of leaning his head back and looking down his nose when he made these kinds of statements. Harry didn't remember that trait in him from before.

"We're here not only to evangelize, but also to set an example," he went on. "The natives do not differentiate between Leo, Lieutenant Subrie and us. To them, we are all whites. We can hardly tell the natives they can only have one wife, and then have Leo defying our authority by doing exactly the thing we say they can't do. The only way we can let the natives know we do not approve of what Leo and his kind is doing is by not associating with him..."

"*Oh, hog wash,*" Harry exploded waving his hand and interrupting Samuel.

"Please don't interrupt me," Samuel said superiorly. "As I was saying ..." Melody came over from where she had been playing. "Go back and play with PJ and Danny a little longer, dear," her father said.

At eighteen she was a woman who was hurt that she was still thought of a child. Moses got up to follow her. He knew what it was like to be excluded from certain conversations for reasons he didn't understand. He went with her trying to lesson her embarrassment by suggesting a game of keep-a-way with Danny and himself on one side, and Melody and PJ on the other.

Samuel Jones watched the two of them leave and then continued. "We cannot have one standard for the natives and another for the whites. If we teach the natives it is wrong for them to have more than one wife, then we have to have the same standard for whites. To associate with Leo socially implies we condone his action. I realize you have to associate with him in business matters—"

"Like selling him your truck when you promised to sell it to Doctor," Alma said interrupting him without looking up from pouring the tea.

From the other end of the station they could hear the truck starting its climb. "They'll be here pretty soon," Harry said, "and there's something I want to say before they arrive, Samuel." He turned in his chair so he was not only looking at Samuel Jones, but also facing him with his whole body. "Leo and Lieutenant Subrie are guests in my house today, just as you are a guest. You are not Director of the Congo field, I am. And rest assured, if any guest in my house is insulted, or embarrassed, by you in any way, I will ask you to leave; not only my house, but this field."

Everybody was suddenly silent. They had never heard Harry reprimand someone in public before. Harry turned and sat comfortably in his chair. At the far end of the station they could hear the truck complete its climb and change gears as it got on the level just below hospital hill.

"Well, shall we play some tennis," Dave said standing up trying to cover the awkwardness. The others were suddenly busy reaching for their cups of tea.

The truck turned between the last two mango trees and stopped not far from where the tea was set up. Leo stepped down from the passenger's side smiling, laughing, and waving a new can of tennis balls above his head. PJ and Danny fell in alongside and Melody and Moses followed them over to the tea table. Leo slapped the can of balls down in the middle of the teacart before starting around to shake hands with everyone.

"I hear you married one of Ronzozo's daughters," Alma said as he bent over to flamboyantly kiss her hand. It was a playful gesture, but everyone knew he had a unique affection for Alma.

"Yes," he said laughing and moving on, "and Victoria is having some problems teaching her everything."

"Which of his daughters did you marry?" Harry asked.

"Obrika."

"I don't think I know that one."

"Ah, Ronzozo has so many wives, who can keep all his daughters straight?" Leo threw back his head laughing and said, "He has so many daughters I wasn't even sure I was going to get the right one."

"Well, you have all our sincere felicitations," Alma said handing him a cup of tea. "We wish you and your new bride every happiness."

"Thank you," he said nodding and blinking back the tears as he took the cup of tea.

Harry, Leo, Doc and Dave walked onto the court with the can of new balls. Lillian turned to Lieutenant Subrie who had taken the empty chair next to her. "And when are you going to take a wife?" she asked. The fact that she said, "take a wife" implied she was referring to his taking a native wife.

"Oh, not until I meet someone as lovely as you, Madam," he said flirting.

Moses watched, amused by Lillian's flirting. As soon as his parents had returned he had put an end to his affair with Lillian. From time to time after that she had tried to arrange occasions when the two of them could meet, but he'd been able to avoid them.

After the Joneses arrived, he suddenly found himself attracted in a way he didn't completely understand to Melody. At first Moses had felt sorry for Melody, but gradually the pity changed to feeling protective of her. It was a new feeling for him, not something he was used to. Furthermore, it was frustrating to want to protect someone it was impossible to protect. It was her father she needed protection from and there was nothing Moses could do about him. Moses knew her father didn't approve of him, not so much as a person, but because of his situation. As far as Samuel Jones was concerned, it was correct to respect the natives, educate them as much as possible, even be friendly with them, but always maintain the line of separation between the races. Including a native as part of the family was going too far. Moses didn't know why Samuel Jones disliked him; he just knew he did.

Melody, on the other hand, felt comfortable only with Moses. If she sensed his protectiveness, she didn't identify it as that. For all of her life she had been the center of her parents' affection. She had been to the United States with them twice when they went on furlough, but aside from that, she had never been far from her home at Bashindi. Now she had been uprooted from her home, told they would not be returning and, worst of all, suddenly found she was unable to do anything right. Throughout her life, as the children of other missionaries were sent home, she remained with her parents being taught mostly by her mother. While other children left, Jumba always remained.

Jumba was the oldest son of their head houseboy. He was four years older than she was and, for as long as she could remember, he had always been there. When she was four and he was eight, he had been assigned by his father to watch over her and play with her. They grew up together. When, on her tenth birthday she was given the pony she had been begging for, Jumba was told to take one of the mules and ride along with her. He was her protector and closest friend. He was also the servant who saddled her pony when she wanted to go riding and put the pony away when they came back. They both understood the relationship, but they were also the kind of friends only two people who have trusted each other all their lives can be. At the age of eighteen, Melody had been taken away from her home, her pony and from the only lifelong friend she'd ever had. After being at Abaru for a month, it was Moses with whom she felt most at ease, safe and cared for.

The men left the court, laughing and drying themselves with little white towels and handed the racquets to the women. There were offers of letting others go first, but finally it was Laura, Rosemary, Alma and Melody. They hit the ball back and forth a few times to warm up, and as soon as they volleyed for serve, Samuel Jones moved his chair to go and sit on the sidelines to shout instructions to his daughter. When it was her turn to serve he reminded her how to stand and to throw the ball high. The rest of the time he was continually shouting, "Watch the ball ... Watch the ball ... Backhand ... Backhand ... You aren't watching the ball. Be careful, dear, she's going to put it to your left. Run up ... Fall back ... Watch the ball."

Melody was pretty good, but his continual shouting made her nervous. Whenever Alma, who was her partner, passed close to Melody she would say, "That's all right, dear, you're doing just fine." But she wasn't doing well and finally Alma shouted. "Why don't you shut up, Samuel, and leave the girl alone!"

Samuel Jones went back to the others, but the game had been ruined. When they left the court, Samuel said sarcastically, "They didn't win the game Melody, you lost it. You gave it to them."

She walked around the outside of the chairs, her head high, but turned away so no one could see the tears. Moses got up from where he was sitting and said, "Let's play some croquet, Melody." They walked over to where the balls and mallets were laying in a pile. Tears dropped from her eyes as she bent over to pick up the mallet. "I'm sorry," Moses said.

"It's not your fault."

"I know, but I hurt inside when you're not happy. I want to hold you and make everything all right. I want to hit people when they make you unhappy."

She bent over the ball ready to hit it. She turned her head to look at him and said, "I wouldn't do that if I were you," she said in a soft quavering voice. "It wouldn't be right, to hit someone, I mean."

They stood for a moment looking at each other, he, standing straight with the mallet hanging from his left hand, and she still bending over with her head turned looking at him, her blond hair falling away on one side. He wanted desperately to take her in his arms and comfort her. She wanted him to hold her, but he couldn't, not with the others there. It would be all right for Uncle Harry, or Aunt Alma, or Doc, or any of the others to hug her, to hold her, to comfort her, but not for Moses. But, he was the one she wanted to hold her. He was the only one, she thought, who cared that she should be comforted.

Jumba had never held her. He had held her hand sometimes to help her climb over rocks, but he had never held her the way she now wanted to be held by Moses. She turned back and hit her ball gently toward the post. He followed behind, hitting his ball close to hers. They went around the course, passing through the hoops, both making sure they didn't get too far ahead of the other.

In the days that followed, Melody stayed away from the guesthouse as much as possible. Sometimes she went and played with PJ and Danny, but mostly she climbed the rocks behind the guesthouse from where she could look over the whole station and dream about being back home. When her parents started arguing again Saturday morning, Melody went to her rocks behind the house. From there she saw Moses leave the Robins' house and head for the schoolhouse. She saw him step onto the porch that ran around the building and then disappear into his classroom. She got up from where she was sitting and started down the path to the schoolhouse.

***

He was sitting at his table wiping the last marks from the wooden-framed slates and stacking them neatly to one side. He turned and smiled when she entered and she said, "They're arguing again."

"I'm sorry," he said standing and then she was in his arms. She felt safe with his arms around her and her head against his chest. She could feel him gently kissing the top of her head and from time to time he would raise a hand to stoke her hair saying, "It'll be all right. It'll be all right."

She cried a little. When she stopped crying she looked up at him and his face came slowly toward hers. She closed her eyes and then felt his lips on hers. Emotions exploded inside her. She pressed her lips against his, and when he tried to pull away, she put her hand on the back of his head forcing him to keep his lips on hers. She felt safe, loved, secure and strangely excited. His hands were on her back, pulling her to him and the more of him that touched her, the better she felt. They separated, finally, and she stood shaking, looking down at her feet and shaking her head slowly back and forth.

"Come," he said taking her hand and starting out of the room. As soon as they were on the porch he let go of her hand. "It wouldn't do for someone passing by to see us holding hands." He took her to the office, which was the only room in the building with a door and shutters on the windows. The door and shutters were not to prevent theft, but to keep the wind from blowing papers around, or to keep small animals, birds, or chickens from getting in.

He held the door for her, looking over his shoulder to see if anyone was watching them go in. It was dim inside with the door and shutters closed. They sat down on the cot where Harry sometimes took a nap. Moses held her. He sat at one end cradling her in his arms. From time to time he would bend forward and kiss her forehead. Twice they kissed and embraced so passionately they had to stop to catch their breaths, but mostly he just held her, and she felt safe and secure. They left when it was time for lunch.

The seduction of Melody Jones took place ten days after the first kiss. It was the Tuesday afternoon before Christmas. Samuel Jones was off on a safari and Melody's mother was helping Laura and Lillian at the class for young mothers. Moses knew Melody was at the guesthouse alone when he went there. Each of them just wanted to be with each other, and the opportunity was too much for both of them.

From time to time, Melody had a vague understanding she was doing something wrong, but there was a sense of satisfaction in getting revenge against her parents. She had almost no sex education. When she had her first period, her mother had explained, vaguely, it was normal for a woman and when Melody got married and had babies, the bleeding would stop. Nor had there been any children her own age with whom she could talk about these things. Any fears she might have had were set aside because she was happy and felt safe when she was with Moses.

1918

CHAPTER TWENTY-SEVEN

At the beginning of March, Samuel Jones was finally talking seriously about leaving. Moses and Melody avoided the subject, hoping if they didn't mention it, it wouldn't happen. What concerned Moses was that there had been no interruption in their lovemaking. With Lillian, he had learned there were times when they had to abstain because of her period. As the weeks progressed and there was no sign of Melody's period, he finally asked her, "Have you bled at all?"

"I did a little the first time."

"I mean your monthly bleeding. When was the last time?"

"I don't know exactly. Not since New Years."

She said it with such hesitation he looked at her with a worried frown and asked, "Do you know what that means?"

"What what means?"

"Not having your monthly bleeding."

He looked so concerned she also became anxious. "Is it bad? Mummy got so upset last month and she said I'd have to go see Doctor Schwartz. So this month, I pretended to bleed."

"How did you do that?"

"Oh, I used the cloths like we always do and then I just rinsed them out as though I really had bled. Is that wrong? I just didn't want to have to see Doctor Schwartz. I don't like doctors."

"If you haven't had your monthly it means you're pregnant. You're going to have a baby."

"I thought you couldn't have a baby until you got married."

"It comes from making love."

Fear came into her eyes and she raised one hand to her mouth. She sat for a moment, pinching her lower lip between her thumb and first finger. The realization of what had happened and how it had happened slowly dawned on her and, with that understanding, was the fear of the punishment bound to follow. "What are we going to do?"

"We'll have to get married. I'll have to talk to your father," he said, but they both knew her parents would never agree to their getting married.

"Is there any way I can *not* have the baby?" she asked.

He shook his head.

"Oh, I wish I had never left home." she wailed, and threw herself against him, clinging to him, sobbing.

***

They sat around the table in the VanVeldt dining room. Harry sat at the head of the table with an open Bible in front of him. Dave Robins and Bill Pontier were on his right. Ernest Wilson and Doctor Schwartz were on Harry's left. Samuel Jones had not been invited and Moses sat at the far end of the table facing Harry. This meeting was to try and decide what to do. All the questions and discussions had taken place at previous meetings during the week since he had first told Dave and Laura that Melody was probably pregnant. They had been hurt, and everyone had cried, and they had agreed it was not likely Samuel Jones would permit them to marry. Dave went to talk to Harry when Moses told them and Laura sat there crying and saying over and over again, "Oh, Moses. Oh, Moses."

Moses had not seen Melody since that night. No one told him, but he guessed from the things said that the Jones had decided to stay until the baby was born. That pleased him. Somehow, during that time, he would at least get a glimpse of Melody and, by listening carefully, he would be able to learn how she was doing.

Harry cleared his throat and said, "Moses, you know why we're here. Not one of us wants to be here, or say the things that are going to have to be said. Before we get started, is there anything more you want to say?"

Moses shook his head. He had said over and over again that he and Melody loved each other and wanted to get married. It had been explained to him just as often that Melody couldn't get married without her parents' permission so there was nothing more Moses had to say.

Harry ran his hands over the pages of the Bible and began to read. "Brethren, if a man be overtaken in a fault, ye who are spiritual restore such an one in the spirit of meekness, considering thyself, lest thou also be tempted." He paused for a moment and then said, "Moses, we have prayed about this, and talked with you and among ourselves about this for a long time. The Scriptures say we are to restore you, but it does not say how we are to do that. Nor is it just you that is involved. However, you are the one that is responsible. You are older than Melody. You should have been protecting her, not taking advantage of her. You are the man. It was your responsibility to protect the woman. We do not love you any less, but our first responsibility is to Melody and the baby that will be born."

He paused and then added, "The Joneses have decided to stay here until the baby is born. They have made it clear they do not want you and Melody to speak, or even see each other again. They have gone so far as to say they will keep Melody locked up in the house if they have to in order to prevent the two of you seeing each other. Some of us around this table may not agree with that thinking, but I think you can understand why they feel that way. I don't think you want Melody locked up any more than we do. What we have decided, Moses, is that until after the baby is born, you are going to have to leave the station..."

"Leave the station!" Moses shouted jumping up. "Where am I supposed to go?"

"Sit down, Moses. We'll get to that in a moment."

"Why should I leave the station? If I have to leave then Lillian Wilson should have to leave, too. She's just as bad as I am."

"Just what do you mean by that?" Ernest shouted, getting to his feet and leaning forward with both hands on the table.

"If I have to leave for seducing Melody, Lillian should have to leave for seducing me."

"You perverted, lying nigger."

Moses had never heard the word nigger before, and so he hesitated for just an instant and then said, "Oh, yes, every Wednesday night when you would go off to staff meeting she would come to my room after her bath."

"Be quiet, Moses," Dave shouted.

"And not only on Wednesday nights, either. Sometimes on Saturday afternoon when you would leave and all the houseboys were gone, and on Sundays when you were at church. The whole year I was living with you she was always coming to my room."

"You're lying!"

"If I'm lying, how do I know she had a red spot shaped like an arrowhead right here just above the hair," he said touching his appendix area.

"Moses! Shut up and sit down," Harry shouted.

"You're a filthy peeper," Ernest said.

"If I'm a peeper, then how come I know you didn't have sex with your wife until three weeks after you were married, aboard ship, in the middle of the Atlantic and you never have sex with her unless she almost forces you. Would she tell that kind of a thing to a peeper?"

"Enough!" Harry shouted. "Moses, sit down and be quiet, or else leave. You owe us a little respect and at least the courtesy not to say those kinds of things in this house."

"Respect? Courtesy? For what? For saving my life? I'd have been better off if my head had been cut off. I'd be better off in hell right now than listening to you people. You want me to leave? I'll leave! And if I ever come back you'll wish you had never saved my life." He turned, knocking the chair over, as he rushed from the room.

Harry put his head in his hands. "Oh, God, what a mess I've made of things." He looked up. "Go after him, Dave, and tell him about staying with Leo."

"After the things he said about my wife you're sending Dave after him?" Ernest shouted. Harry just glared at him, and Ernest stood up, slowly turned and left the room while Doc reached over and patted Harry on the shoulder.

***

Melody Jones stood next to the right fender of Leo's truck, the Diamond-T truck that used to belong to her father. She stood with her hands folded in front of her, looking down at her feet. On the other side of the truck, her parents were saying their good-byes, and she hoped desperately no one would come around and say good-bye to her. She appreciated that Uncle Harry and Uncle Ralph had insisted on the birth certificate, but now that she was leaving, not even that was any consolation. As long as they were still at Abaru there was always the possibility she might see her child, but now that they were leaving, that would never happen.

The child had been born in the white's section of the hospital, and all Melody had seen of her child was the bundle of cloths it was wrapped in, not even the baby itself. She didn't even know if it was a boy or a girl. Her parents decided it would be easier for her if she never saw her baby. In the three weeks since she'd had the baby no one had talked to her about the child because they never had a chance. In the hospital, one of her parents was always with her, and when she left the hospital, they didn't let her leave the house unless one of them went with her. What she learned about her child she heard in the conversations of others. While still in the hospital, she had heard Uncle Harry, Uncle Ralph and her father arguing. "Well, we don't really need your signature, Samuel," Doctor Schwartz had said, "but this child will have a birth certificate." Later on she had heard her father say to her mother, "They don't have birth certificates for natives so why did they insist on one for her? To embarrass us, that's why. To give that bastard our name."

Leo put the last of the suitcases in the truck and the people started coming by her to say goodbye. They all tried to say something nice, but it was a little hard with her mother standing right there. None of them said anything about the baby except Laura Robins. She put her hands on either side of Melody's head as she bent over to kiss her on the cheek and whispered, "Her name is Mary Ruth. I promise she will be taken care of. Write me, so I can write you."

Everybody finished saying goodbye and she climbed into the cab of the truck. She sat in the middle with her mother on one side and Leo on the other. Her father was in back. Some natives lined the sides of the road waving to them as they left the mission heading toward the government post.

They slowed as they approached the post and Melody leaned forward a little to see around Leo and her mother. If she was going to see Moses at all, it would be as they passed through the post. She looked intently as they passed Leo's store, but she didn't see him there.

They left the commercial area of the post and then they were passing in front of the government building with its whitewashed flagpole pole and the black, yellow and red flag hanging limply at the top. They stopped at the border gate and the guard came over and started talking to Leo. Suddenly, Moses was standing next to the guard looking through the windshield at her. He mother started screaming at Moses and her father jumped out of the back of the truck. He started toward Moses who moved around to the front of the truck still looking at Melody. Moses came over to the passenger's side and walked up to the door. Melody tried to climb by her mother while her father pushed Moses out of the way and jumped onto the running board. Melody started to cry, the tears running down her cheeks and landing in her lap.

"You did this. You arranged this delay," Sarah Jones screamed at Leo.

"No, Madam, I had nothing to do with it," Leo said, taking the papers back from the guard. "Better get in back, Mr. Jones. We're leaving now."

"I'll stay right here until we've left this place."

The truck started to move forward with Samuel Jones still standing on the running board.

"I love you," Melody shouted, and Moses started running alongside. The truck moved slowly through the barrier with Moses still following.

"Go faster," Sarah shouted, but Leo just barely increased the speed. Moses held out his arm as though he could somehow take hold of the truck. He finally stopped and stood in the wheel tracks watching the truck disappear in its cloud of dust.

***

At four in the afternoon the whole station was gathered on the VanVeldt porch for tea as they did every afternoon. Harry sat in a wicker chair looking across the porch to the distant hills of the Uganda border. The Joneses had left that morning and, for the first time in months, there was the old tranquility of this time of day. "What are we going to do about Mary Ruth?" Laura asked.

"What do you mean?" Mable asked, pushing the steel-rimmed glasses back up on her nose. Harry ran a hand through his hair. He knew the question was going to come up some time, he just didn't think it would be this soon.

"Laura and I want her," Dave said. "To raise her as our own. Adopt her, even, if that's possible."

My God! Do they always have to put themselves out on a limb to be hurt? Harry thought. Do they know what they're saying? They're almost forty. What did Moses do for them, after all they did for him, except give them heartache? I should stop thinking this way. We have four children who have never given us any trouble. Don't do it my friends. What are you going to do with her? Take her back to the States. Do you think anyone will accept her there just because you gave your life to the Congo? But you two will do it, won't you, no matter what the consequences. "Are you sure you've thought this through carefully?" Harry asked.

"What else can we do, Harry? Should we just stand by and watch her grow up in the orphanage? Or maybe you think some good Christian family will adopt her and raise her up? Are we expecting a native Christian family to do what we don't want to do? Can you see her squatting next to the cooking pot in the orphanage, or in front of some hut, dipping her fingers into the fufu pot? How's it going to look to the natives if she is shunned by the very ones who were supposed to show Christ-like love?" Laura said.

You do cut right to the core, don't you, but the other core is that there are fine Christian homes in Christian America where you will not be able to enter because she's black. It's all very noble for you to come over here and convert them, but don't bring them home to dinner. But I won't remind you of that. You already know it. "I just didn't want you to act precipitously." Lord, what a pompous thing to say!

"Well, we certainly have the clothes and diapers and everything you could possibly need," Alma said, pouring tea into the cup Rosemary had passed to her for a refill.

"It might be a little hard to adopt her right now," Doc said. "It might be a little sticky since the mother has abandoned the child—"

"Oh, Doc, Melody didn't desert her," Laura said, "She didn't have any choice. She would have kept the baby if she could."

"I know, Laura," Ralph said sympathetically, "but whatever the reason, the child was technically deserted by the mother. Fortunately, we have a birth certificate registering her in the consulate in Cairo so she's technically a United State's citizen. But even so, the father would have a right to claim the child. Do you think he would give his permission for you to adopt his child?'

Laura just stared at the floor. Oh, Moses. Moses, Laura said to herself. You were so special. You were such a good son, really. It wasn't right they sent you away. You could come back now. I know everybody wants you to come back. Come back and live with us again. I could help you raise your daughter. That way, we all could have her. We would adopt you as our son and she would be our granddaughter. But you won't come back. We've hurt you too much. Oh, Lord, help us not to hurt Mary Ruth. Are we just being selfish because we want children so much?

"Maybe the best thing is not to talk about adopting," Doc said. "Just take care of the child. If after a certain number of years Moses has made no attempt to get the child, then I think he could also be considered to have deserted the child. The longer he waits to claim her, the better it would be for you under both Belgian law and native law."

1922

CHAPTER TWENTY-EIGHT

The birth of David Jonathan did not come as a surprise; no birth can come as a surprise after nine months of pregnancy, but the unexpected realization she was going to have another child did force Alma to adjust her thinking. They had four living children. Three others had died. Then, nine years after Sarah, their youngest daughter was born; Alma was pregnant again. Doc Schwartz had been a little concerned because of her age, but it turned out to be her easiest pregnancy and delivery.

From the moment David was born, and put in her arms, there was a special affinity between mother and child. All her children were special, but David was the child of their old age. It was not that they were that old yet, but they were getting there. It amused her that they were the oldest couple on the station with the youngest infant. David would still be with them when all the other children were far away. Harry and she would be in their mid fifties before David would have to be sent away to school, and maybe by then, there would be adequate schools in Kenya, or maybe even in the Congo, so David would never have to leave.

1923

CHAPTER TWENTY-NINE

Mbekede sat in his room behind the store smoking a cigarette and drinking a bottle of beer. It was good beer imported from Cairo, rather than the heavy native beer. He was discontent with his situation. Leo's wife Victoria had done her best to teach Mbekede's two wives to cook, but neither of them were as good a cook as Victoria, and she didn't cook food as well as the VanVeldt's cook. Why could black men learn to cook so well for the mondeli, but his wives couldn't learn to cook for him.

He saw no contradiction in the fact that he could hate the mondeli, particularly the missionaries, so much and still desire their life style. He hated the missionaries because they had stolen everything from him. When he was sent from the mission, his love for Melody had turned to wanting to posses her for no other reason than she had been taken from him. He had to be recompensed. He was not interested in mercy, or forgiveness. An eye for an eye and a tooth for a tooth. That was scripture, and that was Africa.

The same was true of Mary Ruth. He didn't love her any more, maybe never had, but he wanted her because she was his. He talked with Leo from time to time about getting her back, and even as he talked, he knew it was just talk. No one was going to help him get his daughter. Leo had explained that if he tried to take it to court, they would probably put him in jail for seducing Melody who had not only been white, but under age. He knew Leo was right, but sometimes it made him feel better to think about getting even.

For a short while right at the beginning, he thought even Leo had turned against him, but Leo explained that taking the Joneses to Juba had been part of the agreement of buying the truck. It had been agreed to long before Mbekede had gotten involved with Melody, and as much as Leo hated to do it, he couldn't break his word.

Soon after he left the mission, Mbekede married one of Ronzozo's daughters whom he named Melody. It was Leo who had talked him into taking a wife. Six months after that he had married a second wife, one of Kitomolo's daughters, a niece to his first wife. Melody bore him three children and Vashti, his second wife, three children. They were both good wives, but they just didn't seem to be able to learn to cook.

He got up from the chair taking another bottle of beer with him and went to his truck. He started out of the post and headed for the mission. It would be teatime there. It was Saturday and they would be by the tennis courts. It excited him to think of the effect his arrival would have on them. Now he was returning to the mission from which he had been expelled six years before. At the time, he thought their word was some kind of law that had to be obeyed. He was no longer the young man they had sent away with only his clothes and some money Dave and Laura gave him. Now he was returning driving his own truck, a truck he had bought from Leo, the same truck that had originally belonged to the Joneses. None of the missionaries had a car or a truck yet. They had motorbikes, but that was not the same as a truck. Best of all, he was returning to get a little revenge. It might not be important, but it would hurt their pride and inconvenience them. And, he might even see his daughter. He was certain that would make them uncomfortable. He passed the church and then turned sharply at the mango tree border and stopped the truck where Leo always used to park it.

He was pleased by the look of both curiosity and apprehension on the faces of all those who sat around the table. There were two couples Mbekede knew by sight and name but to whom he had never been introduced. Whenever the missionaries went to the post to buy anything they always went to Leo's store. Sometimes Laura would go to Mbekede's store, which was Leo's second store, but when Mbekede saw her coming, he would go in back and let the clerk wait on her.

The children ran up to the truck as he climbed out. It was strange how things had changed, but were the same. PJ and Danny now sat at the table with the adults. There were more children than there had ever been before. The two girls in matching blue dresses belonged to Doc and Rosemary. He had seen them all together many times in Leo's store. Ruth and Sarah, who he used to hold with one on each knee, stood back a little from the rest, looking at him skeptically, remembering who he was and wondering if they should run up to him. Mbekede had never seen Mary Ruth, but he knew beyond a doubt who she was. Her hair was curly black and held in two braids at the back of her head. She stared at him wide-eyed and he thought he could see something of her mother in her. She stood out from the other children because of her coloring.

All the men started toward him the instant he stepped down from the cab. They pressed through the children. "You'd better leave now, children," Harry said, "We have to talk with Mr. Mbekede." The children left reluctantly, looking over their shoulders as they went. "What do you want, Moses?"

Moses looked at him smiling, his lips pursed, his head shaking just a little. He waited for a moment and then said, "Well first, I've told you before, don't call me Moses. I want nothing to do with Moses, or the God of Moses, or the people of the God of Moses. And secondly," he smiled broadly, "I've come to see my daughter." He was amazed at how calm he was and it pleased him they all seemed uncomfortable with his being there.

"You've been drinking," Harry said. "I think you better leave now."

Moses stared at him for a moment and then said, "Why? Are you going to make me leave? Are you, who came here to tell us all about the love of Jesus, going to drive me off your property?"

"No," Harry said quietly as Mbekede reached into his shirt for a blue package of cigarettes. He shook one out of the pack and put it in his mouth. It was an act of defiance and he looked at each of them in turn as he put the pack back in his pocket. From his left trouser pocket he took a box of matches, yellow with three bells on the top and blue on the bottom. He slid the box open. It made a gentle scrapping sound as it opened and then rattled as he took out a match.

"That's right," he said exhaling the smoke. "You can't drive me away. I have as much right to walk or drive along the paths, or between the huts of your village as you have to walk in our villages."

They stood looking at him, not answering.

"I didn't come to see my daughter," Mbekede said, "but now that I have seen her, I'm going to come back some day and take her away from you. He took another drag from his cigarette and started walking forward and they separated to let him pass, watching him as he walked away.

Mbekede walked along the side of the house, across the stone bridge over the deep ditch and entered the cookhouse. He sat down on a stool just inside the door. "Pilipo," he said, "of all the cooks you are the best, yet you get paid no more than the worst of the Mondeli's cooks."

Pilipo looked in his direction, but didn't say anything.

"How much do you get paid, Pilipo?"

"Ten franks a month."

"I will pay you thirty," Mbekede said.

"I have a house and garden."

"I also will give you a house to live in. A brick house. You will have two boys to help you in the cookhouse. They will shell the peas and peel the potatoes for you. You will cook for Leopopo and me. He is a white who does not think he is better than us."

Pilipo was quiet for a long time, and Mbekede sat there looking out the doorway. He picked up a straw and started pulling it apart, and finally Pilipo said, "I cannot leave the mission."

Moses threw the shredded straw toward the cook. It landed on the floor in front of him. "It is said Pilipo likes the beer. That sometime when he is going to have the next day off, he goes to Shima's village and drinks from the gourd. It is said that sometimes when he is at Shima's village he lays with women that are not his wife. What say you to that, Pilipo?"

The cook stared at him and Mbekede went on. "If Bwana Van were to know this you could not stay at the mission. It is better if you leave now, before they can learn of it. Come be our cook. You will have a brick house. You will have much room for a garden and get paid three times what you get here and we do not care if you drink a little corn beer. Next week today I will come for you in my truck. Do not be afraid. I will tell Bwana Van he must find a new cook," he said. He stood in the doorway and looked back. "It is agreed then?"

Pilipo nodded and Mbekede left the cookhouse.

1924

CHAPTER THIRTY

The land was tired and burned out. The air had the smell of ashes, and when there was a strong breeze, it carried the dust of dead fires. The dry season fires were over and the land waited for the coming of the wet season rains. There were some green spots along the streams and where trees sent their roots so deep they were not affected by the dryness. Flower borders around the missionaries' houses were watered every day with water carried up the hill.

Kusala stood in the shade of a mango tree. He saw messengers heading toward the station and he knew they were coming to him. The fact that there were two of them meant it was an important message. If one of them were not able to make it for some reason, the other was to keep going. He saw them stop to talk to someone at the edge of the village and then run up the hill. Through gasps for breath he said, "Ronzozo, Chief of the five tribes, Ruler of the north, is sick to dying. His son, Kitomolo, Chief-to-be, has sent us to Kusala. He said to say to Kusala your father desires to see you before he dies. He calls for you. Your father says he would have Kusala and Kitomolo stand together at the burying of their father. These words he commanded we speak to you."

"I hear your words. Rest a while and take food. Then go back and tell Kitomolo that I, Kusala, Son of Ronzozo come to see my father," he said. He found Dave Robins in the print shop and said, "I go now. My father is dying and I go to bury him." He turned and walked away before Dave could reply or ask him anything.

Kusala's wife was on the shady side of the house grinding corn for the evening meal. She looked up at him, her hands still holding onto the grinding stone, and he said, "My father is dying. I go to the burying."

She got up and followed him into the house. He took off his cotton shirt and khaki shorts and reached under his pole bed for the raffia wrapped bundle. He untied the fiber string, folded back the mat, lifted out his leopard skin and wrapped it around his waist. He reached up and took his hunting spear from its place hanging from the rafters. He touched her cheek as he bent over to go out the door.

Walking along, he knew he wasn't a warrior anymore. He might wear the skin and carry the spear, but he had gotten soft. He was not even a hunter. He could still stalk the game, and knew their ways, but his skills were not needed at the mission. Nor could he walk or run as he used to. He was older, it had not been required of him, and so his legs and lungs were soft. His desire for revenge was no longer a burning hunger. There weren't any warriors who would follow him against his brother and he wondered if his promise not to come against his brother until after his father died had been an excuse to himself, because he knew he could not succeed. He went to the white man because he thought in some way he would be able to use them against his brother, but instead they had used him.

The time for opportunities was past. He belonged nowhere. He couldn't sit at the council fires, nor could he sit with the mondeli. They spoke about how important he was, but he still lived in a hut, slept on a pole bed, and ate food ground between two stones. No matter what they said, he knew he was not accepted. Even Moses, who they had tried to raise as their own, had not been accepted. For a man to lay with another man's wife was reason enough to be sent from the village, but they did not send Moses away because he had lain with Bwana Ernest's wife, but because he wanted to marry a white girl.

Both the girl and Moses wanted to get married, but they hadn't permitted it because they didn't think a black man was good enough to marry a white woman. From the beginning, he had made the wrong decisions. What would have been so bad about being the second son, first brother to the chief-to-be? He knew he had not only become soft in body, but also in resolve and will.

He entered the village a little after noon. Kitomolo came out of the chief's house as Kusala approached and stood for a moment in the doorway. Kusala leaned his spear against the house, and Kitomolo preceded him inside. The wives were gathered, sitting on the floor, their legs straight out in front of them, their bodies rocking back and forth as they wailed for the dying. Some had already started cutting themselves to show their grief. Next to the low fire that burned in the middle of the house, the batu-na-dawa intoned incantations to drive away the evil spirits that would leave the Chief's body when he died.

They walked over to the platform on which Ronzozo lay. A leopard skin was spread over his body. Ronzozo motioned for Kitomolo to move to the other side and then opened his hands, and they each took one. It took all his strength to bring their hands together across his chest, manipulating the fingers until they understood he wanted them to intertwine their fingers while each rested a hand on his chest. He put both his hands on theirs and with faint, gasping breaths, so they had to lean forward to hear him he said, "You ... shall live ... in peace ... I, Ronzozo ... have ... spoken it."

He closed his eyes and a relaxation came to his body. He was not dead because they could feel the slow rising and falling of the chest as he breathed. Slowly they pulled back their hands, their fingers slipping apart as they removed them from under their father's.

Ronzozo, Chief of the Five Tribes, Ruler of the North, Keeper of the Lands, Warrior of Warriors, died late that afternoon. It was said he had made himself stay alive until he had seen his son Kusala, and there was speculation as to the special significance of that. The drums started beating, and the death dance began.

The dancing, and the burying and the burning of the old hut was done properly as it should have been done. But there were whisperings Kitomolo's rule would be troubled. The portents were not good. It was the end of the dry season, and the water to make the mud for the new walls had to be carried a long way, which portended struggle. Also, because it was the end of the dry season, what little grass there was for the roof of the new chief's house was not good and would have to be replaced soon, which meant change.

***

They stood on a small rise a short distance from the village. The warriors that had walked there with them were ordered away so they couldn't hear what was said between the two brothers. The time of death was passed. "Our father is with ancestors," Kitomolo said, "and they now know what is between you and me for our father knew it. Tell me, Kusala, will we be at peace, or will you always be against me?"

Kusala didn't answer.

"Almost I would make you chief, Kusala, for there is nothing to be chief of. The mondeli have taken it all away. There are no young warriors. The only warriors left are like you and me and we are too old to be truly great warriors. Things that were, are no more. The young men from the tribes go to be tukutuku for the mondeli instead of being warriors for their chiefs. They go to places they should not go and marry women of tribes they should not marry. They do not come back to the families and the clans, but go after the way of the mondeli.

"When the mondeli first came to our father they said send us men to work and we will pay them. Our father asked if the people work for the mondeli and do not work the gardens how will they eat. The mondeli said with the franka paid they could buy food to eat. Our father said it was the kind of game children would play. Why would men work for the mondeli to get franka to by food when they could work the garden and eat the food without working? But it was not a children's game. It was a game of witchcraft. Everyone now runs to the ways of the mondeli. They put fences around the land and say it is theirs. They say they own the land that belongs to all the people.

"In Matsa they go down into the earth for gold. What is this gold? Yet the mondeli will pay many franka to those who dig the gold. They build them houses. Not mud huts, but brick houses like the mondeli live in. They put iron on the roofs like the mondeli's. They are small houses, but still like the mondeli's. On Saturday nights they bring them corn beer, and every Saturday night there is a dance. They do not dance because of the harvest for they have planted nothing. The mondeli brings in food and sells it to them so they do not know when the time to plant is, or when the time to harvest is any more. They do not dance for the rains for they have not planted anything that needs rains. They dance for no reason except Saturday night is a time to dance.

"And look at you, Kusala. You are a son of the great Chief Ronzozo, yet even you have bowed to the ways of the mondeli. If you had stayed here and taken a wife who gave you no children you could have sent her back and gotten back your bride price. Or if you wanted to keep her, you could have gotten back a portion of the bride price and taken another wife who could give you children. But you now live by the ways of the mondeli. Our father has just died and all his wives have become mine. Because we were of the same day born, you too should have received some of those wives, to care for them, but you live by the mondeli's ways now and can have only one wife. Since you have only one wife who cannot give you children there will be no seed of the great hunter, Kusala. When you go to the ancestors who will you have to follow you there?

"Look, Kusala, and see with the eye of understanding. Men like you who went first to the mondeli were their servants. The children of those servants have been trained in the mondeli's schools and they have no respect for their fathers. With schooling in the ways of the mondeli, they think they are smarter than their fathers because the mondeli gives them better jobs with better franka. And their children will learn even more at the mondeli's school and have even less respect for their fathers. This is a terrible thing that has happened, Kusala. Our sons and our sons' sons reject us and our ways. The mondeli has come and grown like a great evil tree. The white sapling took root and now its roots spread throughout all the earth, its branches and leaves cast a great shadow over all the land. We should have pulled it up by the roots when we could.

"When the first mondeli came we should have killed them. When the second came we should have done the same. One at a time, one at a time, we could have protected ourselves. Now we are only the grass growing in the shade of the tree. They are here now and cannot be pulled up. Their roots are too deep and in the pulling up of them we would pull up our own. The day will come, Kusala, when a chief who will not bow to the mondeli will be removed and be replaced by one who will bow. The thing I must always study well is how much I must bow to remain the leader of my people. I am not your enemy, Kusala. The mondeli is. Return to the place where you belong. Return and take wives who will give you sons who have in them the blood of the great Kusala. Return and help me rule for it is not good for the brother of the chief to make his home in the village of the enemy."

Kusala stood looking the direction of the descending sun. It was not yet sunset, but getting close to it, the time of long shadows. In the stillness of the evening, the smoke from the cooking fires rose and hung over the village like a blessing. It was easy for Kitomolo to say he was not the enemy, but it was Kitomolo who had stolen his birthright and not the mondeli. But he knew in his heart what Kitomolo said was true. He thought he probably would not have been as shrewd and crafty enough to be as good a chief as Kitomolo probably would be. But there was still enough of a sting to what might have been that he could not return just yet. To do so would have been to admit to all those who remembered the past that Kitomolo had been right. It would be breaking confidence with those who knew in their hearts Kusala was the rightful chief.

"I cannot return now," he said. "There are things I must yet do. But know you this; I shall never rise up against you. I shall always be loyal to you and speak well of you. I shall never side with an enemy against you. I, Kusala, first born son of Ronzozo, rightful Chief of the Five Tribes, have spoken it."

There was a flicker of anger in Kitomolo's eyes, and then it burned out.

"And know you this also," Kusala said, "I shall never speak to another person of that which you and I both know to be the truth. Yet if I have sons, I shall tell them, not so they will be against your sons, but because it is their right to know."

Kitomolo nodded ever so slightly. He turned and headed back toward the warriors who were waiting for them, Kusala walking beside him.

1925

CHAPTER THIRTY-ONE

Mbekede sat in the office behind the store drinking his imported beer. It had been two years since he had hired Pilipo away from Harry and Alma, and although there was the satisfaction of eating good food, and knowing he had inconvenienced them, it still was not enough. There had to be some way where he could start to hurt them the way they had hurt him.

It was well after dark when he left the office. He was wearing only a pair of shorts. In the darkness he would look like any other native from the post or even the mission. He walked past the hotel being built. On the outskirts of town, he could see the outline of the half complete church the Jesuits were building.

He walked along the main road. He didn't see anybody, nor did he expect to see anyone. Night was a dangerous time to be out alone. He turned into the mission road. He had been perfectly calm when he left, but now he was beginning to be excited and a little frightened. He walked cautiously, looking every direction. There were no lights in any of the houses. He stopped for a moment between the Robins' house and where the Wilsons used to live. He stood listening to make sure no one was anywhere around and then headed for the Robins'. It had been his house once, his home.

He walked across the yard cautiously and on to the porch. He walked around the porch to where Dave and Laura's bedroom was and stood outside the window. Inside he could hear the sounds of their sleeping. He wondered which room Mary Ruth would be in. He looked into the window of his old room, but there wasn't anyone in there. He walked along the porch to the opposite side of the house and stepped up onto the brick porch rail. He reached into his pocket for the box of matches and struck one. The flare from it was alarmingly bright and the smell of sulfur seemed to fill the night air. He held it cupped in his hand until it was burning steadily and then touched it to the thatch of the roof. He watched it catch, one straw, then two, and three until there was a good little flame burning. He jumped from the rail, leaping across the ditch and ran across the yard. He got to the road and turned to look back, not only to see if anyone was there, but also to make sure the flame was still burning. He saw the flame spreading along the edge of the foot-thick thatch with fingers of flame moving up toward the peak.

He ran until he got to the government road and then looked back and could see the glow of the flames. He walked toward the post. He often looked back at the glow and he had never felt so good in all his life. He felt wonderful. There was nothing that gave him the same excitement and satisfaction as getting revenge. He didn't expect anyone would die in the fire. He didn't want them to die. He wanted everyone to get out and stand by helplessly as everything they cherished was destroyed. He wanted them to live so he could inflict this kind of loss, this kind of hopelessness, on them. He wanted them to have the fear of the fire coming close and being left without anything, just as he had been fearful and without anything when he was sent away.

He walked into his house and lay down in his bed looking up at the ceiling. From the next room he could hear the bed squeaking as his wives rolled over in their sleep. After a while he heard voices outside and he knew they were seeing the glow in the sky and talking about the fire. He heard Leo's truck leave and knew he was going to the mission to offer them help. He wished Leo hated the missionaries the way he did, but he guessed that was too much since Leo was a mondeli himself.

Lying in his bed, Mbekede felt superior. No matter how they treated him, he had always known he was looked down on, never considered an equal. But now he felt equal to them. He had a sense of power. People were responding as a result of something he did. They were responding to something about which they had no choice. He might not see them doing what he intended they do, but they were doing it. Making people afraid was a form of power. Power and wealth, those were the keys. He was on his way to being wealthy. He would also get power.

1930

CHAPTER THIRTY-TWO

The natives started gathering around the VanVeldt home before sunup. At seven-thirty the missionaries began to arrive. Doc, Rosemary and their two girls arrived in their new car. Soon after that Leo arrived in his new Mercedes truck. The Robins came out of the house followed by three houseboys each carrying two suitcases. The Robins weren't taking much with them; there wasn't much to take. They'd sold or given away everything they had, most of it to the Tillmans who were already living in the house the Robins had built. Nor were there any precious things to take. They had all been destroyed in the fire.

Things had never been the same after the fire. Except for the brick walls, everything was new in the house, but for Dave, Laura, and Mary Ruth there was always the smell of smoke in the place. Others couldn't smell it, but they could. Living in that house was a continual reminder of that night, Dave waking up to the smell of smoke and the sound of fire. He had walked out of the bedroom onto the porch thinking there was a grass fire somewhere. When he walked around the corner of the porch he saw the flames coming toward him along the porch roof. He had to run under the fire to get to Mary Ruth's room, which was in the middle of the house. He scooped her up and ran into their bedroom shouting for Laura. By the time they got into the yard, some natives began to arrive, and soon after that the missionaries. There was no thought of running back in to retrieve anything. The fire was moving too quickly. Wearing only their nightclothes and holding on to each other with Mary, frightened and whimpering softly between them, Dave and Laura stood with the others watching their house go up in flames.

For six months after that, the Robins lived in the guesthouse. They moved back into the house when it was restored with a new roof and everything whitewashed, but it was no longer the house Dave had built. New pieces of furniture quickly made in the mission carpentry shop stood where their counterparts had stood before, but there was no friendship, no memories with the new pieces. Getting used to the house, and new furniture, was like breaking in a new pair of shoes. In the thoughts of Dave and Laura was the nagging question and the fear of why the fire had started. There was no question someone had started it. A few months later the newly completed Catholic Church was set on Fire. The Catholics replaced the burned thatch roof with a tin roof. But who was doing it and why?

Laura was happy to be leaving without the prospect of returning. She remembered the day soon after they arrived when she had sat on the edge of her cot in the tent and cried with frustration. She remembered the native woman who had come into the tent and fed her the strange fruit. She had wanted to leave and never return. She had promised God back then, that barring illness or accident, she would give twenty-five years to Africa. She had fulfilled her obligation and she was ready to leave. It was not that she hated Africa anymore, it was just her life there had so many disappointments, the biggest being Moses.

Dave accepted leaving stoically. He didn't want to leave, but it was time to leave. The book of Ecclesiastes said it. "To everything there is a season and a time to every purpose under heaven: a time to be born and a time to die, a time to speak and a time to keep silent, a time to love and a time to hate." And there had been in his life the time for arriving, and now was the time for leaving.

The natives started filing by, each one having to touch, to hang on to the Robins' hand one moment longer. The Robins were not just going to Putu to return, they were going with going. They came all by, men with calloused hands Dave had taught set type in the print shop. There were young men and women Laura had cared for in the orphanage. They were married now with children of their own, and they lifted their children to receive a hand on their head, one final blessing.

Mary Ruth stood behind them with Miriam and Esther Schwartz on either side of her. They were all about the same age. They had played with dolls together. They'd had children's arguments and pulled each other's hair. After the fire, Mary Ruth wore the clothes they had given her. They were closer than sisters, and now one of them was leaving.

"This is for you," Miriam said taking out a plain ivory ring. She pushed it onto Mary's middle finger. "Too big. I guess you'll have to wear it on your thumb."

"And I have something for you, too," Esther said, taking out an ivory bracelet. It was too big to stay on her wrist so Mary put it in her pocket.

"I don't have anything for you." Mary said.

"That's all right, you're leaving. The person leaving isn't supposed to give things."

Mary Ruth bit her lower lips while the tears eased out of the corners of her eyes and down her cheeks.

"It's not forever," Miriam said. "We'll be together again. Daddy says we'll be going to Putu next year, too. We'll be together then."

The last of the natives finally went by and Dave and Laura started saying their good-byes to the whites. Doc and Rosemary, the Pontiers, Mable, Leo, the Tillmans, Sid and Jenny Taylor, the Toumanova family, who had driven the twenty miles from their plantation, and Eddy Schuller, who had been there only six months. And then it was time to say goodbye to Harry and Alma. Laura and Alma just hugged each other while the tears formed in their eyes. There was nothing to be said. It had all been said before while crossing burned out flatlands, over hoes in that first garden, while building the first mud huts, through times of weeping and times of laughter. Their hair that had once been so abundant was thinner now and streaked with gray. They held onto each other as they had so often before in troubled times and that said it all. It was not that they would never see each other again, but an era was ending. They had been together so long, been through so much together; they each wondered if they could go on without the other.

Harry and Dave stood shaking hands, their left hand on the other's shoulder. Dave's once red hair was sandy now and, if possible, he had even more freckles than before. He still squinted his eyes as though looking at a bright light. "Ah reckon ah feel a mite guilty," Dave said. "There's still ah heap to be done."

"We'll just have to muddle through without you," Harry said, and then they, too, had nothing more to say. They walked to the car, Dave sitting in front with Doc while Laura and Mary Ruth sat in back with two of the suitcases that didn't fit in the trunk. Harry said a prayer and then everyone leaned away from the car. Doc started forward, driving slowly so the natives could run alongside. They ran the length of the mission to the government road. He would drive the Robins' to where they would catch the steamer Cairo.

***

Mbekede heard the sound of the car approaching and went and stood in the doorway of his store. He knew this was the day. He had been waiting for the sound of the car. He stood there watching it approach and was surprised when it slowed down and stopped directly in front of him. Dave, Laura and Mary Ruth got out of the car and started toward him. They walked across the gravel road, their shoes crunching with each step, and climbed the stairs to the narrow porch along the front of the store.

"I couldn't leave without saying goodbye," Laura said putting out her hand. A tear overflowed, and she reached up and brushed it away.

"Goodbye," he said shaking hands with Laura and Dave, and then Laura said, "Say goodbye to Mr. Mbekede, darling."

Mary Ruth put out her hand obediently and said, "Goodbye."

"Goodbye, My child," Mbekede said. He wondered how much of the truth they had told her. He watched them as they walked back to the car and for a moment he was touched. They drove away, and he remembered they were mondeli and he was black. It didn't make any difference how nice they tried to sound, or how many tears they shed, they had stolen his daughter from him. They had only brought her around to say goodbye to prove the finality of the fact he would never get her back.

***

Above him the stars were clear, individual, brilliant and absolute. The night sky was too magnificent to let slip away, and yet there was no way he could prevent the dawn from coming any more than he could stop the years from passing. Tomorrow night the stars would again be in their place, and before dawn he would again be in his place in the rocks at the top of the hill. He could come here every morning and see the same stars in their same place and, even though they disappeared with the coming of the sun, they would be there again the following night. Years were not like that. Once they had passed he could not go some place and catch them again as he could the stars.

Years! They had passed without ever asking his permission. He had always known they would, that's what years did, but somehow there should have been a warning attached. It was thirty-five years ago Alma and he had left home for this place. Now home was here, but so much of them was *there*. Fourteen years ago they had taken PJ and Danny to the States, and he had realized at the time their two oldest sons would finish high school, go to college, get married, start families, all without Alma or he there to be a part of it.

So much would happen and had happened without them. Both his parents and Alma's mother had died, and they had not been there. Now Ruth was a missionary in India. Sarah was married to a pastor of a little church in Los Angeles. As the others left, he had been determined there would be something special between David and him.

Whenever he and Alma talked about it being time for David to leave, one or the other would say, "Let's wait a little. We still have time." They were not yet ready to be separated from him. Not just yet. But he knew, even if Alma did not, he had already lost the boy. Lost David as surely as he had lost the others. Rebecca buried in the mud and rain at Bashindi; PJ sitting on the pulpit worshiped by sweet-smelling, pretty-bonneted ladies; Danny sitting in his office collecting good fees for imaginary ills; Esther Priscilla dead before the age of two and buried in the "whites" cemetery on the plateau below Medicine Hill.

Gone. All gone! Lost them all. Even the boy I tried so hard to keep, he thought. Lost him to the heavy smell of gardenias after the rain, to the delicate orchids growing wild in the fields after the first rains of the wet season, to the heat and the damp, to the excitement and the fear, the peace and the quiet. How could two people love the same things so much and not understand each other. David has to leave soon and he will probably return someday, but not to us, but to the land, and the people, and that something indefinable that is Africa. There is something special between Kusala and the boy. It's almost as though David were Kusala's son and not mine. I am being jealous, have been jealous for a long time, he admitted to himself.

1935

CHAPTER THIRTY-THREE

The morning routines were over and Doctor and Rosemary were headed for the house for lunch and a little nap before surgery. She looked down the hill and saw a man staggering painfully along the road. "He's terribly sick," she said, and even from that distance the sight of the man created an unnatural apprehension in her.

"Something is wrong," Doctor said and she knew he had the same thoughts she had. Why was there no one with him? That was unusual. Usually they came with several family members accompanying them. They knew by just looking at him he would not be able to make it to the top of the hill. Doctor called two of the infirmiere and then started down to meet the man. The native stood there watching them approach and then sat down on the side of the road. Rosemary knew he would never get up by himself again. They got closer to the man and the symptoms became more obvious, the stench of the man from the fist size boils secreting their black fluid said it all. One of the infirmiere put his hand on Doctor's arm as though to prevent him from going any further and said, "It is the black sickness, Bwana."

Doc nodded and went and knelt down next to the man while Rosemary and the two infirmiere stood behind him. "What village are you from," Doc asked.

"The village of Chief Lamuwi. Many are sick and many die. The batu-na-dawa cannot save us. He himself has died. A new batu-na-dawa is in his place, but he can do nothing. I come to the munganga to be made well."

Lamuwi's village was two days away, probably four, or five, days for this man. "At what villages did you stop in your coming to the munganga?"

"None. They drove me away with clubs and stones and would not let me stop in their villages," he said, and broke into a coughing fit, spitting blood.

They felt a great pity for the sick man being driven off by armed villagers and yet, at the same time, they were relieved. With a little luck the plague was confined to the one village, but it was here on the station now, and there was no vaccine. Doctor reached over and took the man's hand, held it for a moment, gently and compassionately. She wished he hadn't done that, and yet it so like him, trying to give the poor man some kind of encouragement, and to indicate to the two infirmiere there was nothing to fear. But if the infirmiere didn't know it, she knew the plague was in the last stages of pneumonia, every breath of air that came from his lungs was highly contagious. Doctor looked over his shoulder and told the two infirmiere to go and get a stretcher and said to her, "I wish you'd go to the house, Rosemary."

"Entreat me not to leave thee, or to return from following after thee: for whither thou goest, I will go, and where thou lodgest, I will lodge: thy people shall be my people, and thy patients, shall be my patients."

He smiled a little while shaking his head. She had a habit of adjusting Scripture to make her point. He knew there was no sense arguing with her.

The patient died the next day and was buried less than half an hour later in a grave prepared for him soon after he arrived. The isolated hut on the slope behind the hospital in which he had spent his last living hours, along with the stretcher that had carried him and everything he brought with him was burned to the ground as soon as he was in his grave.

***

For a week the mission station and the government post waited. The tents, chop boxes, and other safari equipment were assembled, and set on the dispensary porch waiting. The word plague was seldom used, but everything waited for the army truck to return with the vaccine Dr. Schwartz had requested from the government hospital at Stanleyville which was almost a thousand kilometers away. The truck was sent with three drivers so they wouldn't have to stop to rest. Every evening and morning, Dr. Schwartz took the temperatures of his medical staff for any sign of fever that might be the first symptom of the plague. With each passing day he became more anxious. What if the plague spread to other villages? Where was the truck? Were they out of vaccine at Stanleyville? But there was nothing they could do but pray, hope and wait.

The merchants, the government personnel from the post, and the Jesuit priests from the Catholic mission, all arrived at Hospital Hill in cars, and trucks right behind the truck with the vaccine. The captain handed Dr. Schwartz a letter which he quickly read. The first part of the letter was technical information about the vaccine. The last part of the letter said:

You are hereby requested, and authorized, to do whatever you deem necessary to confine, and eradicate the plague in your region. Captain Marceaux of the Abaru Army Post has been instructed to give you all assistance possible in supplies and men.

They left the next morning, Doctor and Rosemary, four infirmiere, Harry and Kusala, twenty-five porters, and a native sergeant with twenty soldiers from the army post. They passed though villages quickly; stopping just long enough for Dr. Schwartz to determine if the plague had reached them.

At noon of the second day they found the first corpse lying between two rocks, one arm across his chest, the other arm outstretched as though reaching for something, the body bloated and decaying in the heat. They buried the body and moved on. By mid-afternoon they started passing the rough, pole platforms where the first victims had been placed to die outside the village. They had been the first to die and were only skeletons now picked clean by the vultures.

A half mile from the village they started to smell the stench of death and Dr. Schwartz, Harry VanVeldt, Kusala, and the two infirmiere went on to the village, while Rosemary and the rest of the company stayed a safe distance away to set up camp.

It was a large village of almost a hundred families; the dead lay around the edges. Some had crawled there before they died; others had been dragged there. Everywhere there was the nauseating stench of death, disease and decay. The villagers had long since given up trying to bury the dead. Those who were alive sat in front of their huts certain they, too, would soon become sick and die. There was no reason to keep working their gardens. Any work was considered a waste of effort and so the village was scattered with the dead bodies of men, women and children. Those they tried to talk to glared back at them in angry silence. Death was coming. There was no reason to be civil to the mondeli.

Dr. Schwartz stepped over a body and entered one of the huts. In the interior dimness he could see the body of a dead woman on a crude, pole bed and the body of a child on the floor curled around the bedpost. He took a step and in the darkness kicked a log that banged against a clay pot. A rat jumped out of the dried-food and ran for its hole in the wall. He picked up the log and tapped on the wall and heard the sound of scurrying rats inside. He left the hut carrying the piece of firewood with him. He tapped on the walls of two other huts and in both of them heard the sound of the scurrying rats. He climbed the ladder to one of the granaries set high on stilts. He lifted the thatch lid and peered inside. A large rat jumped for the opening, landing next to his hand, frightening him, so he jerked back almost falling off the ladder. He climbed down the knowing the village would have to be burned. The whole village was nothing but a gigantic maze for an enormous colony of rats. He joined the others and they headed for the chief's hut.

Lamuwi's hut was at the end of the village. A six-foot high pole and wattle wall surrounded it. From the outside all they could see was the thatch roof of the larger than usual hut inside. Kusala opened the wattle gate. Inside Lamuwi sat on a stool, out of the sun, on the small porch of his house. The new batu-na-dawa, surrounded by all his charms and bones, sat on the ground next to him. The whole enclosure was filled with Lamuwi's dead wives and those who had come into the compound to be cured by the batu-na-dawa and remained to die.

They made their way stepping over and around the corpses until they stood in front of the chief. Chief Lamuwi watched them approach and the batu-na-dawa, about to die himself, shook a snake-bone rattle at them, pronouncing a curse on them, and then coughed up blood.

"Sene, Lamuwi, Chief of the Low Valley," Dr. Schwartz said. "I am a munganga. I have brought medicine that will keep the demon of death from entering those who are still well."

"Sene, Munganga. I have heard of you. Is your medicine more powerful than his?" he asked pointing at the witch doctor.

"It is."

"He could not do it," Lamuwi said jerking his head toward the witch doctor. "If you can do this thing, then all that is his shall become yours."

"I do not want what is his."

"So be it. If you can do this thing then all that is his shall become mine."

"You must come with me that I may give you this medicine."

"I do not need the medicine. I am chief," he said pounding his chest.

"It may be the batu-na-dawa has only enough power to protect the chief from the demon of death, but he himself is dying, and when the batu-na-dawa is gone, you, too, may die."

The way Lamuwi glared at him, Dr. Schwartz knew he had mentioned Lamuwi's fear. "He does not protect me," Lamuwi said. "The chief is greater than all. I am chief. I do not get sick."

"Yet you keep him close to you."

"He wishes it so, I permit it so."

"Yet you should take the medicine so all the people will see you are not afraid of the medicine of the munganga and they have nothing to fear from it."

"If they fear the medicine of the munganga, let them die."

"Then there will be none over whom you are chief."

Lamuwi shrugged his shoulders. "They are but trouble to me. A chief is a chief. If there be none to rule, he is still chief."

"It may be that a chief is a chief. Yet even now, half Lamuwi's people are dead. When they are all dead, Chief Lamuwi will be less than the least man. He will have no one to tell, 'Do this!' and they do it, 'Go there,' and they go. He will cut his own wood and carry his own water and cook his own food. He will be as a woman, for he has none to do his wishes."

Lamuwi stared at him for a moment and said, "I will think on it. It would not do for all to die. For their sakes I will take the munganga's medicine. Yet I will not come with you. You must bring the medicine to me."

"I shall give you the medicine at the gate of the chief's house where all can see the love of Chief Lamuwi for his people."

"So be it."

"We must bury the dead," Dr. Schwartz said waving his hand toward the bodies. "It is not fitting for a living chief to sit among the dead. I will need the help of the men of the village to dig the graves."

"It is agreed."

"I shall return and give you the medicine and then to all the people of the village."

"So be it," the chief said and they left quickly, glad to get away from the stench of the compound to the comparative fresh air of the village.

Kusala and Harry went back to the camp to tell the others to bring the medical supplies while Dr. Schwartz and the two infirmiere started separating the healthy from the sick and dying. By the time Harry and the others returned, those who were well were lined up outside the gate to the chief's compound. A small table was set up, the vaccine was ready, and Dr. Schwartz entered the compound to tell Lamuwi they were ready for him.

He was sitting on his stool just as he had been when they had left him. He looked at the doctor and said, "It is not well for a man to take a strange medicine when night is coming upon him."

"Yet it would be well for a man to take a medicine when death is coming upon him."

"The black sickness will not come to me. I am chief."

"You have been talking to him," Dr. Schwartz said pointing to the witch doctor. "He has made your heart that of a woman, afraid of the night. Yet, look at him. Where is his power? He cannot even stand upon his feet. Tell him to stand, Lamuwi," Doc said pausing for a moment and then said, "He cannot do it. Yet he gives you council saying, 'Wait till morning.' He is thinking in the morning he will say to you the day is not right and you should wait a little longer. He is dying, Chief Lamuwi, and he wishes you to die with him. But he will say nothing to you in the morning, for the rising sun will find him as one of these," he said waving his hand taking in the dead bodies.

"He dies tonight?" Lamuwi asked tilting his head to look sideways at the doctor.

"He shall not see another day."

For a moment Lamuwi looked down at the huddled form of the witch doctor covered with the oozing pustules and then stood up and said, "I will take your medicine."

He turned and called his sons from inside the house. The witch doctor muttered something and tried to reach up a hand to stop him but the chief ignored him and he and his sons, the oldest about fifteen years old, followed the doctor to the gate. At the gate, Lamuwi stood for a moment looking at the lines of people. "I am chief," he said. "I do not get the black sickness. Yet I take the Munganga's medicine to show you I do not fear it and there is no harm in it." He and his sons got their vaccination and went back to their house.

The lines started moving by the table, men in one line being taken care of by Doctor, and women and small children in on the other side of the table vaccinated by Rosemary, all of them apathetic and without hope or any belief the medicine would do any good. They moved up, got vaccinated, and walked away because the chief had done it and told them to, and because the soldiers forced them to. They didn't believe the medicine would help, but since they were going to die anyway, what harm could the medicine do?

The next day half the men of the village with the soldiers dug graves while the women carried out the bodies. As soon as a grave was deep enough bodies were dropped in until they were within three feet of the top and then the dirt was thrown in covering them. The first day they were reluctant to dig the graves, but they did it because Lamuwi had told them to and the soldiers forced them to. By the second day, when no one else had come down with the sickness, they were more cooperative and more cheerful. They were able to bury most of the dead, but there were many in the village whose bodies were so decomposed they couldn't be moved. Doctor didn't have the heart to make them carry out body pieces and he was anxious to get on with the burning of the village.

They started cutting down trees and tall grass. On the third night they heard wailing coming from the village for those who had died and they knew the villagers were confident enough they would live.

On the fourth day they started piling the trees and grass in a circle around the village. Inside the village they made several piles of grass and branches down the center of the ilolo with trails of grass that would carry the flames to each hut. Dr. Schwartz and Kusala again went to visit the chief. He sat on his porch watching them approach through the open gate of his compound. His oldest son sat on a stool next to him.

"Sene, Chief Lamuwi," Dr. Schwartz said, "I have chased the sickness from your village. None have become sick since they took my dawa."

"It is true. Yet the sickness might have gone away of itself even if you had not come."

"Not so, Chief. The sickness is carried by the rats and the fleas of the rats in this village. And you have many rats and fleas."

"I have much of everything."

"The rats and fleas must be killed to kill the sickness."

"The rats of this village belong to me. Yet they do me no good. They eat food in the granaries and bite babies in their sleep. If you are able to kill the rats, I will let you kill the rats."

"We must kill all the rats and all the fleas; even those that hide in their holes. We must burn the village."

"No! No one burns the village."

Dr. Schwartz sighed and started again. He explained again that the disease was carried by the rats and the fleas, the fleas bit the people and the people became infected. The only way to get rid of the rats and the fleas permanently was to burn the village. When he was through Lamuwi's answer was still the same. "The village will not burn."

Kusala explained it in detail telling how the tiny flea was comfortable and warm in the gray fur of the rat. Then the rat scratched it out and it landed on the cold floor, shivering and waiting for the warm body of person to come along. The flea jumps on to the person, bites the person to get the food of the blood and the person becomes sick and dies. He ended with, "I am Kusala, brother to Kitomolo, Chief of the Five Tribes. Kitomolo says the village is to be burned."

"I know you, Kusala. You turned against your brother and joined the mondeli. If it is the word of Kitomolo the village be burned, it will be burned, but you do not come with any word from the village of the Great Chief Kitomolo. You come with the mondeli. The word of

Kusala means nothing to me for he is no longer in his place as brother to the chief. I am chief here. The village shall not burn. I, Chief Lamuwi, have spoken it."

"It may be what you say is true. That I am now with the mondeli is well known. But all know I do not use the name of my brother in vain and all know I do not lie. The village will burn. I, Kusala, have spoken it."

As far as Dr. Schwartz was concerned it was a stupid contest of wills and the longer he stared at Lamuwi the angrier he became. He forgot for a moment he was a missionary sent to preach the Gospel and heal the sick. He was only a doctor who had become disgusted and angered by the stubbornness and unconcern of an unimportant sub-chief. He suddenly filled with anger. He hardly came to Kusala's shoulder, but he seemed to grow a couple of inches, the compassion in his eyes was replace with a righteous fury when he said, "I have with me the tukutuku who will help me. At the setting of the sun I shall burn this village, Lamuwi. It shall burn to the ground so all that remains are ashes. So get you, and your sons, and any of your wives who still live out of your house, Lamuwi, for as surely as the sun shall set the village will burn. I have spoken it." He turned and strode away. Behind him he heard Kusala saying, "Kitomolo says you are to build your new village in the valley of the blue flowers. He gives you that valley for this," and then he, too, turned and followed the doctor out.

Outside the compound, Dr. Schwartz ordered the soldiers to start evacuating the village immediately. He didn't want Lamuwi to have time to tell his people not to leave. When the soldiers told him the people were all out, Dr. Schwartz, Harry and Kusala walked around the outside of the barricade of grass, branches and logs. Most of the barricade was built higher than their heads. They checked the ground carefully to make sure there were no bare spots of earth through which a rat might escape. The villagers stood around in a festive mood waiting for the fires to be started. They smiled at the munganga and his friends. That their hut was going to be burned down was not a great bother to them. If the munganga wanted to burn their hut in payment for saving their lives, it was quite all right with them.

The sun was setting as they finished their circuit. There was no reason to wait any longer and Dr. Schwartz told the sergeant they could go ahead. The sergeant sent the soldiers with firebrands lighting the barricade. The grass, leaves and twigs burst into flame, igniting the branches and then the logs. The wood of the barricade settled down to the ground burning hot and furiously. They threw the firebrands to the thatched roof of the huts inside, the flames jumping from one hut to the other. The thatch roofs burned off quickly, almost explosively, leaving the geometric frames of the burning rafters. The flames worked down the wall poles and into the interwoven fibrous vines that made up the structure to which the mud was applied. The mud coating started to crack and break away from the vines and poles to which it had been attached. It was then the rats started to come out, first one by one, then in pairs, then in swarms, the gray color of the rats matching the color of the ground they ran over so in the flickering firelight it looked as though the earth was heaving from the heat. The swarms moved between the centers of heat, toward the barricade, then back into the village, turning, circling, melding, separating, reversing, always swirling to get away from the fire. And the people watching kept moving back as the heat increased.

The roof rafters fell in, walls fell out, and the poles supporting the granaries burned through, dropping the round, mud granaries to the ground so they split open pouring out their flow of grain. Some of the rats caught fire and ran among the swarms setting them on fire. In other places, the bodies of dead rats could be seen in little mounds among the ashen timber.

Two hours after the fire was started the village was nothing more than a huge bed of coals, accented occasionally by a section of mud wall that had refused to fall. It was a standing section of the chief's hut that reminded Dr. Schwartz of Lamuwi and he became strangely overwhelmed by a fearful uncertainty. He couldn't remember having seen the chief at all that afternoon. He had not been among the villagers who were there when the fires were lighted and who watched as the village burned.

He walked, despite his fears, toward the end of the great bed of coals where Lamuwi's hut had once stood. He didn't know what he expected to find. He half envisioned an accusing form rising from the coals to denounce him, but he wanted to find something that would prove Lamuwi had left before the fire started. Many of the villagers were settling down in little family groups, starting a fire to cook an evening meal, spreading mats where they would sleep that night on the ground. Rationally, he knew the thing to do was to go to them and ask if any of them had seen the chief, but at the same time he didn't want to put in their minds the thought that the chief had been burned in the fire.

He heard Harry and Kusala come up behind him. "There's nothing more to be done, Doc," Harry said. "Come have some supper. We're all waiting for you. Rosemary's worried about you."

"Where's Lamuwi?" he asked Kusala. "I want to talk to him."

"He has left. Some say he has gone to speak to Kitomolo against you."

1936

CHAPTER THIRTY-FOUR

David and Kusala left for Kitomolo's village the day after Harry and Alma left on a trip to visit some other stations. None of the missionaries would miss David. If any of them asked where he was they would be told he was somewhere with Kusala, which was as good as being with his own parents.

They entered the village at mid-day and slowly walked to the large hut at the end of the village where Kitomolo sat in the shade of his porch. Two of his sons stood behind the chair. Kusala raised his hand. "Sene, Kitomolo, Chief of the Five Tribes, Ruler of the North. I bring him with me of whom I spoke."

"Kusala, son of my father, you are welcome. My house is yours while you are with us. And you, my son, favored of Kusala, you, too, are welcome," he said looking at David.

"I thank Kitomolo," David said.

A woman came out of the hut carrying two stools for them to sit on, took their bedrolls, and went back into the house. Kitomolo and Kusala talked idly for a while and then the chief turned suddenly to David and said, "Why do you wish to become son to the son of my father?"

"He has been a father to me and I wish all so to know."

"And what says your blood father to this? Will he know of this?"

David paused before answering. It would not do to answer so important a question quickly, without any thought. "He does not know of it," David said after several minutes.

Kitomolo also paused before asking the next questions. "Why have you not told him? Think you there is shame in what you do?"

"No, My Chief, I am not ashamed."

"Would he object?"

"I have not asked him, but I think he would. He would not understand why I do this thing. He would think I want Kusala in his place."

"Do you understand why you do this in opposition to your father?"

"As I am able, I understand."

"Do you think your understanding greater than that of your father?"

"No. My understanding is different from that of my father."

"One must weigh carefully that which he does against the will of his father. You must give me good reason to let you do this thing."

David waited for a long time before he answered, and then he said, "It is known to all people, My Chief, that the father of your father, Chief Kimulu, made war because his people were being taken by other tribes and sold to the white robes to be made slaves. Your father's father defeated Chiefs Kesalengo, Sesengi, Junjuju and Kimi. It is well known that at the last great battle with Dumodo, your father's father proclaimed a man belonged to the land whereof he was born. He took no slaves, but demanded the return of his people and formed this great nation of Five Tribes over which you now rule. I was born of this land. The first words that passed my mouth as a crawling child were in the language I use now to speak to you. Even today I speak the language of Kitomolo and his people better than the language of my blood father. I am of this land and I am entitled to the rights of the land where of I was born."

"You speak too boldly of rights which are not yours. You are an intruder who lives on my lands out of the kindness of my heart."

David waited the appropriate length of time and then said, "My father was the intruder who your father, the Great Chief Ronzozo, did not choose to chase from the land. Your father cut the blood with my father. The covenant of blood is forever, from one generation to the next. When you became chief you did not drive my father out. You kept the covenant between your father and my father. Because you and your father permitted him to stay, you gave your consent to my being born of this land and of your tribe. I say this not to be disrespectful of my blood father or of you, but to explain why my father would not understand. He is of another land. I am of this land. Because I am of this land, I desire to become the son of Kusala."

There was silence for a long time. Finally the chief said, "You speak yourself well and I accept your words as they are spoken. You are permitted that which you desire. Go now and prepare yourselves."

***

The afternoon rain ended and one of Kitomolo's sons came to get them. They followed him out of the hut. Neither Kusala, nor David, was wearing anything. According to ritual, that was the way it should be for when you are born into the world you are wearing nothing. And, when a child is conceived the parents have no clothing. In front of the hut, Kitomolo sat in his tepoi high on the shoulders of his bearers. Around his waist was his leopard skin and around his neck was a skin of black and white fur covering his shoulders and chest. On either side of him was a column of forty men carrying spears and shields.

David and Kusala fell in behind Kitomolo and his two sons as the procession walked the length of the village and then turned right toward a grove of eucalyptus trees. There was no sound except the swishing sound of the grass as they moved through it. When they got to the grove, the whole village was gathered around the edges. As they entered, the two columns of warriors separated, walking around in a curve while the bearers carried the chief across the clearing to where a group of the elders were sitting on the ground. They set the chief down in front of the elders facing the way they had come. Kusala and David waited while the two columns filed by them to stand in a circle along the edges of the grove. In the center a small fire was burning. The Chief gave the signal and six drummers started beating on the conical shaped drums. Kusala and David walked in opposite directions half way around the circle and then turned to face each other.

The batu-na-dawa danced back and forth in front of the chief. He was covered with the skin of a leopard, the face tied to the top of his head, the forelegs tied to his arms. He jumped back and forth, bending forward then jerking up straight, waving his arms and throwing his head. The tail and hind legs of the skin swirled and flopped as he danced.

Slowly, the tempo of the drums increased, and the batu-na-dawa danced faster and faster. The warriors behind them turned and danced in unison in a circle, their right hand on the shoulder of the man in front of them, their spear and shield carried in the left hand so the circle was enclosed in a chain of shields. David and Kusala walked to the fire and raised their arms, clasping their hands across the fire. They danced sideways around the fire, always keeping the fire between them, the smoke from the fire rising through the oval of their arms. The batu-na-dawa left his place in front of the chief and came and danced behind them chanting loudly.

A little before sunset the batu-na-dawa stopped and all sound and motion ceased. The assistant brought over the knife and an elaborately carved rod. He gave the knife to the batu-na-dawa who took Dave's hand and made a cut on the side of the knuckle of the first finger. He held the hand over the fire and made sure none of the blood fell to the ground, but into the fire. He made a similar cut on Kusala's hand. The batu-na-dawa took the rod, held it over the fire, and Kusala and David grasped the rod so the two cuts were touching each other. The blood mixed and flowed over the rod and dripped into the fire. The batu-na-dawa turned to Kusala and said, "Your home shall be his home, your possessions his possessions. Your tribe shall be his tribe, and your understanding his understanding. Your wives shall have him as a son and your children shall greet him as a brother. Instruct and train him carefully and hold him in respect for he has freely consented to be your son."

He turned to David. "Kusala takes you for a son. His home and his possessions become yours. His wives will receive you as a son, and his children will accept you as one of them. He will teach you the laws and ways of our people. You must respect, honor and obey him. You will protect his home and, in time of war, fight by his side. His enemies are your enemies and his friends are your friends. Your responsibility is great for you are a son of choice and not of passion. Your name in the tribe shall be Logoro, son of Kusala."

Someone brought over a flat black stone. The batu-na-dawa handed the rod to his assistant and held the stone while David and Kusala rested their hands on it and Kusala said, "I, Kusala, son of Ronzozo, take you Logoro as a son, swearing to fulfill all the duties of a father to a son."

Then David spoke. "I, Logoro, submit to you as father. I will honor and obey you as is fitting for a son. I will be at your side in time of need, and give you comfort in your old age."

The ceremony was over. The medicine man took some cobwebs out of a pouch hanging from the string around his waist and put them on the cuts to stop the bleeding. They headed back to the village. There would be dancing the whole night.

***

Almost exactly a month after the adoption, the wet season came to an end. Ordinarily it would have gone on for two more months, but just when the rains should have been getting to be their best for the sprouting seed, they dwindled to little afternoon sprinkles and then stopped all together. During the first week of no rains, there were dances in all the villages to honor the spirits in the hopes of flattering them into starting the rains again. By the second week, the young shoots were turning brown and there was talk of bad times ahead. Chickens, lambs, goats, and sometimes even calves, were killed and sacrificed on pyres in an effort to appease the anger of the spirits.

After a month the people didn't sacrifice any more. Even if the rains did come, it would be too late to save the crops that had died in the dry, hard earth. Now they guarded their animals as a source of food. Even the dogs that usually ran loose in the village were claimed and brought into the house at night. Sitting in the shade of their empty granaries, they wondered what they had done to anger the spirits. There were some who in secret thought the adoption of the mondeli was what had displeased the spirits.

CHAPTER THIRTY-FIVE

The long heat was everywhere. There was no food except with the mondeli. It angered Kitomolo that the mondeli were taking better care of their people than he was. His people were reduced to forging for roots and grubs and snails along the streams that still had water in them. Once a month, Leopopo, who had married Kitomolo's sister, Obrika, would bring him a truckload of wheat. They would talk about the long heat and when Leopopo left, Kitomolo would distribute the grain to his village. But it was not much. When this time was past, the people would remember the mondeli had taken better care of their people than Kitomolo had.

At the post a truck arrived every week with corn for the garrison. The supply sergeant sold a third of it to Mbekede who, in turn, sold it to whoever had the franka to pay for it. In addition, Leo's and Mbekede's trucks were continually going back and forth to Juba and bringing back Egyptian wheat. Not everyone had franka to buy the grain. Some came with goats, chickens, and even cows to exchange for some grain. In normal times they would have gotten two months supply of grain for a cow, but now they got only two weeks. But they had no choice. If they killed a cow it would have to be eaten in four days or it would spoil. There were some who had nothing to trade for grain and so they offered to exchange their children for food. In the villages the old and the weak were dying of starvation.

In the sixth month of the long heat, Nicholas Toumanova met with the whites from the post and the mission with a new scheme to get food. He proposed a hunting trip to the Dungu River where there was plenty of game. With the extreme dry heat, if the meat was cut in strips of not more than an inch thick, it could dry before it spoiled and stored for long periods of time.

They left the following Monday. There were four trucks in all. Leo had two trucks and brought his two sons, Mbiyama, his Masai gun-bearer, and natives to clean and carry the game. Harry, David and Kusala, with the mission natives, were in Eddie Schuller's truck. Nicholas and Boris Toumanova lead the convoy in their truck. They camped that evening on the edge of a valley two kilometers from the river.

They left well before sunup to take their places overlooking the river. They lay in the brittle grass, waiting for the beginning of day that would bring with it the herds that came to drink. There was not a sound, except the sound of their breathing.

David lay on his belly, propped up on his elbow, his right hand resting on the shaft of his spear. Next to him one of the natives had his rifle. It was Kusala who had insisted he bring the spear, and he understood the reason for it. His elbows began to ache and the ants crawled annoyingly over and up his arms and legs.

The night began to dissolve away and he could see the trees individually instead of a wall of black. From the corner of his eye he saw a head next to him turn slowly to the right and he looked that direction. A small herd of wildebeest, not yet in range, paraded slowly toward the river. They walked in single file almost exactly alike in color and shape and comically uniform in their jerking, mechanical motion. From the other direction, they saw a herd of hartebeest headed for the river. They were closer to Eddie and his group. They waited for other herds to arrive and then Kusala raised a hand pointing toward the river. They looked and saw a kudu bull just getting up from where he had spent the night.

The kudu stood grandly and confidently, the long spiral horns shining in the morning's first light. They could see him sniffing, testing the air until he knew he was safe. He stood magnificently, as only a grand kudu bull can stand, his horns reaching back four feet into the air, the long shaggy beard running along his neck from his chin to his chest. In the morning sunlight, his gray coat took on a pink hue. He took a few steps, his head high, the horns leaning back over the fluid moving body as though the entire five hundred pounds was floating along suspended from the horns. He stopped and stretched himself, his front and hind legs apart, his back swayed, then he brought his feet back firmly under himself and shook vigorously. He walked nonchalantly into the river up to his belly and slowly drank. He raised his head and walked out, the water dripping from his chin, beard and belly. He shook the water from himself and then rose on his hind legs to reach the tender green leaves at the tops of the shrubs.

They started slowly down the hill crawling on their hands and knees. Harry released the safety on his rifle and Kusala shook his head and pointed at David and then at the kudu. Harry looked at Kusala, frowning, and the natives smiled knowingly. David crept forward uncertain, but determined. He had killed a wart hog once with a spear, and some other smaller things, but never anything as big as a kudu. A spear was the hardest weapon to use, but in front of his father and the other natives, Kusala had committed him. If he missed his father could, of course, shoot it, but his shame would be great.

He moved ahead slowly, Kusala, his father and the others staying in their place. He wished there were a breeze, but it was perfectly still. Any little draft could suddenly spring up from any direction and be just enough to carry his scent to the kudu. He watched the animal, timing it. How long it was on his hind legs varied depending on how far he had to reach for the food, but the amount of time he was down chewing was constant, and he always finished chewing and swallowing before he went to another bush. He would have to throw the moment the kudu came down on all four legs.

The distance got shorter; sixty yards, fifty, forty, thirty. He was close enough. Maybe too close. Still on his hands and knees, he pulled his left knee up to his shoulder and then leaned back so his weight was on his feet. Carefully watching the kudu, he gently bounced the spear until it settled perfectly balanced in the palm of his right hand. His left arm rose slowly as his right arm went back. The only part exposed above the grass was his left arm and his head. He hung there poised, his arms and shoulders one straight line, the blade of the spear just inches from his face, the words running through his mind: The left arm must point the way, and in your mind you must see it go before you throw.

The kudu lowered itself and in one fast, fluid motion David was rising, his legs and body pulling his arm and the spear, his body twisting with the arm adding its thrust, the last quick flick of the wrist just as his right foot landed well in front of his left foot. The moment it left his hand he knew it was a good throw. It entered the kudu in one straight thrust of the combined weight of head, shaft and counterbalance. The full length of the head and barbs entered the stomach area just below the backbone and behind the ribs.

The kudu galloped off, the long shaft bouncing grotesquely at every step causing the blade to slash and tear at his innards. He brushed against a tree in his flight hoping to dislodge the spear from his side and there was a loud crack as the shaft snapped and twirled off into the grass. He rushed away, nose out-thrust, his great horns flat along his withers, and a foot of splintered shaft protruding from his side. There was no reason to hurry after him. He would run until he fell exhausted from loss of blood. When he tried to get up again, he would be too stiff to move.

The running of the kudu had frightened other animals and almost immediately he heard his father, and then others down the line, opening fire bringing down animal after animal. David went and retrieved what was left of his spear and then started following the kudu's trail. They found the bull lying next to a dead anthill, the buzzards already circling low over it, and the large, fat, blue flies swarming around. It tried to get up as they approached; rising to its front knees, and then fell over. Even lying on the ground dying, the kudu kept his head lowered and moving, the long, sharp, pointed horns shaking menacingly. A couple of men walked up behind it and grabbed the horns and it was all they could do to hold the head still. It lay there, not making a sound, watching them with its quick moving eyes, its front legs with sharp hooves slashing wildly while Kusala drove his spear in at the base of the neck until it reached the heart. Blood gushed out in great spurts soaking the gray mane and changing it to almost black. The fountain of blood died to a trickle, all motion stopped, and the deep brown eyes stared accusingly at the victors.

David yanked what was left of his spear from the dead body while the natives started dressing it, slashing its belly open and pulling the blue, purple and white guts onto the ground. They tied the legs together and slipped a pole through to carry. They tied the head and horns up so they wouldn't drag on the ground. They started back toward the others and Kusala said, "You did well, my son. Soon you will have to kill your leopard and then you will be a man."

1937

CHAPTER THIRTY-SIX

The rains had lasted a month longer than usual as though to make up for the drought of the year before. At the end of the rains there was a message from Kitomolo saying he wanted a meeting at the stream halfway between his village and the mission. Kusala had no idea what the meeting was about, but he pointed out it was not a good meeting since the chief didn't invite them to his village.

Kitomolo arrived with three drummers in front pounding out the walking beat. Kitomolo rode high in his tepoi and behind him, in wardress of skins and spears, were fifty warriors. It was before noon, which meant he wanted to get the business over with quickly and get back to his village in the same day. The bearers grunted as they lowered the tepoi to the ground. Harry walked over and said, "Sene, Kitomolo, Chief of the Five Tribes. I and those with me greet you."

Kitomolo returned Harry's greeting. He rose slowly from his tepoi and made his way to the large wicker chair Harry had brought expressly for Kitomolo to sit in. The chair creaked as he settled into it and two of his son's took their place behind him. He greeted everybody appropriately and then said, "Leave us now. I would speak alone with Kusala."

Everyone moved back far enough that they could not hear what was said. Kitomolo looked toward the stream for a while and then said, "I come to ask you again, Kusala, to return with me to the place where you were born and sit by my side as brother to the Chief."

Kusala waited the appropriate time before answering and then asked, "Why come you now to ask me this?"

"The government man at the post has insulted me. With tukutuku and much show he comes to my village. With no respect he comes to my village. He stands before my hut and calls to me like a dog. In front of many warriors and all the people of the village he shouts at me. He accuses me of calling away his tukutuku and of stealing bunduki. When I do not answer he takes the gangilo that stands before my house. He shouts so all can hear, saying when I return his bunduki he will return my gangilo. All my warriors have heard his shouting and have seen me insulted and I cannot let it pass. There are many who think I should have killed him as he stood before me. It may be I shall have to make war. If that should be, it is not good that the brother of the Chief be in the village of the mondeli."

Kusala waited for a long time before answering. "You must think hard before you do this thing, for to make war will be the end of the Five Tribes."

"That I know. But I also know I cannot let the insult lie for then I will no longer be Chief, and then, too, it will be the end of the five tribes. The Chiefs will fight one another and it will be as it was in the days of our father's father. At the least, I must kill the government man at the post. If I do not, the people will say I fear the mondeli and their tukutuku."

"If the mondeli apologize, will you rest at peace?"

"If they do humble themselves and with proper ceremony return the gangilo and do me honor equal to the insult, I shall let it rest."

"I shall speak to Bwana Van."

"Bwana Van cannot make right what was done by the post man. The government people must make right the wrongs. Do you come with me?"

"I cannot."

"Do you come against me also?"

"Upon the death of our father I swore to you I would not come against you. But of all men, only Bwana Van, and Logoro do I trust. And I do not leave my son until he has killed his leopard and become a man."

"Do they know what is between us?"

"I have told only Logoro, for it is his right to know."

"It is not enough to say you will not come against me. To sit in the village of the mondeli will be seen as you not joining me. I know I cannot win against the mondeli in open battle. We shall kill and run, kill and run. They will never know when or where we come next. As quickly as we come we shall be gone. It may be after much bloodshed they will come and make right the insult. But it may be they will never do that, and I know then the people will get tired of the fighting and I will never win against the mondeli and the tukutuku."

"Would it not be better to find another way?"

"There is no other way. If I do not go to war I am not chief because I let the insult lie. If I go to war I may be defeated. They shall kill me, and put another in my place. It is better to go to war than to do nothing. If I do nothing, all is surely lost. In all ways it is the end of the Five Tribes."

They were silent for a long time and then Kusala said, "Kitomolo, listen well to what I have to say. Upon the death of our father I swore not to rise against you. Our father asked that of me and I agreed. Now I ask two things of you."

"Speak."

"If there be war no harm will come to Bwana Van and his people. Our father cut the agreement of peace in blood with him. We cannot go against that."

"So be it. And the second?"

"I shall tell Bwana Van of what the government man has done. It may be Bwana Van will talk to him and he will make right what he has done. How much time do you give Bwana Van to do this?"

"If Bwana Van can do this it would be a good thing, but the government man is stubborn and will not listen to the advice of elders. Yet I will wait. I will speak to the elders and chiefs of the way of it. The moon in the night is now near to round. I give until it is again round. Beyond that ..." Kitomolo opened his hands, palms up and shrugged a little.

"It is enough," Kusala said.

"I go now," the Chief said and stood up.

Harry and David walked with Kitomolo to his tepoi. He sat down, and Harry said, "Go in good health, Kitomolo, and may we meet again before the sun has made so many times its way across our lives."

Kitomolo stared at him for a moment and then said, "May you and Logoro also go in good health. And know you this; between you and me, and between your people and my people, there will always be peace. My warriors bear witness," he said waving a hand toward his warriors. "I, Kitomolo, have spoken it." The bearers raised him to their shoulders, the drums started to beat, and they left the direction they had come.

***

They made the turn around the circle of whitewashed stones with the flagpole in the center and stopped at the bottom of the steps to the main building. Two privates ran down the steps to open the doors to their car and David followed his father up the steps. The guards on either side of the door came to attention as they passed and a sergeant led them to the commandant's office, announced them, and then stepped aside to let them pass.

The captain came from behind his desk to shake hands and then indicated for them to sit down. "What can I do for you, Reverend VanVeldt? I hope it is not another plague," he said leaning back in his chair.

"We met with Chief Kitomolo yesterday. I understand from him that a few days ago you paid him a visit—"

"Yes, he was arrogant and uncooperative," the captain said interrupting with a wave of his hand.

"How's that?"

"I mentioned to you a few weeks ago that five of my soldiers had deserted. They took five rifles and two thousand rounds of ammunition with them. They were of Kitomolo's tribe, so Kitomolo must have know something about it."

"Did he?"

"When I told him about it he didn't come out of his hut, didn't even answer me."

"He says you came to his village uninvited, that you shouted at him and insulted him in front of the whole village."

"I don't have to have an invitation to go to some village."

"He is a chief, Captain. You must know there are certain protocols one observes when calling officially on a chief."

"He's just another native to me."

Harry sat there for a moment clutching the arms of the chair and breathing deeply to control himself and then said, "He also says you stole his gangilo from in front of his house."

"I didn't steal it. I told him he could have it back as soon as he returned the rifles and the ammunition."

"I cannot believe you do not know the significance of taking a chief's gangilo."

"And you, Reverend VanVeldt, don't seem to know the significance of five rifles and 2,000 rounds of ammunition."

"Captain Marceaux," Harry shouted jumping up. "Are you really as stupid as you seem or are you trying to create an incident?" Harry leaned over the desk, his hands spread on its smooth surface. "I have lived in this part of Africa since before you were born. Apparently you do not understand what you have done. The gangilo is the symbol of a chief's authority. To take it is equivalent to declaring war. He is demanding an apology, and the return of his gangilo."

The Captain stood up slowly. "First of all, Reverend VanVeldt, if you were not of the clergy you would not still be in this room. I am an officer of the government of this country and I am not stupid."

"I apologize for that. Of course you are not stupid, just uninformed."

"And I do not apologize to natives, especially not to one who demands it."

"You don't seem to understand, Captain. He has been insulted beyond measure. He is gathering his warriors. If he does not receive an apology he will get revenge. He will probably start with killing you and Lieutenant Pelant."

"Reverend VanVeldt," the Captain said patronizingly, "you are unduly concerned. I am certain he would not try anything so foolish, and if he did, I am sure we can handle it."

"With what, the army?"

"Absolutely."

"Do you expect your native soldiers to back you against Kitomolo? Besides, why let it come to that?"

"May I suggest, Reverend VanVeldt, that you worry about their souls and I'll worry about controlling the natives and the military."

"Are you refusing to apologize?"

"Yes!"

"You are indeed a fool," Harry said and walked from the room so fast David had to jump up and run to catch up with him.

"What are you going to do now?" David asked as they drove away.

"We're going to Matsa to see Colonel d'Entremont. As soon as we get home pack a suitcase. You're coming with me."

"I am?"

Harry nodded. "We leave first thing in the morning."

CHAPTER THIRTY-SEVEN

David sat alone on the front porch of the colonel's house. When they arrived, they were shown to their rooms and David purposely took a long time with his bath so he wouldn't have to go with his father and Uncle Eddy to visit the missionaries. He watched the yard boys pouring pails of water around the roots of the shrubbery beside the porch. It was four in the afternoon and beyond the low, brick wall the road was filled with natives going home after work. From behind him he heard a soft, almost far-away voice say, "Ah, bonjour." He rose, turning, and saw Madame d'Entremont coming along the porch toward him.

"Bonjour, Madame," he said.

"It is so good to see you again, David. Welcome to Matsa." she said putting out her hand. "Is your father here?"

"He's gone to the mission station,"

She walked past him, her white gown drifting softly as she moved toward the chair. He waited until she was seated and then sat down again and noticed her feet were bare except for gold sandals. Her toenails were painted red. The missionary women never painted their nails or even wore lipstick. Even the women at the post only painted their nails on special occasions like Christmas or New Years, but not on an ordinary weekday. The one time the d'Entremonts had been at Abaru he didn't remember her nails having been painted.

The houseboy arrived with a tray of bottles and glasses and she fixed David a grenadine and soda while she asked him about the trip. He thought she was the most beautiful woman he had ever seen. Her long, black hair was piled high in a braid on her head and held in place with a gold band. Her dress was folds of light, white material gathered and held at each shoulder by a gold pin. She had a gold cord around her waist. Her voice was soft and sounded far away, and when she laughed, it was a high trilling sound like the call of some unidentifiable bird in the night.

Colonel d'Entremont and the children arrived together, all with a freshly scrubbed look, and the children were talking excitedly about the trip to Abaru. Their father gallantly prepared them drinks, a grenadine and seltzer for Jacques and an orange squash for Monique.

Jacques and Monique both looked like their mother, especially Monique who had her hair arranged exactly like her mother's. Through dinner David kept looking at Monique. He couldn't keep from looking at her. The time they had been to Abaru, the twins were seven, and both those times David played mostly with Jacques and hardly noticed her except when she pestered them to be allowed to play with them. Now at twelve, he thought she was as beautiful as her mother.

They left the next morning right after breakfast. The colonel insisted David and his father ride with them in the big touring car, leaving Eddy Schuller and Kusala the only ones to ride in Eddy's truck. The native driver sat by himself in the front seat. Pierre, Cecile and Harry were in the middle, the three children in the back seat with Monique sitting between David and Jacque. People turned to watch as the convoy with the colonel's car in front, followed by Eddy's truck and then four army vehicles with the soldiers and their equipment, headed north out of Matsa.

They arrived at Abaru late in the afternoon and Captain Marceaux came running down the steps as the big car came to a stop in front of the building. He hesitated for a moment when he saw Harry and then hurried around to Pierre's side and saluted. Pierre responded by touching the brim of his helmet with the tip of his swagger stick.

"I didn't know you were coming," the captain said opening the door for Pierre. "I shall have quarters prepared for you and your family immediately."

"No," Pierre said getting out of the car. "We will be staying with Reverend VanVeldt. Lieutenant Pelant is your second in command here, is he not?"

"Yes, Colonel."

"Have him present himself to me immediately." The captain sent the sergeant to call Lieutenant Pelant and Pierre said, "I understand you have Chief Kitomolo's gangilo. You will bring it to me please."

The captain told one of the soldiers to go get it and d'Entremont said, "No. You will bring it to me personally." Marceaux saluted smartly, turned on his heels and headed back up the steps.

Pelant arrived, saluted, and then the two officers stood silently until Marceaux returned. Pierre took the gangilo and asked, "Was Lieutenant Pelant with you when you took this?"

"No, Colonel."

Pierre turned and put the gangilo in the car, the children having to duck down so it could rest in the middle of the car on the tops of the two back seats. He turned and called Marceaux to attention and every soldier in the sound of his voice came to attention. "Captain Marceaux, you are, as of this moment, relieved of your command. The reason for this action is the insulting of Chief Kitomolo and the taking of his gangilo. Yesterday I wrote General DePaul at Stanleyville explaining why I am relieving you of command. You are to report to him as soon as possible. I shall travel there as soon as I can. In the meantime, until you find transportation to Stanleyville, you are relieved of all duties and confined to quarters. Do you have any questions?"

"No, Sir."

"Very well then, you are dismissed." Pierre turned to Pelant. "Lieutenant Pelant you are now temporary commandant of Abaru."

"Yes, Colonel."

"I hope to shortly call on Chief Kitomolo. Do you know he is gathering his warriors and is demanding an apology?"

"That is the talk, sir, and I believe it to be correct."

"Why did you not send me a message with that information?"

"The captain specifically ordered me not to do it, sir. Since I knew Reverend VanVeldt was already on his way to see you, I did not feel it necessary to disobey the captain."

Pierre nodded. "My trucks and men should be arriving shortly. Three squads for an honor guard. You will billet them until we have word from Kitomolo that he will see us," he said getting back into the car. Lieutenant Pelant saluted as the car pulled away.

CHAPTER THIRTY-EIGHT

Kusala, Harry and David stood to one side of Kitomolo waiting for the soldiers to arrive. They came into view around some of the temporary huts at the far end of the village, two lines of men marching in step. In front of the columns was the colonel and the sergeant major, each of them with their swagger stick in their right hands held so the tip of the stick rested on their shoulders. Behind the colonel was the flag, the wide fields of black, yellow and red drifting a little in the breeze toward the soldier who carried the gangilo. Kusala had said, "It must be carried respectfully, but not held upright as though its authority was yours." Behind them were the soldiers with the boxes of gifts, and behind them the bugler, the drummer, and then the rest of the soldiers. They marched in two perfectly straight lines to the edge of the village.

When they entered the ilolo, the sergeant raised his swagger stick and then jerked it down; the soldiers seemed to melt together. When they separated the colonel and sergeant major were in front. Behind them in a line were the bugler, flag, gangilo, and drummer. Behind them were the four soldiers carrying the gifts and then all the remaining soldiers in one straight line taking up the whole width of the ilolo. They all moved exactly the same, even to the swaying of the black tassels on their red fezzes. They moved up the length of the village without a sound except the beating of the drum and their bare feet hitting the packed earth.

They stopped with Pierre and the sergeant a few feet from the braided grass rope that lay on the ground in front of Chief Kitomolo. It was suddenly quiet. The sergeant shouted the command and the rifles with exact precision were slammed to the ground, each butt spurting up a little chunk of dirt and dust where it hit. The sergeant shouted again and he and the colonel saluted; every soldier raised his rifle holding it straight up and down in front of him while the drum rolled and the bugler played. They stayed that way until the drum and bugle stopped and then they lowered the rifles to the ground.

The sergeant stepped a little to one side, turned sideways, gave a command and the soldiers raised their rifles at an angle across their chests while at the same time there was the loud clicking of every bolt being slid back. The rifles were raised to their shoulders, pointed at exactly the same angle into the sky, and all the rifles exploded together. A round blue cloud hung for a moment at the muzzle of each barrel and then it drifted away in the light breeze. Fifteen times, at exactly the same time, the rifles were fired and then were lowered again. Pierre stepped forward until his toes were almost touching the grass rope. He waited until Kitomolo finally nodded and then he started to speak, waiting between each phrase as Harry translated.

"To Chief Kitomolo, Ruler of the Five Tribes, I bring greetings from the Great-Chief of all the mondeli. The Great-Chief wishes for Kitomolo good health and long life. He has told me to say we hold Chief Kitomolo in high regard. He who offends Chief Kitomolo offends us. Any mondeli who offends Chief Kitomolo we throw from us for we know you to be a friend. We return to you now the gangilo of Kitomolo. That it was ever taken is a great wrong which we would make right." The soldier carrying it handed it to the sergeant, who handed it to Pierre, who handed it to the warrior who stepped out from alongside the chief. Kitomolo inspected it and then sat holding it in his left hand.

"The actions of the captain were done without our knowing. The taking of Kitomolo's gangilo shames all mondeli and we ask you to forgive us. The one who did this terrible thing has been sent away in disgrace. He will be punished and greatly shamed. We hope Kitomolo will know our hearts are right toward him." He stopped waiting for some response from Kitomolo, but Kitomolo just stared straight ahead. Pierre started to speak again.

"Because of your help in time of need and friendship at all times, I have been instructed by the Great-Chief to give to you as a token of the high esteem in which we hold you, the coat of high office. In all of this land there is no other coat like it. Only a few men of the greatest authority in the lands across the sea may wear such a coat, just as here, only you are permitted to wear the skin of the black and white monkey upon your shoulders."

Pierre motioned to the soldier who brought the box forward. Pierre and the sergeant slowly unfolded the cape. Approving "aah's" escaped from the warriors who had crowded in closest behind the soldiers. Pierre and the sergeant walked forward, crossing the grass rope, the cape draped over both their arms. Kitomolo rose grandly as they approached and Pierre had to reach up to drape it over the chief's shoulders. The cape was made of red satin with a wide, black, satin collar. Two yellow satin stripes ran from the shoulder to the hem and a heavy gold braid ran along the front edges and around the hem. A gold clasp closed it at the top. The "aah's" increased as those further back saw their chief in the red cape with all its trimmings and then stopped abruptly when he took it off and handed it to one of his sons.

Pierre and the sergeant turned and walked back and the chief sat down. Pierre returned carrying a heavy medallion attached to a chain and hung it around Kitomolo's neck. "As the robe is the symbol of authority, this medal is the symbol of power. They are small tokens as the glowing coal is, but a poor token of the greatness of the sun. As the coal is poor, so are these tokens, but as the sun is great, so great is our respect. To accept these tokens you do honor us."

Kitomolo took the medallion from around his neck and handed it to another one of his sons. He waited for a long time and then said, "To accept these tokens I do indeed honor you, but I have not yet decided if I will accept them."

Pierre waited the appropriate length of time and then said, "I ask Chief Kitomolo to be patient with me for what I am going to now say, I say of myself and not for the Great-Chief of all the mondeli." He waited while Harry translated. When Kitomolo nodded he went on.

"Many years ago, when I was but half the years I am now, I stood, much as I do now, before your father, the Great Chief Ronzozo. Then, as now, there was a mondeli who did wrong. Then, as now, there was talk of war. You were there when I cut the blood with your father, the Great Chief Ronzozo. It was an agreement that was to last as long as we both should live. He is now gone to his ancestors and that agreement has come to an end. Yet, in my heart, I am still in agreement with your father.

As I had deep respect for your father, so I have deep respect for you. The insult done you cannot be undone, just as words spoken cannot be brought back. The thing done cannot be undone, it can only be forgotten. To ask you to forget it is to ask a great thing. I would like to give you a gift. It is not from the Chief of the mondeli, but from me. Of all the things in my house it is one of the most precious for it was in the house of my father, and in his father's house before him. It is not something anyone could buy from me, but I would give it to you. I do not give it to Chief Kitomolo to buy his forgetfulness, but to show him how important it is to me he forget the wrong done him."

Kitomolo sat for a long time looking intently at Pierre. If he were to refuse the gift before he had seen it, it would not be an insult to Pierre for he had said it was precious to him. But if he were to accept the gift, he would also have to accept the cape and medallion. The cape and medallion were shown with no substance and not acceptable considering the insult. Yet he couldn't help but wonder what was concealed under the plain cloth covering. Finally, he nodded and said, "I will accept your gift."

Pierre motioned to the first soldier who brought up his bundle. Pierre lifted off the cloth, handing it to the soldier, and took the elaborately carved, curved-legged stand and set it in front of Kitomolo, moving it around until he found a place where it wouldn't wobble.

The soldier brought up the second bundle, and Pierre unwrapped it and set the highly varnished, gold lettered and decorated box on the stand. He opened a door and, taking out a brass crank, placed it in its hole in the side. He wound it up and then opened the lid. He took out a shiny brass disk more than a foot across and set it in place on the turntable. He released the brake and the disk started to turn, the needles on the disk hitting the teeth of the metal comb of the music box.

Many years before Leopopo had given Ronzozo a box that made the same kind of sounds. Leopopo's gift had only been a little larger than a woman's hand, and its sounds weak. This box was the length of a man's arm in all directions and the sound was strong and full.

Kitomolo got up from where he was sitting and walked over to the music box looking down at the turning disk. Pierre showed him how to wind it up and start and stop it. Kitomolo handed his gangilo to his son, and after working the music box himself and sampling all three of the disks, called for the cape. He put on the cape and hung the medallion around his neck. The gift was acceptable. Ever since the little music box Leo had given Ronzozo had stopped working, Kitomolo had wanted another one. Now he had a great one. No other chief had anything like it.

He stopped the music, raised his hand, and a stillness fell over the crowd. "The words spoken today were true. I accept them. The gifts are sufficient. I accept them. The insult done is forgotten. I, Kitomolo, have spoken it." He sat down, and stools were brought for Harry and Pierre to sit down next to him. He raised his hand and the warriors moved on to the ilolo and started to dance.

***

From Kitomolo's village they could hear the celebrating as they sat at the camp table in that pleasant moment before dinnertime of day. There was the sound of the water running in the stream and the call of the birds returning to the treetops. They were sitting quietly, think about the events of the day. Finally, Pierre broke the silence. "It is hard to believe it has been twenty-eight years since you and I sat by this stream. Do you remember that day, my friend?"

Harry nodded, thinking of the letter that had arrived telling of Angelique's death. Then, like now, Pierre had come because of the good possibility of a native uprising.

They were silent again for a while and then Harry said, "I shall not soon forget this day."

"Nor I," Pierre answered, "but there are not many others who will remember it. In a few months no one will even think about today, except possibly Kitomolo and you and I. And maybe it isn't as important as we think it is. Maybe today was just a lot of foolish antics on our part. That's the trouble. You never know if something is important until it becomes a catastrophe. Today is not important to anyone except you and I because there was no incident, no bloodshed, no death. Any record of it will soon be forgotten. Oh, I will file my report, and because Marceaux has some political connections back in Brussels, there will be a little discussion in Leopoldville about how to deal with both Marceaux and me. I have been in the Congo so long now I have outlived most of those who were here when I arrived, and longevity demands a certain amount of respect." He chuckled a little. "Marceaux will probably be sent home and get some kind of commendation for his service in the colony. My report will be filed somewhere and then in a few years it will be thrown out because some clerk will not think it important enough to keep. In Brussels it will be filed away somewhere to collect dust. I know somewhere there is some sort of record that Pierre Guilluame d'Entremont entered His Majesty's Congo Service, and finally became Commandant of the Matsa Garrison and District Commissioner. But aside from that, no one knows much of what we do." He raised his tin cup and took a swallow of whiskey.

"Well, I never expected recognition or honors in this life and I'm always a little surprised when I do get some kind of honorable mention," Harry answered.

"Ah, do not misunderstand me. My dreams as a child were not to volunteer for service in Africa. But now I would not exchange this spot and this table and this day for all the parade grounds of Europe. And you, my friend, would not exchange it for all the churches in America."

"That's very true," Harry said and they were silent again. They sat looking off into the distance, two distinctly different men, yet so much alike. Harry, with an almost gaunt face and a head of gray hair badly in need of a haircut, one of his thin-fingered hands resting caressingly on the Bible on the table in front of him. Next to it was his dirt-smudged brown helmet and a tin cup of cold tea.

On the other side of the table was the colonel, stocky and muscular with wavy gray hair and neatly trimmed gray mustache. In front of him on the table was his swagger stick, the brown helmet with its gold crown and lions of authority and a cup of warm whiskey. There was between them a mutual admiration. It was not in what they said, but there was an invisible respect as if the two of them knew something no one else knew, had done things no one else had done, been places no one else had been before them. They were, without having planned it, or even being conscious of it, the real pioneers. There was within them something that grew and grew until they had to do what none had done before. They heard an inner voice that said, "Go! Do!" and so they went, not really knowing why, only knowing they must. They were gray-hued now, serious-eyed, thoughtful, and unafraid. The fires of youth and the bright illusions were gone. They didn't care. They had done what they had to do, and it was enough.

Now they were just the shadowy figures of a forgotten dream, the fading colors in a painting that had never hung on a wall, the nameless, faceless, enduring pioneers. They were the ones who had gone before, opened the door, and showed the way. No one would ever know what they had done, and they didn't seem to care.

1938

CHAPTER THIRTY-NINE

It was early November and the sky seemed to be settling to the earth in a bank of dark clouds. David stood by the living room window wondering how it could stay so dark for so long. At home, when it decided to rain it got cloudy and rained, but here it could stay dark for days with no rain. Finally, after a week with no sun, it had started to snow. "Oh, look, David," Aunt Laura had said excitedly, "the first snow. It's the first snow you've ever seen, isn't it?"

He answered as politely as he could, but he couldn't get excited about the snow. It was insecure and nondescript specks of white floating on the gusty wind against a backdrop of leafless trees, almost black in their despondency.

He liked Uncle Dave and Aunt Laura. He had been living with them for the summer while his parents were traveling. Now, he would be staying with them when his parents went back home. Uncle Dave often took David with him on his speaking trips, and as they drove along, Uncle Dave would tell stories about the early days. He was glad he wasn't staying with his brothers PJ or Danny. They didn't seem to care about home at all, but from the way Uncle Dave talked, he knew he wished he were back there. In a way, Uncle Dave had helped David understand why he couldn't go back home with his parents.

He was angry with his parents when they had left Abaru and he knew he wouldn't be returning. He had been angry because they had taken him away before he'd had his chance to kill a leopard and become a man. Even Kusala had said it was time to leave, and that, too, had hurt. Today his parents were starting back and he was being left behind. He didn't want to have to say goodbye. He was afraid he might cry, and he didn't want to cry. It wouldn't do for someone old enough to kill a leopard to cry. He wished Mary Ruth was there, but she had said her goodbyes at breakfast and rushed off to one of her classes.

He heard the others coming down the stairs, Uncle Dave in front carrying two suitcases and then his parents. His mother came over to him, put her arms around him, released one arm, and then they walked toward the front door with one arm on his shoulder. They stopped to put on their coats and she held his for him, buttoning it up for him, making him feel like a little boy, but also special in some way. "You are such a beautiful young man," she said and leaned forward and kissed him on the cheek. She smelled of the cologne that was part of his earliest memories of her. Her hair was gray and she had wrinkles around her eyes and neck that he hadn't noticed before. They all walked out the front door to the car. His parents talked for a few minutes with Dave and Laura as though there were some last minute things that had to be said. Finally, they said their goodbyes, and his mother turned to him. She stood looking at him for a moment with her hands on his shoulders and then she hugged him tightly, kissed him on the cheek, then released him and climbed into the van.

His father put an arm around his shoulder, squeezed him and said, "Goodbye, Son. I'm going to miss you terribly."

David nodded and his father bent over to kiss him on the cheek. David threw his arms around his father. David clung to him until the tears were pushed back and then he let go. His father patted him on the shoulder and then walked around to his side of the car.

"We'll take good care of him," Laura said.

The car started and then pulled away from the curb moving slowly down the street. It was the only vehicle moving between the lines of stark, leafless trees that grew on both sides of the road. He stood on the sidewalk with Uncle Dave and Aunt Laura watching the car until it disappeared around a corner several blocks away. He wondered if his mother had looked back from time to time, or if his father had seen them in his rear-view mirror.

When they went inside he went up to his room and flopped down on his bed. He reached for the little packet of letters from Monique he kept in the drawer of the nightstand. Those last few months before leaving Abaru had been the best time of his life: killing the kudu, the trip to Matsa, and the apology to Kitomolo. After the safari to Kitomolo's village, the d'Entremonts had stayed with them for two week. During that time he knew he had fallen in love with Monique. He had never said anything about it to her, or anyone else, but after they left she had written a thank-you note and they had continued to write to each other. In the last letter she had told him her father had retired from government service and they had moved to a plantation in the hill country on the approaches to the Rift escarpment. He took her last letter, with all its description of the land and the people and the events, and read it again and felt he was still connected to the place by the letter. He read it several times and then went to the desk and started a letter to her.

Dear Monique:

My parents left today. They are starting back to Abaru. They left me with Uncle Dave and Aunt Laura. They aren't my real aunt and uncle, but they went to Abaru a long time ago. They were with my parents when they first went to Africa. You never met them because they went to Putu before you came to Abaru. I guess I'll be living with them from now on.

Did you get my last letter? I wrote when I first came to stay with Uncle Dave.

Your farm sounds simply super. I wish I could be there. I know I said that in my last letter, but it's true. I don't like it here. It was snowing this morning when my parents left. Just a little snow, but I don't think I'm going to like snow. I already don't like the cold. I wish I were back at Abaru. Please write me often because I like to hear about all the stuff on your farm and everything.

Say hello to Jacques.

Your friend,
David.

He put the letter in the envelope, sealed it, addressed it, and then sat staring at it as though it could somehow transport him to where he wanted to be. He turned and reached under the bed and slid out the trumpet. He opened the case slowly and took out the shiny, brass instrument. It was the golden color that had first attracted him to it. He crossed his arms holding it to his chest, something that was part of home even more than Monique's letter. He slowly unfolded his arms and raised the trumpet to his lips and started to play. The notes came out soft and slow, carrying with them the ache of having been deserted in a foreign land.

1944

CHAPTER FORTY

The radio, dark gray in color, sat in the corner of the living room close to the window. For half an hour every day there was always twelve to fifteen people crowded around it with those who got there first getting the seats closest to the radio. At exactly one minute of four Harry would turn on the switch. The two dials with their wavering needles would glow yellow, and the speakers would squeak and rattle until Harry had it tuned precisely, and then they would hear the deep, resonant sounds of Big Ben striking the hour. After the sounds of the clock were the words, "This is the BBC, London ..." and then the news.

It was in there, staring at the dark gray box with its yellow dials and black knobs they heard the devastating reports of the invasion of Denmark and Norway. A month later there was the news of the invasion of Belgium and the Netherlands. They heard of the defeat at Dunkirk and ten days later that German forces had occupied Paris. They heard Prime Minister Winston Churchill speak to his countrymen. Almost all they heard was of losses and defeats. It was by way of the BBC they learned of the attack on Pearl Harbor. They were all Americans, but somehow the attack on Pearl Harbor didn't seem as personal as the bombing raids on London.

Slowly, the news began to change. There was the English and American invasion of North Africa and within nine months Rommel and his troops were driven out. There was the invasion of Sicily and Salerno and the capture of Naples. There were times when the news created anxiety. Other times there was cause for optimism. But most of the time it seemed things had not changed much from the day before and they wondered why they had made the effort to get to the VanVeldt house only to strain so hard to hear what was said between the squealing and crackling. But always, no matter what the news that followed might be, there was something reassuring about the sound of the clock over the House of Commons striking the hour and the words, "This is the BBC, London ..."

On June the fifth, nineteen forty-four, the most important news they heard that day was that Rome had been liberated by the United States Fifth Army the day before. There were also the usual reports of bombing attacks on enemy installations in France and Germany.

CHAPTER FORTY-ONE

David VanVeldt lay in his bunk with his hands clasped behind his head. Outside it was drizzling. They said tomorrow would be the day, but they had said that for the past three days. Everyone knew there was going to be an invasion; the only questions were where and when. The first time the word came down that tomorrow would be the day he had been so frightened he hadn't slept that night. He was sure the other three men in his room hadn't slept either. The first time they were not called at three-thirty he wondered if they had been over looked. At six-thirty they were told the invasion had been postponed because of weather.

The last letter from Monique was in his pocket. Over the years the letters had become more frequent. When he was in high school there had been four or five letters a year. In college it had grown to almost one a month. Three days after graduating from college he was sent to Officers Candidate School. Three months later he was commissioned as a second lieutenant in the infantry and he sent her an official army picture of himself. After that they wrote each other almost every week. In the dampness of England, her letters told of sunlight and coffee crops and arguments with her brother, which were all part of home.

The door flew open and the unshaded glare of the overhead light bulbs suddenly filled the room. "This is it, Gentlemen," the Captain said. "Your companies will be assembling in half an hour. There's breakfast in the mess hall if you want it." He was gone and the four of them sat up, slowly rubbing their eyes against the brightness of the light.

David sat with both feet on the ground scratching his head with both hands thinking that at least he had gotten a good night's sleep. One of the others walked over to the window and, peeking behind the blackout shade, said, "It's still rainin' fer Christ's sake."

The day was beginning to dawn when they boarded their ship and they were told the invasion had started; the first troops had landed. They were below decks for the crossing and when they came on deck, David could see ships in every direction. From the ships the landing craft ran in lines, one behind the other, to the beach. He could hear the sound of gunfire, a background noise to orders being shouted. It was his company's turn to go over the side and he put his leg over the rail and started down the rope netting. When he had been practicing on the wall from which the rope net was hung it had not been swaying back and forth like the side of the ship and the ground hadn't been bobbing up and down like the landing craft below him. All along the side of the ship, men with helmets and full packs were making their way down the netting to the landing craft below. David got to the bottom of the net. The landing craft was rising toward him on a wave and then falling away. He jumped, landing in the bottom, and lost his balance falling to one side. He got up quickly and moved to the far side to get out of the way of the men coming behind him. The craft filled and pulled away, leaving men hanging on the net while another craft moved in below them. There was nothing to do but feel the vibration of the engine, the rising and falling on the channel swells, and to think. He hoped no one knew how terrified he was.

He felt them bump bottom, then the ramp at the front fell down and they were wading toward the beach. The water was almost waist high. To one side he saw a landing craft with a shell hole in its side, its ramp still down, useless and abandoned. When they got to the beach there were jeeps and guns and even tanks abandoned and useless. He saw men lying dead in the sand, arms and legs blown away, and he was glad he had not been among the first waves to land. The beach commander waved them up the beach while medics carrying stretchers with the wounded ran toward them.

He kept running forward, across the beach and then across a narrow road to a wall of scrub growth and trees where they were pinned down. There was the sound of rifle and machine gun fire and the sound of heavy mortars. He crawled on his belly close to the forward edge. Across the field, a hundred yards away, was another line of trees and shrubs where the enemy waited. Under cover of the trees, the troops lay on their bellies with their rifles, machine guns and bazookas all pointed toward the trees on the other side. From time to time they would hear a barrage of shells headed toward the other trees and then it would quiet down for a while. They were told they were waiting until they had enough men.

Across the field came a barrage of big gun fire. Some of the shells passed over their heads to land on the beach behind them. Others broke branches off the trees. Some landed among the troops. He saw men on either side of him killed, a hole in their chest or parts of their bodies blown away. The shells come over and then exploded above them, sending shrapnel every direction. Where were the tanks? Where were the guns that could do the same thing to the enemy across the field? he thought. The barrage decreased and he saw the men running out from under the cover and start across the field. He heard his captain shout, "Move out," and everyone was on their feet running toward the enemy.

In front and on either side of him he saw men fall. It looked like they had just stumbled and fallen forward and he suddenly found himself in front. He didn't know how he'd gotten there. He looked to either side and behind him to make sure he was not alone; the whole field was filled with men running the same direction he was.

He was holding his forty-five in his right hand and wished he had picked up a rifle from one of those on the beach who'd no longer need it. He saw a splash of dirt and blue smoke. It all happened at once, the blast and the sudden stinging, burning on his left side. He looked and saw his arm dangling by some flesh and the whole left side of his body a bloody mess. He dropped his forty-five and put his right hand to the stump of the arm hoping to stop the blood from flowing. He felt himself getting weak, waves of unconsciousness coming over him as he fell forward. The last thought he had was that he had been cheated. He had come all this way and hadn't been able to fire a shot. He should have killed one of the enemy. It would have been better than killing a leopard that prepared you for the real enemy, he thought. He hadn't killed his leopard. Instead, it had pounced on him from out of nowhere, spots of black and yellow in blue smoke, its teeth mangling his arm, its claws tearing up his body.

CHAPTER FORTY-TWO

They sat in their chairs talking until they heard the generator stop, then they quieted and turned in their seats to face the radio. Harry came in and took his place in front of the radio, flipping the switches and then gently turning the dials. He had to attend to the dials all the time because the broadcast tended to drift off. They heard Big Ben striking and the reassuring words, "This is the BBC, London. The Supreme Headquarters of the Allied Expeditionary Forces announced today that the invasion of Europe from the West has begun ..."

"Hallelujah," Paul Heller shouted slapping his knee. "This is the beginning of the end. Hitler is doomed. In one year it will all be over in Europe."

They became more and more excited as they listened to the quotes from the communiqués from General Eisenhower and reports from some who had been there when the troops first landed. Alma listened along with the rest of them, frightened more than excited. David was there somewhere and all she could do to help was to silently pray, "Oh, God, don't let anything happen to him." The others gradually seemed to remember Harry and Alma's youngest son might be among those who crossed the channel that day and became a little less vocal in their excitement.

When the news was over, they went out on to the porch for tea as they always did. Alma poured tea as she always did. Not one of them said solicitously, "David will be all right," because that would have been trite. They all wanted desperately to believe it and did believe it. Alma also wanted desperately to believe it, but somehow couldn't.

CHAPTER FORTY-THREE

Harry and Alma were the first to arrive for Pierre's birthday and, after freshening up from the long drive, they sat on the porch with the teacart and drinks tray close by waiting for the other guests and catching up on personal news. During the past ten years they had gotten together at least twice a year. Sometimes the d'Entremonts would go to Abaru and sometimes the other way around.

"And what do you hear from David?" Pierre asked. "Monique had a letter from him just before the invasion of Normandy, but we haven't heard anything since."

"You haven't heard anything more recent than that?" Alma asked looking at Monique.

"No, Madame. The last letter I got was dated the day before the invasion."

"We've received one letter from him since then," Harry said. "He was in a hospital in England. He said he had been wounded a little and we were not to worry. But it was more than that. We got a letter from Dave and Laura Robins. David put them down as the ones to be notified. I guess he thought the army wouldn't know how to get information to us," Harry said smiling with a jerk of his head. Pierre knew Harry had been hurt when David had put the Robins down as next of kin. "David also told the Robins he was only slightly wounded, but the army had notified them he had lost an arm..."

"Oh, no!" Cecile exclaimed, "I'm so sorry, Alma," and Pierre saw the look of shock and fear in Monique's eyes as she raised her hand to her mouth.

"Where is he now?" Pierre asked.

"We don't know. D-Day was more than two months ago and that one letter is the only one we've gotten from him. We don't know if he's still in the hospital in England or if they've shipped him back to the States."

"Excuse me," Monique said and got up and went inside.

"It takes so long for the mail to get to us," Alma said. "When we write we have to send it to the Army Post Office in New York and then they send it to England. It seems so ridiculous for the letters to have to cross the Atlantic twice. If he had only told us the name of the hospital in London we might have been able to write to him directly."

Pierre got up and went to look for his daughter. He found her in her room sitting on her bed. She wasn't crying, just sitting on the bed looking at the floor. He walked over and sat down next to her, putting his arm around her. "Why couldn't he have told me, Daddy?"

"He probably didn't want to upset you."

"It's going to be hard for him."

Pierre nodded and thought it would be hard for anyone.

"Yes, it will be hard for him, My dear, but he has the steel to overcome it."

"Oh. Papa, I'm so scared." She turned toward him, burying her face in his shoulder, and started sobbing. "I love him, Papa, and now maybe he'll think I can't love him because of his arm."

1946

CHAPTER FORTY-FOUR

Through the dust clouded windshield of the surplus army truck, David VanVeldt could see the buildings of Abaru ahead. The feelings of hope and excitement which he'd had at the thought of coming home became tinged with doubts and anxiety. After he was wounded, he spent several weeks in hospitals, first in England and then in Washington D.C. In the hospital in Chicago, after he had returned home to Dave and Laura's, they had tried to fit him with an artificial arm and hand, but it was an awkward thing of plastic and leather held in place with straps. As far as he was concerned, the looks and limited use of the artificial arm was not worth the weight and the nuisance of the straps chafing against his shoulder and chest.

As the truck came to a stop at the border station, he wished he had cabled his parents he was returning ahead of the others. He wanted to spend some time alone with them before the d'Entremonts got there. He knew Monsieur d'Entremont had cabled them that he and Monique were going to get married, and again when they had arrived in Paris, but because of the traveling, they had not heard from his parents. He wondered how his parents felt about his marrying Monique. It was not something they had ever had an opportunity to discuss. He had never been able to tell them how, after dinner at an oceanside restaurant, Jacques, Elizabeth, Monique, and he had gone walking along the beach.

It was a cool April evening with the moon shining on the water and the waves breaking on the beach. The four of them turned to walk onto the pier. David and Monique stopped where they could look down to the spot where the water lapped the land, while Jacques and Elizabeth continued on to the end of the pier. They leaned on the rail for a while, watching the water ebb and flow, and when they straightened up and looked at each other, he realized the sparkle in her eyes was from the pier lights reflected in tears. She stood there, tall and slim, her black hair falling around her shoulders, the breeze blowing loose wisps around the edges. It startled him to see her crying. Like her mother, she was always so regally graceful and in control. He couldn't think of any reason for her to be crying. "What's wrong?" he asked.

"Are you ever going to come home?" she asked.

More than anything else he wanted to go home, and at the same time he knew he was in love with her. "What would I do? What kind of work could I get? How would I live?"

He wanted to ask her to marry him, but he was afraid of her answer. In all their lives they had only been with each other three weeks, two weeks during the Marceaux incident when she was just twelve and he was sixteen, and again now when she was twenty. Despite all the letters, did they know each other well enough for him to ask her to marry him?

"Maybe you could work for Papa," she said.

"If I come back will you marry me?" He couldn't believe he had said it. He had asked the question almost banteringly, while at the same time amazed he had dared to ask it, even jokingly.

"Oh, yes," she said throwing her arms around him. He put his one arm around her, feeling the restriction of his left sleeve tucked and pinned inside the jacket pocket preventing him for raising the stub of his left arm. She released her arms and held his face in both her hands, standing on tip toe, pulling his face down to hers, kissing him on the lips, and cheeks, and eyes, and nose, saying "Oui, oui, oui."

"Are you sure?" he asked when she finally let him go. It was too hard to believe.

"Oh, yes. I'm sure. You can ask Jacques. I have loved you from the first time I saw you when I was just a little girl. I have never loved anyone else. I will never love anyone else."

He had cabled his parents that he was coming home with the d'Entremonts and getting married, but he couldn't help but wonder how they felt about it.

They passed through the checkpoint and entered the town. He was amazed at how much bigger it was than it had been when he left. He had somehow thought it would always stay the same. He had the driver drop him at the hotel. At the desk he paid for one day and a bath. The porter carried his duffle to his cabin. He handed the porter a set of the new bush jacket and shorts to be pressed and then sat on the foot of the bed polishing his shoes while waiting for the bath water to arrive.

He bathed, dressed and crossed the lawn to the main building. There were no guests in the lobby and he crossed to the other side of the building, stood on the porch and looked in both directions. There were several cars and trucks, mostly surplus military vehicles, parked alongside the road. He crossed the road, and walked to Leo's store. Inside it was exactly as he remembered it. Leo was sitting in a rocking chair behind the counter reading a paper that had arrived just that day from Juba. When David left, Leo's black hair was beginning to be salted with gray, but now it was pure white. Only his eyebrows were still dark. A native clerk came toward him. David ignored him and walked to corner of the counter and said, "Mr. Papadopolis."

Leo looked up slowly from his paper. "Yes?"

They stared at each other and David had the sudden fear that, since he had not told anyone he was coming, his parents might be gone on a trip. "Do you know if the VanVeldts are at home right now?"

"Why wouldn't they be?"

"They aren't away on a trip, are they?" he asked and saw Leo look at the end of his left sleeve which was just long enough to cover the stump of his arm.

"You are David!" Leo said, dropping the paper and jumping up from his chair. He rushed around the end of the counter and threw his arms around David, pounding him on the back, and then leaned away, keeping both hands on David's shoulders, looking at him. "Your parents told me you were coming with the d'Entremonts and getting married. Are they here?" Leo asked trying to see around David to the road.

"I came on ahead."

"And you didn't tell your parents you were coming?"

David shook his head.

"Shame on you. Shame on you! You should never do anything like that to your parents. Never again. But it will be a great surprise, won't it," he said excitedly, and then calmed down a little and slapped David's left shoulder. "Your papa told me about this. I'm sorry." Then he was exuberant again and added, "But a little thing like that isn't going to stop a man like you." He dropped his hands and told one of the clerks to get him a can of tennis balls from the shelf. "I shall take you home myself. This will be great fun seeing your father's face when he sees you."

They stopped in front of the long school building and a mototo cutting the grass confirmed Bwana Van was still at the school. Leo led the way along the porch, motioning for David to stay behind him. He stepped into the office while David waited outside. Harry looked up and said, "Well hello, Leo. What brings you here this time of day?"

"I have a present for you," Leo said placing the can of tennis balls on the desk. "Let's go play some tennis."

"Now? Are you out of your mind? I can't play tennis now," Harry said waving toward the pile of papers on his desk. Looking at Leo questioningly. "I have too much to do. Beside, it's much to hot to play tennis now. Later, Leo. This afternoon when it's cooler."

"Well, in that case, I'll have to try something else to distract you from your books and papers," Leo said, stepping back to the doorway and motioning David to come in.

David walked into the middle of the room and Harry sat there for a moment staring unbelievingly at his son. He started shaking his head and pushed himself up from the desk. He came around the desk and they threw their arms around each other. They hung on while their eyes filled with tears. They let go after a while and Harry leaned back to look at his son, seeing him blurred through the tears. He kissed him on both cheeks and then hugged him again.

"Give my regards to Alma." Leo said waving. He turned, smiling broadly and walked, almost skipped along the porch to his car. He called the oldest of the mototos who was cutting grass and gave him the duffle bag out of the back of the car. "Take this to the house and then go tell Kusala that Logoro has returned."

"Well, we'd better go see your mother," Harry said when Leo left. They walked silently along the back path behind the church from the school to the house. His mother was waiting for them in the front yard standing with her hands folded in front of her. They walked toward her and then his father dropped behind. He and his mother stood looking at each other and then she raised her arms and said, "Come here, you rascal."

They clung to each other, and when her tears had stopped, she gently let him go and stepped back. She looked at the butt of the stump just barely visible below the cuff of his bush-jacket sleeve. "Does it hurt at all?" she asked.

"No. Not a genuine hurt," he said. "Sometimes it has a funny tingle in it. Not a hurt so much as an irritation. Sometimes I feel as though I have an itch in my left hand and when I go to scratch it, there's no hand there to scratch."

She reached over, put her hand around the butt of the arm and started to cry silently. "Please don't cry, Ma. Please! It's all right. But please don't cry."

She moved her hand away, took a handkerchief from her apron pocket, daubed her eyes and blew her nose. "Why didn't you tell us you were coming? Where are the d'Entremonts? Last we heard from Pierre we didn't expect you for another two weeks."

"They're still in France. Monsieur d'Entremont is working with his brother to buy some stuff for the plantation. I was getting tired of waiting around and I was anxious to see you and dad."

"You should have cabled us you were coming on ahead. If we had been away and anyone else had been the first to welcome you home I would have been furious. Don't you ever do anything like that again."

195

"Yes, Mother."

"Now go say hello to Kusala and then come right back.

Kusala was waiting for him at the corner of the porch. He had just arrived from the village where the mototo had gone to get him. "You have come home," Kusala said, and if it wasn't for the voice, David would not have been sure it was Kusala. Kusala was bald and the hair over his ears was white. The worst part was that the once strong, tall Kusala was now bent over with arthritis and leaned on a cane. The fingers that had taught him to shoot the bow and arrow were gnarled to the place where David wondered if they could even hold a cup.

"Yes, Baba, I have come home."

"And you have become a man."

"I did not kill my leopard."

"Killing leopards is for those who cannot do greater things."

"I did nothing great."

"Your father has told me of the battle of that day. He has shown me pictures of war and the day and place of your battle. For a man to be there and not run on a day like that is greater than killing a leopard."

He reached over and put his hand gently on Kusala's gnarled, right hand. "Is there much pain?" he asked.

"It is always with me."

They started to come then; those he had grown up with came with their wives and young children. Others who knew his brothers and sisters and who had been with the mission as long as Kusala came and David was special to them because of all of the children he had returned. The missionaries came; all of them were more reserved than the natives.

It wasn't until after dinner that he and his parents could be alone. "Have you decided when you and Monique are getting married?" his father asked.

"We haven't decided. Monsieur and Madam d'Entremont wanted us to discuss it with you and everyone. Monique would like it to be around Christmas. She say's it would be the best Christmas present she ever got."

"Well, yes, Christmas would be nice. It will be nice to have one of our children a little closer than half a world away," his mother said looking down at her plate so no one would notice the moisture beginning to collect in her eyes. She had been seen crying once that day and that was quite enough. It was not just the excitement of the day that had her close to tears, but also the thoughts of the future. She had never attended one of her children's weddings. She had never seen one of the grand children growing up, but had only seen them at five or six year intervals when visits seemed to have no connection to the one before, or to the next. Now one of them had come home. She had never admitted it to anyone, but this youngest, the son of her old age, was her favorite.

***

On a chilly November day she had left him standing on the curb of a little town in the middle of North America. She had turned around as the van pulled away and looked back through the rear window. Through the distortion of her tears he had looked so forlorn despite the arm Laura had placed protectively around his shoulder. Would he ever forgive her? Would any of her children forgive her? Some of her children had understood. Others had just forgotten her, not in the sense that they didn't know who she was, but in the sense that she and Harry were no longer important to them. Looking back through the oval, rear window of the van that day, she was sure she would never see her youngest son again. She knew she and Harry would never return to the States and, if David was at all like his brothers and sisters, he would not return to Africa. Looking back through the window she had been angry with God, and angry with Harry, for separating her from her baby.

He had not written much, less than the other children. It was Dave and Laura who had kept them informed as to how their son was doing. She had been hurt when she first learned he was writing to Monique more than to his own mother, but now she was pleased and grateful. It was Monique's letters that brought David back.

***

"You know, David, I don't know Monique very well, and maybe I shouldn't say this, but I will always love her because she brought you back. That day when we left and I looked back, and saw you standing there was one of the saddest days of my life. I was afraid I would never see you again. It was almost as though you had died. That's how much it hurt. And because we were the ones that were leaving, it was as though I had killed you myself. Can you ever forgive me?" she asked looking up and putting her napkin to her eyes to catch the tears.

He got up and went over and put his arms around her shoulder, his cheek resting on the top of her head, held her for a moment and then went back and sat down. "It was snowing that day. I think that is one of the reasons why I hate snow so much. I guess that's why I moved to California. Not a day went by that I didn't wonder when and how I could get back."

"I'm sorry, son." his father said.

"It was good being with Uncle Dave and Aunty Laura. Uncle Dave wanted to be back here as much as I did. He used to take me with him lots of times when he was speaking somewhere and we would talk about everybody and everything. He told me one time that you left me in the States because you thought it would be best for me. Did you think it would be best for me to stay with Uncle Dave and Aunt Laura?"

"At time we thought so," his father said. "It was what everybody did. Then the war came and people were afraid of sending their children off to school. Since there were no high schools they started teaching their children at home. On some stations parents got together to teach different subjects and we realized there would have been no reason to leave you in the States. Your mother and I could have taught you right here. Dr. Schwartz could have taught you science. Mr. Pontier could have taught you architecture and engineering. Of course you wouldn't have a recognized degree, but maybe that's not as important as we thought it was back then."

"All I know is I'm back, and that's all that matters to me."

"Do you have any idea when the d'Entremonts will be arriving?"

"In a week or ten days, I expect. He's taking care of some financial things with his brother, Francois, and buying a surplus German army truck and a car. I guess he plans to ship them as far as he can, and then he and Jacques will drive them the rest of the way."

"Do you drive at all?" his father asked.

"Oh, yes. Uncle Dave taught me to drive. I can hold the wheel steady with this stump," David said grabbing the stub of his left arm, "when I have to shift."

They were silent for a moment and then tears came to Harry's eyes and he said, "I can't think of one important thing I taught you. Uncle Dave taught you to drive. Your mother taught you to read and write, and ...," he looked at the kudu head hanging over the fireplace, "Kusala taught you how to throw the spear."

"Oh, no, Dad. You taught me how to play the trumpet. You have no idea the number of times when I was in college, and then in the army, that playing the trumpet brought me home. Of course, they wouldn't let me take it with me at Normandy, but when I was in the hospital in England, one of the nurses found an old bugle for me, but you can't play many notes on a bugle so I started playing the harmonica. You know, I think it is the only instrument you can play with one hand."

1954

CHAPTER FORTY-FIVE

The death of Leo Papadopolis did not come as a surprise to anyone. He was over seventy and for more than a year had been weak and mostly bedridden. He refused to go to either the Catholic or the Protestant hospital. He protested he had lived his life his own way and he was going to die his own way, in his own bed, with his family gathered around him.

Turned sideways in the corner of the front row, Alma noted the church was filled mostly with whites. Every missionary and merchant from the post was there. The few blacks were Leo's family. Victoria and Alice sat in the front row with their seven lighter skinned sons and daughters. Behind them were Leo's grandchildren, and great-grandchildren, becoming progressively darker with each succeeding generation. Seated in the very back, Mbekede looked straight ahead. Alma didn't recognize him at first and when she did, she couldn't help but think of how old he had gotten. Mbekede was never seen around Abaru or in his stores anymore. Looking over the congregation, Alma realized most of the people didn't know anything about Moses Robins and the Jones girl. The merchants had all arrived after the incident, and aside from Mable Guetz, Doc and Rosemary, the other missionaries might have heard about it, but they couldn't have identified Mbekede as the man. At the end of the service Mbekede didn't file by for one last look, but was out the door and disappeared as soon as the service was over.

Alma saw Mbekede again at the graveside standing behind the family. There were Leo's sons and daughters with children and grandchildren all on the other side of the open grave; the blacks were on one side and the whites on the other. Behind and above the group of black faces was Mbekede's face. It seemed to her his stare was filled with hatred and anger. Maybe he had a right to be angry, she thought.

She stepped out of her place and crossed to the other side. She took a place at the end of the front row standing next to one of Leo's black daughters-in-law. Even in death, the coffin of a white merchant was on the side of the grave where the whites had gathered rather than on the side where his black family was gathered. She guessed her gesture hadn't meant much, but she had to do it. She thought when the service was over she was going to make it clear to Harry, and everyone else, that when she died, she wanted to be buried in the native cemetery on the other side of Medicine Hill.

CHAPTER FORTY-SIX

Breakfast at the plantation was regularly served at nine-thirty on weekdays. It was a time when the whole family got together; Jacques and David came in from getting the day's work started and the children took a break in their lessons. Pierre and Cecile now had eight grandchildren ranging in age from six to the youngest ones, which were both two and were born only a month apart. There was a teacher for the four older children and a governess for the two younger ones. It was a time when the adults held the children on their laps and listened to what they were learning.

Breakfast was the family time of day. At lunchtime Pierre and the boys discussed the business of the plantation and by dinnertime the children were already in bed. They were just starting to eat their fruit when they saw the car approaching along the road that led to the house. They didn't give it any thought. People in the area knew what time they had breakfast and just dropped by. There was always an open invitation to breakfast at the d'Entremont's. Breakfast was simple, and always the same, fruit to start with and then rolls and croissants just out of the oven with butter and jams and lots of rich, black coffee mixed with steaming hot milk. If guests arrived it was just a matter of splitting another papaya or pineapple and putting another tray of croissants into the oven.

Gordon Bixley from the mission at Kasengu got out of his car and waved as he walked across the polished cobblestones. He stopped at the top of the stairs. "I have bad news, David, Your mother had a stroke at a little after five this morning. Your father wants you to come home as soon as possible."

"Is she still alive," he asked jumping up and spilling his coffee.

"When we received the radio call this morning she still was."

"You must go. Right away," Monique said jumping up.

"Don't wait for anything. I'll pack your things and we'll come later. Don't wait for us. Go now! Go now! No. No. I'll come with you. Mama will pack our things for us. We must leave right now."

He sat in the passenger seat letting Monique do the driving. It was just five years ago that this same Gordon Bixley had come to tell him that Kusala had died and then less than a year ago he got the news the Leo had died. He had been to both those funerals and he had an overwhelming fear that he was on his way to another one.

***

There was no road to the native cemetery. The whites' cemetery had a way into it so cars could pull right up to the gravesite. The graves in the whites' cemetery were all in nice straight rows, one grave right next to the other. If Alma had been buried there she would have been buried next to Leo Papadopolis. Many thought that would have been appropriate. They had been friends a long time.

She had come home from Leo's funeral furious. "It was disgraceful, Harry. I'm ashamed. I'm ashamed of myself and everybody on the mission. Not you, Harry. You were where you belonged, conducting the service. But the rest of us, we separated ourselves from them for no other reason than they were black. Leo was our friend and we refused to stand alongside his widow! Do you know why, Harry? Do you know why?"

She was standing in the middle of the living room shouting at him and pounding her fists into the air. "Because we think we're better than they are. It's disgraceful." He had heard her on these kinds of tirades before and knew better than to try and stop her, "When I die I don't want to be buried in *that* cemetery." The way she exploded the word *that* conveyed all the scorn she could feel. "You have to promise me, Harry. I will not be buried there. Not unless we start burying the natives there, too. Promise me, Harry! If I die before you do, please promise me you'll bury me in the native cemetery."

"I promise," he said, and they had both sat down and decided *they* wanted to be buried with the natives. He had presented their views at the next staff meeting and even typed up a copy of their wishes, signed by both of them, and given it to the new Field Director. The others had accepted their views without comment. It was a nice gesture, but when the time came they were sure neither Harry nor Alma would really want the other one buried over there.

***

It was a large funeral. The natives were mostly just those attached to the station and there were merchants from the post. But missionaries had come from almost every station. There were times when they had felt Harry and Alma were in their way, were doddering old folks that had to be tolerated, but they respected longevity and Alma had been like a mother to almost all of them when they had first came out as recruits.

The service was conducted entirely by the native pastors. A man who was just a boy when Harry and Alma arrived gave the eulogy. He explained how he stood with the curious, watching them even before

Kusala had joined them. The pallbearers were the head houseboys from the various homes on the station. It was all the way Alma had said she wanted it. "I don't want the whites to do a single thing, Harry. I want the natives to put me to rest."

The pallbearers carried the coffin out of the church with the native pastor, Harry and David behind the coffin. They walked the length of the station and up Medicine Hill passing the entrance to the white's cemetery. They crossed the open area between the doctor's house and the hospital and started down the path on the other side. It was just a narrow footpath. Natives were usually just wrapped in a blanket. The pallbearers had trouble keeping their footing carrying the coffin around the boulders.

They set the coffin on the slope of the hill next to the grave. There were no even rows here or neatly built brick borders, just mounds of earth scattered around the hillside wherever the family thought best. Some of the graves had little piles of stones at the head. They had dug Alma's grave high up on the slope not far from where Kusala was buried. Seeing the location, Harry thought it was appropriate. The native pastor took his place and the people started to sing.

Doc said Alma had gone painlessly and Harry hoped it was so. He had rolled over in the bed the night before and the full impact of her being gone had flooded in on him. Everybody had been considerate and kind doing what had to be done, except the most important thing of filling the void and removing the hurt. Alma, Alma, how could you have done this to me? How will I ever be able to get along without you? It wasn't fair of you to do this. Who will straighten me out in private so I don't make a fool of myself in public? Oh, Alma, Alma, Alma. What am I to do next? I'm glad you're there. I'm glad all the aches, and pains, and tears are over, but oh, Alma, I miss you so much. I really don't think I can go on without you.

He looked around at the crowd on the hillside. They were standing in little clusters on the steep slopes between the mounds that were graves and the boulders. There was almost an equal number of natives and whites and they were standing next to each other, blacks next to whites in little groups of two and threes, or five and six. Oh, Alma, how you would have loved to see this. But then you can see it now, can't you? How like you to have accomplished more in one day than I have been able to do in fifty years. What am I supposed to do next, Alma? I really don't know what to do next.

1957

CHAPTER FORTY-SEVEN

They had run out of supplies before they could get to three of the villages Doctor wanted to get to, and he was upset about that. "I hate to think there are people who need us and we didn't get to them. Maybe we should just pick up some more supplies and head out again."

"We're not going anywhere until you've had some rest," Rosemary said firmly. The last time they had been on furlough the doctors had warned him of his heart condition, and ever since then Rosemary had had all she could to keep him from doing too much.

They arrived at the mission mid afternoon. Harry was there to meet them and walk with them up the hill. "I'll expect you for dinner," he said as the porters laid down their loads on the dispensary porch. "Come whenever you're ready. We'll hold dinner until you arrive."

The infirmiere and houseboys unpacked the hospital boxes. "Guzali went home a week ago. Ruta died in the night five days ago. Paulo is better. He'll be leaving soon." The list went on and on. "There are many who wait to see the munganga."

"I am returned now and will see them all in the morning."

"There is one girl, Bwana. Very sick. By her mother she was brought. For three days she has been trying to give birth. The midwives can do nothing for her."

"I will see her," the doctor said. Bring her to the surgery."

"It can wait till tomorrow," Rosemary said.

He ignored her and Rosemary followed him silently toward the operating room. She hoped he would let her do the operation. Not because she wanted to do an operation, it would probably be a simple caesarian, but because he needed to rest. She was not a doctor. Everything she had learned after nurses training had been from him. She had worked beside him every day of their lives. First he had started by explaining everything he did. When other missionary wives were darning socks, she was practicing surgical knots. When they were reading magazines, or novels, Rosemary was reading medical texts. Then he had stood beside her, directing her every move until finally he stood so as to assist her when she was doing a procedure.

The complicated ones he did himself, but a caesarian was not complicated.

In the operating room the infirmiere directed the family as they brought in the girl and laid her on the table. The family was ushered out; they stood on the porch with their faces pressed against the glass windows. The girl was having contractions, clenched her fist, writhed, and moaned. "Contracted pelvis," he said after examining her. He pressed the stethoscope against the stretched stomach. "Baby's still alive. Good heartbeat," he said straightening up, and lifting the stethoscope.

They went and stood in the door of the scrub-room that looked down on the compound of huts where the native patients stayed. Once they were out of intensive care they usually refused to stay in the hospital separated from their families. "After the conditions of the past month it will be good to get back to a clean operating room again."

"Why don't you let me do this one, darling?"

"You're as tired as I am. I'm okay, I feel fine."

The hot water arrived and they went in and started scrubbing, Dr. Schwartz, Rosemary, and two infirmiere. They stood in a row, their faces to the wall, bent over the little metal washstands with their white enamel basins. Two houseboys reached in between them to retrieve the basins, rinse them out, put them back on the stand, and add more clean water. They helped each other into gowns and masks and went into the operating room. The girl, who had never worn a piece of clothing in her life, lay under two sheets.

Rosemary started the chloroform, turned it over to the head infirmiere, and came and stood across from her husband. The sheets were turned back exposing her stomach and upper legs. Rosemary painted the protruding, black stomach with tincture of iodine and then washed the iodine away with alcohol.

"Scalpel," Dr. Schwartz said and with a single, swift, uninterrupted sweep, he cut a line from just below the umbilicus, straight down the middle to just above the top of the pubic bone. He cut cleanly through skin, fat and silvery-blue fascia. For a moment the flesh lay open and clean and then a few vessels seeped blood and had to be tied off. Another incision through the linea alba, then through the peritoneum, and the uterus bulged out through the retracted incision in the abdominal wall. He made a one-inch cut in the thick, muscular wall of the uterus. The blood started to flow and he inserted two fingers into the hole to guide the blunt-nosed scissors as he lengthened the incision to four inches, the blood pouring over everything as he went. He got rid of the scissors, reached in with his right hand up to the forearm and pulled the baby out, feet first, guiding the arms and head through the incision with his left hand. Rosemary tied off the umbilical cord, cut it and carried the baby girl to a nearby table, sucked the secretions from the baby's nose and mouth and the baby wailed.

One of the infirmiere took over the cleaning of the baby and Rosemary went back to help her husband sew up the incision and put on the dressing. The patient was moved from the table to a bed and wheeled to the recovery room.

"Well, that went well, dear," he said heading for the scrub-room. He took off his cap and mask and threw them in the laundry basket. He stripped the gloves from his hands, threw them in the wastebasket. He took three steps toward the recovery room, gasped and clutching at his chest, sank slowly to the floor.

She ran across the room, "Oh God in heaven, please, no." She knelt down beside him doing all she knew how to do for a cardiac arrest victim. Finally, she leaned back and picked up his hand, still powdery and wrinkled from having been in the surgical glove, and sat stroking it. He lay there, looking up at the ceiling, his hair tousled from yanking off the cap, the eyes that had always been so full of kindness, empty now. After a while she reached over and lovingly closed the lids over the eyes and then looked up and said to the infirmiere who were standing around her, "The Munganga is dead."

She started to get up and they rushed over to help her. She walked out of the room onto the hospital porch and then turned and said, "Put the Munganga in one of the rooms."

She walked away from the hospital toward the house, the head infirmiere beside her. She walked straight and fast. There were no tears, only the shaking of her jaw as though she were shivering, her teeth clenched against her in-turned lips. She didn't want to have those thoughts, but they came to her. How futile it all is! It was useless, a waste. A fifteen-year-old girl and her baby are alive and my husband is dead. What can they do for all the people that are waiting to see the munganga in the morning? What can they do about the three villages we didn't get to? What can they do about the hundreds that will die in the years to come because the next closest doctor is over a hundred miles away? What a waste. What a sacrifice. There is nothing beautiful about sacrifice. It is just stupid. I should have insisted he wait until tomorrow. I should have insisted he let me do it. Would that have changed anything? He's with the Lord now. We've known for a long time about his heart. He wouldn't stop when we first learned of it, and he wouldn't have let anything stop him now, she said to herself.

They got to the house and she turned to the native infirmiere who had walked with her and said, "Go tell Bwana Van," and then she went in the house and closed the door behind her. The infirmiere grabbed Rosemary's bicycle from off the porch, he didn't feel it would be right to take the Munganga's. Because her bike was so small, he could only ride it standing up in the pedals, his body bent forward over the handlebars. He started peddling swiftly, down the back path between the boulders where the gardenias were in full bloom, past Mabel's house to the road, past the magazine, the print shop, and the houses of other missionaries, not stopping, and peddling as fast as he could. At the school and the church, people watched him curiously as he went by, then falling in to run behind him because he was in such a hurry. "Bwana! Bwana!" he shouted as he tore across the VanVeldt's yard, "The Munganga is dead. He did an operation and then went to be with the Lord."

Even before Harry could get in the car to go to Rosemary, the long drums started to beat the slow, erratic rhythms of the death dance announcing the Munganga had died. "Stop the drums," Harry said to infirmiere.

"It cannot be, Bwana. All know there is no dancing here. We have no other way to tell them. He was well loved. It is their right to know he is gone."

The mission drums stopped after an hour, but before the drums were silent people from miles around were making their way toward the Hill of the Two Steams. They came, some of them walking in mutual defense groups through the night. Some came because they, or a member of their family, had been treated and kept from dying by the Munganga. Others, who had never seen the munganga personally, came out of respect for the good things they had heard about him. They came with their sleeping mats in one hand, their walking spears in the other, and their wives carrying the food, pots and children. By dawn the one hundred yards between the hospital and the Schwartz's house and down the sides of Medicine Hill was filled with people.

***

At precisely six o'clock in the morning, Rosemary Schwartz received the first of the viewers. Bill Pontier stood at the door controlling the numbers. They entered five at a time and Rosemary conducted each group over to the unpainted, raw-wood box. Doc lay with his hands crossed over the Bible that lay on his chest, a sheet covering his waist and legs, copper-colored, metal-framed glasses over his close eyes, his sandy colored hair more neatly combed than anyone had ever seen it before. Harry and some of the other missionaries were in the room with Rosemary. Harry had strongly suggested she sit in a chair at the head of the coffin and he would escort the people in, but she had insisted it was her responsibility.

She stood straight and dressed in her starched, white, nurses' uniform, which was all anyone there had ever seen her wear, except sometimes at church on Sundays, or away at some other mission station on vacation. She would thank each person for coming and, looking at her little gold wristwatch, give them exactly one minute. Then Harry would lead them out the back door telling them the service would be at noon at the church while Bill allowed the next group in.

They were all allowed the same amount of time: the important and the poor, the known and the unknown. She didn't know many of them, but she did recognize Chief Lamuwi. They had not heard from him since they set his village on fire to destroy the rats that carried the plague. Dr. Schwartz had been concerned that Lamuwi had been killed in that fire. They had never found his body, but there had been so many dead bodies in the village when they torched it they could never be sure if Lamuwi had stayed in his hut as he had vowed. She stood looking at him, thinking this minor chief could have saved her husband a lot of anguish and concern if he had made himself known earlier. Lamuwi had done it on purpose. She wanted to reach out and slap the face of this man standing there with three of his sons, looking down at the body of her dead husband.

At noon the viewing came to an end and the six infirmiere, who were to be the pallbearers, came into the room and picked up the casket with the lid still off. They walked out the front door, across the lawn to the road halfway between the house and the hospital, and led the crowd down the hill. They walked the mile from the top of Medicine Hill to the church slowly with the casket open and held low rather than on the men's shoulders so those along the road could look into the casket as it passed.

Samuelle Adengo, who had been raised in the mission orphanage, gave the message, and when he was through, the whites were permitted to file by the coffin and then the lid was nailed in place. The pallbearers carried it out of the church and back along the palm lined gravel road followed by the missionaries and priests and then the throngs of natives.

The cemetery, and the whole side of Medicine Hill, was filled with people. Harry conducted the graveside service and after the coffin was lowered, the people started filing by to throw a handful of dirt in the grave.

The crowds left and Rosemary and the missionaries walked back to the VanVeldt house. Rosemary would stop every few feet when someone wanted to tell her of how wonderful the Munganga had been. Several times Harry tried to stop them but Rosemary said, "No. No, Harry. It's all right. They're not bothering me."

They got back to the house and sat down on the porch at almost exactly the same time as the drums had started to beat the day before. Shortly after that the afternoon rain started. "Is there anything we can do for you, Rosemary," Harry asked.

"Do, Harry? What else is there to be done? It's all been done. You know he would have been fifty-nine next month? I had a special birthday present I had brought all the way from home without his knowing about it ... and two from the girls. I don't know what I'll do with them now. The medical safari was hard this time. I knew I shouldn't have let him do the caesarian, but you know how stubborn he could be at times. Well, I guess he's made his last safari, the last, long safari home." She sat silently, then staring at one spot in the floor, the others saw her tears.

1960

CHAPTER FORTY-EIGHT

Everyone had tried to discourage Pierre from going, but since he had been officially invited, he was insistent on being at the ceremonies when independence was finally granted. He hadn't been quiet about his concern for independence, but since it was here, he was in many ways as excited as any native. Jacques drove his parents to catch the riverboat at Stanleyville that would take them to Leopoldville.

At the plantation they heard news of the riots that broke out in Leopoldville on Independence Day. They waited anxiously for word from Pierre and Cecile while all around them the whites were leaving. By radio they learned that with the quick departure of the Belgian government and with no trained natives to replace them, public services broke down quickly. When government employees didn't get their paychecks they went on strike, which broke into riots. At Leopoldville the garrison staged a protest against Lumumba's policy of keeping white officers. The commanding general ordered another garrison to put down the Leopoldville protest and they, too, mutinied. Like a line of dominos, every garrison in the country mutinied against their white officers. The soldiers went on a rampage, looting stores and army supplies and attacking and killing officers and their wives. Five days after the mutiny started, Lumumba gave in and fired all the Belgian officers. He replaced them all with NCOs. Every soldier was promoted one rank, which left an army without a single private. Mobutu was made general of the army.

When after a week they hadn't heard from Pierre and Cecile, David and Jacques decided it was time for them to leave. They argued about it, but it was finally agreed David would stay behind in case Pierre and Cecile came back. They left in three cars with eight children, Jacques, Elizabeth, and Monique along with the governess and the tutor.

David stood on the porch waving as the cars drove away. He had no doubt he would survive, but if things got as bad as they had in other places, his family might not. He could out run anybody chasing him, but his family could not. He could hide in ways and in places where he would never be found, but he couldn't hide his family. They would be safe, and when it was time to return, he would still be there.

There was also the concern for the native workers. They were ready to defend themselves and the plantation, but those loyalties could be dangerous and it was better to also let them go. With the family gone, the natives would also feel free to leave.

A week after Jacques and the others left, Moise Tshombe, Premier of Katanga Province, declared his province was seceding. David waited one more week and then decided that since he had not heard anything about, or from, Pierre and Cecile, it was time also for him to leave. The homeland he had returned to with so much hope and expectation had erupted into riots and tribal civil wars.

CHAPTER FORTY-NINE

Mbekede sat at the head of the table in the office of the African Supremacy Party in Stanleyville. He had moved there a year before Independence. Gray had taken over half of his curly black hair, but he was still lean and hard and there was a fire in his eyes that made people listen to him when he looked at them. He had become a wealthy and powerful man and he often thought if the mondeli had not refused to let him marry the mondeli girl, he would now just be some insignificant pawn of the mondeli.

His rise to wealth began when he went to live with Leo and his rise to power began when he married a daughter of Chief Ronzozo. A year later he married a daughter of Kitomolo, chief-to-be. In the next four years his two wives had given him three sons and four daughters. After the birth of his third son he began marrying the daughters of lesser chiefs. He didn't bring these wives to Abaru, but built houses for them right in their father's villages. He had many children by these wives. He provided well for these families and made frequent trips to visit them, always bringing gifts for his wives and children.

As his wealth increased, his sons grew older and became his agents in the various villages. They not only conducted his business, but they were also his spokesmen. If a native was whipped, it was pointed out a mondeli had ordered it. If a person who was working for the mondeli got hurt on the job, the person was just let go and replaced by someone else. Everyone knew if someone were helping you work on your house and got hurt so he couldn't work anymore, you were responsible for him and his family. But the mondeli didn't do that.

The Second World War had also been particularly good to Mbekede. During the North African Campaign, Abaru was a stopping place. Thousands of troops passed through Abaru on their way North to join Montgomery in his campaign against Rommel. Mbekede catered to those troops. There was the official government hotel, which was frequented by white officers, but all the other bars, restaurants and brothels, were operated by Mbekede. He had "whites only" bars, and brothels that were managed by light skinned Indians and staffed by the blacks. From the villages, his agents supplied him with woven baskets, mats, ivory and ebony carvings, animal skins, and any anything else he could sell to the troops passing through. Endless convoys of great, sand-colored trucks passed through daily and prices for everything skyrocketed, and Mbekede was in the middle of high prices.

The war also helped Mbekede's cause. Soldiers passing through from other parts of the continent told about how they were driving the whites out. Indian troops talked about independence in India. By the time the war ended, Mbekede was the spiritual leader of a militant group that exceeded twenty thousand dues-paying members committed to the total expulsion of the mondeli from the land. There were many more who didn't pay dues, but were in agreement. The mondeli had to go and the blacks had to become the rightful rulers of the land that was theirs.

Now, sitting in the party headquarters in Stanleyville, Mbekede knew it was time to move. His protégé, Lumumba, had advised caution and moving slowly, but now less than ten weeks after independence, Lumumba was no longer in power. The government, what there was of it, was in shambles. Mbekede looked around the table. "It is not enough just to be in control," Mbekede was saying. "We must push forward. Mobutu is totally involved in fighting Tshombe and has no troops to come against us. Our first move will be to get control of Kivu Province. We must accomplish that before the New Year. I intend that we start 1961 in control of both the Oriental and Kivu provinces. General Tingwembi will be responsible for the Kivu conquest. In the meantime, Colonel Mabalu is going to raise an army of Simbas. They will be the most ruthless lions who ever spread through the land. This army will become part of the invasion force, but the main purpose of the Simbas is to rid the land of the mondeli's influence. It is no longer enough just to rid the land of the mondeli. We must rid the land of his ways. Every black who supports and protects the mondeli must be wiped out. Every convert to the mondeli god must be killed if they do not reject the mondeli's god and their Yesu Kristu. Any person who ever worked for a mondeli must prove they are worthy of our trust. For the time being we will take the help the Russians have offered us and then, when we no longer need them, we will kill them, too." He smiled, pleased with himself. "After all, they are also mondeli."

1964

CHAPTER FIFTY

Since independence shortwave radio communications had become a way of life for the whites who had returned. Every station, plantation, and business kept in touch with each other by way of radio. Rosemary slipped into a chair next to Harry just as Tom Wright finished his prayer and turned on the radio. The radio crackled and then the voice said, "All stations, this is QG-24, Stanleyville."

The caller was Al Jackson who was director of the Unreached World Mission with headquarters in Stanleyville. "Get out while you still can. This Simba activity is not like anything we have ever seen before. Yesterday, Simba trucks came and confiscated all the food and furniture out of our houses. Some mission natives were killed and all granaries emptied. They've taken our vehicles and put guards outside our houses. We are prisoners. We had the radio hidden, or they would have taken that, too." There was a pause and then panic in his voice. "They have just broken into the house again and you can ..." The transmission stopped, and just before the radio went dead they could hear shouting and banging in the background.

The radio was quiet for a moment and then Tom Wright spoke into the microphone broadcasting. "This Tom Wright from Abaru. Now we will take the roll." He started calling each station to make sure they were on line and all right. He was halfway through the list when he was interrupted.

"QG-32 Abaru! QG-32 Abaru! This is the United States Consulate at Kampala. Do you read me?"

"Yes, Kampala. We read you."

"Is Reverend Thomas Wright there?"

"This is Tom Wright."

"Mr. Wright, the Ambassador strongly advises all Americans and Europeans of your mission to leave immediately. The Mission headquarters in Philadelphia has been advised of the situation and they concur. They have asked us to tell you they are ordering all your mission personnel to leave Zaire. The Simbas are taking hostages of all whites and have informed the United Nations they will be killed if certain conditions are not met. Have your people pack lightly as they may have to abandon their cars and walk through the bush to get out.

The embassy cannot over emphasize the urgency of these instructions. You have no time to delay. Do you understand?"

"Yes. I understand."

"Notify all stations they are to evacuate immediately. The situation is desperate."

"I understand and will comply."

"This is Kampala, out."

With the orders from Kampala there was a moment of dumbfounded silence, suddenly everyone was talking at once. Tom Wright had to shout to get people to quiet down while he finished taking the role by radio of all the CAM stations, making sure they had heard the message from Kampala. When he was through he turned off the radio and said. "Remember what I just told you, God said to Joshua. Well, He's saying that to us now. Be of good courage. Now let's decide who will be riding with whom."

"Well, I can't leave," Rosemary said. "I've got three patients that can't be left without medical attention."

"Let the infirmiere take care of them."

"They are not qualified."

"We'll talk about it later," Tom Wright said.

"Nothing to talk about. I'm not leaving," she said and walked out. She didn't expect Tom Wright to understand. The patients were her responsibility. Dr. Wentworth had left the day before to go back to his station and left them in her care.

Driving back toward Medicine Hill, Rosemary thought how strange it was that everyone was now about to run from the army of a man who had been raised by the Robins' in their own home, as their own son.

The big Mercedes automatically shifted down as she started up the hill. The Medicine Hill road came out almost exactly halfway between the house, and the hospital, and as she leveled off at the top, she saw there was a crowd gathered at the hospital and she turned in that direction. Some of the people came running toward her, and Yoane was at her door even before she came to a stop. "It is Pastor Adengo, Madamu." Samuelle Adengo, the one who had preached Doctor's funeral service because he had been one of Doctor's favorites. "He is very sick. Coughing out food and he is hot with fever. Pain in the stomach, and then down here," Yoane said pointing to the right, lower side of his abdomen. "I think it is the no-use finger."

She smiled a little even as she rushed to where Pastor Adengo was lying on the gurney. Yoane had seen more than one appendectomy. Once he had asked Doctor what it was he was removing and Doctor had said, "A no-use finger. It does nothing, Yoane. It is of no use except to sometime get infected and have to be taken out."

"It is not the way of God to made a no-use finger," he said smiling secretly, "it may be the mondeli have not yet found the reason for it."

Her examination confirmed what Yoane suspected. "Get him ready, Yoane. We have to operate right away. Is the water for washing hot?"

"It is always hot, Madamu. The munganga said the fire was never to go out."

She nodded and went to the lab. She thought this was not the time to tell her infirmiere that all over the station the mondeli were preparing to leave. She found a piece of paper and a pencil and wrote:

Dear Harry and Tom.

Pastor Samuelle Adengo has just been brought in with acute appendicitis. I must operate immediately. There is no question now I won't be able to leave with you today. I'll follow as soon as I can.

R.S.

Outside she found an older mototo. "Run with this," she said handing him the note. "Show it first to Bwana Van then to Bwana Wright. Now hurry. Run!" and the boy ran toward the house, the note clutched in his hand, heading for the back path that would lead to the mission road.

She and Yoane and two other infirmiere were just finishing scrubbing-in when Tom Wright burst in. "How long is this going to take," were his first words.

"Probably an hour, or more, Tom."

"Well then I guess we can wait for you," he said as Harry walked in behind him.

"I won't be leaving today," she said matter-of-factly.

"Why not? After the surgery is done the infirmiere can take care of him and the others."

"Why should they stay if I don't stay, Tom? How many of the mission natives are getting ready to leave?"

"I'm staying, too," Harry said his eyes flashing.

"No, you're not, Harry," she said. "I'm sorry, but you can't help me in anyway and I would feel responsible if anything happened to you. I don't want to hurt your feelings, Harry, but let's face it, my dear friend, you are eighty-five years old. I really would prefer it if you don't even consider staying. You would just be one more thing I would have to think about."

He knew she was right. All he could do if he stayed was give her moral support, and that wasn't worth much when the first thing the Simbas would do would be to keep them apart and not let them see, or talk to each other.

"Well, you're not staying either, Rosemary. As soon as this surgery is done we are all leaving," Tom said.

"Get out of here, Tom. You're in the way. I'm not leaving and that is final." She didn't have time to argue with him.

He accused her of being defiant and not submitting to his orders and those of the home office. He finished by saying, "Well, I will not be responsible for you if you stay, Rosemary."

She thought, and wanted to say, I'm not asking you to be responsible, Tom. Besides I think God is far more capable of being responsible for me than you are. Instead she said, "I understand, Tom."

"Come on, Harry," he said and stalked out.

"It's been a blessed and exciting time we've had together, Harry," she said as she slipped into the gown the infirmiere was holding for her.

"What can I say? I'd like to stay, but I understand how I might be more in the way than a help to you. You know what they're like. You know what you're doing."

She smiled a little. "I know what my God is like, Harry, yours and mine."

He nodded. "Until we meet," he said, the tears welling up in his eyes.

"Till we meet. Here or there, either way it will be blessed," she said pulling on the gloves and he turned and walked along the porch to his car while she went into surgery.

CHAPTER FIFTY-ONE

At the plantation David and the others heard the instructions from Kampala. They had the women start packing while he and Jacques called in the houseboys and all the foremen and told them everyone was to leave the plantation and go to villages so the Simbas would not know they worked for the mondeli. When all the natives were gone they hid their guns and some gold and silver in the manure pile behind the barn. They took what paper money they had and divided it equally between everybody so if anything happened to one of them, the others would still have a supply. They all crowded into two cars and started for the border.

It was a little after ten in the morning when they came to their first roadblock of logs across the road. There was a dozen Simbas there. Five had rifles and others just seemed to be lazing around under the trees. Those with rifles stood in front of the logs with their rifles pointed at the approaching cars.

Jacques and David got out and walked toward the Simbas. From the Simbas' reaction, it appeared they were the first people to be stopped. The Simbas didn't seem to know what they should do next. They had all been drinking and they were all shouting instructions at each other. They asked for a road pass but didn't know what a road pass looked like. But the leader did know that the passports David and Jacques showed them were not road passes. They argued and haggled for several minutes, but the leader insisted they would have to go back to Bunia to get the road pass.

Dave and Jacques were about to get back into the cars when two of the rebels stepped in front of them and ordered everyone else out of the cars. They started searching the cars, under the seats and dash and in the glove compartment. They opened the truck, taking out the suitcases, opened them, throwing the contents on the ground. One of the men took a bra, held it to his chest laughing and then threw it to one of the others. They started throwing the clothes back and forth to each other, laughing and shouting. One of the rebels grabbed the hat from off Suzanne's head and threw it to one of the others. Suzanne reached up trying to catch the cap as it flew through the air and the man that had taken it reached over and ripped open her blouse; the buttons popping through the button holes. She threw her arms across her chest protecting herself and shuddering with fear. Jacques and David started toward her, but two men pressed their rifles against their chests. Sarah instinctively started to run toward Suzanne to comfort her and then stopped, frightened that the same thing might happen to her. They were both fifteen years old and had grown up together and were closer than sisters. The four youngest children were huddled behind their mothers with their arms around each other. They looked around from time to time, but mostly they kept their heads buried in each other's shoulders. The older brothers Stanley and Antoine also had rifles pointed to their chests.

One of the Simbas grabbed Sarah and pushed her over next to Suzanne. He ripped open Sarah's blouse and then pulled it down so it acted as a rope binding her arms to her sides. One of the men reached down into the cleavage of her breast grabbing the bra and yanked so the clasps broke and the bra hung down across her stomach, leaving her breasts exposed. The one who had pulled the bra off grabbed one of her breast and laughed as he squeezed it. Both girls were bare from the waist up and the men were all standing around them squeezing their breast, not fondling them, but painfully torturing them, laughing at the girls crying.

Dave and Jacques stood there getting angrier, but they were helpless. All the men had rifles pressed against their chests and there was nothing they could do without getting killed. Monique and Elizabeth both had a man on each side holding them. With one hand the men held tightly onto the women's arms while they ran their other hand freely over the women's buttocks, stomachs and groins. Their hands were still on the outside of the skirts, but that was because they were more interested in what the others were doing to the girls. Dave knew he had to get their attention away from the girls before sexual desire and lust became stronger than revenge.

Dave started lowering his one arm. The rebel stopped looking at what was happening to the girls, poked him in the chest with the point of the rifle, and shouted at him to get his hand up. Dave nodded but kept slowly lowering his arm and the other rebels started looking his direction because one of them was shouting. Dave reached into his back pocket and pulled out his wallet. His guard reached for it but Dave jerked back his hand, turning the wallet upside down letting the five, ten, twenty and hundred frank notes drift slowly to the ground. His guard lowered his rifle trying the catch the money. The others, seeing one person getting all the money, lost interest in the women. They hadn't been paid in months and they hadn't seen that much money at one time in all their lives. As soon as the gun was taken away, Jacques took out his wallet and started throwing the money in the air. Stanley and Antoine did the same thing. Money was floating around on the wind and the rebels laid down their rifles and those who had been under the tree jumped up and started running after it.

The rebels jostled and pushed each other in their chase after the money and the whites rushed for the cars. Gravel flew as both cars backed up turning around. They had to back up twice to make the turn. Some of the Simbas started shouting at them and a couple started shooting. Everybody ducked down. Most of the bullets missed, but one came through the back window and out the front of Dave's car as they sped away. Monique and Stanley, who were sitting in front, started pounding out the shattered windshield so Dave could see. Five miles down the road, Dave blew the horn three times and both cars stopped to check everyone was all right and brush the glass chards from the seats. The girls had their blouses buttoned again but stood with their arms crossed protectively across their chests.

When they started up the long driveway to the house they knew something was wrong. They came to the wide, cobblestone drive with the great mango tree in the center. As the cars crawled slowly around the drive they could see all the windows had been smashed and the porch furniture broken. They went by the house and took the road to the barn. While the others stayed in the car, Dave and Jacques dug their plastic wrapped guns from the manure pile. The barn was empty and the milk cows and steers were gone from the pasture. They couldn't tell if the workers, or the Simbas, had taken the cattle away.

They drove back up to the house. They left the engines running with Monique behind the wheel of one car and Antoine ready to drive the other while Jacques and Dave entered the house. They climbed the steps slowly, looking both directions. Dave said, "They're gone. It looks like we left just at the right time." He put the pistol back in the holster and started through the house.

Inside all the furniture was smashed. The glass cabinets with the china had been pushed over. In the bedrooms, drawers were pulled out of dressers and clothes scattered all over. The Simbas had left behind the clothes they couldn't use. They walked out of the pantry to the back porch and both of them stopped and stared for an instant, and then Jacques turned and vomited. The head houseboy was hanging stretched between two pillars of the back porch. He had been expertly skinned alive. The skin was completely missing from his armpits to his hips. Blood and fluid ran from his red muscles and white tendons and down his buttocks and legs. Flies swarmed on the blood and raw flesh. Jacques stopped vomiting and straightened up. "Go make sure none of the others come back here," Dave said "and don't tell them what happened."

He waited until Jacques was gone and then he walked over to Faruna. He was still alive but unconscious. He took the pistol from his holster and put it to Faruna's head and pulled the trigger. He put the pistol back in the holster, took out his knife, cut the cord to one leg, and then to the other. He cut the cord to one arm and the body swung down and slammed against the pillar. With only one hand there was no way Dave could cut and hold the body at the same time. He cut the last cord and the body dropped, hitting the porch rail, and then rolled over and into the ditch. He jumped over the rail and taking one of the wrists pulled the body into a storage shed behind the house.

He came back and got the rest of them out of the cars. The closest boarder crossing by road was seventy miles away and everybody from all the mission stations and plantations would be headed for it. The best way out would be the thirty miles over the mountains to Lake Albert. They changed into hiking clothes and heavy boots and left with each of them, even the youngest, carrying a gun and their pockets bulging with ammunition. On their backs they each had a knapsack with extra sox, a jacket, and canned foods. Dave led the way with Jacques bringing up the rear. They walked up the slopes between the coffee trees and then left the plantation behind.

In the early afternoon they stopped at a small cluster of trees and had something to eat. Far below them they could see the plantation buildings and the neat rows of coffee plants. It was the middle of the rainy season and everything was alive and green. It had never looked more serene and beautiful.

"It's going to start raining soon. We'll stay here until night fall," Dave said. "Jacques and I will stand watch. The rest of you try and get some sleep. We'll travel at night when the Simbas are less likely to be on the move and sleep during the day."

It was dawn of the fifth day when they climbed the last hill and looked down on the lake below. The sun was just coming up on the other side, sending shafts of light through the clouds. Below them they could see the small clusters of huts in the villages and the canoes pulled up on shore. Across the lake they could see the line of the other shore, Uganda, safety.

Throughout the morning they kept looking down at the villages through the binoculars to see if there were any signs of the Simbas. They started down a little after noon and arrived in the village just before five. Even before they got to the village, the natives were coming out to greet them. The chief said that sometimes a patrol boat stopped, but he didn't know if they were the Simbas or the Nationalist, but there were no Simbas in the village.

They started across in three boats with outboard motors just after sunset. Once they heard a patrol boat approaching and they waited silently as it went by. In the darkness it chugged by with light shining from its windows. In the darkness there was no way of knowing who it was.

Day came and they drew close to the shore with villagers waving to them as they approached. As they got close the natives ran out and helped pull the boats to shore. They stepped out into safety.

CHAPTER FIFTY-TWO

Kamuwelli, son of Kitomolo, Chief of the tribe, stood in front of his chief's hut. His father had died ten years ago, five years before Independence, and he had become chief in his father's place. For a few years there had been pleasure in being chief, but that all ended when Independence came. With Independence everyone wanted to be chief. There was a way a person could become a kind of chief if the people voted for them. He didn't fully understand voting, or what kind of a chief voting made a person, but he worked hard going to the villages and getting the people to promise to vote for him. People knew him, and his father, Kitomolo, and his father before him, the great Ronzozo. The people clasped hands in agreement and vowed they would put their mark for him. But they had broken their vow and had not voted for him, because if they did he would have been elected as a representative to his provincial assembly. He didn't understand what a provincial assembly was, but he did know his people didn't vote for him.

Almost as soon as independence was declared, tribes started fighting against tribes and chiefs against chiefs. Chiefs of tribes that had once been part of the Nation of Five Tribes were now enemies, each one trying to be greater than the other. Those who had been elected to power tried to remove those who were chiefs in the tribes and villages. Chiefs retaliated by having elected officials removed by having them killed. It was no longer possible to know who would be in power from one day to the next. Now standing in front of his chief's hut, he knew his time had come. Simbas had gone through the villages of his tribe and then finally had accused him to his face in front of his village of being an enemy of the revolution. He didn't know exactly what it was he had done that was against the revolution, or what he could do to correct his error. He just knew they would be coming soon to kill him.

As soon as he saw them entering the village with their bunduki in their hands and wearing the monkey fur armlets, he went into his hut and took off his mondeli clothing of khaki shorts and shirt. He put his leopard skin around his waist and the black and white monkey skin over his shoulders. He could, with total pride, be scornful of them when he was dressed in his manhood leopard skin and chief's monkey skin. For all their talk of getting rid of every mondeli influence, they still carried the mondeli's bunduki and wore mondeli clothes. He took his spear and went and stood at the entrance of his house.

He stood straight with his spear in his hand, the butt of it resting on the ground next to his right foot. In his left hand he held his gangilo. He waited calmly for the bunduki that were pointed at him to speak their death. He wondered if he would hear the sound before the bullet reached him. He was not afraid of death, but rather disappointed and a little sad. They would install someone else not related to him in the place of chief and would not even bother to burn down the old house and build a new one for the new chief. Some of his wives would be afraid, and would deny they had been married to him.

His father, Kitomolo, had lived a long time and Kamuwelli had grown sons with sons of their own when Kamuwelli became chief. Things had already begun to change by then and there was nothing he could have done about it. He had been chief for less than ten seasons and he wondered if there was something he could have done. He felt somewhere he had failed, but he didn't know exactly where it was. He would be going to his ancestors soon and would have to account to them. He would have to explain to them how he came to be the last of the line of chiefs that had for so long ruled over the Five Tribes.

CHAPTER FIFTY-THREE

By the middle of November the world had gotten tired of Gbenye's threats and refusal to negotiate for the release of the hostages. Intelligence reports showed conditions were so bad in Stanleyville that black hostages were killed daily and their flesh sold for food in the market. It was believed the white hostages were all still alive.

On November 24, 1964, Tshombe's mercenaries launched a heavy attack from all directions against Stanleyville. At the same time, six hundred Belgian paratroopers were dropped into the center of the city from United States planes. Mbekede was informed as soon as the push started at the outskirts of the city and, almost immediately, heard the sound of the planes overhead. He went down the hall to Gbenye's office, but Gbenye and all his staff were gone and none of the soldiers knew where they were. From a window he saw the paratroopers dropping. He gave orders to release all the white hostages and as they started out of the building he shouted over the loudspeakers to the guards and soldiers, "Kill the hostages. Shoot them all. Don't let them escape. Kill them all: men, women and children, kill them all." But the paratroopers were just beginning to land and the rebels first started shooting at the paratroopers and then turned and ran. The hostages streaming out of the prison started to run for cover. Mbekede grabbed an assault rifle and ran out of the building. Firing from the hip, he started mowing down the hostages. A sharpshooter paratrooper took aim and fired. The bullet entered the front of Mbekede's head, shattering his face and blowing the back of his head away.

The Simbas were no match for the force sent against them that day and were soon throwing down their guns and their monkey skins and disappearing into the population of the city and then fleeing to the shelter of the great Ituri forest. Gbenye escaped and was never heard of again. Mbekede had been able to kill twenty-nine hostages with the assault rifle before he was killed himself. Later that day the bodies of more than fifty hostages that had been cannibalized were found.

After it was all over a Belgian officer, who had seen the massacre of the hostages, stood looking down at Mbekede's body and said, "He came out of that building over there shouting orders. Was he anyone important?"

One of the natives who was going to drag his body away for disposal said, "That is for the ancestors to know."

CHAPTER FIFTY-FOUR

It was 10:22 when she heard the truck grinding its way up the hill. It had been three days since the Simbas arrived and had smashed all the equipment in the dispensary, including the generator, and made her prisoner. The Simbas guarding her heard it, too, and roused themselves enough to appear to be guarding the house. The truck made the turn to stop at the front door. Simbas jumped out of the back; the replacements for those who had been there the day and night before.

From the passenger's side a heavy man, dressed in complete fatigues and a peaked military cap with a star on it, lowered himself ponderously to the ground. He stood next to the truck, his hands on his hips and shouted, "Abominable Mondeli, come out."

Rosemary stepped out onto the porch, put her helmet on, and went over to him. Under the peak of his cap she could see the tribal marking along his forehead. He glared at her through squinted eyes. "Don't I know you?" she asked looking up at him. "You are Mololamu, first son of Chief Lamuwi."

"I am chief now. My father is dead."

"I am sorry to hear that. If you had brought him here we might have been able to stop the sickness. And your brothers, are they well?"

"Would you have cured him with fire like you did our village?" he asked sarcastically ignoring the question about his brothers. "I have come to see the sick. I think you say there are sick here when there are no sick so we will not kill you. Show me."

The families on the hospital porch grew silent as they approached, some disappearing quietly into the shrubbery and down the hill, the rest eyeing them fearfully as they walked by. Mololamu walked into each of the patient's rooms, looking at them critically. It was obvious they were seriously ill. He didn't talk to any of them. Back out on the porch he turned to Yoane and the other two, and said, "You are people of the mondeli. When she dies, you die."

"We are batu-na-dawa. Infirmiere," Yoane said. "We do what we must do to help the sick."

"You are of the mondeli's medicine, not of our medicine. You will die." He turned to Rosemary and said, "You will care for the sick, but when they are well I will burn your village just as you burned mine," he said waving his arm to take in all the buildings on Hospital Hill. "Until then, I will burn one building every day," he said and turned away.

She watched him walk away thinking he must have been a teenager when the village was burned, but she couldn't specifically remember him from the burning. It was from Doctor's funeral that she remembered him.

***

She was standing on the back porch the next day seeing the columns of smoke rising from the other end of the station when she heard the truck grinding its way up the hill. She went inside to get her helmet and put it on as she crossed the front porch. She was waiting for him. When the truck came to a stop Mololamu climbed laboriously down from the passenger side and said. "I have set the school on fire for so it was I spoke it."

"So you spoke it, so it is I see it."

"It has come to me that one of your sick has died. You could not save him."

"The funeral is this afternoon. Mololamu should come and see that there is no fear in his family for he has gone to heaven and is in the presence of God. "

"There is no heaven," he scoffed. "He is with his ancestors. But they will have nothing to do with him for he has brought great shame on his family for believing the lies of the mondeli. Forever he will walk alone, for none on the other side will have anything to do with him for the shame he has brought on them."

"No, Mololamu, He walks among the angels and is of the family of God."

"The God of the mondeli? I have heard of your God. I have been to the Catholic school at the post. But I have learned the truth about the mondeli from Mbekede. Your God is weak and cannot save you. And when I am ready, I will kill you and we will all know your God does not care for you."

"Mololamu, son of Chief Lamuwi, do you think it a great thing to kill me?" she asked, her soft gray eyes blazing. "It is no great thing. You are large and I am small. You are strong and I am weak. You are young and I am old. You are a man and I am a woman. So to kill me will be no great thing. But I tell you now, Mololamu, you shall not kill me. I shall live to see my children and my children's children. I shall go to my grave in peace and you will know my God has delivered me, and I shall live to tell of it after you are dead." She wondered how she had dared say that, couldn't believe she had said it, and then she thought that maybe she would be rescued. It was quite possible. The Simbas could be driven out of the area before all the patients were better. With no radio she had no idea what was going on in other places. Maybe the United Nations and Tshombe's forces were defeating the rebels and soon Mololamu and his followers would be heading for cover.

He threw his head back and laughed and then turned and climbed into the truck.

***

She was jolted awake by the sound of gunfire right next to her. Usually she heard them coming before they got to the bedroom. They were shooting around the room, laughing at her startled shock. She didn't know if they entered quietly specifically to startle her, or if she had been so tired she didn't hear them enter the house and her bedroom. With their guns they motioned for her to get up. She was embarrassed they found her lying down. She stood up and they motioned her over against the wall. For a moment she thought they were going to shoot her, but instead they started shooting at the bed. They strafed back and forth across the bed. The mattress actually bounced with the impact of the bullets, the material being ripped apart, bits and pieces of it filling the air, feathers from the pillows floating erratically. They stopped and left the room, laughing hilariously at what they had done.

She sat down on a stool and stared numbly at the destroyed bed. The dust and flying feathers had settled. There were patches of the bed that appeared to be intact, but most of the bed looked like it had been clawed apart with the springs popping out through the torn material. In the light of the single kerosene lantern the springs looked like curly worms crawling out of the blue and white mattress. She wondered if it would be better if she turned the mattress over and decided it wasn't worth the effort of trying to find out. The bullets probably went through the bottom as well as the top and when she turned it over the springs would just pop out on the other side. Well, there are plenty of beds at the hospital, she thought defiantly, and grabbing the lantern headed for the hospital.

The Simbas followed her as they always did and then she realized that beyond the Simbas there were others following her. Yoane was suddenly beside her. "Is Madamu all right?" he asked.

"God is good. I am well. How is it you are here?"

"We have people watching you. There is nothing we can do, but we watch and pray. When we hear the shooting we all come to see that you are still well."

"Did you know someone put food in my house during the funeral?"

"We knew of it."

"Say my thanks to those that did that."

"It is not needed. That you are alive is thanks enough."

"They shot my bed. Back and forth so it is a bed no more. I shall sleep at the hospital the rest of the night."

"When it is day we will make up one of the rooms at the hospital for you, or we will move one of the hospital beds to the house if Madamu wishes it."

She thought about it for a moment. Somehow she didn't feel right about letting the Simbas drive her out of her house. To spend one night in the hospital was one thing, but to move there was quite another. "We shall see," she said, but she knew she was not going to move into the hospital permanently.

***

Rosemary Schwartz sat in the broken chair in the living room reading a study by Oswald Chambers. It had been three weeks since the Simbas arrived and the last of the patients had been discharged the day before. It was hard to concentrate. She would read a couple of sentences and either start to fall asleep or look up because she thought she had heard something. She had started for the hospital again about nine o'clock. She didn't have anything to do there. She had no reason to go there other than she had gotten tired of sitting in the house. But as soon as she stepped off the porch she was confronted with rebels telling her that that there were no patients, she was not to leave the house. When Mololamu arrived, he would decide if she could leave the house.

She heard the truck starting up the hill, stood up, picked up her helmet, and started out the door. At the edge of the front porch she put on her helmet and walked a short distance into the front yard. If she was going to be killed, she wanted it to be where everyone could see her. The truck didn't come all the way to the house like it usually did, but stopped at the top of the road halfway between the house and the hospital.

Mololamu lowered himself from the cab; the relief Simbas jumping down from the back gathering around him. He said something to one of his men who came running toward her. He stopped a safe distance from her and gleefully ordered her, and the men surrounding her, to get over to the hospital.

"You have no sick in the house of medicine," Mololamu said.

She didn't answer him.

"If there are no sick, then there is no need for the house of medicine."

She looked at him, knowing what he was thinking, and felt worse about the burning of the hospital than she had about being killed. "There is always need for a house of medicine. People don't stop getting sick because the mondeli are gone. There are those who could use the things of the house of medicine for the good of the people."

"We have our own batu-na-dawa. We need nothing that is of the mondeli."

He walked her to the hospital, nodded to his men, and they started smashing the plate glass windows of the operating room. Some rode gurneys around the porch, laughing and waving to the others. They smashed everything they couldn't move with sledgehammers, threw the autoclave and baby incubators through the windows down the cliff. When they were through, they started setting the mattresses and bedding on fire.

Smoke poured out of the hospital rooms, blackening the whitewashed walls, and she heard the crackling of the furnishings catching fire. Flames started coming from the windows and reached up to the open beams of the roof. Someone went by her with a firebrand that he threw to the thatch roof of the dispensary. It caught quickly. It became too hot to stay there and they moved away from the heat. The foot thick thatch of the dispensary was consumed quickly, leaving the rafters burning until they fell in setting the benches and tables in the dispensary on fire.

He made her stay there for more than an hour. There was an ache in the pit of her stomach as she watched. From time to time she would look down so as not to look at the flames, the smoke, and the settling soot. Mololamu would yell at her to look. One time when she didn't look up he reached over and grabbed her chin, raising her head so she had to look.

When there was nothing left except coals, burning beams and gray smoke rising straight in the still heat of the day, Mololamu said. "You may go to your house now. If you come out of the house you will be shot. I have told my men."

She walked back to the house, the new contingent of Simbas following her. Behind her she heard the truck start heading down the hill and she wondered if they were going to set other buildings on fire. When the church and the school and other building had been burned she had been angry. But with the burning of the hospital she felt hurt. It was like something had been ripped from inside her, something she didn't even really know was there, something that had been growing there for forty years.

***

In the darkness she heard the front door open and she quickly sat up looking at her watch. It was early. Eleven forty-seven. They were usually later. She turned up the lantern and just managed to be standing when they entered the room. They started shouting at her, accusing her of killing people in her hospital and asking her questions to which she had no answers. Between questions they would fire short bursts, laughing when she jumped at the sound of the guns.

"Where is the money? You stayed here to protect your money. Where is it? Tell us, or we will kill you."

"I have no money and I have no fear of death." They left after forty-five minutes. When she saw the last one through the front door she turned down the lantern and flopped down on the bed.

It was a terrible dream. Mololamu was standing over her ordering her out of bed, and then it wasn't a dream, he was really there. "Get up, Madamu Munganga." She had not heard the truck arrive. She sat up while swinging her legs over the side and stood, aware that there was a brightness coming from the living room that eliminated any need for her to turn up the kerosene lantern. She looked at her watch. It was two in the morning. She thought that was late enough at night that there was not likely to be any of the mission natives keeping watch over her house. Mololamu was the only one in the room and that, too, was different. He had never been involved in one of the night harassments before. Usually the others all came in laughing and shouting at her. "In there," he said pointing to the living room door with his rifle.

She walked into the brightness of two Coleman lanterns, one set at each end of the mantle piece, filling the room with their bright, white light. Opposite the fireplace, standing along the front wall were two more Simbas, smirking at her as she entered the room. They were quieter than usual and she realized they were sober. Mololamu took his place next to them, indicating with his gun that she was to stand along the opposite wall. Suddenly the room was filled with the deafening sound of their automatic weapons. She instinctively turned toward the wall, her hands over her head. She stood between the fireplace and the wall to her bedroom thinking, If this is it, well I'm ready, Lord. At the same time she was saying aloud, "The angels of the Lord encamp round about those that fear Him and delivers them."

She squinted one eye open. All around her the plaster was falling away from where the bullets were hitting the wall. It seemed they were firing on either side of her and above her, the plaster from the wall falling on the top of her head and shoulders. They're playing games with me. Trying to scare me, she thought, but the expression on their faces was not that of someone teasing, or trying to scare someone else. They kept firing, the shots coming from the three automatic rifles sounding like a roar. They were strafing back and forth across her, and yet she was not being hit. Above the roar of the shooting was a purring, whirring sound like a lion purring, only different.

Gradually, she became aware of them and she was filled with a strange awe. There, in front of her, between her and the Simbas, there were men. They were tall, but they were not like any men she had ever seen before. Nor was she sure they were really there. They were entirely white, a blue-white that she could see through, but they were moving between her and the Simbas. The guns were aimed right at her, but none of the bullets were hitting her. Bullets were hitting all around her. She saw one of the figures in white reach over and take the end of a rifle and point it away from her.

One by one the Simbas stopped firing, their automatic rifles sinking slowly to point at the floor, staring at her unbelievingly. Mololamu was the last to stop firing and when he slowly lowered his rifle, the figures in white disappeared. She started to smile, Mololamu and the Simbas staring at her unbelievingly. She smiled, tears streaming down her face, and said, "Mololamu, my God will not let you kill me."

He turned and ran from the room, his men following him, leaving their gasoline lanterns behind. She stood for a while in the brightness of the room, hoping the angels would come back. She had experienced "the power of the age to come." She had been permitted to glimpse into the realm of the heavenlies. She was awed and humbled and thought she understood a little what Shadrach, Meshach, and Abednego had experienced in the fiery furnace; what Daniel had experienced in the Lion's den, and what Peter had experienced when he was led out of jail. He had granted her to understand what they had understood. Her God had sent His angels to deliver her. She stood there filled with awe, reverence, and gratitude. She stepped away from the wall finally, and felt a rock under her foot, a piece of plaster, or brick. She looked down and saw a thumb-size pebble, gray in color. She bent over and picked one up. From the feel of it she knew it was a piece of lead, misshapen, and flattened from hitting something. She clutched it tightly in her fist, stepping reverently over the rest of them, and went, and turned off the Coleman lanterns. She went back and lay down on the bed. She was at peace, with no fear, but she could not fall asleep. She was too filled with wonder. She wished there was someone she could tell about it, but she knew that most people would not believe her. It was between her and her God and those blessed few who could believe for such things.

***

The sun was well up when she awoke. She sat up, startled by how much light was outside her windows. She looked at her watch. Nine o'clock. She had slept soundly, and more than that, peacefully. Things began to come back to her and she looked in the palm of her hand, but the piece of lead wasn't there. It must have been a dream. She rushed into the other room. The two Coleman lanterns were still on the mantle and on the floor, in front of where she had been standing against the wall, were the slugs. She knelt down, her old bones and joints protesting silently, her knees hurting against the hard, brick floor. She started picking up the slugs, but there were too many of them. With both hands full with spent metal, she went over and got the cosmetic case. She dropped what she had in her hands inside the case and went over to pick up the rest of them. All in all, there were eighty-six of them, not to mention the hundreds imbedded in the wall. She knelt there, her knees aching, running her fingers through the slugs as a child would run fingers through marbles.

She suddenly realized that it was getting late. If he were on time, Mololamu would be arriving soon. She closed the lid to the cosmetic case, took it into the bedroom and hid it under the bed. Sliding the case under the bed, she saw the one that had fallen from her hand when she fell asleep. She opened the case and dropped it inside with the others. She went to the bathroom to wash up and came out trying to brush wrinkles out of her uniform.

She got her Bible and headed for the living room. She stopped short when she stepped through the doorway. She hadn't noticed it before, but the wall was pockmarked from floor to ceiling with bullet holes. The area immediately around where she had been standing was almost bare of plaster from a concentration of firing, while there was not a mark on the wall directly behind where she had been. In the bathroom she had thought she would have to clean up the mess they had made, but now she knew she was not going to touch it. The plaster on the floor was going to stay right where it had fallen. To sweep the floor would in some way desecrate what had happened.

She walked over to the fireplace and took the two gasoline lanterns from the mantel. She walked out of the front door and set them on the ground just beyond the large, flat stones that formed a bridge across the ditch that ran all around the house. The Simbas were more alert than she had ever seen them at this time of day and they eyed her cautiously.

"These belong to Chief Mololamu. He forgot them here last night. See he gets them," she said and went back into the house and sat down to read her Bible.

She heard the truck starting up the hill and she stood and went to the door to watch. She had no intention of going to him if he called, but as far as she could tell, Mololamu wasn't in the passenger's seat. The rebels jumped out of the truck and those who had been on duty ran to climb in and the truck drove away.

When she turned back, Yoane and Pastor Alibe were standing in the doorway to the dining room. They had come in through the back while the Simbas were changing the guard. "Madamu is well," Pastor Alibe said. It was both a statement and a question.

"Yes. I am well. The angels were here last night. They stopped the bullets from hitting me," she said pointing to the wall.

They stood looking at the wall, nodding their heads solemnly, though they didn't seem at all astounded by it. "So it is we prayed, so it is it happened," Pastor Alibe said finally. "There is talk among the Simbas that you cannot be killed. We are praying now that they will let you go."

For an instant she wondered if she wanted to be let go. It was here she had seen with open eyes the salvation of the Lord. She had been uniquely privileged. Nevertheless, what she had seen had not made God more real and precious to her than He had been before, just more astounding.

"We shall keep you company until the night comes," Yoane said and they both sat down cross-legged on the floor.

She sat, understanding they couldn't be seen leaving in the daylight without the chance of being shot. She thought how nice it would be to have someone to talk to, especially with two men who had prayed, and believed, and seen their prayers answered. They would leave after dark when they would not be seen by the Simbas.

CHAPTER FIFTY-FIVE

Shimmering heat waves rose off the three lane gravel road that was the main road through the town of Yei, distorting the goats, chickens, people and vehicles that moved along or across it. There was no wind and the heat rising from the road and the tin roofs was like invisible smoke that burned the throat and lungs. In the center of a cluster of buildings in the middle of town was the hotel. It was more a bar than a hotel. The whole lower floor, surrounded by a porch, was a drinking room with two bars on opposite sides. There was a space void of tables and chairs that ran the full length of the room from the front double-doors to the back doorway of the same size. That open space divided the natives from the whites. Inside, the fans caused a stirring in the hot air, creating the impression it was cooler than on the porch. The hotel had electricity, but no running water.

On the porch of the hotel, Harry VanVeldt sat with his son David at a rail-side table. A board with chess pieces was set up between them, but no one had moved a piece for more than an hour. Harry looked tired; his ancient face topped with thin white hair was resolute despite the fatigue. Across from him, David kept running his hand through his long blond hair. Harry and David were the only occupants of the porch.

So far the news from Abaru had been good. They had been in Yei for five days and from the drivers of trucks that came through from Abaru, they were sure Rosemary was still alive. They didn't know anything more than that. None of the people they had talked to had been anywhere near the mission station. The Simbas were still in control of the government post and the mission and the drivers didn't want to go near there or give the Simbas any reason to be suspicious of them. What the two on the porch were waiting for was someone Harry knew he could trust.

In Kampala, people had told Harry he was too old; that there was nothing he could do. Tom Wright had specifically ordered him not to leave Kampala. He had asked the questions tentatively, discretely, "Don't you think we should maybe go back to Juba or Yei and see if we can get her out?" He was testing to see if there was anyone who might be willing to go with him. It was not that he was afraid to go alone, but he had gradually come to admit that at eighty-five, there were some things he couldn't do as easily as he used to. His left hand, disfigured with arthritis, was limited in what it could do. Changing a flat tire, which in the past would have been nothing, now was a chore.

And it would have been nice to have someone to help him with the driving. But when he had been ordered not to leave Kampala, he had parked his car two blocks away from where they were staying so no one would hear him starting the motor if he were to sneak away in the night.

The Central Africa Mission people were staying at the CAM rest house and David and his family was staying at a hotel three blocks away. He had been to see them every day since the escape so he was certain they wouldn't think it strange if he stopped by to see them again. He hadn't told David what he was planning because he didn't think David should be separated from his family right away. But within a few minutes of being there, Monique had said, "Dad, what are you up to?"

"Up to?" he exclaimed trying to act ignorant. "Can't I come and visit my son and my favorite daughter-in-law and my grandchildren without you getting suspicious?"

"You were here earlier than usual this afternoon and just the way you answered the question makes one suspicious."

"So? I wanted to see you all again," he said shrugging his shoulders.

"Dad, you're fidgeting. That's not like you. David, he's up to something. Find out what it is."

"I know what it is. He's planning to go back and see if he can get Aunt Rosemary out."

Harry looked from one to the other.

"Reverend Wright talked to me. Said you might try something like that and I was supposed to try and stop you."

"I see." Harry pursed his lips, nodded his head a little looking down at the floor and then looked up and said, "Don't try to stop me, David. It won't do any good."

"I'm not going to stop you, Dad. In fact, I'm coming with you. I already have my duffel packed."

"You didn't tell me anything about this," Monique said.

"I didn't want to worry you. I wasn't sure if Dad was really going to go or not. You know I have to go with him," Dave said.

"I know," Monique said resigned to the idea.

"You're not coming with me," Harry said. "You belong here with your family."

"Don't forget, Dad, Aunt Rosemary helped bring me into this world."

They left the next morning. He was filled with a sense of gratitude to David for coming, to Monique and his grandchildren for letting David come, and to God that David had come back to the Congo instead of staying in the States like his other children had. He had a migraine and it was hot, but he was sitting across the table from his son and for that he was exceedingly grateful.

Most of the time since they had gotten to Yei they sat at the same table, talking or playing chess, but looking up every time they heard a vehicle approaching from the direction of the Zaire border.

Harry stood up slowly because of the pain in his joints, certain it was the truck he'd been waiting for long before he could read the name, Papadopolis et Fils, on the door of the cab. It was a blue, fairly new GMC ten-ton truck with a white canvas over the back. David ran into the road, Harry following behind, and stood, waving their arms, forcing it to stop. The truck pulled over to the side and David jumped onto the running board on the driver's side while Harry climbed into the passenger's seat. The driver looked at him frightened. On one side was a one-arm man holding on with his one good arm and on the other side was a white haired old man. There was nothing to be frightened of really, except these were frightening times.

"You are Imbego Papadopolis, the son of the son of Leo Papadopolis, is that not so," Harry said.

It was a statement more than a question. The young man nodded.

"Is Madamu Schwartz still alive?"

"It is said she is. I have not seen her, but there are those who say they have seen her."

"Are there still sick people at the house of medicine?"

"I do not know. I think there is maybe one left. Maybe he is already gone. It is said she will be killed when all the sick are gone."

"Do you think she could escape?"

"Oh, no! I am told she is watched day and night. It is said Chief Mololamu himself has said he will kill her."

The statement that Rosemary would be killed was not unexpected, yet it was a shock to hear the words said. "Is there no way someone might be able to get her out? Will the Simbas accept money for her? Can they be bribed to let her go?"

Imbego sat with both hands on the steering wheel, his head turned toward Harry, his forehead pulled into a worried frown. "It may be the Simbas would do that. They have nothing to do in Abaru and they have not been paid for a long time. I, and all my brothers, have to be careful. They want things from the store, but they cannot pay so they take it and say they will pay later. It may be they would sell her," he said nodding seriously.

"How much will it cost?" David asked leaning down to speak through the window.

Imbego shrugged his shoulders. "There are many who would have to be paid. The little people would have to be paid only a little. The important people would have to be paid much. Chief Mololamu would require much. I do not know what it would cost. I have never done this before." The last sentence was spoken as though it was an interesting business concept that had not occurred to him.

"Where are you going now?" Harry asked.

"I go to Juba. I take oil seeds. I get supplies."

"How long will you be there?"

"In tomorrow I come back."

"Good. You go to Juba. Hurry back. When you get back to Abaru, you ask how much it will cost. Will you do that?"

He nodded his head hesitantly, cautiously, as though considering the danger involved.

"Do you know who I am?"

"Yes. You are Bwana Van."

"Are there any who will help you in this?"

He nodded again and said, "My brothers and my father and uncles. All know you were good friend of Leopopo, the father of my father's father. Many people in Abaru do not like the Simbas. But we must be careful. We cannot let them think we care about Madamu Schwartz. We cannot let them know you are wanting her. If they think you are wanting her, they will ask much. If they think you do not much care to get her, they will want to get a little money for her instead of killing her, they will ask little. It may be they will think they can get more pleasure from the money you pay for her than the happiness of killing her."

Harry nodded, thinking Imbego was probably as good a trader as Leo had been. He slapped Imbego on the knee in a fatherly sort of way and said, "You go to Juba and do your business and I will start getting the money to buy Madamu Schwartz. I will always be at this hotel," he said pointing out the windshield. "As soon as you have news come back. I will pay you for your time." He opened the door and climbed out of the cab while David jumped off the running board. Imbego pulled away and they stood by the side of the road watching the truck leave, headed for Juba.

CHAPTER FIFTY-SIX

The afternoon sun had forced them away from the table right next to the rail, but they still sat where they could watch the only road into Yei from Abaru. They watched as a Volkswagen bug, faded now from ten years in the African sun and covered with dust, made its way in front of the hotel and then turned into the drive that would take it to the back of the hotel. Through the distortion of the dirty windshield, Harry thought the face looked familiar, but he knew he was imagining every face coming from that direction to look familiar.

It had been four days since they had talked with Imbego and they were beginning to be anxious. They had watched the Volkswagen with interest, but what they were really looking for was a Papadopolis truck. They were surprised then to see Imbego come through the front doors from inside the hotel. He walked to their table quickly and sat down without even returning their greeting. "I have talked with Chief Mololamu. He is even now on his way to meet with you. He is ready to sell Madamu Schwartz to you."

"How much is he asking?"

"It is said he tried to kill Madamu Schwartz and could not do it. I do not know how it happened, but that is the talk."

"How much is he asking?" Harry asked again, suddenly afraid that they might not have enough money.

"I have talked with him." There was the sound of a car on the road and Imbego looked the direction of the sound. When he was satisfied it was not Mololamu's truck he turned back. "It would not be good for him to see me talking to you. He said to me he will ask two thousand American. Zaire money no good."

Harry let out a soft whistle. He didn't have that much.

"It is my thinking he will let Madamu Schwartz go for five hundred. He has not said this, but she is an embarrassment to him. If he gets money, he can say he did not want to kill her, but kept her alive to get the money. Do not agree to what he asks until he cannot ask for any less. I must go now. I will come back when he is gone," he said getting up, looked anxiously down the road and disappeared into the hotel and to his car parked behind it.

It was hard for Harry to contain his excitement and his mind was racing on how best to deal with Mololamu. He had never been able to drive a bargain or haggle over the price of an item.

They saw the truck, a battered old Dodge, heading for the hotel, and they knew it was Mololamu even before it stopped. Mololamu got out of the passenger's side, followed by his driver and three other men from the back of the truck. They climbed the stairs, Mololamu heading straight for the table, his men following him. When he was five feet away Harry and David stood up and Harry heard himself saying, "Chief Mololamu, you know me. I am Harry VanVeldt. You come to talk with me. That is good." Mololamu nodded. "And this is my son. Do you know him?"

Mololamu scrutinized David, taking in the blond hair, tanned skin and missing left arm. "I do not know him."

"It may be you do not know him with knowing, but you know him with hearing. He is the one adopted by Kusala, brother to the great Chief Kitomolo, before the time of the great dryness. You have also heard how, when he was just of sixteen seasons, he killed a great Kudu with only one throw of the spear. That was during the great dryness when many died because there was no food. It was the talk around many cooking fires. He was taught by the great hunter Kusala, son to Chief Ronzozo, brother to Chief Kitomolo. You see this," Harry said grabbing David's stump just barely visible below the edge of the short sleeve. "The arm was blown away in the great war of the mondeli. Sit down with me Chief Mololamu. We have much to talk about, for our families go back many seasons."

Mololamu's eyes narrowed and he motioned his men away as he lowered himself heavily into the chair.

"It is said you have burned houses on my hill and made one of my people prisoner. I do not know if that is true, but so it is I have heard it. If there is truth in what is said, then you have broken the cut of blood between me and the great Chief Ronzozo," Harry said.

He held out his left hand, showing the scar of the incision made over fifty years ago. "Look, there is the mark of the covenant I made with Chief Ronzozo."

Mololamu bent forward a little to look at the extended hand.

Harry grabbed David's stub of a left arm and raised it a little toward Mololamu. "If his hand were still here you would see the mark of his adoption to Kusala. My son is by blood covenant of the brother to Kitomolo, son of the son of Ronzozo."

"Ronzozo is dead. Kitomolo, his son, is dead. The nation of the Five Tribes is no more. All that now is, is Simba," Mololamu said sitting up a little straighter and drawing in his breath. "What was between you and Ronzozo is no more."

Harry waited for a moment, staring at Mololamu and then said as a patient teacher reminding a student of a forgotten truth, "Chief Mololamu, the cutting of blood is not like the agreement made over the cooking fire, or even the council fire. The cutting of blood does not end when a man dies, or a tribe is no more. It is forever." He put his hand on David's shoulder. My son, and my son's sons, must keep the covenant for as long as it is remembered. When I cut the blood with Ronzozo, and our bloods mixed, I was in covenant with every other person who cut the blood with Ronzozo. Did your father, Chief Lamuwi, cut the blood with Chief Ronzozo or with his son, Chief Kitomolo?"

He paused to give time for Mololamu to answer, knowing that in all likelihood somewhere along the line there had probably been a cutting of the blood. Mololamu stared back at him, eyes narrowed, and Harry knew he was not at all happy with what he was hearing.

"Mololamu, you are the son of a man who cut the blood with a man who cut the blood with me. You are in covenant with a mondeli, Mololamu. Did you know, Mololamu, that the blood I cut with the great Chief Ronzozo, was not just to me and my children after me, but also to all those who would join me at the Hill of the Two Streams. The Madamu Munganga Schwartz is under my covenant."

"She burned my village."

"Chief Kitomolo himself said your village was to be burned. I was there. Your village was full of disease. The disease had to be killed. The only way to do that was to burn the village. You are alive today because of the medicine given to you by Munganga Schwartz and the land given you by Kitomolo was better than the land of the old village.

"Mololamu, if a cutting of blood between people of different tribes is sacred, then it is not so if cut with the mondeli? One who breaks a covenant must give account of it to the ancestors, is that not so Mololamu?"

"Madamu Schwartz is well," he said. "We have not harmed her."

"That is good," Harry said leaning back in the chair. "Mololamu, I would like the Madamu Schwartz brought to me. If he will do it, it is my desire that Imbego Papadopolis bring her to me." Harry got almost chatty. "Know you, Mololamu, that the mother of Imbego's father's father was daughter to Kitomolo? So he, too, is of the covenant."

"I did not know that."

"It is so. She was of the name Obrica. But it is hard to know them all, for Kitomolo had many wives, and many children by his wives."

"Of a truth, that is so," Mololamu said, hoping the conversation was taking another direction.

Harry reached into his top bush-jacket pocket and took out five $20.00 bills. "Mololamu, I would like to pay you to help Madamu Schwartz come to me. Here is one hundred dollars American. I will ask Imbego to bring her to me. When he does, I will give him four hundred dollars more to give to you. Of it all that will be five hundred for you to help Madamu Schwartz come to me. You can trust Imbego to give you your money. You can trust me to give him the money, for are we not all brothers by the cutting of blood?"

"But you are a mondeli."

"That is so," Harry said nodding his head and looking as though the thought that he was white had just occurred to him. "I do not know if it is so, but it is said by all the Logos, and by the Lugbara, and by the Kakwa, and even by the Azande, which all other tribes agree are the lowest of all tribes on the earth, that if one breaks the covenant, the evil he did will come on him four times greater. I do not know if that is true, for I have never broken a covenant, but I would not want any evil I do you to come on me four times."

Mololamu reached over and took the money. "It may be I can help you," he said and stood up, shouted at his men, and headed for his truck.

CHAPTER FIFTY-SEVEN

Rosemary saw the boys playing in the front yard kicking the ball back and forth as they had done so often in the past three weeks. Almost every day they would come by, leaning into a window to shout taunts at her so the Simbas would not get suspicious. When they left there would be a couple of hard cooked eggs, or a tomato, or an ear of corn or something else to eat. She watched them, smiling to herself, wondering what it was they would leave this time. In addition to the anticipation of what she would find on her windowsill, there was pleasantness of having friendly people close to her.

They bumped, shoved and kicked, so full of life and energy. Sometimes the ball would get kicked away and they would all run as fast as they could after it. She watched them moving the ball, kick by kick, closer to the house. The Simbas sat on the rocks in the shade of the mango trees. A couple of them got up when the ball came their way and kicked it back to the mototo and then sat back down on the rock laughing.

The ball flew away through the entrance to the porch as it had so many times before and she wondered that the Simbas didn't get suspicious. The boys came running onto the porch, pushing and shoving each other to get to the ball. They kicked it back and forth along the front porch and then the ball bounced around the corner. She went from the living room to the bedroom waiting to see the hands come through the window. Four hands, one at a time, cautiously put something on the windowsill. It looked like three eggs and a tomato.

After checking that no Simbas were on the porch, or looking her direction, she went over and picked up the eggs. When she picked up the tomato, she saw a small, folded, piece of white paper under it. She thought it was probably a note of encouragement from Pastor Alibe. She unfolded it, a half sheet of paper that had been folded four times until it was only one by two inches square. It was dirty and damp from the sweating hand that had carried it. Tears came to her eye as she saw that it was in English, written in block letters.

AT 10 A.M TOMORROW A GREEN VOLKSWAGEN WILL ARRIVE. BE PREPARED TO LEAVE. PACK ONLY THE BAREST NECESSITIES IN A SMALL CASE. AS SOON AS YOU SEE THE CAR, LEAVE THE HOUSE AND WALK TOWARD IT. DO NOT TALK TO ANYONE, OR WAVE TO ANYONE, OR LOOK AT ANYONE. BE

READY!!! GET IN THE CAR AS SOON AS IT ARRIVES. THE CAR WILL NOT WAIT!!!

She read it over three more times. It was hard to believe. It was not addressed to anyone, or signed by anyone. She didn't recognize the writing and she wondered for a moment if it was a trick of some kind. She sat down on the edge of the bed, holding the small piece of paper in front of her, letting the tears stream down her face.

CHAPTER FIFTY-EIGHT

Rosemary stood just inside the front door waiting. Now that it was time to leave she had mixed emotions. It was not that she wanted to stay any longer. It was just that all the special things in her life had happened here. It was here her children had been born. She knew she would never be back and so there was the void that comes with leaving anything in which one has invested so much of their life. There was nothing to take with her. The silver-framed pictures that had been on the mantel were gone. All the things she and Doctor had collected that marked the passage of their life together had been destroyed, or stolen. Memorabilia, once so precious to keep the memory alive, were all gone. At the same time, the little lead slugs she had in her little case were tremendously precious.

From time to time she looked at her watch and on several occasions she thought she heard a car approaching, but maybe it was just something passing on the government road a mile away. At two minutes after ten she wondered if she had read the note correctly. She considered going into her case to get it, but she knew what the note said. She had memorized it.

Ten fifteen and still no car. Maybe they had gotten the day wrong. Maybe the mototos had delivered the note a day, or even several days, ahead of time. Maybe it was just a cruel trick the Simbas had thought up. No, it couldn't be that. They didn't know English. She couldn't bring herself to give the Simbas credit for being that clever. She looked at her watch again. Ten twenty, and then she heard it, the unmistakable sound of a Volkswagen starting up the hill. She heard it shifting down to make the climb. Oh, God, let it make it. Let it have enough power to make it up the hill, she prayed. She watched it crawl over the crest to the flatness of the hilltop and turn toward the house. She clapped the helmet on her head, took one last look around at the bullet-scarred wall, picked up the case, and walked out of the house, across the porch, and onto the drive.

The car and Rosemary approached each other. The Simbas stood up, talking among themselves, shouting at her to go back in the house. The car stopped alongside her and she threw the little case through the window into the back seat, opened the door and climbed in, her helmet getting knocked off as she got in. It went rolling and bouncing, along the gravel drive away from the car that was moving again almost before she had the door closed. Imbego made an abrupt turn rushing for the road while behind them the Simbas' started firing at the little Volkswagen Bug. They careened down Medicine Hill road much faster than Rosemary thought safe. At the bottom of the hill he slowed down a little, the car rattling as it made its way along the gravel road.

They drove down past the two brick columns that had once held the mission sign at the intersection with the government road. Imbego didn't say anything and seemed nervous. Rosemary didn't try to talk to him.

In town, the natives lounged around on the steps and porches of buildings as though waiting for something to happen. The normally bustling street was quiet without the usual business going on. When they approached the gate to the road out of town, Imbego tapped a signal on the horn, the gate was raised and the Simba guard waved them through. A mile further, Imbego breathed an audible sigh of relief and said, "It is safe now. We have just crossed the border. Bwana Van is waiting for us at the turn by the big rock."

"Bwana Van?" she asked both surprised and yet believing he would be the one she could count on to come after her.

"Boyo, Madamu. Bwana Van and his son."

She saw the blue Subaru, the two men leaning against it. They stood up as the Volkswagen approached, and broke into smiles when they saw her inside. She jumped out and she and Harry ran to each other as fast as it is possible for the old to run. They embraced as only those who have been through things together can. They separated finally and she hugged David. It had been years since she had seen him.

Imbego stood next to his car, the engine still running. Harry reached into his pocket for the four hundred dollars and held them out to Imbego. "This is for Mololamu," he said.

Imbego took them, counted the bills and put them in his pocket.

"And what do I owe you, Imbego?" Harry asked.

"Nothing for me, Bwana Van. I do it for friendship and because what Mololamu and the Simbas did is wrong."

"Leo, the father of your father's father was always doing things for us out of friendship," Harry said.

"It is for that I do it. Your friendship with him is well known in my family. I go now, Bwana Van," he said, got into his little car, turned around, and drove away from them.

Harry held the car door for her and then got in the front next to David. "Imbego tells me they tried to kill you," Harry said.

"Yes," she said quietly, leaning forward and resting her hand on the back of the front seat. "I'll tell you all about it, Harry. After a bath and a good night's sleep I'll tell you all about it. I want my mind to be clear when I tell you. But you can't tell everybody. Not everyone will believe it. Some will say I imagined it, or was hallucinating, but I wasn't. But it is far too precious a thing to just lay out on the table for everyone to look at and wonder if it was real. It is only for you and me, Harry, and those who can believe. I'll tell you all about it in the morning," she said and leaned back in the seat smiling, safe and at peace.

1965

CHAPTER FIFTY-NINE

Harry VanVeldt drove the little Peugeot slowly toward the town of Abaru. The secession of Oriental Province under Mbekede had come to an end six weeks before when Stanleyville had been liberated, but the Congo was in chaos. There were refugees and shortages everywhere. Industry was at a standstill, mines closed and plantations deserted. Pockets of Simba resistance were still strong in many areas. Tribal and regional warfare was going on with scores being killed every day. Whites were advised it was not safe to return and none had.

Harry was aware of the situation, but he was sure he would be safe. Simbas were no longer active around Abaru. He had spent Christmas and New Years with David and the others in Kampala.

He approached the white gate slowly so they could see him coming. When he got there the guard was surprised to see him, but not unfriendly. The guard remembered him and after a quick look at his papers waved him through and he headed for the mission.

He turned into the mission road and then up to the top of Medicine Hill. He stopped in front of the burned hospital buildings and took the back path to the black's cemetery. He stood for a few moments next to Alma's grave. He went back to his car, drove down the hill and along the palm lined road the length of the station and parked the car under the mango trees. The tennis court and lawn was overgrown with grass more than a foot high. He walked through the burned-out skeleton of a house he and Alma had lived in for all of their life together. On the back porch, the little generator, that for twenty years had supplied power for the lights and radio, was missing. In every room, what furniture remained, was smashed. In the living room there were ashes and pieces of charred wood in the middle of the cement floor. The Dulcetone was smashed with all its forks missing and pieces of it scattered around the room. One of its spindle legs was half burned in the middle of the room. It was the destruction of the Dulcetone that seemed most personal. It had been the first keyboard instrument in that part of the world. He had spent years at that keyboard. Others had later brought pianos, but they had always needed tuning, while the forks of the Dulcetone were never out of tune. The only thing that hadn't been disturbed was the head of the kudu David had killed so many years ago. It was still above the fireplace. He was pleased with that.

He stepped out onto the front porch and saw a mototo standing in the front yard. Harry waved and smiled and was going to say something when the child bolted and ran away. He went and got the car, driving it right on to the front porch, thinking Alma would never have approved of that. He was just starting to unload his camping equipment when they started to arrive; houseboys vying with each other to set up his cot and camping equipment on the wide porch and cooks working in the roofless cookhouse starting fires to cook his dinner. When they were through, they sat on the porch talking long into the night. He fell asleep that night to the sounds of home: a cricket chirping, mosquitoes buzzing outside his net, the beating of a distant drum, and once he thought he heard the roar of a leopard.

He woke up before five as he always did and headed for his rock at the top of the hill behind the house. The path was overgrown and he had to pull himself along in many places. He had to scramble on hands and knees in places and had to stop, rest and catch his breath several times before he got to the top of the rock. He stood panting tiredly as the sun began to break over the horizon. In the villages on either side of the hill, smoke was beginning to rise from the cooking fires of the few who had returned after fleeing to escape the Simbas. He looked down at the burned out buildings of the station. He had been there when every one of those buildings had been built. He remembered the first hut Kusala had helped them build and that they had lived in with Dave and Laura. Laura was dead and Dave was in a nursing home outside of Chicago. Poor Dave, you never did get back to your mountains of Colorado.

The land became bathed in the soft yellow of early day. To the north were the seven hills of the Sudan border and to the east the distant volcanic mountains of the Uganda. Three miles away to the northeast were the buildings of the town of Abaru. To the west and south the lone and level grasslands stretched endlessly away. He remembered when they had seen Leo coming from that direction. Standing now, looking over the rocks, brush, and openness of home, he knew he had not returned to get things started again, but because he didn't feel right anywhere else.

He went and sat down where he had sat so many times before in his lifetime and wished he had brought a pillow. The rock was hard, but he had to sit and rest his tired, old legs. He leaned his head back against the rock behind him and closed his eyes. He would rest them just a moment before he started to read.

Alma. Alma. Alma. You have no idea how I've missed you these past eleven years. What are we to do? Our Congo is in such trouble and I don't know what to do about it. I'm too old. You were here to help me before. We did what we could, it just wasn't enough. Or maybe we went about it the wrong way. Africa, Africa, how good you have been to me, and how troubled you now are. Will you ever again know peace?

***

The natives were not surprised when they didn't find Bwana Van at home when they came to prepare breakfast. They were used to his going up to the rocks and after Madamu died, he had started taking long walks, sometimes going all the way to the post. But when he didn't come back by eleven, they sent people out to look for him. They found him where he had fallen asleep leaning back against the rock. In his right hand he was holding his Bible with his index finger inserted between the pages, making the place where he had been reading.

The funeral was the next day. There were not many people in the walls of the burned-out church for the service. Less than a fourth of the families had returned to live in the mission villages. There were no mondeli at all. A native pastor conducted the service and walked ahead of the blanket wrapped body to the cemetery. The small company sang as they went, singing hymns Bwana Van had translated for them and first played for their fathers on his trumpet. They carried him over Medicine Hill and down between the rocks on the other side and buried him in the native cemetery between the graves of Alma and Kusala.

GLOSSARY

Askari – Native soldiers in German East African army

Batu-na-dawa – Medicine man sometimes called a witch doctor by the mondeli

Bunduki – Guns

Dawa - Medicine

Dhoti – A pre-sized length of wrap-around cloth

Fufu – A staple food being dried, boiled, or as flour made from maniac root.

Gangilo – Chief's staff often elaborately carved and decorated with animal teeth, feathers, twisted metal or other significant items.

Ilolo – Area running the length of the village with huts on both sides and the chief's hut at the end.

Infirmiere – Native hospital personnel with on the job medical training.

Mondeli – Caucasians

Mericani – A course white muslin produced in the US and preferred over the Indian variety

Mototo – A teenage child

Munganga – Doctor

Putu – Homeland of Caucasians

Sene – Hello

Tepoi – Carrying chair similar to a sedan chair only carried on the bearers' shoulders.

Toto – Infant or toddler.

Tukutuku – Natives who are Belgian soldiers

About the Author

The author, Paul J. Stam, was born in the northeast corner of the Belgian Congo where he grew up listening to the accounts of the old timers some of whom were the first whites in that part of Africa. Just before the end of World War II, when he was 15, Paul came to the United States with his parent.

After graduating from high school he enlisted in the U.S. Navy, serving aboard a destroyer during the Korean War. His tour of duty completed, Paul attended the University of Minnesota and later joined the staff. Among other things Paul has been a foundry worker, salesman, university teacher and administrator and sailboat skipper. Paul is now retired and lives in Hawaii.

Paul is also the author of **A River That Is Congo: Of Rulers and Ruled** published by All Things That Matter Press and available as a Kindle, Nook and audiobook.

ALL THINGS THAT MATTER PRESS, Inc.

FOR MORE INFORMATION ON TITLES AVAILABLE FROM
ALL THINGS THAT MATTER PRESS, GO TO
http://allthingsthatmatterpress.com
or contact us at
allthingsthatmatterpress@gmail.com